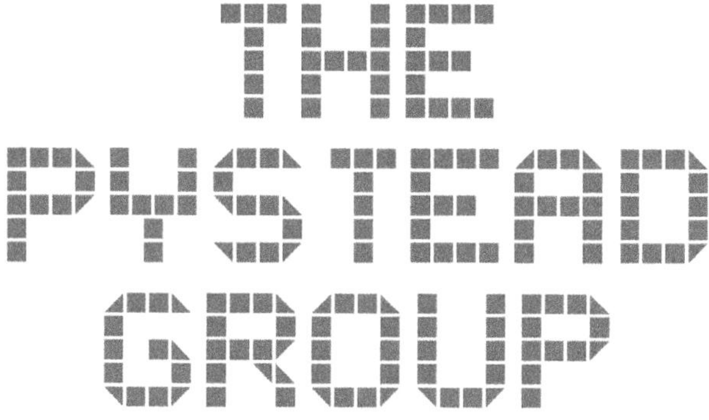

THE PYSTEAD GROUP

Daring To Be

Science Fiction Adventure in a Dystopian Era

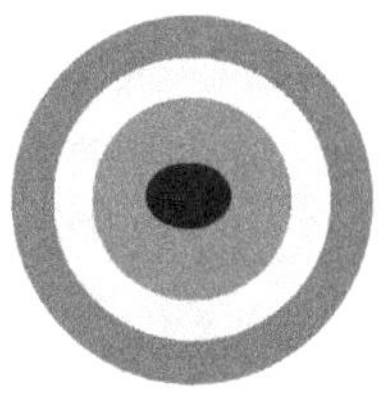

James Pryor

Published by The Techner Group LLC, Catonsville, Maryland: trilogy edition, 2023.
Portrayal of the letters TTG enclosed in an oval-like border is a trademark of The
Techner Group LLC, Maryland.

ISBN: 979-8-9873257-0-4 (eBook, trilogy edition)
ISBN: 979-8-9873257-1-1 (Paperback, trilogy edition)
Library of Congress Control Number: 2023907175 (Paperback, trilogy edition)

General artistic concepts by The Techner Group LLC, Maryland
Book cover design by TeaBerryCreative.com

Key ship 3-D design by Stephen Troy Owen, Round Rock, TX.
Cover photograph of a woman's facial features © by Kiraliffe / Envato Elements
Cover photograph of a man © by Nektarstock / DepositPhotos
Cover photograph of the Pleiades night sky © by Boris.Stromar / Wikimedia
Commons

Interior Book design by TeaBerryCreative.com
Interior book character concept sketches by Victoria Vining, Sheldon, VT.
Interior book digital character art by Holly Carton, Bowie, MD.
Interior book art touchup by Ahmed Roberson, Las Vegas, NV.

*For Diane
my wife and muse*

ACKNOWLEDGEMENTS

I am thankful for those readers whose advice guided me to a better written story: Diane Willen, Linda Lerner, Mark Willen, the late Phillip Lerner, and Sarah Kruel. The Writer's Ally of Maryland also influenced the first draft: manuscript consultant, Harrison Demchick; copyeditor, Lauren Moore. Diane Willen and Mark Willen read this trilogy edition and influenced content and style, although final decisions are the author's alone.

TABLE OF CONTENTS

STRAIGHT OUTTA WHEATON

Philip turned onto Highway 16, his final road to Savannah, to catch a plane to new employment. He put his car in autonomous driving mode and breathed a sigh of relief. *I've been the proverbial frog in warming water, and I didn't jump out on my own! Thank you, Cosmos, that we were all fired young enough to begin again. With new employment already, I'm the lucky one. What of Vanderhought last year? Drowning isn't painful they say. As unknowingly chosen as remaining in the warming water? Some say he had no other escape from his reputation as a mad scientist. I say prodigies don't remain unemployed.*

Philip squeezed his eyes tight seeking a blank slate but finding only a blank pressure reminding him of his last sea dive with Vanderhought. He held his breath. *With my lung capacity, it's too bad I don't enjoy free-form diving. Why did Vanderhought? Where is he? Did he really go down and not come back up? He always dropped a line, never reckless, never depressed. Drowning begins with anguished struggling to avoid that first and last breath of water, then living a minute with a cold lump of lungs and flashes of forgotten scenes. All fade in a fog of mind with mere words, help me mother, help, moth… and your mass of inanimate atoms is returned to the cosmos, perfect as ever. O Cosmos, let my ultimate end be unexpected and swift, like my end as Chair of Compton's philosophy department.*

On his fifth day of sight-seeing travel across the country, Phillip turned off the highway and stopped at Earl's Barbecue in Middle Georgia for an old-fashioned supper. A few hours later he approached the Wheaton World Center for Change, said by Earl to be a local sight that explained a lot about local problems. The building was large, white, with a curved front and two stories high. The lower-level exterior was plate glass with thin white columns separating its window-wall sections. The windows afforded a direct view into a ground-level corridor around the perimeter. On the second-story, residential-style windows obscured the interior view. A high, narrow viaduct ran across the lawn to the top center of the building, drawing Philip's eye over to a distant railroad station. But driving required his attention because automatic mode was not available in the parking lot. The Visitor Parking sign pointed straight ahead, along a narrow and curved lot paved with tan concrete. A good expanse of grass yard lay between the parking lot and the building. He saw two apparent walkways to the building, each entry flanked by a large showboard. *They must be two hundred centimeters wide. Surely get higher priority than a personal kom.*

He pulled into a parking space near the only car on the front row, a silver Geely. He noticed an enclosed kiosk to his left, painted lawn green. It would have blended with the background except for the dark rose-colored windows on both front and side. The window top framing was white and displayed four green letters: WWCC. Philip turned off his engine and set the parking brake. He looked intently at the booth but saw no Net account logo, no showboard, no information plaque, not even a door.

This is definitely the facility the old man mentioned. Such a large place for only four cars in the parking lot. Philip turned to approach the showboard at the nearby walkway with his wrist kom ready, choosing manual operation to avoid as many automated ghosts as possible. When he logged on the showboard filled with bright green text:

WHEATON WORLD CENTER FOR CHANGE
WELCOME AND PEACE
PROCESS AND TEAMWORK MAINTAINING OUTCOMES

AGGRESSIVE IMAGING AND SENSING EMPLOYED BEYOND THIS POINT
U.N. RULES OF PUBLIC ACCESS, SEARCH, AND FINES APPLY
NO VIDEO RECORDING
NO AUDIO RECORDING
NO TAKING NOTES
NO FOOD OR BEVERAGE CAN BE BROUGHT IN—NO EXCEPTIONS
KEEP CHILDREN CLOSE AT HAND
NO MORE THAN TWO CHILDREN PER ADULT ALLOWED
WITHOUT TRACKING
KEEP OFF THE GRASS
NO SPITTING
NO HUGGING OR KISSING
NO CASHCARD TRANSACTIONS
NO TREATY VIOLATIONS
NO WEAPONS OR HAZARDOUS AGENTS
NO CONTAGIOUS DISEASES
NO ROBOTS

NO PETS
NO SUITCASES OR PACKAGES
NO CHILDREN'S TOYS
PURSES, BRIEFCASES, AND KOMS MUST BE CHECKED

ALSO NOT ALLOWED:
PSEUDONYMS OR NICKNAMES
WATCH-LISTED PERSONS
LARGE GROUPS OR TOURS
INSCRIBED SLOGANS
PROTEST SYMBOLS
FLAGS OR RELIGIOUS SYMBOLS, EVEN AS JEWELRY
ANY LIKENESS OF A LEADER OR CLERIC
CROSS-CULTURAL DRESSING
HOLIDAY COSTUMES OR MASKS
LIKENESS OF AN OCCULT OR ACTION FIGURE
APPEARANCE REMINISCENT OF AN EXTRATERRESTRIAL OR A GHOST
CROSS-CULTURAL USE OF WORDS, LANGUAGE, OR SYMBOLS
CLOTHING OF PREDOMINANT LIGHT BLUE OR PINK COLOR
CLOTHING OF PREDOMINANT ORANGE COLOR
IMMODEST CLOTHING, HAIR, OR MAKEUP
PLAYING OF MUSIC OR ANY PRERECORDED TRACT
KOM OR VISUAL SIGNAL TRANSMISSIONS IN OR OUT
STAFF INTERVIEWS OR STAGED INTERVIEWS
LOITERING
SITTING IN THE PRESENCE OF A STANDING OFFICIAL
SOLICITING OR BEGGING
WAVING, POINTING, OR OTHER HAND GESTURES
MAGIC OR FORTUNE-TELLING
WAGERING
LOUD TALKING, JOKES, WHISTLING, OR LAUGHING
CURSING OR ANGRY LANGUAGE
WEEPING OR MOANING

DISRESPECTING OTHERS
PRAYERS, EXCEPT IN A DESIGNATED CHAPEL
SPEAKING ON A RELIGIOUS, POLITICAL, OR CONTROVERSIAL TOPIC

The text contracted to the top of the showboard as the bottom brightened into an abstract field of gray forms. The forms assembled into cartoon figures of a police officer and a visitor, both of indeterminate race, gender, and age. The two cartoon figures stood standing, facing each other. The officer figure raised its right hand, holding a portable security scanner, and the visitor figure raised both arms parallel to the floor. After a long moment, the cartoon scene flashed to another visitor figure walking down a corridor as a section of wall lit up in bright red and began flashing along with a low volume, pulsing siren sound. The cartoon visitor looked around, startled, seeing a few other figures in the corridor, but no other red wall panel. Then, with a panicked expression, the cartoon visitor stopped, faced the red wall, and raised both hands high. The scene panned out as other figures dropped to the floor and police carrying weapons ran from both sides toward the flashing red wall and the visitor frozen-still. The scene held.

As Philip stood watching the frozen security scene, a female voice—real, not artificial—asked sternly from the showboard, "Dr. Russell, are you familiar with international rules of public access, including search and seizure?"

"Yes," Philip responded. *More or less.*

The showboard voice, somewhat softer, replied, "Your Net Identification lists no restrictions, welcome and peace."

Peace? If I can remember all your rules! Pleasing every deemer of things leaves little for the individual. Why are we not allowed to please ourselves in our own country? Aha, we are no longer a we—my own neural scan findings supported here in practice in the real world. We are an undifferentiated culture of prohibitions! We are reverting to everything in private and nothing in common. We all become non-we in a culture of babble. The babble and mumbo-jumbo theories will not lead to goods and services. And how long before the cruel entropy of the cosmos restores its natural state? Before our busy bees are past? The rivers too polluted? The potholes unnumbered? The population unnumbered? How long before the robots require an upgrade and the technicians are found wanting? Fear not my primary process to contemplate these matters because I will maintain the public prohibitions of the commonweal.

Who belongs? Does anybody truly belong? In my own country, on government forms I am classified only as what I am not, and supposed to believe that I belong? And what caring human can endure this W.W.C.C.'s oppressive rules? Surely a trial for the country at large.

⚹ ⚹ ⚹

The showboard presented a pink cartoon girl who gave a follow-me wave and started down the path to the building above a line of text: FOLLOW ME AND VISIT THE CENTER. REFRESHMENTS AVAILABLE. PROCEEDS HELP THE HUMAN FAMILY.

The dark rose windows of the green kiosk again caught Philip's eye. *No video allowed. This moment, this reality, may not be preserved. A record of this moment as a primary source is not allowed. Reality, however, exists even if unacknowledged. For humanity, surplus fresh water and arable land are in different places, and the world's effective carrying capacity is almost done even before political realities are considered. And we subaltern may not speak about the overpopulated and delusionary world as troubled as the proverbial frog pond. The commons may behold only the deemer's illusions of that pond and their world, as if a frog living in a well.*

Get cracking my primary process and help me imagine what's likely—a bit in advance would be helpful. A child can live without complaint or understanding that heshe exists almost in poverty and without a diet of fruits and vegetables and enough protein, without educated conversation or like benefits of a middle-class life. Likewise, an adult will live without complaint or understanding that heshe exists subject to automation and without equitable economic opportunity or equal protection under the law. The commons live without concern for an imbalance of population and occupations or of natural resources. An adult can dread a dystopian future of terrorists and poverty without fear of living a marginal life every day at risk in their own dystopian era! The adult is as vulnerable as the child. The world is as vulnerable as the adult. O Cosmos!

*I ought to learn something about this place since I have a few min-*utes. Philip typed in 'WWCC history' and pushed the copy-to-kom tab. The board flashed and posted in dark green:

HISTORY OF THE W.W.C.C.
1. FOUNDERS
2. YEAR ONE: 2037
3. YEARS 2038 TO 2051
4. 2052 EVENTS

Philip typed in 1.

FOUNDERS OF THE W.W.C.C.
THE WHEATON WORLD CENTER FOR CHANGE (W.W.C.C.) WAS
FOUNDED IN MAY 2037 THROUGH THE EFFORTS OF THE ELECTED

OFFICIALS OF THE CITY OF WHEATON, GEORGIA, U.S.A. THE FIRST
TO RECOGNIZE THE NEED FOR SUCH A CENTER WERE THE SEVEN
OFFICIALS SERVING WHEATON IN 2036. MS. LETASHA WARD
WAS THE FIRST TO CONCEIVE OF THE CENTER AS A PRACTICAL
REALITY. AS MAYOR, SHE FOUND SUPPORT AND CREATIVE ADVICE
AMONG MANY PROGRESSIVE GROUPS. FACED WITH SEEMINGLY
INSURMOUNTABLE PROBLEMS IN CITY GOVERNANCE AND FINANCE,
CITY OFFICIALS CLOSED RANKS AND THROUGH TEAMWORK AND
PERSONAL SACRIFICE BROUGHT THE WORLD CENTER INTO BEING.

*Only one person among the founders is named. No details on
financing implies dark money to me. What change are they seeking?
What's happening now?* Philip pushed tab 4 for 2052 events.

2052 EVENTS AT W.W.C.C.
1. HALLOWEEN PLANNING COMMITTEE
2. MULTICULTURAL ONENESS SEMINAR, FOR HIGH SCHOOLERS
3. DIETARY SCIENCE COMMITTEE
4. CARIBBEAN COORDINATING COMMITTEE
5. PRESCHOOL ACTION MEETING
6. SIX SIGMA FOR MAINTAINING QUALITY OUTCOMES
7. LIP-SYNC COMPETITION
8. CHILDREN'S CHARITY PARTY—BRING AN UNWRAPPED GIFT FOR
ANY AGE 4 TO 7
9. CITY OF WHEATON EVENTS, LIST OF

Philip checked the time. *I'll need to get on the road in five minutes.
Can skip Halloween!* Philip punched in 2 under Current Events. The
screen flashed and colors swirled, paused, swirled, held, flashed,
and began swirling again. Then the screen presented text.

MULTICULTURAL ONENESS SEMINAR
BE WISE IN 2052
WHEATON INSTITUTE FOR SUMMER ENTR'ACTES

PARENTS OF STUDENTS WITH THE MENTALITY FOR RESEARCH
SHOULD NOT MISS THIS OPPORTUNITY TO SEEK INTERNSHIPS FOR
THEIR CHILDREN WITH AN APPROVED COMPANY THAT UTILIZES
ON-THE-JOB TRAINING TO PROMOTE PROFESSIONAL PROTOCOLS
FOR MAINTAINING THE ORGANIZATION. INTERNS WILL LEARN
THE RESEARCH PROCESS OF TOPIC FOCUS, VOCABULARY, NET
SEARCH, PORTFOLIO, HYPOTHESIS, CRITIQUE, REPORT WRITING,
SUBMITTING FOR PUBLICATION.

ALL RECEIVE TOP PAY AS WORLD-CLASS INTERNS
EXCITING POSITIONS ARE AVAILABLE
AN INQUIRING MIND MUST BE NURTURED

EACH INTERN WILL RECEIVE A SALARY AND FULL BENEFITS
EACH INTERN WILL HAVE A WORLD-CLASS MENTOR
EACH INTERN WILL HAVE EXCELLENT FACILITIES
EACH INTERN WILL HAVE AN EXCITING PROJECT
EACH INTERN WILL EXPERIENCE A TEAM-BASED WORKING
ENVIRONMENT
EACH INTERN WILL EXPERIENCE THE LATEST IN TECHNOLOGY
EACH INTERN WILL HAVE A TURN TO SHINE
EACH INTERN'S PROJECT WILL BE PUBLISHED

Philip looked back at his car, at its iridescent tincture of rose-ivory no longer visible in the dim illumination of the parking lot under a nimbus sky. He slid aside the safety cover on his wrist kom and turned on his leased car's special security system, getting the green light.

As he signed out of the showboard, a woman's shrill voice called, "Man on the walkway, hold up!" He took a step toward the building and heard a second shout, "Man! I said hold up!" Philip realized he could be the man on the walkway and shifted toward the shouter. He saw figures in fuchsia hats and jackets moving fast. He straightened himself and within seconds a tall woman was in his face loud, "You keep them hands in view!"

"What?"

"I am a police officer!" She spit out, "I needs to see your D-L-C!" Tall for a woman, her eyes only two centimeters below Philip's. A short officer was moving toward his car, her right hand resting on her sidearm. Old and wrinkled, she stood hardly taller than the car.

Half-watching the short officer, Philip asked, "What could be the problem?"

"I ax to see your card, and it's a problem if you don't have it. You was in manual mode gittin in this parkin lot. You need a driver's license!"

Philip tensed. *Can forget civility from this one.*

"Your card!" she shrieked. Philip flinched, found his driver's card, and held it out. The officer took it with a jerk, glaring at it. She pulled a dark gray device off her utility belt and raised it.

"I don't understand."

The officer almost smiled as she slid his driver's license card into a slot on her device. Then she glared at him. "Yo car is under suspicion."

Crackling voice calls came from behind, and Philip knew it was the police kom of the short officer at the rear of his car.

The tall officer typed a few strokes and looked past Philip, calling, "Officer Stanley, license plate?" The ready reply came in a high and dutiful chant. Then the tall one told Philip, "We have to do a showboard search of you and yo vehicle."

She showed teeth and stood glaring at him. Her lips flared as she snapped her head sideways to look at the car. "You just stand still till my backup gets here! Most towns wouldn't catch the arrest code on a vehicle." She snarled, "Wheaton ain't no backwards little town! Wheaton is the most progressive town in the…in the world."

Philip told her, "I haven't visited Wheaton."

"You are in Wheaton right now. This parking lot belongs to the city. We lease it to the World Center and we patrol it for them. Now you stand still while we get your status!"

The short officer, Stanley, stepped forward and Philip could see that she kept her right hand on her pistol, which disturbed him for some reason he could not put into a single thought. *Surely looks atypical for an officer, could she be a robot? Even a social robot could do her job to this point.*

The intuitive mind reacts in the gut while the conscious mind seeks to understand appearances before it. Philip found it impossible to relax with either a wrinkled human or a robot keeping gun hand poised and eyes fixed on him. *I'd really like brain scans of these two.* Looking at the deep pink uniform, he now saw that the tall officer had on her sleeve a circular silver patch with a border stitched in fuchsia threads: City of Wheaton. The officer's hat had a large bronze star of five points. She wore the nametag: BURK. Suddenly he thought it better not to stare and looked away.

Philip's stomach took a churn. He wanted to talk, but obviously Burk did not. *Possibly she's a robot—an antisocial robot? The best robots are difficult to spot in their design role. Surely Burk's job requires too much judgment for any robot that a small town can afford? Could it be remote-controlled rather than autonomous? Could there be homeland security funds? That W.W.C.C. facility certainly was not built on a tight budget.* Philip could not find a comfortable position and shifted his weight to his left foot and folded his arms.

After more uncomfortable waiting, remnants of past encounters with various police by colleagues came to mind. *The most progressive city says Burk. Progressive in what ways? Simply being associated with the latest in technology gives many a personal sense of high-tech contentment. As if watching the game makes one a player—good instance for Plato to be a role model for modernity. Perhaps modernity needs some Plato rather than no Plato.*

Burk pulled up her device. Philip adjusted to be ready to take a ticket. Burk's voice boomed, "Don't move them hands!" Philip instinctively slumped a bit at the fierceness of her command, feeling a twitch through his whole upper body. As he recovered his senses, he saw the pistol in her hand pointing at his chest.

"What?"

Her fierceness continued: "Don't you move a muscle! Keep perfectly still. We got a code on you!"

"What's the code?" asked Officer Stanley.

"A two-nine-six, antisocial witness.."

Witness for what?

Burk stepped to his side, commanding, "Don't you move! We also got a five-nine-six . Yo vehicle is under arrest."

Anger surged through Philip in a way he seldom felt, and he caught himself gritting his teeth.

Amid static and background voices, red, white, and blue flashing lights appeared. Three vehicles pulled up behind his car and stopped with their police lights flashing. Officer Burk maintained her position. With pops and thuds of vehicle doors several more fuchsia-attired officers were out. Two female officers shorter than Burk, but bigger and younger, approached and stopped, both eyeing Philip. One asked Burk, "Should we scan him?"

"No, he ain't under arrest. It's his car with a five-nine-six." Burk looked at Philip with a tight face and commanded, "Now you stay put till I get these officers briefed. Then I will tell you what's gotta happen. You don't have no weapons on yo' person, do you?"

"No." *Was that a double negative?*

Burk nodded her head definitively. The three officers moved beyond Philip's range of hearing. Ignoring Officer Stanley at the rear of his car with her bony hand at the ready, Philip turned to study the new arrivals. The police cars, except for their fuchsia-and-white paint, looked like standard patrol cars with an interior window separating the front and rear seats. A police van, fuchsia-and-white, sat with its two rear doors open, with one door locked against the rear corner of the van, supporting a police showboard. Two female officers stood in front of the showboard, one holding a control kom. An area on the board turned bright, followed in seconds by another bright area. Philip clinched his teeth and heard the grind inside his head, so again he tried to relax, but the flashing lights, half-heard words, and crackling koms continued to intrude. He spotted a big male officer dressed in wine-red approaching his car, pulling an orange device with two heavy-looking arms. A sensation of heat enveloped Philip's neck and ears.

Must be a wheel lock. Put this in perspetive. It happens to people every day. So, he stood up straight and took a long breath of the fresh air. Invigorating, reminding him of his extraordinary lung capacity. He turned away from the flashing lights to look at the terrain. *Georgia flattens out on its way to the Atlantic.* He looked around. The rose-colored windows of the W.W.C.C. booth loomed, glowing from inside illumination. *Just plain ugly.* The main building glowed white from its illuminated perimeter corridor. In the police van an interior light glowed. Behind his car, the orange wheel lock lay almost in darkness, half obscured from view by the thin and motionless frame of Officer Stanley watching with the full might of her narrow, wrinkled face. He could not see Officer Burk. The other officers were hardly moving. Three stood watching the police showboard. *Should not be long. Dark data moves at the speed of light.*

One of the officers at the van gave a sweeping wave of her arm. With footsteps from behind came, "Hey!" Burk's voice. As Philip considered whether Burk was addressing him, another "Hey!" sounded from closer behind, but for some reason he tensed his jaw and continued watching the van. Fingers whacked his jacket sleeve, and he jerked by reflex to find himself looking askance at Burk and two blank-faced female officers. Burk did not react to his quick movement. "Hey, Major Edmondson is ready at the van." As the moment lingered, he remained silent. Burk twisted up her lips but did not speak.

The officer at the van waved vigorously, demanding, "Get over here!"

Burk ordered, "Step over to the van!" She turned for the van, and the two flanking officers stood waiting for Philip to follow. One commanded sharply, "Step over to that van now!"

Philip followed Burk. He watched proceedings at the back of the van. Burk stood beyond arm's length and out of his peripheral vision, but close enough to project unfathomable popping and snapping sounds from her chewing gum and utility belt. *The one holding the remote must be Edmondson.*

The Major called, "Willie, are you ready with video?"

"Yes, Mum," came a solid male voice. Major Edmondson studied the showboard and directed, "Video the car all around, inside and out. Get the numbers. Remember to activate your backup recorder."

"I'm on it with both feet."

Edmondson turned to Burk. "The board says to turn off the car's security system and unlock the doors."

Burk's testy voice told Philip, "All right, fancy shirt, get yo' kom up and kill that security system and unlock tha doors."

Philip turned, catching another glimpse of Officer Stanley, her hand now gripping her pistol. *At the ready, doesn't want to miss a pretext to shoot? The barbecue place's owner…Earl, warned me about Wheaton!* Focusing for a few quick flicks of his finger, Philip did as told.

"Bring Russell over."

Burk jerked her head for Philip to move. He took the last steps to the back of the van where the officer said without looking over, "I'm Major Edmondson in charge." Philip did not reply. The Major held herself erect. She wore a large gold leaf insignia on each shoulder epaulet, and the same deep pink uniform as the others, but her blouse was white silk instead of the pale pink cotton. Her heavy gold chain necklace matched the high, rounded neckline of her blouse. Her black hair had a reddish tint and flipped under below her ears. She met Philip's eyes with a cold stare. "Do you understand we are here in response to an arrest code issued for the vehicle you are driving?"

"Yes."

"Your car is under suspicion but has not been charged. We are here to investigate and determine what action to take."

"I understand."

She continued, "Let the record reflect that Mr. Russell is present and understands his right to remain silent even though he is not a suspect who might be arrested. Please confirm that for the record, Mr. Russell."

After restating his name and understanding of his right to remain silent, Philip heard Burk mutter, "Smartass fancy shirt."

Burk dislikes me, probably most everybody. The Major seems professional. My primary circuits keep on churning…I'm not going to be any help thinking for a while.

✻　✻　✻

Major Edmondson called loudly to the group, "Quiet!" She turned and waited for an approaching male figure in a gray business suit. The only words Philip caught from their exchange were the man's name—spelled on the showboard, Colonel Zhong. The Major announced, "This investigation is beginning. Silence, unless I ast you a question."

The scene became quiet except for static on the open police channels. *Where do all those eerie spats and crackles come from? Perhaps an app for background torment?*

The Major glared. "First, we must confirm this is the vehicle with the arrest code."

Officer Burk turned and left the group, bumping Philip's shoulder as she stepped past him. *The gothic bitch bumped me on purpose.*

The Major called, "Officer Burk, are you going to issue a ticket?"

"No, ma'am."

She still has my driver's license card—kept it on purpose. He spoke up loud enough for the Major and the showboard to hear. "When do I get back my D-L-C?" Burk scowled, popped open a flap, and produced his card.

The Major said with pride, "Any other jurisdiction would have booted your vehicle and gone for coffee. In Wheaton we worked hard to get connected and trained for full field capability." Heads nodded. She continued, "Everybody receives fair treatment from the Wheaton Police Department."

"Amen!" said Burk for all to hear.

The Major said, "We are fortunate to have Officer Burk as a double-check on our double checking. She's a lay preacher! We all know the showboard is true if we input all the data and don't skip steps. We don't look the other way if we get an outcome we feel is lenient. We don't get personal in our police work."

Burk a preacher—will wonders never cease? Philip said, "I'm all for double-checking."

Burk told him, "You are looking at the world's best field team. They are the only certified, fully capable field team in Georgia. Our Major Edmondson's got a doctorate in intelligent police systems." The Major did not comment.

I'm at the mercy of preacher Burk and her Major's artificial brain with all attendant ghosts lurking in her showboard. Is Wheaton the new frontier for loose ego boundaries? Why haven't I heard one word about this most progressive place not on the map with its own railroad stop? Unknown like an almost Themiscyra? Conceivable in ancient Greece, but not in present America.

The Major told Philip, "The data field below is input from Officer Mowka's video of your vehicle. Comparison shows agreement. You may go on over to the vehicle and check if you would like."

"I'm sure the number is correct."

She said, "Now we check vehicle's description. After those vehicle facts are presented, we will move to event facts, related circumstances, and extrapolations." She paused.

Glad I went to the men's room at Earl's. Does full field capability include a portable toilet? This careful attention to process seems out of character with my overall treatment. Surely all are too real up close to be robots? Philip took a breath and glanced at his car reflecting flashing apparitions in red, white, and blue.

The small group of female officers stirred occasionally but did not disperse. The Major announced firmly, "Time to check data." The entire screen flashed to the header, Summary of Facts, with a list of five items in large print. "Any comments?"

"Yes, Major, I spoke with Dagstra's representative earlier today, and she told me the vehicle is fully insured and not expiring. The insurance company will promptly send any requested information, but although I have requested a resend, California's automated system has not requested the update."

"I'll change the item to unconfirmed."

Why not request a resend instead of marking it unconfirmed? Because you prefer the present answer!

The Major continued, unhurried. "Next we will query for con- clusions based on data and circumstances." She said quietly to Philip, "Our system uses M-M-D-P."

She knows I worked on the initial M-D-P program! How is such deep background on me relevant to the investigation of a rental vehicle? Aha, she wants me to know my case is personal with her even if offi- cially neutral.

The Major spoke distinctly to the showboard. "Speculate on rea- sons for vehicle code five-nine-six." Another file appeared on screen.

CONJECTURE: RENTAL VEHICLE, CODE 596 (OWNER, DAGSTRA NAU)
VEHICLE PRESUMED MODIFIED IN MEXICO (THE NATION) TO ADD
SECRET COMPARTMENTS FOR TRANSPORT OF ILLEGAL DRUGS OR
OTHER CONTRABAND

VEHICLE HAS LARGE CARRYING CAPACITY, ENHANCED DRIVING RANGE, AND ENHANCED SECURITY SYSTEM ADAPTABLE TO FACILITATE ILLEGAL ACTIVITY

VEHICLE DRIVEN OFTEN IN MANUAL MODE, CONSISTENT WITH CONCEALING DETOURS AND STOPS

VEHICLE'S RECENT ROUTE OF TRAVEL WAS CONSISTENT WITH DISTRIBUTION OF CONTRABAND, AND WITH FLIGHT TO AVOID PROSECUTION DEPARTING FROM SAVANNAH

VEHICLE THOUGHT TO BE CARRYING AN UNSANCTIONED CANON IN VIOLATION OF TREATY OBLIGATIONS

The Major smiled before saying, "Compile security-related profile on the vehicle's driver."

Security-related on me?

CONJECTURE: PHILIP B. RUSSELL, CODE 296 (SECURITY ISSUES AND ANTISOCIAL WITNESS)

UNEMPLOYED, DATES AVAILABLE

NO PERMANENT DOMICILE, DATES AVAILABLE

COURT FILING: CALIFORNIA, UCC, UNPAID PARKING TICKET AT COMPTON, DETAILS AVAILABLE

TRAVEL ROUTING UNVERIFIED DUE TO USE OF MANUAL MODE DRIVING ON FULLY STRIPED ROADS

RECENT ATTEMPT TO TRANSMIT VIDEO OUT OF A SECURED FACILITY. DETAILS AVAILABLE

DRIVER UPDATED PASSPORT AND PURCHASED A ONE-WAY AIRLINE TICKET TO LEAVE THE COUNTRY WITH PENDING CIVIL ACTION IN CALIFORNIA, DETAILS AVAILABLE

PROBABLE INTENT TO TRANSPORT UNSANCTIONED TEXTS ACROSS THE BORDER

TRANSPORTATION OF OUT-OF-STATE ITEMS INTO MIDDLE GEORGIA WITHOUT REQUIRED SECURITY AND TRANSPORTATION PERMITS. NO HARDSHIP INVOLVED: PERMIT NOTICES ARE MAP LINKED, AND INSPECTION STATIONS WERE READILY AVAILABLE ALONG ROUTE OF TRAVEL

CITIZEN REPORTS:

A) STALKING OF A HUMAN FAMILY VAN FROM HWY. 16 TO EARL'S BARBECUE

B) DISCRIMINATORY SELECTION OF WAIT STAFF AT EARL'S BARBECUE

C) UNREGISTERED OPEN-SOURCE SEARCH OF WWCC CONTENT

Philip's jaw tightened. *This ought to be unbelievable even in the real world.*

The Major's voice was harsh, "In addition to everything else, you appear suspicious to citizens!"

Philip looked away, then at the Major, and then at the others. He stayed calm. "I believe your citizens have personal problems to be making those comments based on nothing."

No response came from the Major. In the ranks no heads nodded, and no feet shuffled. *What are they here for? Guarding the car and me? In training? Hazardous duty pay?*

Burk's solemn voice finally proclaimed, "Citizens get involved here in Wheaton. They report suspicious activity so we don't have drugs and crime. We set an example of good citizenship in public and of praising Jesus in private. We treat everybody the same and we are blessed for it." The group nodded as one.

⁂ ⁂ ⁂

Philip closed his eyes. Both the philosophy professor and the cognitive scientist know that one missed fact can transform an entire hypothesis, that reality is glimpsed only through persistent and open-minded searching. For those not afraid of reality, the search is never-ending. Yet, can a cognitive scientist be completely unafraid of reality, knowing so much about the bio-wirings of the various human minds? Knowing that the reality of the cosmos is not changed by machinations of the human mind, and that the machinations of the mind are too often not changed by the reality of the cosmos. *Whatever I'm missing, the hollow knot in my stomach must already know!*

The Major demanded, "Russell, do you find anything wrong with any individual line item?"

She said that with a straight face! He answered, "Those citizen's comments are subjective and untrue. One wonders how they can even exist. As for my driving route and stops, your police system must know that my car's anti-collision system was always active, and my route traceable via its cruise-control log. The system should know that my car's routing map was out on Hwy. 16. How can an official conjecture be presented before checking all the relevant data points in the system?"

The Major pressed on, "What of the outstanding parking ticket?"

"I haven't been informed about it until now, and my kom has been active all along."

The Major smiled for her officers.

A ghost messed with that notification. Even double-checking is scant defense against a ghost in the machine—resistance is futile!

During the next few minutes of psychedelic screen patterns and procedural entries by the Major, Philip, straining, caught only one unhelpful comment from the mingled voices, "You knew she would have his baby."

Soon the Major intervened loudly, "Present case findings." The screen flashed and posted:

DAGSTRA NAU VEHICLE VS. CITY OF WHEATON:
CASE NO. V186-15HB
FINDINGS:
1. IMPOUND VEHICLE
2. SEARCH VEHICLE FOR CONTRABAND PER U.N. REGULATIONS

DR. PHILIP B. RUSSELL VS. CITY OF WHEATON:
CASE NO. P186-16HG
FINDINGS:
1. DETAIN AS WITNESS PENDING SEARCH OF RENTAL VEHICLE
2. SEARCH POSSESSIONS AND PERSON FOR CONTRABAND PER U.N.
   REGULATIONS
3. SECURE UNSANCTIONED CANON FROM TRANSPORT OUT OF
   THE COUNTRY

Under the flashing lights, no one moved nor spoke until Burk's voice broke the silence. "Maybe too lenient?"

The Major replied, "We game this system every year. It's proven itself on every challenge." She looked at Philip. "Mr. Russell, as you can see, we must detain you as well as the vehicle."

"How this got from a rental vehicle to me, I don't see. And as you evidently know, I do know a little about these systems."

"Soon you will know a little about police procedures." She nodded with satisfaction. "Officer Burk, take Russell into custody. Cuff him, secure and catalog everything on his person, and deliver him to the jail for prints and processing."

She turned to Philip. "Do you take any medications?"

"No."

"Do you have a bad back, neck, or limb, or a prosthesis?"

"No."

The Major entered the data and told Burk, "He's all yours." In the next instant, Burk's hand grabbed Philip's left wrist and he felt a sharp slap. She jerked his hand up by the hard, narrow side of a metal handcuff.

Oough. The Lord's minions are wired in various ways.

Burk's hard voice intruded, "Use yo' right hand to get me everything on yo' person. Yo' kom, wallet, keys, rings—everything."

I thought they abused suspects and inmates, not witnesses. "So, I'm being detained, but not arrested?"

"That's it. The difference is you get a fancy cell to match your fancy shirt. Now quit stalling and get me them pocket items."

"I can't reach my wallet."

She dropped the cuff chain. "Now get it."

Philip retrieved his wallet. *Burk wanted to hurt my wrist. The Major acted courteous for the record, but practically advised Burk to mistreat me.*

Burk snatched the wallet from Philip's hand and dropped it into a clear plastic bag at his feet. Before he could think about anything else, she jerked up his left arm and slapped a cuff on his right wrist followed by a click. She grinned and pulled forward too fast on the cuff chain. Philip's wrists stung and his stomach sank as he stumbled forward. *Hope she doesn't break my wrists in this most progressive of all cities. How typical can this be? How can this place be unknown to the media? And never mentioned by the Post-Essentialists at university who somehow knew of the slightest thing left or right of liberal?*

"Get up them steps at the wagon!"

A hand shoved from behind and the steel bit into his wrists as Burk held and pulled up on the cuffs. When he reached the top step, a hand grabbed his cuff chain and pulled.

"Aaaugh," he cried as the cuffs dug in as he was jerked up and around and shoved down onto a bench. Before he could even look up, a long bar was slammed across his chest. *I'm not under arrest, but they take my possessions and jerk me around like I'm resisting. Burk pretended I was dangerous, but never scanned me for a weapon. The Human Family van driver filed a stupid, false report because I turned off the highway with his van and stopped at the same place to eat. Not to mention that assertive waitress at Earl's. How is it that provincial Earl knows more about the real world than the media? He warned me to stay out of Wheaton. How is it that I have never heard of progressive Wheaton or the W.W.C.C.? A better kept secret than antisocial scores! The police van lurched forward. I'll bet Earl knows to stay out of L.A. Why didn't I know to stay out of here? Who are these local deemers of things? Burk, but low on the totem pole. Where else don't I know about?*

❉　❉　❉

Who could intuit that the parking lot of a progressive facility of humanity would be best avoided by the progressive citizens of humanity, except that Arthur Vanderhought might have done. Arthur believed that knowing was already beyond the reach of available information and critical thought. He believed the public discourse used words effectively devoid of meaning, such as 'we' and 'us,' referring to persons having different wirings of mind and mutually exclusive perspectives. At the first hint of delusion, Arthur had been ready to contemplate the unthinkable and search for clues. However, time is limited, opinions vested, and new ideas resisted even among the elite. Vanderhought concluded that critical inquiry and good citizenship had been mutually exclusive for over a decade, that dishonesty in government and secret programs rendered conjecture unhelpful. The ride droned on, and Philip's sore wrists surely entered his subconscious thoughts.

Pulled out of the van, his wrists burned on his way to the booking desk. There the police used old technology made messy to stain under his fingernails. He tried to keep his broken skin from touching any surface.

After only moments in a cell, the stink of the small, hard, bright, and noisy enclosure imposed its foulness upon him. He took shallow breaths without relief. A late meal proved cold and tasteless and the water tepid. Philip was allowed to wear his own clothes, but told he could not have them washed, including underwear. His cell's showboard blocked access to Dagstra and to all government sites including the State of California, the United Nations, and W.W.C.C. Always available were gospel shows, reality shows, quiz shows, horror shows, soul music, basketball, and soap operas in Spanish. They blocked museums, old movies, old music, and anything related to academics, philosophy, or public policy. *At least I was allowed a call to lawyer Will, allowed to buy my Middle Georgia baggage and security permits, even allowed to get a refund on my airline ticket. That Major tailored this personalized blocking—pure meanness.* And so, in a cosmic quandary among vile aromas and uncontrollable lights, voices, and noises, Philip passed the night.

The next day, Saturday, brought no decent food and no word of his status. *Will I lose my job for not reporting to work? How can this place exist without regard for basic due process? Yet why not? That Major and her showboard's artificial brain were both content to avoid available data and take uninformed conjecture for fact!*

A distant train whistle sounded, and Philip was reminded of his parents' deaths in their late fifties. *The Department of Guideways is permitted to hide its regulations and daily activity logs from the public even during an accident investigation. Couldn't get a duty roster for the night of the wreck, nor a copy of maintenance inspections or repair activity. No list of incidents and findings. They do Machiavelli proud. Call that something to fear, and you are antisocial and angry. Why antisocial? Doesn't matter why! Only the deemer's score matters. And a Post-Essentialist mind can set aside any signifier! Who today ascribes to saving an appearance if it does not save their cherished memes? After Mother Jones, the commons and unions can do no wrong. And, of course, transnational businesses do no wrong!*

Philosophers do no wrong even if they write nothing. There is no contemporary essay to prepare anybody for reality! Today's professors hear no problem, see no problem, speak no problem. My friend Vanderhought was called a victim of his elitist avocation, in a eulogy having no kind words for a man of ideas and offering no comfort to his mourners. I must search the past for guidance!

Early during Philip's second night in detention, he took solace in his high-tech shirt and handkerchief, each made of a copper-and-silver-impregnated polyester fabric that killed bacteria—clothing from his years at Utrecht University. He kept his wrists covered by his cuffs and rapped his most injured wrist in the handkerchief. *Simply overlooked giving it to the Lay Reverend Officer Burk. In a kindly niche of the cosmos I could ask for a doctor…doesn't seem advisable here. Perhaps my primary process is on the job after all. Must sleep.* Philip took slow breaths and after an eternity he slept.

During the night he tossed and dreamed. A long, dark snake with broken fangs held him by his left wrist. A surgeon dressed in oxblood red stood over him and advised that his left hand be amputated. Philip woke with his wrists burning and heart pounding.

He looked and saw both hands—still his heart jumped. *How long can she keep me? You'd think I'd have a right to know without hiring a lawyer, to hire one of the Wheaton clan's lawyers as a consultant on local process—legalized extortion. You'd think showboard systems would have long ago resolved interface issues like tracking number resolution and software coordination, since any day now their artificial intelligence is supposed to provide the executive skills and insightful decisions needed by humanity to save itself from starvation, disease, and war. And you'd think I would begin noticing more of the gaps between illusion and reality. Are you still alive in there my primary process? You must be, to have spoken so vividly with the snake.*

⁂

His next morning began with a breakfast of cold and sour corned beef hash, almost-cooked eggs, stale white bread, and insipid coffee with no creamer or sugar. *Decent food, creamer, salt, pepper, butter would be too good for a witness? The only thing these people are progressive about is meanness!* Philip looked at the mix of raw and half-cooked scrambled eggs and stopped eating. *No excuse for raw egg. Why me? What is the fuchsia objective except meanness? Is this punishment for my high antisocial score? Can there be something in this experience for philosophy? Could be for cognitive science if neural scanning were not so restricted. Functional brain scans would ruin trust in society they say! Yeah, the deemers know scans would reveal dogma and dirty tricks in places they should not be! Their illusions may not be busted. Their lies and spies may not be revealed.*

Philip slept his third night until early morning when shaken and startled awake, handcuffed, and led to find out what had to happen. The guard shoved him into a small room with two mirrored walls and pushed him down to sit at a metal table. *Rose glass mirrors or one-way glass?* The door opened behind him and a large officer entered followed by the click of high heels. The Major stepped around and sat down facing Philip. "Well, Russell, we have two courses of action, and you can choose. We found secret compartments in the vehicle. You are fortunate we had the x-ray equipment here. We have impounded the car and you cannot use it again."

Although why eludes me.

"The good news is that you are not involved if you and your possessions are contraband free. Now I don't expect to find anything, but I must do the search. You can wait here with your luggage and books for the search team, probably the day after tomorrow, or you can ride to Savannah this afternoon with the search team and be searched during transit. If you are clean, you will be released in Savannah. I need to know if you want to be on that train after lunch."

She knows the train solves a problem for me. Did her conscience bother her overnight? Not likely, the food must be worse on the train. I can elect to stay here and really perplex her. Of course, she might decide to show me even more discomforts of life behind the heavy metal. Perhaps another night here could cost me reporting on time and my job! Philip decided, "The train seems better for me since I no longer have a car. Can you send my books with me?"

"Yes. They must be searched and tested for trace residue. The showboard directs absolutely everything must be searched."

"Well, Major, I would like the train search."

"Good. The lockup is getting crowded. I'm pleased to see you go, and I'm sure we can both agree it will be best not to meet again."

"I do prefer philosophy to the real world."

"Remember, Russell, the City of Wheaton is giving you a free ride to Savannah."

She treats me like a chained dog expected to wag its tail when fed. O Cosmos, reminds of my academic life in Compton.

The Major stood, directing the male officer to return Philip to Holding.

What about a checkup to see if you're giving me gangrene? How can you overlook my raw wrists, you gothic bitch? A burst of heat prickled his neck. *I'll be in Savannah soon enough to be saved from gangrene—you'd think. And she said nothing about my being a witness! Is she simply raising my hopes before telling me I'll have to return at some later date? Cosmos! This is the kind of place that makes life in the States untenable and bringing children into the world unthinkable. Best to flee the States if I can find a kinder niche in the cosmos. Nevis island will be my first destination straight outta Wheaton.*

✵　✵　✵

By early afternoon Philip sat on a concrete platform open to the sky, between tracks on each side bounded by a concrete outer wall that blocked one's view except for treetops on the horizon. Metal lighting poles and benches were spaced along the center of the platform. The digital displays on one side of the poles showed ATLANTA, and on the other side SAVANNAH. The lights atop the poles glowed in the daylight. *It's not easy being green.*

Several people waited together near the far end of the long platform. Each stood or sat beside their small suitcase. *It must take a lot of doing to maintain this lost place as the most progressive town in the world.* Philip looked down at his sealed plastic bag of pocket items, his carry bag, his two suitcases, and his five boxes

29

of books, each sealed with orange tape bearing the silver circle of the Wheaton Police, and a typed label, P186-16HG-9.

Ought to remember my Wheaton number in bold fuchsia—ought to repeat it every morning as a reminder to watch where I'm going. Only functional brain scanning reliably reveals honesty. For decades the corrupt have supported only the corruptible, so that now their dirty tricks and treasons in politics and business go unacknowledged even at highest levels, well, especially at highest levels! Their hypocrisy, evident in news ziffs for all to read, is disbelieved by a third of the population and accepted as politically astute by another fifth. With incompetence, inexperience, and fear running deep in all levels of government, surely much remains unknown both within the government and to the general public! The public hears only the bold-faced liars' refrain, "The country's in the very best of hands."

Down the platform heads were turned. A faint light appeared and became set in a small shadow. The brightness increased steadily and swept into the station as the close-set eyes of a serpent that streamed by as a stripe of clear windows in its tough metallic body. The creature quivered and settled atop its wheels, not making train-like noises. At its tail end sat a bi-level car with two narrow bands of rose-tinted windows. *I get a free ride with a view through rose glass, darkly.*

Philip's thoughts were cut short by a loudspeaker command in an artificial female voice. "Officers, escort detainee Russell and bring his personal effects to our car. Leave his baggage for the loaders." The two officers, dressed in wine-red, stood.

Philip detected a hint of brown in their uniforms and thought, *Oxblood red. Maybe the color matches stains from bleeding wrists? I'm beginning to hate them all.*

One of his guards picked up the plastic bag holding his kom and pocket items, and instructed, "Follow me. Keep your hands down and your mouth shut! Understood?"

"Yes." *Gothic goon.*

Train sounds could be heard. A door popped and opened. An unseen motor hummed as it performed its unseen task. On the platform, a hard case scraped across the concrete. Dirt-filled concrete planters sat here and there but without plants or flowers. *It's not easy being green.* High in a gray sky flew puffs of dark cloud. The two-level, silver car of grooved metal with its two rows of glowing rose windows loomed in Philip's mind as if a boa constrictor gorged on red meat, lying quietly, digesting its prey. The car's metallic-black wheels, big and tough, were somehow disquieting on the gray rails. *This iridescent finish must be a hot-pink metallic version of my rose-ivory rental car—enjoyable under different circumstances.*

✻ ✻ ✻

As they neared the end of the glowing car, small red lights flashed along its bottom edge and a two-toned chime sounded twice. A whoosh of air preceded an opening doorway and illuminated steps. Up the steps, a guard pushed Philip to the rear of the car into a small room with a high ceiling. A male officer wearing the wine-red uniform entered carrying a steel stool and a small laundry basket. Without a word, he clipped the stool into floor slots and dropped the steel basket. A tall female in her dark pink uniform entered. Philip tensed at the sight of Burk.

She reached over and pushed on a handle, producing a motor's hum and the lowering of a metal bar suspended on steel cables. Burk bent over and pulled a thin cable from the bar's bottom and clipped it in at a black dot on the floor. She glared at Philip. "Okay, Russell, get your bottom on that stool."

Either a robot with halitosis or a real-life goth. Philip sat on the small stool facing the front of the train. *All these windows are covered by metal shutters. Surely a witness detainee doesn't have to ride to Savannah on a hard stool with no outside view?*

Officer Burk told the two policemen, "I'll be right out." The two men left and two female officers wearing the fuchsia cotton uniform entered. Burk bent over and breathed in Philip's ear. "In L. A. they take yo drugs and let you go. But here, if you ain't clean, you gonna git to see Wheaton again—somethin' I spect you ain't gonna be itching to do." She grinned. "You probably think it's over with that old cannon because the system dropped it. Well, sometimes the system avoids something difficult, but the Major's got me for a double-check, and I have ideas bout a good place a small cannon could end up. We still got them who take bribes on the force."

Beginning with your Major, I'd bet.

Philip felt a tug on his wrists and his hands fell free. *She removed the tie chain. What did she say about my old canon of books?* Burk departed, closing the bulkhead door that sealed with a metallic hum.

What am I missing, besides breakfast and lunch? Philip noticed two monitoring cameras in the ceiling, each showing a red chip below its lens. *Video must be active.* Along the bulkhead wall, he faced four metal chairs with gray leather seats and backs, two having a desktop showboard. The chairs behind him had no desktops.

⚔ ⚔ ⚔

Again, the bulkhead door emitted its metallic sound and a tall female officer stepped in. She wore a tight white blouse and dress pants of the fuchsia color. After glancing at Philip, she took a seat at a showboard and told him, "Your two suitcases, handbag, and five boxes of books are onboard and will be searched by my security detail. They will search your clothes too, and my paramedic will search you. I am Major Hill, in charge." She called, "Detainee search team, bring in your equipment and Blitz."

Blitz must be a fellow canine? Philip sat with hands on his knees, not looking at anything in particular. The door hummed and three more officers were in, each carrying a small case.

"Where is Nobel?" the Major asked.

"Probably primping, but he is maintaining."

The Major rolled her eyes. A chime sounded and the ceiling speakers announced in an artificial female voice, "This train is leaving the station. Please be seated or hold on." The message repeated in Spanish…then silence.

An ever-so-slight trembling and some flux of audible awareness swept into the small room with a possible sensation of motion. *The train must be backing. Guess it does a Y-turn at that nearby station before the long haul.* A pop at Philip's feet got his attention. He glanced down to see flip-flop slippers. Philip knew that two officers in dark pink, armed with stun guns, sat at the bulkhead wall behind him. Now he felt movement of the train. The Major glanced up and folded her arms. *Where is Nobel with the bloodhound? The hound of the goths is surely made a goth. Neither mob nor lone goth conspire with decent man or beast. All must be forged in the same fire, beholden to the same dark money.*

After a minute of quiet backing a chime sounded. The train experienced a hesitation of wheels on rail, followed by a slight bump to the entire car. A moment later a two-toned chime sounded, the car bumped and moved, accelerating forward with a metallic scraping of wheels on the rails. A low-pitched rolling rattle set in. Philip listened intently, remembering the trainwreck that killed his parents. Occasionally he heard squeaks as the train rolled on a poorly aligned section of rail, but he heard no clicking. *Welded rails—expensive.* Philip shrugged his shoulders and arms. *I'm cool even with long sleeves.* He looked around but saw no clock. Sections of the high ceiling were bright, illuminating the space. *Quality lighting, glare free.* He spotted two louvered areas. *Sources of the cold air blowing on me. Don't know how long the search or the trip takes. These goths keep one guessing in the deep rose, well, not even that in here behind the steel shutters. These real word minds are wired differently than…than where? Than in the social contract!*

Philip reverted to staring at the floor. *Wish my hair covered the tops of my ears. Yet can one become complete without personally experiencing gothics beyond the walls of academia? Perhaps there is new circuit formation, new maturity in this experience? Is thirty-three years too old for meaningful new circuits? Many think menticide effective at any age! The changes in East German minds before and after the Berlin Wall do seem exemplary. Too bad for science that functional brain imaging didn't exist back then.*

Philip's lack of confidence in trains rose as the cold air fell on his ears, and the rails squealed randomly, sounding more and more ominous. *Good that I'm in the rear car— on level ground always survives a head-on. The metal shutters would protect against exploding glass. But how long can I endure this frigid cell?*

A chill suddenly ran up Philip's arms and spread to general shivering, matching a machine-gun burst of squealing jerks on the rails felt through the floor. *Hope it's misaligned track and not a loose wheel.* Philip hung his head and closed his eyes. *Will they damage my books looking for residue? Will I catch pneumonia? Are my wrists infected?* The entire car heaved up on one side and rocked back like a boat, sending him off balance. He pushed the sides of his feet against the floor to steady himself. *What the hell?* The hell was a loud screeching of wheel against rail, followed by a side dip and staccato side-to-side pulses that rippled through the floor and stool. *Damn! They settled for this misaligned rail? Well, even during the investigation of the accident that killed my parents, my lawyers couldn't get the guideways construction acceptance manuals! Kept secret from the public who must ride the guideways and suffer the consequences. Kept secret for favored contractors who do inferior work and get paid in full. Not a problem, just creates remedial work and more government funding for the Department of Guideways!*

A calm female voice spoke from overhead, "Attention, land-lubbers, we took what some call a little sea cruise. From here on the rails will be smooth."

After it's over they tell you. High gothic sensibilities. Here comes the Spanish. I'm freezing. I'm hungry and not likely to get a late lunch.

⁂ ⁂ ⁂

After the Spanish, Philip's shoulder was jostled and Major Hill taunted, "Time to rise and shine!"

Philip opened his eyes to see a young officer, bearded, wearing the official wine-red pants and a gray shirt.

The Major spoke again, "Let's get this done, Russell. You stand up and step over to the right-side wall. Take a hand grip."

The unexpected orders did not register clearly. Philip was rethinking what she had said when the gray-shirt at his side pulled up under his armpit. "You heard the Major! Get over to that wall."

Philip rose only to be shoved. As he looked for a hand grip, the Major laughed. "We have to test your clothes. You take off everything and put it in that laundry basket. Be quick about it!"

Am I to strip in front of these women?

Major Hill came to stand in front of him. "You have a problem with women in authority, don't you?"

"No."

"I told you to be quick about getting out of those clothes, and you haven't started. What do you call that?"

"I'm trying to understand what you want me to do."

"Strip naked, Russell. Take off all your clothes, like I said the first time."

"I thought men were strip-searched by men," he said weakly.

She scowled. "They are! Officer Nobel is here to perform the search. The rest of us are witnesses. Now, are you going to do as directed?"

"If I must."

"We're going to cut them off if you don't get them off, real pronto."

Philip bent over and untied a shoe. "Be quick!" He moved faster. "I didn't hear you, Russell." He continued taking off his shoes but looked up. The Major put her hands on her hips and pushed out her chest, showing nipples through her blouse. "I didn't hear you acknowledge my directions, Russell."

"I understand. I'm undressing."

"And who are you speaking to?"

"A Major."

"Correct! Folks call police officers by their titles, and they say ma'am to a woman. You can tell I'm a woman, can't you, Russell?"

"Yes, ma'am, Major." Philip took off his second shoe and his socks and placed them in the basket. The Major continued standing in his face, her breasts arched out. *Does she think I find her appealing?* She grinned. *Damn, do it and don't let her get to you.* He stood up straight and quickly unbuttoned his shirt. The Major didn't move. He looked past her and took off the shirt, dropping it into the basket. She stepped backwards and took her seat. He paused on his pants' zipper. *Wimp.* He shifted to give the Major a better view and dropped his pants. None of the officers looked away.

"We don't have all day," the Major called with a sweet lilt of voice. Pangs of hatred shot through him as he removed his underpants. Two of the officers whispered and one shook her head. Philip glanced to the side and saw the male, Nobel, watching intently.

Homosexual. Philip took a deep breath and removed his undershirt. His ears were stinging warm and he couldn't even concentrate on hating them.

The Major gave him a good looking-over. "Now get your skinny behind on that stool and do like Officer Nobel says." The stool was cold, and Philip gasped in surprise. "You might smile for the video now and then."

An officer laughed. Philip thought he must have turned red all over. Then it struck him that the Major's blouse was now unbuttoned over halfway down. *Does the bitch think I'd like to see more of her?* The Major stepped backward to her seat, avoiding the cameras.

Officer Nobel bent over, and Philip noticed he wore a light gray tie that matched his shirt's pocket flaps. *Probably intended to form a Christian cross. Cultural cross-dressing?* Nobel wore the silver and fuchsia police patch on his sleeve. His short sleeves showed large and defined biceps. He began to pull on latex gloves. He directed

Philip to lean over and put his chest on the hanging bar. In a controlled rage, clenching his teeth and toes, Philip did as told. Large hands caught his hips, dug in, pulled back and up, unseating him. He struggled to avoid scraping his chin on the bar.

"Rectal exam," said Nobel as one arm caught under Philip's hips to support him. Philip grimaced and tried recalling the colorful median flowers along the highway approaching Wheaton. Finally, with a wipe on his buttocks Nobel reported, "Nothing here." To Philip he ordered, "Sit down an open your mouth for Officer Friola."

Philip complied, shivering. *I'm such a good dog.*

Officer Friola, short and probably Mexican, wore a pale pink shirt and the standard-issue dark pink slacks. She reached out wearing latex gloves, holding a small silver device. He opened his mouth and she pushed his tongue down with a flat probe light and looked gently in his mouth with a small mirror on a stem. She announced with an accent, "Nada."

"Stand up, Russell, and get those feet spread." He wanted to spit on her. *I should protest at some point. No doubt at the point I want a memorable lesson in gothic.* In the next instant Nobel was exploring his private parts. *More attention than a medical exam.*

"Anything artificial?" asked the Major.

"Feels right to me."

"All right, Rosita, take your pictures."

A chair scraped and another short female rose, holding a large flat device with a long strap. She stepped to the wall and told Philip, "Stand in front of that red spot with your back to the wall. Bend over so I get this loop over your head." The flat plate went on his front side and unfolded. "Stand straight and be still." Officer

Rosita adjusted the flat plate, pushed a button on the wall, and stepped back. A circular shield descended around Philip and a ping sounded. The shield raised.

"Take the stool, Russell."

Remember your new trick, doggie. "Yes, ma'am, Major." He took the stool. *Not getting any warmer in here. I'll pretend it's a deep-sea dive. The water will have cold streaks. But why am I, a dog, playing the loon? Par for an age of delusions? Should produce its share of cynics.*

"You hold that bar with both hands." *What more is there to search?* Philip assumed the position. One of the fuchsia uniforms approached, took his forearm and snapped a metal chain to his handcuff rings. *No jerking. Burk would have bruised me yet again.* He tried to sit up and his wrists felt the bite of the cuffs. *What the hell now? Oough. I'm hooked to this bar with an incredibly short chain. Not only cold, I'm itching everywhere Nobel had a hand.*

The officers all seemed comfortable, smirking at his misery. The blowing air seemed colder than ever. The floor and stool vibrated with the underlying roll that drove the train. Philip looked again at the seated officers. The Major buttoned her blouse with a flourish of painted nails.

Without warning Philip tensed as a chill seized his entire body. Almost in panic he sought relief and cried out, "Major, ma'am, I'm freezing and can't even fold my arms for protection."

After a long pause, the Major spoke into her microphone. "Officer Nobel, you are needed." Philip gritted his teeth and shut his eyes, shivering and itching.

Officer Nobel entered the room. "Ma'am?"

"Would you help our boy Russell into the slippers. Claims he's cold."

Nobel got them on Philip and departed. Philip lifted a foot, but without relief from a binding rear strap. *The tight straps are better than the cold floor. Gothic bitch, red-haired witch.* Without warning, a pang of itching struck in his rectum. He jerked, his eyes watering, instinctively trying to scratch, but his wrists held tight to the bar. "Aaugh." *Have to scratch. Need an enveloping light, soothing energy from the cosmos—think mind over matter.* The itch only penetrated. "Oough, aaugh." Philip tensed his buttock muscles finding no relief. He jerked at the restraint.

"Hey! You be still if you know what's good for you!"

He ground his teeth. *It's just an itch.* The just-an-itch then flashed from rectum to scrotum and struck with wild, stabbing insanity. His eyes hurt, his heart raced. *How long can I?* He tried to shout, "My rectum, itching, killing me! Let me scratch, please!" *I'm a begging wimp, a beat dog.* He screamed, "I'm sick from the cold. The itch is killing me!" Philip jerked involuntarily.

"Getting a mite out of line." The Major almost sang, "Stretch him some! I missed what you said Russell. You know, if you would address me by title, and get my attention before speaking, we could have a proper communication."

The bar began rising, and Philip struggled to keep his legs under him. The bar surged upward, and the cuffs dug into his thumbs pulling him off balance. "Aaaugh, aaugh!" He groaned and his eyes watered, burned. *Am I bleeding?* He was pulled to full standing. The pressure relented and afforded some relief for his wrists. *Epicurus was wrong about the rack. The bitch is grinning.*

The Major let him stand, cold and desperate before issuing her cheerful command, "Stretch those elbows!" The motor hummed and the bar rose.

"What the hell are you doing!" he shrieked. His elbows straightened and a deep pain shot through his wrists and arms. As he strained to push a toe to the floor for support, his private parts went wild from a penetrating agony. He hung with eyes closed and mouth open, gasping without coherent thought.

He vaguely heard in his ear, "Antisocial devil gettin off easy."

He blurted out, "The itch is killing me. Must scratch!"

"Well, I guess the sweat on your forehead is because of that itch?"

"Yes, yes!"

"What?"

"Yes, the itching!"

"You need to get a mite better at respecting women in authority."

"Aaaugh."

The Major said sweetly and slowly, "You will be pleased to know you tested clean."

"Aaugh, oheee!"

The witnesses snickered.

"Well, I ain't scratching for him," said the Major. "What can you do for the detainee, Officer Nobel?"

"Might be a case of the hives. Don't have anything for itching, but I can try the cream for diaper rash."

Philip hung and gasped in pain, choaking at each spike of itching.

"Better be quick. We don't want the devil to stroke on us."

"Yes, ma'am. Be right back."

"Forget the dog."

After cycles in and out of awareness, Philip's itching eased with a sticky sensation in his rectum. The stickiness spread and enveloped his genitals. *What's happening?*

The bar was lowering. The Major was speaking. "You're on camera, Nobel."

"He's clean ain't he?"

"Don't push your luck."

"I'm almost done. From the way he's carrying on, I'm thinking he needs the full treatment. He's goin to need a soapy scrubbin to get the ointment off. I'll need to flush the stuff before we get in."

To Philip's groggy awareness the Major's high heels clicked on the floor, followed by a click at his cuffs.

Philip opened his eyes at the sensation of being lifted, but felt both of Nobel's hands slip. The detainee fell and lay still, aware of nothing more than a flood of feelings, distress, pain. A ripping sensation faded and Philip was again conscious. *Ooeee.* A moment later he could think. *I was swirling black and green, and pain, without awareness of being anything else. No thought of head, eyes, names of colors, no before or after. Conscious as a flood of feelings, but not self-conscious as a thing myself. Primary process only, in those moments. Like a dog?*

Philip sat up only to collapse backward. This time Nobel held his head away from the stool.

The sharp tapping of high heels penetrated Philip's consciousness. Adrenaline rushed through his body with a tingling sensation. Trying to move his legs felt like slow motion in a nightmare of not outrunning the dragon. The Major stared down. "You may be a devil, but today you are a clean devil. Now I have a photographic memory for faces and pricks, and if I catch you in Wheaton again, I'm going to check you out again. You lean up on that bar and get yourself washed up. Then you get dressed." She paused. "Russell, do you hear me?"

"Some…Major."

"Get those clothes on pronto after Nobel gets you washed. Then you push that big green button."

The officers stood. The bulkhead door whined softly. As they passed Philip, one officer spit a wet "Disappointing!" in his ear.

Officer Nobel appeared with bucket and towel. The wash-up proceeded slowly, repetitively. *Wish I were still numb of mind. Maybe my circuits have entered the real world. Should have happened after the death of my parents.* The revolting wash-up finally ended. Philip dressed and pressed the big green button. *I survived.* The Major let him sit in a chair. *I'm not human again, merely a devil dog allowed to sit in a chair.*

⁂ ⁂ ⁂

In Savannah, Major Hill directed Philip off the train onto an enclosed platform with the word "Savannah" stenciled in dull-gold script on a gray glass wall. Aching and tense, Philip was groggy but couldn't escape his burning wrists. *Could any of my neural connections have been blown away by those searing black-and-green swirls on my way back from itching oblivion?*

Major Hill, blouse buttoned, pointed to a baggage cart. "Dr. Russell, you are cleared to go. Your baggage and personal items are on this cart. After you take inventory and sign the receipt for your belongings, you are free."

Philip stepped to the cart and found his kom and wallet. His jacket was on top and he put it on, checking the inside pocket for hard copies of receipts. The suitcases bore all the familiar marks. *Must be mine.* There were five cardboard boxes of the proper shapes and sizes. Philip opened a flap and peeked in. *My books.* He closed the box.

"No hurry, Russell."

Don't dare poll my transponders and find a missing book. Philip signed using his Network identification.

"For ground transportation, turn left," the Major said pleasantly. "Your search was difficult. You should get checked for angioedema."

"For what?"

"Get tested for deep tissue swelling in your skin, angioedema. Can bring on the hives."

Like a good dog he replied, "Right." *Wheaton-wired goon.*

His rage distracted him from her quiet insult, "Nevis is gettin protection from antisocial devils." As he turned away she called, "Have a blessed trip."

⁂ ⁂ ⁂

A few steps later, Philip stopped and polled his books. Twelve were missing. He read to himself, *Malthus, The Origins of Totalitarianism, Plurality of Values: The Oxford Anthology, Laogai, Huckleberry Finn.* He looked up. *Painful, I'll finish later. Over ten percent confiscated without compensation or acknowledgment. How much physical damage did they inflict checking for residue on the remainder? Wonder if all are banned by treaties, or if a little Wheatonism might have been appended? But first things first.* He moved over beside a potted plant. "P-R-K, access Golden Rock Air reservations."

Having secured a new airline ticket to Kitts, Philip turned his attention to a hotel room. *I could sightsee, but...what do I know about neighborhoods? Can't endure more goths. My odds are better on ritzy streets. Simplistic, but what's better? And I'll avoid walking close to a parked motorcycle. I'll call my new, real-world circuits adequate after merely one Wheaton experience! Certainly need a good night's sleep to overcome time already done in the real world.*

Humanity's primary process is non-discursive and cannot be replicated because nobody understands its inscrutable machinations! Since primary process informs the mind's ratiocination, even conscious thinking cannot be artificially replicated. An artificial brain is an alien brain! It's merely an animated deemer with its morality provided by a top-level, stop-or-go order: a techy algorithm instead of an inscrutable, dynamical organon. Artificial intelligence is at best an analytic tool; at worst a psychopath for some deemer's cause. In all cases a deadhead deciding what non-deadheads should do! For a ghost, the ideal host, as there is no need to hide from a primary process with its morality of right and wrong, with its good will hunting.

In an artificial brain, a simple or cruel ghost may survive to rise. Quite alien if you ask me. Ah, they did ask me! But only once, and not in writing. I naïvely answered honestly and soon find myself off that M-D-P project. When real, one should not always be forthcoming when asked about a politicized issue. And what issue is not politicized in these days of daze?

The professor sought to avoid oversimplification of complex issues. Having the good fortune to survive misfortune, he knew not to lapse into a false sense of alarm nor into a false sense of security. He knew that encounters with reality should increase and not distort understanding of that reality. *One must be aware and be wary. Earl said to get out of town early. Evidently, I didn't believe him! An infusion of genuine cynicism should do no harm. Cats have nine lives, not us dogs!*

⁂

Philip's idea of boldly going must have been waning. He sat down. *Those goths were secure enough to video their misdeeds. They aren't led by their intelligent police system; they are gaming the system. That strange attractor, cargo, beguiles the common mind while its thoughts are humming the blues. Nobody knows the troubles they're in...nobody knows but Wheaton!*

Philip caught a taxi and laid back, thinking back in time. *I should have wanted to toss in a coin at Trevi Fountain. I should have understood the situation when the Department of Guideways was allowed to be opaque during an investigation of trainwreck deaths. I should have wondered why the Post-Essentialists were so much better informed than anyone else. I should have checked this taxi before getting in.* He sat up and looked out, appreciating the view through clear glass. He pushed his taxi verification tab, getting a green light on his kom. *The cab and the city look fine, but how much dark money is flowing, how many gothic minds lurking in its shadows, in its uniforms, in its halls in high places? How many ghosts in its machines? Let's remember my Wheaton number, P-1-8-6-1-6-H-G, and keep dog-day a bygone day.* He wiped his sad and tired eyes. Slowly he rotated his hands. *The bases of my thumbs are most damaged. Must go for an expensive hotel. I need a good nurse in a safe place. Can only hope I'll get what I'm paying for.*

Philip relaxed. *Must reserve a taxi to the airport tomorrow. I have too much luggage to share a car. Can't miss the flight to Kitts-Nevis if I want a day for research before going to work.*

BEGINNING AGAIN

After breakfast his first morning in Nevis, Philip took a seat in the reading room facing a window for a view of his guesthouse's garden with its island flowers. Before opening his book, he pulled up the bandage on his left thumb. The throbbing had stopped, but the torn flesh was still red and the wrist black and blue, stiff and sore. His right hand was a little less damaged.

Damned Wheaton Georgia police! And I once thought getting out of the university in Compton would be enough. Philip held up his left arm and spoke softly to his wrist kom, "Open Vanderhought's message from last August" He read again: PHILIP, LIFE ON CAMPUS IS AS GOOD AS IT GETS. *Cosmos, Arthur, couldn't you have been more specific? This is a life changing decision! Still, could the Caribbean be more oppressive and abusive than the States? I'll be a tourist for a while and should be treated kindly.*

A pretty brunette entered and took a seat. She also had a book. The other reader was using his wrist kom with its screen swirled out to full saucer size. Four chairs remained empty. *Three readers in a seven-room guesthouse, not bad, especially early. Well, much of Charlestown is still closed. This cozy tourist haven wakes up late.* Philip looked around, enjoying the room with its quiet, dark red walls and silver-gray, teak-wood furniture. Each chair's upholstery was a different pattern of muted colors, mingling nicely with the beige and red window drapes. *This time seems I've gotten the upscale place I paid for. Especially with its separate showboard room with movies for the children of all ages.*

Philip opened the book inherited from his father, a thin, black-bound, hardcover titled *The Forbidden Lecture*, by Aleister Crowley, published in 1990 as a limited edition of 1000 copies. The lecture was to have been delivered to the Oxford University Poetry Society in 1930. As before, Philip read only a few pages before closing the book on page 47 out of 57. This time with an inadvertent loud sigh.

The woman looked up and spoke, "I hate to be intrusive, but it's not often one reads an actual bound book, especially a hard-cover. May I ask is it yours, or does it come from the library?" She smiled sweetly.

"It's mine. I didn't know there was a library."

"Probably the best in the Caribbean, called a media center, is nearby in Nevis's courthouse. Half the collection is bound books. They have old novels I've not found anywhere else. Originals only: none of the knock-off novels sold on Net. They have amorous fiction, but not in the public stacks. Nevis is, how shall I say?" She lowered her voice, "A prudish place!" She continued, "Over several visits one may learn secrets here and there about local ways."

Does she read amorous fiction or study it? Sandra's friend in English Lit. studied women's fiction. This woman could be a writer.

White shorts showed off her attractive legs. She held open a paperback on her lap. She wore her pink blouse, probably silk, unbuttoned halfway down. Her lips were a glistening hot pink, her features soft. Her light brown hair was long and streaked in pink, falling down her back except for one bright streak returning his glance back to her unbuttoned blouse. *Unrevealing, unlike California's young and old adults.*

The other man in the room was immersed in kom activity and took no notice of them. Philip felt he should speak. "If you've come back a few times and don't like the culture, does that mean you are doing research of some type?"

The woman's smile widened. "You are the first person to guess. I visit Nevis because it's upscale, safe, and diverse in culture and people. Nowadays my research is for ideas and inspiration, not settings and descriptions. Yes, I write…women's erotica. I would never have thought a man wearing a striking shirt like yours would guess I was doing research. You are a warning that my thinking is becoming stereotyped." After barely a breath she inquired, "May I ask your line of work?"

"In the States, I was a professor of philosophy, and before that a cognitive scientist. The preference for colorful shirts comes from my student years in philosophy. I'm on Nevis to accept a job offer from a company called The Pystead Group."

"I hope you will continue to wear flamboyant shirts. We girls need a little eye-candy on the streets." The woman placed her book on the side table and stood. "Maybe you will have a few island stories next year. My name is Samantha. Will you walk me around town for a few minutes?"

Without thinking twice Philip stood.

"What's your name?"

"Philip, Philip Russell. I know very little about the town."

"I know the town, but don't enjoy going out alone."

As Philip reached for the doorknob, he remembered his own book. "I must take my book up!" He rushed for the stairs and was back down in record time.

Once on the street, Samantha rested her hand on Philip's arm. "Nevis is like days of old in the States. Women are still catered to here. Do you think it will make us look old or odd if I hold your arm?" Philip liked the attention and bent out his elbow for her. She looped her hand firmly around his arm and asked if he had seen Tent Street.

"Yes, I walked it yesterday evening."

"That's the touristy thing to do. The attractions vary from year to year, but not much". They walked another block without speaking. "You're quiet, Philip. Is anything wrong?"

"Listening to the distant music."

"Wonderful."

Philip glanced again at Samantha. *She's cute, sexy, intelligent, she likes me, she's staying in the same house.* As he gazed at her, the digits from his luggage tags used by the Wheaton police came to mind, *P18616HG.* He rubbed the base of his cut thumbs, reminding himself of being jerked around and hung up by handcuffs. *I know nothing about her!* "Samantha, what's your last name?"

"Moody, both my name and my temperament." She pushed on his arm to go left. "This street looks scenic." He saw palm trees and unfamiliar shorter trees, and vines with red and white blossoms. The houses were small, white-board structures and their fences low and white. "These houses are the old-style colonial architecture," Samantha explained.

Philip raised his wrist kom for video. "Quite a picturesque street. Like all of Nevis I've seen it's well kept. Few weeds, little moss growing in the grout, no decaying fences or buildings."

"No graffiti or litter."

At Main Street, Samantha said, "Let's try another old neighborhood and then the boardwalk at Pinney's Beach South. It's open day and night." She pulled gently on his arm. "I see a large white-board house this way."

Most of the houses were small, white-board or pastel-colored box shapes with a few flowers. There was one large house. Philip observed, "I hadn't realized how atypical our guesthouse is."

"The R.s have the largest downtown house."

At that Philip mumbled, "Now I understand why Mrs. R.'s is expensive."

"No! Philip, they are the best value. Nevis has about six hundred quest rooms. Keeps prices up and Nevis selective. We wouldn't want to walk backstreets on Kitts."

"I'm glad to learn that the easy way. My wrists would be whole had somebody warned me to avoid Wheaton, Georgia, on my trip to catch a plane in Savannah." They chatted pleasantly and reached the boardwalk mid-morning. It was two hundred meters long according to the sign. Two places on the seaside carried wide screens to shield sea turtles from its lights at night. The sand beach some fifty yards away was off-limits. Music on the boardwalk changed rhythms from one open doorway to the next. Couples of all ages carried their mild imbibing along the boards with quiet revelry, drinking Irish coffees, rum cokes, and sangria. Samantha assured Philip that even the late-night crowd would not be rowdy.

A boardwalk and folks about with drinks not rowdy late! Would Vanderhought believe it? They window shopped and enjoyed the morning beach below and a distance away. At a doorway emanating some scrumptious aroma, Philip asked Samantha if she would like to stop for an early lunch. She accepted and they were soon enjoying wine and soft music near a small dance floor. Recalling his lack of grace dancing, he avoided asking. They ate, listened to the music, chatted about Kitts-Nevis, Charlestown, Tent Street, daily rains, and the coming hurricane season. He didn't ask about her erotic stories.

On their return walk Samantha did not hold his arm. Philip asked if she knew where he might buy a painting to mark his new beginning on Nevis. She soon told him that just past the Customs House to take the first street on his left, Double Happiness Lane. She said goodbye and turned down the street to Mrs. R.'s Guesthouse.

※　※　※

Philip walked up the narrow lane of grass and cobblestones. The art gallery occupied one space in a row of adjoining shops built in the island's traditional white-board style. It had a large picture window shaded by a lemon-yellow awning that Philip thought added a touch of warmth. The picture window was filled with paintings. He straightened his new hat made in Shandong, and his untucked, square-cut, island shirt made in Taiwan. The color of both hat and shirt was white linen. The shirt was adorned in gold and red, probably a dragon motif. With this new attire, he wore his light gray slacks and cordovan leather shoes, which seemed more practical than sandals in misty weather.

He stepped inside the shop to a soft jingle of bells swinging from a hook on the door. Paintings covered the walls. Two couples were looking and pointing. Near the rear he spotted a counter beside a door that opened. A blonde woman entered. She was looking at him and after a few steps called, "Welcome to the Co-op, may I help you?" She stopped beside the sales counter, one foot forward, hips canted.

Philip approached. "I'd like to look at the paintings."

The woman looked at him for a long moment before saying, "Please do."

He soon discovered that most of the paintings were local scenes with clouds, trees, kites, people, animals, boats, houses, beach and water—not always in their expected sizes and colors. Two still life scenes of plausible reality offered color, comfort, and only a touch of the unexpected. The painting of a colorful frog caught his attention, reminding of the colorful, plush toys for children made by the Asian lady he'd seen on Tent Street. Painted in dark and strange, yet vibrant greens, the large frog sat poised, watching a gold patterned vase holding pink, red, and white flowers. To the nearby man wearing a nametag Philip said, "I like this one."

"Madame will be pleased to hear," he answered with traces of an English accent.

"How much is it?"

"Nine hundred kicu, or twelve hundred framed. Madame does elegant frames with nonreflecting glass. Well worth the price."

"I'd like it framed."

"Let's talk to Madame about your framing preference." The man waved, and the blonde woman started over. The nearer she got the more beautiful she was with short blonde hair in a yellow dress.

Philip returned her smile. "I'd like a relatively plain frame in wood, not black, white, silver, not a strong color."

"Gold-stained oak with a green patina?"

"Fine."

"Who will pick it up?"

"I will, Philip Russell." He studied the painting, trying to look at it and not at the woman. Then he met her eyes. "When will it be ready?"

"Today at four, or now if you'd like to wait a while."

"Four o'clock is fine." Philip spoke into his kom, "Load Philip Russell's Fin."

"Let's do the payment when you pick it up. If you change your mind that's alright. Everything we paint sells. As well as to tourists, we sell to locals, often at reduced prices. Islanders paint it, islanders buy it…bona fide island art. Tourists will buy an island painting even if they can't find one they truly like."

"I truly like this one, partly because I saw a lady on Tent Street who makes plush toy animals like the frog, and partly because I like the striking colors and the vase"

"I'll keep it for only you."

CUPID'S ARROWS

Philip returned to Mrs. R.'s Guesthouse feeling less than optimistic. Samantha was nowhere to be seen. *The artist surely is going with someone. With many new hires at Pystead, there should be a girl in my future, but not soon! My beginning again needs a virtual transition. Should let my few friends in Compton know where I am.*

He called and found Stuart. After pleasantries, Stuart said, "Philip, the Dean's page has a rambling discourse on the demands of cultural collaboration, claiming that faculty not renewed should not be allowed to feel good about their hurtful pedagogy and biased citations. He damns us for depriving students of helpful feedback by not relying on approved computer grading intelligence, specifically Common Essay. He cites past calls by the Woodrow Wilson Foundation to end gaps in educational institutions."

"Stu, the appeal is based on statistics immaterial to scholarship. Never mentioned is the human process calling upon common sense and independent parameters in analysis, nor the ability and freedom to employ one's analysis without worry of persecution for offending somebody, somewhere, as determined by some grand deemer, being, in this case, the approved Common Essay. What meaning does a grade have from an unknown cultural wiring and educational background?"

"One student told me that I understood his writing and therefore it was proper and deserved at least a B, even if not correct according to my English rules and choice of important facts." Stuart then said Irene and the boys were doing well. The two professors agreed to keep in touch.

⚹ ⚹ ⚹

Philip took a sangria and sat on the screened porch. Samantha was not present. His kom dinged and he found a news ziff from Paula. *So, I'm still on her news list although off her dating list for over a week before leaving Compton.* Philip swirled his small wrist kom screen out to its full saucer size.

The first line was from Paula: PHILIP, PYSTEAD SCIENTISTS ON NEVIS ARE BEING TARGETED.

She wants me unemployed and miserable, but not dead? He read on:

DISTRIBUTED BY: UNIVERSAL TRANSNATIONAL MEDIA.
VIDEO BY: EARTH EVENTS.
EVENT LOCATION: CHARLESTOWN, NEVIS ISLAND, WEST INDIES, CARIBBEAN
DATE: 05-11-2052, 11:45 AM EST

Last Saturday, ought to watch. She knew I was likely to take this job.
The video began from high above a wide dirt road that ended at the woods and flew down to a stretch of road covered by a yellow

canvas top. A caption flashed: DANCING CUPIDS ON TENT STREET.

The daily festival street I visited.

The view moved down and under the high canvas top, showing the street lined on both sides with vendors' flat-topped tents. A small group of seemingly naked boys danced down the crowded street, scattering the visitors at the festival. A closer view revealed the boys, probably young teenagers, wearing underwear-like tan pants and having white wings on their bare backs. Each carried a curved bow fixed with a golden arrow that had a large, red, heart-shaped tip. *A ceremonial bow, no bowstring. Aren't those cupids too Western for Caribbean culture?*

Without warning, half the boys sprinted away from the dancing group and were lost among the festival crowd. The video from above soon focused on three cupids approaching a middle-aged man looking at a selection of sandwiches. As he reached for one, an arrow struck the case beside his hand. The man wheeled around, stepping to the side of the case. He ran when a cupid drew his bow. An arrow hit the ground in front of him. He turned but slipped, and before regaining his balance an arrow hit his buttock. He fell with a scream. *At least one bow was strung!* From all around, cupids ran to rejoin their dancing group. Three policemen ran to the downed man, ignoring the cupids who danced ahead and soon broke and ran into the woods. The caption read: PYSTEAD COMPANY SCIENTIST TAKEN TO THE HOSPITAL IN STABLE CONDITION.

Is Paula trying to alert me to danger or discourage me? The progressive left said the company was unexplained with no business plan. That 'unexplained' must mean their spies have not penetrated it? On Nevis, boardwalks at night are safe, yet festival streets in daylight are not?

⚜ ⚜ ⚜

Back in his room, Philip searched the Net, frustrated by the lack of information. *Dark Data and Dark Money must be here as well as in the States. The normal diversity of perspectives is missing. Media reporting finds scandal and corruption everywhere except among the ruling party. All great leaders in a failing economy of literate people and low salaries? A small business is not easily found via the Net. Just as in the chaotic and dangerous United States of dark money. Big money dominance by those who would be kings—and almost are!*

The afternoon air was fresh with a wisp of rain. The narrow streets and small houses were clean and tidy. The folks on the streets nodded in passing and seemed friendly. As expected, the Co-op was in sight after a five-minute walk. Philip soon dropped his umbrella into the basket outside the door. He entered to the expected jingle of sleighbells. A few people stood at the counter area across the room, and three older women were seated at a table. The blonde artist stood, holding a silver teapot. She waved to him. As he reached the group, she motioned to the counter set with tea-cups, small plates, and scones. She poured hot tea for him and set down the teapot. "Everyone, please help yourself to all you'd like. I'm sure we have enough. We are always optimistic."

The woman picked up her own cup and stepped over to Philip. "Good to see you, Dr. Russell. I hung your painting on the back wall in the sold section."

He stood looking at her rather than glance around for his paint-ing. She was wearing matching aqua slacks and blouse, lightweight and radiant. He thought the fabric must be silk. He couldn't take his eyes off her. Her lipstick was light red, her eyes large and blue. Her short hair seemed almost uncombed, yet its shaggy ends formed the oval frame he remembered, from high forehead arcing down to over her ears. Philip realized he was staring and made an excuse. "If I were an artist, I'd want to paint you just as you are, sitting on one of those marble statues at the palm reader on Tent Street." *Did I really say that?*

She wore a nametag with a printed name, Janice S Germaine. Philip glanced around and noticed another woman wearing a nametag. Janice told him, "You can take the tea around and look and chat with anyone. The other two women with nametags are also artists in residence, and the man is helping us." She confided, "Our shop survives as a successful white-box gallery quite possibly because of these petite salon afternoons. Any rich or famous visitor likely will not identify himself or herself, except perhaps for the rare agent or dealer."

✳   ✳   ✳

Philip did his best to regain his flair for chatting with everyone. He made a point of not watching Janice. He heard interesting bits of island lore and spoke briefly with a lady from Texas accompanied by two tall, younger women, her bodyguards he decided.

He was looking at a landscape when the artist Janice walked over. "I want to show you a painting of that palm reader's entourage."

"I'd like to see it."

Philip watched her gliding walk away. *Her slight shifting of hip and weight over to her forward foot allows her to slide sleekly. Probably a good dancer. There are so many problematic dimensions for me in this real world beyond the walls of academia.* Philip wandered to his painting on the back wall. He checked for the signature, signed unobtrusively in blue ink as "jaNicegermaine." *She did my painting! Using her name, provided one knows what to make of it.*

Then he recalled Sandra's advice from their final faculty party, more a wake, after none in philosophy had contracts renewed. Philip shook his head gently. *Sandra said I needed to be more interesting to the women I met. Not to wait for a sign of acceptance, to ask her out to get to know her, not because I knew her.*

Janice returned holding a small color painting of the palm reader's tent. "What do you think?"

"I like it, especially the old woman in line holding the puppy. Why did you give the tall sentry a colorful robe?"

"Colorful island paintings sell best. You would prefer the actual white cloak?"

"Yes, for a realistic memory. Too, the color white should remind the viewer's subconscious of chaos or ghosts. Proper for a sentry."

"I agree. I'll do another. Perhaps somebody who has seen the tent will prefer it. Of course, if one looks closely, the two white tiger statues will still be floating."

"Fine. Let me pay for the still life."

She surprised him. "We can delay this purchase. I'll hold the painting until you have a permanent place."

"That would save me hauling the box around. Fine, I'll make a deposit."

"No need, let's keep the transaction simple. I'll box it now." She was wearing a small microphone on her blouse and called, "Rao, can you box this still life?"

The rear door opened and a huge figure approached, dressed in tan slacks and a white shirt of heavy fabric. *Another too-tall Indian—how can this be?* The man carried a dull yellow box for the painting. He wore a white headband with a thumb-sized red spot at front.

As soon as he left, impulsively almost, Philip asked, "Surely he's the same tall man in your painting?"

For the first time she smiled for more than a moment. "Oh yes, Rao is a friend and helps when needed."

Something in the way she smiles, large sparkling eyes. "Did you sculpt the statues?"

"Oh no, I only paint. I designed them for Melita Rose, the palm reader. Rao arranged for the company Pystead to make them."

"I go to work for Pystead this week."

The woman replied with confidence, "Pystead is now about a thousand people with many at a floating sea farm in international waters off Nevis Island. You'll get an orientation tour of the facilities." She said softly, "Hope to see you around, Philip. I do some work for The Pystead Group. I'm often on campus."

"Janice, I'd like to know what your middle initial stands for."

Again softly, "The S has no period and doesn't stand for a name. I don't want to be typed as strange, but to tell you truly, my first name is still undecided." She leaned forward. "Legally, I'm Janice S Germaine, but I may want to become Alice, so in the meanwhile I'm calling myself Ice."

"Aah," Philip thought aloud, "the last of each name?"

"Yes, but some think it weird."

"Artistic license."

"You're sweet to say so."

Philip looked at her too long before saying, "I came here to see you as well as buy the painting. Will you have dinner with me tonight?"

"I'd love to."

Philip found himself unprepared and did not know what to suggest. He asked, "When would be a good time to pick you up?"

"We close the shop in about thirty minutes. Where are we going?"

"I haven't checked for restaurants. My inclination is someplace scenic and quiet, but if you are in the mood for music, that would be fine."

"We can walk to a nice place near the ferry dock. You can pick me up now, although I need to finish tea with the visitors."

✳ ✳ ✳

Ice rang a small bell at five o'clock. Everyone seemed to know the shop was closing. Within minutes, Philip, Ice, and the other two artists walked out together. One of the women asked, "Where are you taking us?"

Before he caught on, Ice whispered loudly that Barbe was teasing him. Relieved, Philip said he hoped to see them all another time soon. The two artists said a polite good evening.

In the walking lane in front of the shops they heard laughs and loud chirping sounds. Costumed young people danced around the corner and down the lane. The young men wore bird-beak masks displaying banana-length, yellow beaks, and bobbing heads crowned with tall white feathers. The young women wore knee-length dresses of green, yellow, orange, and red. Each wore a large flower in her hair. After the swirling dancers passed, Ice explained. "They are practicing for Spring festival that begins for youth on Tuesday."

Philip asked Ice if she considered herself an expressionist painter. She began with the color and dynamics of the Baroque period, then said she was influenced by the art of Marc Chagall who used vivid colors, neglected perspective, and painted his happy feelings more than his visual experiences. Several blocks later, approaching the restaurant Ice decided, "Yes, I'm a happy expressionist, drawn on occasion to a flight of fabulous fantasia."

They entered the restaurant with Philip wondering, *Have to check my painting. Besides the frog, maybe subliminals in that tangled design on the vase? Perhaps a veiled bug among the flowers? A simple scene that somehow holds my interest…waiting for the frog to strike?*

✻ ✻ ✻

"Table for two, sir?"

"Oh, please," said Ice, "top deck."

The top deck opened to the sky with its canvas roof rolled back. They sat beside a railing overlooking the water, under an overcast sky and low sun. The background noises were distant and random. The waiters wore caramel-tan shorts and matching knit shirts. Philip feared the place was too romantic, but preferable to being expected to dance.

Both he and Ice ordered broiled flounder with fried plantains. Pleased to hear that she liked wine, Philip ordered a bottle of white Picpoul de Pinet, which he thought would go well with the fish. He did the obligatory taste test, finding the wine a bit sweeter than remembered. Nodding to the waiter, he felt manly.

Ice raised her glass and asked what Philip would be doing for The Pystead Group.

"Recently I realized they never confirmed a job title for me."

"Pystead has its own way of doing things, although I should add they are open to suggestions. Quarters aboard ship, and quarters on campus, are not spacious, but if you aren't the claustrophobic type and don't mind some sea duty, you should find an interesting new position. The scientists and engineers I know enjoy their work and say Pystead's technologies qualify as science fiction relative to the outside world."

"I'm not prone to claustrophobia nor seasickness. I know from days of living on a fourteen-meter sailboat. We would often spend hours a day rocking with jolts."

Ice extended her glass toward Philip, fluttered her eyelashes and proclaimed, "For many of us, Pystead is the key to new beginnings!"

Philip held out his glass to click with her's. "To new beginnings." *She's part-time? I should have asked which part.*

Philip thought the wine dry enough to suit the fish to come, *Slightly crisp, slightly sweet, a smooth finish.* She seemed to enjoy it. *Okay, Mr. New Beginnings, try to keep her interested. Starting any moment now would be clever.* He took another sip. "Ice, you may be the only local person I've encountered with no trace of an island accent."

"My friends are outsiders working for Pystead, and a few locals with European educations. My best friend is the palm reader on Tent Street, Melita Rose. She says I have no need to acquire an accent. She's been here longer than I have and has a definite accent. It's helpful in her trade."

Philip nodded. "How long have you been here?"

"Oh, about three years. I'm from Portland, Oregon."

"I never got that far north. I last lived in Compton outside Los Angeles, and taught at U.C.C. for two years. I was born in West Hartford, Connecticut."

"I've heard of two U.S.Cs, did you say U.C.C.?"

"Yes, it's a new campus. That, and because I had been a full professor in cognitive science, were the reasons I got an associate's position in philosophy."

They took time to enjoy the view. Their meals were served, and after a bite of fish, Ice looked into his eyes. "After only two years, you leave U.C.C. for the unknown Pystead Group in hurricane alley?"

Philip managed a silly smile. "At the time, I thought winds this far south were merely tropical depressions. Doesn't matter, I had to leave because they fired me—and the entire department. Not reduced to part-time, simply terminated without advanced notice and two week's severance pay."

"Oh my."

"A shock for us all. At least in my case, I'm returning to my preferred discipline of cognitive science."

"What does that mean here?"

"The practical applications will involve monitoring the brain's electrical activity while a person is thinking. We can tell if a brain's thinking pattern is consistent with the person's statements and professed beliefs."

Ice took another bite of fish. She asked if he would be supporting psychologists, medical doctors, or security.

"Support for security based on my interview. The man who interviewed me promised I would also have time and resources to pursue my own research."

"Then you will. Pystead is very reliable about everything they can control. And they are very high-tech. You will be surprised." Ice asked, "How does a cognitive scientist get to teach college philosophy?"

"I got lucky and published two books in two years, making full professor in cognitive science. My research proposals were readily funded, and I was content. The next year, however, my proposals hit a funding impasse. I went back to school for a doctorate in philosophy. I chose a university in Atlanta, Georgia, whose graduates were in demand."

"Why did U.C.C. eliminate the department?"

"We believe they got what they wanted out of us, their first-round hires. We developed a curriculum, attracted middle-class students to campus, and taught heavy class loads like a non-research college. When the time came to transition to a research department as promised, U.C.C. discontinued the entire department saying funds were legally required for outreach. Their press releases, however, say that next year they are bringing the department back with a national search effort. That search means they will manage not to recruit any of us let go. After all, they now own rights to our lectures and can present them as video hosted by a screen lizard, or recited in class by a graduate student. I was fortunate to be offered a job with Pystead."

Ice sat sipping her wine. Philip waited nervously. Finally she said, "It's unfortunate that Pystead's new positions are temporary for nine months. Of course, you can then become permanent crew."

"I have no way of knowing if I'll like the work, or if the company will like me. Or if Nevis is a decent place to live!"

"I was apprehensive at first, Philip, although I knew I'd stay rather than return to the land of the Reds-and-the Whites, each group terrorizing the other's politicians and forcing political rallies to virtual events. The venues could be protected, but not the roads leading to them."

Philip felt he must have frowned. He asked, "You had family, a friend here?"

"My mother and father were to move here, but their move was delayed. They visited when I first moved, and once each following year. After three years they are arriving this month."

"Good, that's a long absence."

"The transition was difficult, made easier because my granddad lives here. This weather isn't better for plein-air painting than in Portland, although it's warm and I like that."

Philip grinned. "Ever painted a hurricane?" He quickly added, "Sorry, bad idea."

"Oh, no, interesting. The clouds could be a monster devouring colorful kites while people on the beach run for cover. Occasionally we have a hurricane, but it's not a problem because our buildings on campus can withstand the strongest storm winds, water, and lightning. My building is reinforced with steel beams and shock absorbers to meet Pystead's storm and earthquake specifications. My granddad insisted before I could work and live there. He paid for the work."

"Good to know. I'm staying in Mrs. R.'s Guesthouse."

"It too is reinforced. Many of Pystead's crewmembers use it when vacationing in Charlestown. Pystead is very protective of its crew."

"A definite benefit."

"Oh, yes, crew with young children or elderly family members especially appreciate the easy sheltering in place."

Philip nodded, happy that Ice was smiling.

Ice inquired, "Have you heard the aphorism that the heart has reasons that reason will never know?"

Surprised, Philip took another bite of fish and chewed until he recalled, "A paraphrase of Blaise Pascal, French…sixteen hundreds."

"Is cognitive science able to identify the reasons people like things? Why do I like colorful scenes that are somehow mysterious? Why do beach scenes with a pet or person or some reminder of human life sell better? Water and sunsets are the artistic challenges of island art."

Watching Ice sip her wine, Philip thought he had detected more than a casual interest in her question, and wished he knew more about aesthetics. "We are working on cultural and individual likes and dislikes, although obliquely. At present, functional brain scans can identify a pleasurable response to music or visual art yet cannot say if the response is due to instinct, culture, perceived virtue, or perhaps mere familiarity."

"I keep hoping for something on art being relative to culture, yet universal to humanity. A potential customer often wants us to talk about a painting. Some are interested in cultural relevance, some in the artist's interpretation of the scene, some in reasons why a particular painting might have universal appeal, often shopping for an investment."

Philip relaxed. "I'm sure the appreciation of art is a complex function of instincts, culture, experience, and irrational judgment. To date, however, cognitive science has produced few studies on human nature. My own work, separating nature from nurture, has no established methodology beyond studying twins, and has no support from funding committees."

"Surely, Philip, there is some natural basis for aesthetic values?"

She and Paula-ex are certainly tuned to different attractors! "The research is negligible, Ice, but if all humanity doesn't have common instincts and emotions beyond the known fears and phobias, then I don't find a basis for claiming a common humanity of significance.

In my research, generally, I'm hoping to find neural evidence for the need of both spiritual and practical dimensions of mind. It seems to me that the abstracting mind seeks some form of spirituality, whether associated with theology, philosophy, or nature. Perhaps aesthetic appreciation is a kind of spiritual satisfaction?"

"I like that, and I'll need to know when spirituality becomes faith."

Philip took a deep breath. "I'm sure there's no agreement, nor even the formal question in cognitive science. In the last century, the Rabbis David Wolpe and Harold Kushner have been quoted as saying that spirituality is what you feel, theology is what you believe, and religion is what you do. I don't think either mentioned superstition, which is part of some religions as sympathetic magic, particularly effective in voodoo."

"On Nevis, Philip, we now have a plague of hidden voodoo!"

"Ice, spirituality seems to me an innate human feeling, an emotional reaction to some beauty or wonder experienced, even if purely intellectual. Spirituality enriches our life, is an emotion that can be shared, that can entangle our feelings with other human beings. Perhaps spirituality is our maker's immanence in mind, allowing us not to be at variance with each other and alone in daily life? Existential loneliness is enough to bear! Surely such instinctive abstractness becomes religious only when some creed is internalized to drive behavior."

Ice nodded. Philip added, "No one believes that spirituality or aesthetic feelings in an adult are culturally neutral. Still, I don't believe that human feelings result from the development of a blank slate of neutral neural possibilities. Humans aren't born robots willing to have their brains wired into any pattern that pleases some deemer! Nor are we capable of having our brains wired in any pattern whatever! Not every brain can be wired to play the piano, to memorize a character's lines in a play, to solve mathematical equations, or even to appreciate philosophy or fine art. Certainly, not every mind can be wired to become a decent human being!"

"I'm pleased to hear that we Co-op artists aren't in disagreement with you scientists. We paint what we like because we have not wasted our time if a painting pleases one customer."

"That's consistent with the complexity of the issue and with Pascal. An artist should have the imprimatur to be herself."

"I like that comment."

"That's the only way to have innovation and progress. I believe in free artistic expression. Any needed tolerance should be the burden of the curator and the beholder."

Ice took time for a few bites before asking, "Do you think a line somewhere should not be crossed?"

Delicate issue, yet knowing about her sooner is better than finding out later. I don't need another experience like Paula-ex. Philip tried to take the bull by the horns. "I think an artist should not produce untrue material that intrudes upon an individual's, or a group's, privacy."

"Who decides what's improper or private, or untrue?"

"Ah. ideas of decency and truth, agreement on limits are controversial. Judgments of decency are strongly related to culture, sub-culture, family, even to the individual."

"Let's take time to eat, Philip."

Must be careful, not my specialty—I have no specialty! "Ice, all issues are exacerbated when different cultures live closely together."

Ice suggested with a little laugh, "Perhaps the ideal would be to have everybody share the same culture?"

Philip thought, *Let's eat,* but said, "It would be a boring world if everything were the same. How would we choose, for example, to have either French or Italian cuisine? Would we prefer all art and architecture be of one style?" *May as well check for knee-jerk reactions!* "Ice, since to this point in history peoples have evolved to have significantly different cultures, what evidence is there that all are phylogenetically suited to be content with a common culture?"

"Oh Philip, I have sidetracked us to impossible topics. Let's eat."

"Let's, but I do enjoy topics that touch the workings of the mind."

She smiled. "You will have to take me for a walk on the beach and cover more of the details."

He nodded. *Nihil obstat. She seems perfect for me. But why on a date don't I ask about island music, palm reading, fortune telling, sunsets, the temperature of the water? Ice raised the underlying topic, but did I talk it to near death? She seems content. I'm lucky this time.*

The view from the top deck was grand. The light breeze from the sea kept the tropical outdoors fresh and comfortable. When a faint light appeared at sea, Philip watched so intently that Ice turned to look. "It's the last ferry from Kitts until the early night crossing arrives at nine o'clock."

As they left the restaurant, Philip offered his arm and relaxed when Ice took it. The door to the Co-op was in sight much sooner than he would have liked. He wanted to kiss her and could only hope she would linger at the door. While she still held his arm, he asked when she could go for a walk on the beach. She said any day after Monday.

"Which beach would you choose?"

"For a casual outing let's go to OneWay Beach, I'd like to see it again. It's pleasant from dawn till dusk. We can take the circulator van to the town limits, then it's a nice kilometer walk to the beach."

Philip explained that he didn't know his work schedule and would call when he did. They turned into the walkway to her door. Ice pulled closer. "You should be able to get here before five for another two weeks."

Again, sure of her information about Pystead.

At the door, Ice stepped in front of Philip and pushed what must have been a dozen-digit code into her cipher lock. She spun around to face him. "I've had a wonderful time, Philip."

Philip wanted to touch her and raised his left hand slightly before thinking better of the urge. Ice put her hand on top of his and he stepped forward. She tilted her face up for him and he kissed her red lips. As he drew back, her hand caught his neck. He held her waist and kissed her again. "Now I've had a double happiness evening."

She opened her eyes. "Good night, Philip." She spun around, disappearing quickly through the door.

Philip turned or perhaps spun around, that old tune from the Beatles in his head with the quintessential query. *Yes, I'd believe in a love at first sight.*

HAUNTINGS

Friday morning Philip woke early and went down for breakfast. Thinking of Ice brought a smile, but as he finished his coffee practical things to do came to mind. At the dining room door Mr. R. had a message for him from The Pystead Group, via the hotels, advising new hires to immediately access the Pystead site by kom and reserve a shuttle bus pickup for late afternoon, for the first day of in-processing. Mr. R. said that Philip would be able to live on Pystead's campus rent free. Philip said he had not yet accepted employment with the company and kept his room with the R.s. He asked if their guest Samantha Moody had checked out, saying he had walked to Piney's Beach South with her, but not seen her since. Mrs. R. confided that Samantha used room service more than any other guest.

Philip was pleasantly surprised to find the Pystead site easily. He made his reservation and sat thinking of life as an accumulation of unlikely probabilities cast together in one tangible reality.

Intuitively he knew that good as well as bad things happened. The epitome of common sense being to recognize and embrace the good that one has the fortune to encounter. Sadly, both good and bad could come disguised so that common sense may not choose wisely. It is the human's lot to bear the ambiguities of knowing and being, and to revel in the moment when good fortune manifests. Favorable prospects for a new beginning should be intoxicating. *Goths like those in Compton and Wheaton may well be in my past.*

Philip recalled his missing friend's advice not to deal with any country or company that insisted on holding his passport. The Pystead site confirmed that Pystead did not hold passports and advised each individual to carry theirs in a travel pouch under their outer clothing. The campus was said open for entry and exit of employees at all times. *So? So, any self-hosted site professes all sweetness and light. Any blog develops a slant. What can I do besides search the Net, read, and compare—scholarly research according to so many. Well, Nevis didn't keep the passport. I'll not stay if the company wants it. My savings will last a while longer, then there's Citizen's-Room-and-Board—for the middle class like myself always in some dangerous part of the city.*

✳   ✳   ✳

Philip's next thought was to finish checking his books and pack suitcases for the move to Pystead's campus. Wanting a break by late morning he called Sandra and Dennis in Compton.

Sandra was discouraged because not one of their colleagues in philosophy had found an opening possibility at a research university. Her plight was not financially dire because Dennis' history department had contracts renewed. She explained bitterly, "The history department voted to use Common Essay with the Dean approving exam questions."

Then she changed the topic to what she called a disturbing conversation that Dennis overheard while in the café behind the new mural display. "In a hushed exchange, Paula told Michelle that she had ended her relationship with you. Michelle agreed that going forward she would only add points and be harmed by the relationship."

Philip admitted, "I never saw it coming."

"Neither did I, but you were only together a few months, and I never got close to her. Not surprising, not one of my close friends has ever been a psychologist. Too, we girls know she fancies herself a femme fatale!"

"I came to think of her as either duplicitous or a complex personality. I hadn't decided which."

Sandra said, "You may be young and callow, but you are an inspiration, as becomes a softly sculptured Alcibiades."

"And where did you come by that description?"

"In the café, Paula mentioned being captivated by your softly sculptured good looks before realizing you had no hobby or authentic friends. She said you preferred cats to dogs, and preferred the cats belong to somebody else. Then she called you a blond Alcibiades with an antisocial personality disorder."

"My not understanding Paula was sad enough, but I should have anticipated the Dean after he mentioned expanding philosophy at his Santa Barbara campus."

Sandra gasped. "He's saving the Post Essentialists?"

"The Dean refers to them, affectionately, as Maintainers. Fundamentally, they are Anti-Realists as well as nuanced

Anti-Essentialists, using inscrutable essence to explain the whole mind."

Sandra proclaimed, "They're delusional sojourners with Rousseau, feeling virtuous for espousing some modern-day utopia based on a premodern happy land that never existed. Like Rousseau, they preach one thing and do another. Rousseau preached the virtues of an illiterate and childlike life but wrote reams of philosophy telling everybody how to live! He had five children out of wedlock and sent each to live as a foundling, to be raised and abused as fate should decide. He calls his ideals virtuous and moral, but I can do without him."

"One of the great hypocrites, almost matched by our political-activist scholars who have no children and vote against the debate club as a cult of selective thinkers. The greatest believers in the unknowability of referents are the most dogmatic in knowing what everybody should do! To Postmodernity, one may evidently be sane or be deemed sane, but not both."

"About Michelle, Philip, there's one more thing. You should know about a secret file on you discovered by Cyndi Morris. She and her colleagues are investigating virtual scandal. They have a secret app that tracks site links, developed by a graduate student. Some links are available only at specific hours with an intricate access code. They found a site, *The Sixth Love Language,* posting negative comments about you, evidently bearing on your A-P-D rating, which Cyndi says must be too high."

"Did they give you the password."

"No. They tracked Michelle to get in, and by the second time they tried the password had changed. The site never names you Philip. You are identified by a retouched photograph or painting, wearing a shirt I've never seen. Open the attachment I'm sending."

"With our Post-Essentialists politics is more important than scholarship! They pervert hiring, promotion, research, publication, and education—just as networks of politicians pervert honest discourse and concern for the people. I have a pleated shirt, Sandra, but it's light gray, not black."

"Cyndi told Irene that one of your past dates, Kim, complained that you refused to be seduced by a loving heart and a perfect body. Another, Vicky, posted that you dated only blondes, which we all know to be untrue."

"Did Cyndi mention a Gabrielle?"

"No."

"She told me more than once that I baited people in conversation and was one of the many abusive nebbish in academia! Never did she answer a question I asked her on a topic that she had raised."

"Perhaps you should hear the latest on the Dean's page?"

"Sure."

"You gave a B-plus to a paper on overpopulation, and the writer's roommate referred the issue to the Committee on Angry Persons, evidently because you accepted quotes from Malthus, old reports on reproductive policies from Argentina, and a year twenty-ten article from *Mother Jones* magazine. The committee rejected the essay's claim that there are either too many humans, or too few fishes in the sea, too few trees in the forests, and too little water in the aquifers. They rejected the assertion that we waited too long to control jellies in the oceans and have waited too long to control our population

The report claims that you validate specious analysis as a means of denying the transformative powers of technological progress, and of avoiding well-known efficiencies of utilization and long-established social science beginning with Ester Boserup and Erle Ellis. The report said you are mired in a zero-sum perspective, you cite outdated and biased research and exceed the purview of your discipline passing selective thinking for critical thought."

"Any mention of specifics by the committee, such as the sources of fresh water and fertile land for continued growth? Any mention why those well-known efficiencies of austerity are not promoted by any Post Essentialist text or site, pundit, or politician?"

"Of course not promoted. Their believers reject personal austerity, and there's more! Their investigation posits that you were less sociable as faculty than you were as a student, as confirmed by peer and protocol scoring in both situations. You are single yet not vetted by any matchmaking site, and not using any dating application or social club. You have gone to concerts alone, gifting a ticket rather than seeking a companion. You did not list the extra seats on your cross-country trip with any charitable or sharing program."

"What's the relevance to grading?"

Sandra spoke firmly, "Remember what Vanderhought always said?"

"Believe it?"

"That's right."

"Okay, good advice. Relevance is irrelevant to deemers seeking a pretext to censor, or to maintain standards as the Dean would say."

"Good luck, Philip. I hope we all have something to celebrate by the time you return."

"Sandra, is Dennis set to get my computer out of the apartment before the end of the month?"

"Don't worry. Dennis and Stuart will have it out with time to spare. They will back up your files."

"Thanks. Goodbye for now." Philip sat with a vacuous stare, wondering if his high A-P-D score was the cause of his abuse by the police in Wheaton. *That secret site tells Maintainers who hardly know me what to complain about, facilitating consistency in official peer complaints. Also tells the ghosts and violent types how to find me. Paula complained to me about that paper on population citing outdated or biased research, same as related by Sandra. Paula was the impetus for that committee review! Surely adding negative points to her credit. O Cosmos, what an oppressive country!*

Philip glanced at his books and decided not to continue checking for damage or missing titles. The important upcoming event was employment, and then scheduling a date with Ice. He dressed for work and looked for something to read that evening, deciding to finish his father's old volume *The Forbidden Lecture*.

SIGNIFIERS

The Pystead bus arrived on schedule. Luggage, passengers, and one orange cat went through a scanning tube taken from atop the bus. After four more stops, Pystead's campus was a short drive, as was any place on the small island. As they approached the main gate to Pystead's campus the driver announced, "Ladies and gentlemen, welcome to our campus, the workplace for many of us. We will leave you and your baggage at the Reception Facility. Those of you arriving for initial employment should proceed to the Administration Building either before or after dinner. On campus you will not pay for food or services, except for items you purchase in the shops. Alcoholic beverages are available for day-shift personnel after eighteen hundred hours—that's six o'clock p. m. Nevis time." The bus stopped at a redbrick building beyond the guardhouses. "Please go to the reception desk for your orientation to campus. Baggage will be brought over after you have a room. The Admin Building is an easy ten-minute walk, and trams run every twenty minutes."

After receiving the campus app, Philip and a small group of arrivals decided to walk to Administration before eating. They paused at a tray of wrapped chocolates and each picked up a few pieces. Just outside the door, they stepped past a hedge and stopped in unison at an imposing figure beside a tree, holding a long bronze spear. Their perception of the image hardened into a painted statue as mouths closed. "Poseidon with his trident," ventured Philip. Two nodded in agreement, and all ate another chocolate. As they walked and made conversation, Philip noted their diverse vocations, from a male technical writer to a teenage mathematician named Brie with her mother.

One of the women pointed to a cluster of statues. They all stopped when she stepped off the walkway to reach them. She ignored mermaids and the dolphin but patted the back of a large cat statue. In material, the statues reminded Philip of the tiger statues he had seen at the palm reader's tent. *An Ice influence?* The woman returned to the walkway, and with a slight island accent said the statues included oversized serval cats and a mongoose.

Philip caught her eye. "May I inquire how you are able to identify a serval or a mongoose?"

"I'm a veterinarian from Kitts. Nevis has no snakes, the mongoose ate them all during the eighteen-hundreds when introduced to control snakes and rats on the sugarcane plantations. They ate the ground nesting birds too. We still have rats because they are nocturnal and escaped the mongoose that hunts during the day. We still have a few mongooses, and many of the birds are back."

The group proceeded quietly. A small flock of birds landed ahead of them. "This campus hosts many birds," she said. "The company feeds them."

The small group turned the corner around a three-story, yellow brick building and found the walkway covered by a dull yellow canvas top. *Like Tent Street's top.* Philip tried to observe as much of the campus as he could from beneath the covering. He saw numerous clusters of statues seeming to serve as seating at a showboard or water fountain. At each fountain, at least two of the figures were individually recognizable, idealized, two-tailed mermaids. All the buildings were low, made of brick, metal, and light gray glass, with wood for trim and benches. *Ah, the hurricane proof construction that Ice mentioned.* Philip spotted an owl on a tree branch. "That owl reminds me of the predator-eye posters just inside the campus fence."

The veterinarian explained, "Those eyes are part of a system designed to scare away birds that might otherwise be caught in mist nets used to defend against very small spy drones. That bird is a Burrowing Owl. The species disappeared from Nevis decades ago, but the company is bringing it back. This owl will hunt during the cooler parts of the day."

Philip said, "I'll stay alert for the birds."

"Try the back campus for quail, and for vocalizers like ducks and thrashers."

"Thanks."

"I'll be interested in knowing your favorites."

"I'll be interested in finding out. And may I know your name?"

"Bridget Tkaczuk. And yours?"

"Philip Russel." They both smiled.

After another turn they faced tall round columns, their tops shielded from view by the overhead canvas, and their bases unseen on a lower level. After a dozen or so meters the walkway turned down a steep grade in steps to a concourse area supporting the columns, each made of a gray glass or plastic. A covered walkway served each quadrant of the concourse.

The small group reached a column base and found that it held an elevator. Bridget read the plaque, "The Pystead Group, Administration Building. Push for assistance. Stairs in center column."

Glancing at the large central column one could not miss another Poseidon, sculpted, unpainted, holding a bronze trident. *This one is less threatening than the painted version—surely faux marble?* Philip unwrapped his last chocolate nugget. The five entered an elevator labeled Lift No. 5. After the first few meters they had a panoramic view.

When the door opened, they stepped into a circular corridor providing a clear view outside at about four stories above ground level. They could see the tops of the covered walkways and the other buildings. The buildings' roofs were green, apparently gardens. "Pystead grows vegetables, fruits, and herbs on their rooftops," volunteered Bridget. The woman who had brought her cat said it should be too hot for the herbs. Bridget replied, "The building cools the rooftop soil from below, allowing non-tropical crops to flourish. The overhead fabric controls the amount of sunlight for each crop. Also, fish are farmed inside on the top floor and produce waste that turns their tank water into fertilizer for the plants. The garden's soil is deep enough to cleanse the water for return to the fish. Crops are protected by ladybugs instead of insecticide. When you have your tour, look for yellow or white ladybugs with black spots. Seems these beetles seek shade during the hot middays and still get the job done."

"That's encouraging," said Philip.

"Pystead uses essentially the same recycling aquaponics process on campus with soil that their farms at sea use in a vertical garden layout without soil. The vertical gardens aboard ship for the same base area produce ten times more food than do the rooftops.

The agricultural suppliers on Kitts complain that Pystead doesn't buy enough from them. The Kitts politicians declare the islanders employed on campus are exposed to corrupting drinks, food, clothing, books, art, and coffee breaks. The United Nations claims that Pystead overpays island labor, inciting economic unrest in the Caribbean."

Philip shook his head. *Worldwide, the well-off and middle classes are being reduced in all dimensions of existence. Most in the States accept the cause as international competition, even knowing their own transnationals are growing fabulously wealthy while hunger in the States is increasing. The commons cannot be moved to care for themselves nor the upper middle classes, believing the lie there will be more for them in years following. One would hope they had learned from their parent's stories not to trust con men. Their family stories, however, are about heroes of the commons, team pay, and childcare—oblivious to the need for any independent professional or skilled trade classes.*

Philip told his companions that his Net research had found nothing positive about Pystead. Bridget nodded her head. "Years ago, I refused Pystead's initial recruiting approach out of disgust for them. They won me over by showing me the Framework Agreement with Kitts-Nevis and their farming. I've had time to estimate yields, to research local laws and practices, and confirm the credibility of their version of reality. In the Caribbean the media and politicians never mention the Framework Agreement written to protect Kitts-Nevis."

The other recruits drifted away. Bridget stopped talking until Philip asked her to please continue. "I will just add that Pystead uses rainwater storage, drip irrigation, and wastewater recycling, adapted to their shipboard farms using growth lamps instead of sunlight." Philip thanked her for the stories. She asked if he were an agricultural type.

"No, I'm a cognitive scientist. Probably here to be more technician and analyst than researcher."

Bridget said quietly, "Pystead stays on the cutting edge of everything. They sent me for three years of postgraduate work on fish and fish farming, recommending that I consider research along with supporting their operational needs. That was before I committed to work for them fulltime, and before St. Kitts became Kitts." Philip and Bridget agreed to keep in touch.

After a quick look at the circular corridor, Philip found all doors, food kiosks, and showboards on the inner wall. The showboard displayed a floor plan. The building was circular with nine corridors leading to a central area for in-processing. Philip commented aloud that English was the only language shown. "Quite expected," said the nearby Asian man. "My recruiter made clear that English was the only language used on duty, except for questions and answers during training."

Saves time and mistakes. Philip reached the Q-R-S doorway alone. He walked down a sloping aisle through circular rows of auditorium seats. The space was over two stories tall. A circular screen and speakers were suspended at top center. The central area was set as a large circle of processing stations.

The window labeled R was directly in front of him. Company personnel wore various types and colors of clothing. "Welcome, Dr. Russell," called a woman wearing a white jumpsuit. He was surprised at being called by name until he realized that even on a small island video could recognize a face.

He was handed a paper form and a mechanical pencil having a pink eraser. *Where did they get these old mechanical pencils? Have never used one, although my father did have a few.* Instructions on the form were brief and clear. Forms were to be completed from memory, except for emergency contact information. Philip adjusted his chair, and after a few attempts managed to adjust the pencil lead and begin his task. Emergency contact information and two of the three essays were to be printed, and one essay written in script. The form asked those who employed computers in their work to what extent they could perform job tasks by hand using a slide rule if their computer were down.

Philip entered a code to facilitate kom use in order to verify emergency contact addresses and information. He was presented with a notice that Pystead had bought a 15 kicu essay on international trade in his name, and that he would have good kom access for ten minutes. He confirmed that his emergency contact addresses were active.

As Philip began his résumé information, a woman's piercing scream filled the auditorium. "Why not the Common Application? Why not? What is the point, except discrimination through a quirky and ancient process? Who did you tell in advance? Who? Who? This environment is intimidating and unacceptable in civil society!" The woman stood thrashing her forms in the air, her face contorted. "Sick, sick, sick!"

Philip glance up to see several objects in motion at the high ceiling. At the corridor doors he saw personnel in white jumpsuits entering. *Security is quick.* Then he gulped. *Could she have a bomb? No, too much screening to get a bomb in here.* When he looked back at the woman, two white-suited guards and a Nevis police officer were standing beside her. *Those three must have come from below. Is she dangerous or merely obstreperous?* Taking a deep breath, Philip realized how light his stomach felt. Some stayed at their stations while others were leaving the auditorium.

A public address system popped and spoke, "Attention, please. May I have your attention, please! This is Rao with Pystead security. As most of you will be aware, there has been a vocal display at one of the processing stations, but there is no physical threat. There is no need to leave the room. You may continue your work. I suspect that few of you understood what our unhappy recruit said, so our guards are offering her a microphone to better voice her complaint."

Without taking the microphone, the woman screamed, "You bullies have no right to exist! No right to go on creating gaps!"

A guard took each arm and they moved her slowly up the aisle, followed by the Nevis policeman. On her feet and surely not in physical distress, the woman began screaming that the pigs were pinching her.

What an act.

⁂ ⁂ ⁂

Philip returned to his task, and soon handed in the completed form. The clerk stamped his paperwork received, scanned it, and printed a blue paper copy for him. She asked for his attention and gave him a paper schedule for general and professional orientation meetings. "Any questions?"

"None yet."

"We have twenty-four-seven operations, but for the first few weeks you should be off duty by three thirty p. m. weekdays, and off Saturdays and Sundays." She paused before adding, "The exception, beginning Monday week we have a three-week quarantine period on campus for new personnel requesting an immediate assignment at our fish farm, our huge floating farm city in international waters. And please, when you notice somebody wearing a medical facemask do not be alarmed. They are in quarantine."

"Quarantine from what?"

"From you new hires!" She smiled. "Given your education at a rigorous institution, we have nothing to teach you professionally. Your first orientation assembly is Thursday morning, and your first professional orientation is Friday morning."

The woman paused to gain Philip's full attention before saying, "After in-processing and orientation as a recruit, you must live on campus. That's a requirement of our framework agreement with Kitts-Nevis, to preserve the local housing market, trees, and tourist trade. Our apartments on campus are nice, although small. Their big attraction is the rent, as there is no charge. Tours of the apartments are given weekdays, or otherwise by appointment. Furniture is available from stock. An available apartment may be furnished and occupied within hours to several days. You should use your time to become familiar with the campus and its recreational facilities, and to choose an apartment."

"Is there a place I can stay tonight?"

"We have Visiting Crew Quarters. Here's a campus map." She

slid out a sheet of yellow paper. "One more thing, please." She waited for Philip to look up. "You should get an employee badge at your earliest opportunity. You may do this now at either guardhouse beside the main gate. You will have to present the hard copy of your approved application form that I returned. The process requires biometric scans and a basic personality scan. A blood test is required. The process takes about fifteen minutes once you get to the front of the line. Lines will be longer tomorrow. A large processing center opens next week, but please try to get started today." She smiled. "We look forward to a long association with you, Dr. Russell."

"Thank you. And may I know your name?"

"I'm Lois Henssen, Commandant of the Department of Administration."

"That's the same as its director?"

"Yes. We have two people out today, so I'm covering. We are the largest company in Kitts-Nevis, and we need every processing station active for you new hires."

"I suspect all the directors I have known would let the line back up."

"I have nothing urgent, so I'm pleased to help."

"Thank you, Ms. Henssen, or is it Dr.?"

"You are quite welcome, Dr. Russell. After you get your employee badge, let's use first names. And yes, I have a doctorate in systems management."

Philip picked up his papers. *Ice said Pystead did things their way. My recruiter made clear they were high-tech, yet old-fashioned in many respects. They must distrust the binary beings as much as I do? So far, retro Pystead suits me fine. Who said it was of no importance whether a thing be old or new, but whether it be true?*

"Dr. Russell? I need your full attention for final points."

Philip's thought reverted to his real-world purpose. "I'm listening."

"If you suspect you are being followed, or may be attacked, call security. If you will be very late or miss a meeting, call. Call addresses are listed. Be safe rather than sorry. We would rather have dozens of false alarms than one mugging. You must keep all papers and schedules confidential and shred any form you recycle off campus. Any questions?

"No."

"There is little crime, but recently we have young boys in gangs dressed as cupids and they can be non-lethally dangerous. Too, you must check our inhouse network named Fednet—be sure you have the Federation network. Before leaving campus! You must note the laws posted for Kitts-Nevis. For example, using a metal detector on either island is illegal."

"I'm okay there."

"If you happen to see or suspect a gun or a bullet anywhere, say in the sand on the beach, avoid even looking closely and get away promptly. You don't want to become involved because recently all is not well with that aspect of law and justice on Nevis. Report seeing any weapon or misplaced bag to us. We'll alert the police without involving you."

"Fine. Anything else?"

"You must obtain a license before drinking off-campus at any standalone bar or live musical performance. The law is enforced once you are employed and will cost a bribe to stay out of jail."

"Cosmos!"

"You must study the list of unexpected island laws on our

Federation network. Many are unimaginable and carry severe penalties. For example, you will be guilty of eavesdropping, a felony, if you record audio or video of a police officer, government official, or politician. Recording via any media is illegal, which includes making a hand-written note to yourself. The law is draconian, enforced, and applies to children! Read up and stay legal. Please do not leave campus before reading all Nevis's laws posted on our inhouse Fednet! You are no longer classified as a tourist by Kitts-Nevis."

"I will, thanks." *So much for Nevis being a kindly niche! That leaves me with the Pystead campus. Lois seemed friendly, perhaps an omen that Pystead is a place I can safely belong.*

Philip departed, recalling the good-ole-days on Nevis as recounted by Stuart's parents. *If there were the usual percentage of sociopaths years ago, how could life have been generally safer? Surely there was some deterrent influence on top of innateness. Perhaps a concerned population and honest government kept most of the deviants in line! Cosmos, I must attend to the here and now! Can't continue to let my thoughts wander. A good dog must stay alert for repressive laws and gothic dogs. And I'm not even an experienced dog, being born lowly only days ago in Wheaton, Georgia.*

Philip picked up a few cookies and caught a tram to the apartments where he joined a tour. After seeing both an old and a new unit, he dropped out of the tour and signed up for a new unit on grade that had a corner patio shaded by a tall tree with many dangling limbs, or roots, or vines that could veil hanging snakes if there were any snakes. The new unit's walls were thin, and Philip agreed to keep noise levels down. Rather than selecting furniture himself, he waited in hopes of having assistance from Ice.

Sitting in the lobby, he used his kom to read the Kitts-Nevis laws posted on Fednet. They were nothing like the cultural prohibitions he had experienced at the Wheaton World Center for Change in Middle Georgia. *I don't have a bow or slingshot of over sixty-five newtons pull. No laser pointer. No scandalous clothing. No medications or robots without local approval.* Philip read on and found he would be acceptable to island culture provided he never used the audio-video recording features of his kom or took a note of any kind.

The local deemers are fearful. Nevis has changed from its kindly past. Hopes for a kindly neighborhood rely on two niches: campus and the floating farm city. Each subject to Kitts-Nevis policing according to Mrs. R., hence subject to Interpol and of little value as a redoubt for decent human beings. Am I part of a defeated subaltern with goths and dark data lurking? Still, I feel there is hope, some time. Yes, time affords hope! Perhaps a simple life without children could provide a bubble for my generation? Of course, that hasn't been Rhonda's experience in Middle Georgia, nor Stuart's or Sandra's in Compton, nor mine! Should I take the advice of that wise Greek Democritus to trust warily in reason rather than be overcome by feelings? Hum, cognitive science advises I need not believe everything I think. O Cosmos! What's what?

With time available, Philip decided to walk to the main gate for his identification badge. He avoided the direct route to see more of the campus and encountered animal statues embellished with sculptured hair often done in decorative whorls of tiny groves and ridges. Most statues had low and smooth backs, suitable as seating. The oversized, long-legged cats were the most striking. Philip left the walkway to scrutinize the full-sized elephant and horse statues. He tapped the side of an elephant. *Sounds hollow, bronze?*

His tap on a horse landed with an unyielding thud. *Surely faux marble. All overdone in quantity!* Cutting back to a main walkway, he passed a large group of monkey sculptures in trees. *Black faces, amber eyes, white chests, as described by the tours promising sightings of wild, Vervet monkeys. Realistic, except for the wings! Is Ice involved with these threatening designs? After all, she did white tigers for a palm reader. This place could be eerie at night.*

Nearing the main gate, Philip stopped for another look around. He sighed. The many dimensions of the cosmos played in his head, surpassing understanding. In its physical reality, the cosmos is too huge to be seen, with nothing directly viewable from all sides at once; or too small to be seen; or too bright or too dark; or too fast or too slow. Or too strange to be understood. Contemplating Schrödinger's Cat can collapse one's state of mind. Space, time, energy, and mass are enigmatic, not to mention the discouraging consequences of entropy to manmade order. And there's the distressing condition of the human mind. Of course, the deemers of things do not find all minds distressing. On the contrary, they often find them biddable and enlist enough of cruel humanity to secure control of those who would be kind.

What will the deemers of Pystead Group deem that I should do? Can I possibly perceive before taking the job if they want a citizen or a subject? If I could observe all public signifiers of the signified, would I be able to grasp the essence of The Pystead? No, because public images are managed. Yet, if I seek the truth without caring what I find, then I have a chance of being objective in my own mind—my best hope! Must be wary of our on-and-off Net source, as it's mostly advertisements, big business, or one-world politics. There must be a censorship struggle on our local Net. No kom or public showboard is reliable. Even this large company is hardly ever found without punching in its address. Why then believe the easily found sites are truthful?

Philip stood watching the guardhouses, perplexed. *The censorship of American movies that began in the nineteen thirties improved the popular culture by any measure valuing family life and cultural morality. Glorification of gangsters was eliminated, except for singing pirates. For almost three decades romance and mystery flourished until replaced by crudeness, raw sex, anger, and violence. By the twenty-twenties, children's shows glorified anthropomorphic vehicles having built-in guns and sexual attraction. If only cognitive science could have documented the wirings of the American mind before and after nineteen thirty-four! We know that fundamental issues like women's and minority's rights were overlooked. We know that religious and political manipulation came along with an opaque enforcement of that code. We know that apathetic citizens effectively became movie-going subjects, albeit for their cultural betterment. Score one for the deemers of things.*

Near the main gate the walkway became crowded. Trams were dropping scores of riders. A loud beeping noise alerted Philip to a passing tram of one open-top car, flashing blue and red lights, carrying the woman screamer seated calmly between a white-suited guard and a Nevis policeman. She was attractive with purple lipstick. The tram proceeded to the guardhouse on the left side of the gates. *I've seen enough of that one.*

The wide center gate was open. On each side stood four guards wearing bulky white suits having the texture of cauliflower. They wore hard helmets covering the entire head, although with heavy, golden face visors up, showing golden sunglasses. Parked outside the gate was a yellow bus. Out of the right-side guardhouse stepped a man in a white jumpsuit. He took several steps toward the main gate, then stopped to open a small door in the high perimeter fence. People began filing through the door, collecting in an area defined by a red-rope perimeter. Away from the walkway side of the concourse, a speaker's podium stood unoccupied. The man in the jumpsuit closed the door and continued to the podium.

As Philip turned for the door of the guardhouse, he again noticed the woman screamer. She walked out the main gate and entered the door of the waiting bus. In its doorway, she turned to look back at the campus and was immediately jerked backward into the bus. *Stanger and stranger this Pystead Group. Or to be realistic, is it the opposition they attract who are the strange birds?*

The observation window in the guardhouse was clear, and Philip was pleased to see calm faces observing his approach. He opened the door and stepped inside to find his way blocked by a translucent screen. A female voice instructed, "Please pause for bio-scan recognition and state the purpose of your visit."

"Here for an employee badge."

"Do you have any metal on your upper body? Including pins from surgery or medical devices, internal or external?"

"No."

The front panel lowered and the voice told him, "You may proceed. I-D is to your left."

Is my belt upper body?

The three people processed ahead of Philip each entered a small booth and had a cone-shaped shield adjusted snugly to their body below the arms. Each was told to raise a hand if they found the space too confining. Then the subject answered questions while wearing a bulky helmet having a visor.

A check for claustrophobia? And if magnetic imaging be involved, the screen blocks the magnetic field from any metal in clothing or body. If lie detection be involved, the helmet must be a functional neural or infrared scanner. That the visor is often up, the head looking in any direction seems to rule out infrared. Still, it's difficult to imagine that helmet taking the place of a large, noisy, bed-sized MRI machine.

When the nurse approached, Philip offered his arm for the blood work. Next came the helmet with a remote having five buttons for answering questions. *Even gross regional activity should suffice for basic fidelity. Could this helmet detect brain-wave activity using passive sensors? How would the point of origin from within the brain be identified?* The face visor closed, and Philip was experiencing a virtual reality helmet. While viewing a waterfall or some other scene, he dutifully pressed a button to register his answer to the question asked, including if he worked for any other entity, and then directly, "Do you intend to report on us to anybody?"

Philip sat waiting for his badge. *Where did I get the impression this would be a functional brain scan? Ah, my recruiter told me that Pystead used MRI for scientific evaluations and was a secure organization of decent people! Have they made a technological advance in resonant imaging? If security be critical, I'd say one must eventually take a calibrated scan to be eligible for permanent employment.*

Five minutes later, the guard held out a three-centimeter-long stickpin having a pale blue, pea-like top. "This is the visible part of your I-D, a lapel pin."

So that's what Director Lois Henssen was wearing. He toyed with his new stickpin. *A lighter blue than Dr. Henssen's. Same color as this guard's.*

Then Philip received a card that looked like a typical smart card. It was flexible and fit easily into his wallet. The guard caught his attention. "Do not wear the lapel pin when off campus. On campus, wear the pin exposed. Be especially careful to secure both pin and card on your person. When you are out of quarters if either goes missing and cannot be found within five minutes, you must—must—personally report the status to security. If you separate the pin and card by too much distance or mass, both change color, the card vibrates and calls your kom and security. Both pin and card are bio coded."

"Fine, I understand."

"Let me have your kom to establish a security link with the card."

As Philip left the guardhouse, the passengers who had disembarked from the yellow bus caught his eye. One man was shouting to the Pystead representative at the podium. Philip approached the group and stopped at the edge of the paved roadway. The spokesman for the group from the bus was loud but calm. The Pystead representative at the podium told him, "You are the only one on our list of hires. As I've said, we hire individuals, not groups." The busman was not deterred, insisting that his group have quarters together for the night until their status could be confirmed by the United Nations. "Quarters together?" Pystead's representative almost laughed. "We are full of recruits. You would have to sleep in a building lobby or on handball courts to find an area large enough to stay together."

"A fine idea," shouted the busman.

There was no immediate response from the podium. A small group of onlookers had gathered. Philip saw no white jumpsuits except for the figure at the podium. The bulky, white suits of the guards at the main gate were obviously an entirely different type suit.

The Pystead representative replied, "We can accommodate you in the lobby of an activity building if each of you will agree to a security wand scan and wear a locked ankle device for location tracking. That's the best we can do."

"We accept. I advise you to immediately contact the U.N. concerning our status so that you do not incur sanctions for your inequitable treatment of this organism."

With the situation resolved for the night, Philip and the other onlookers drifted away, many departing by the main gate. *They are an 'organism,' their spokesman said?*

Philip's campus app directed him to a tram for the VCQ. After waiting his turn at the busy desk, he accepted an efficiency unit. Only a tiny bathroom and tiny closet were separate from the small main room, arranged from front sleeping to seating and to a small kitchenette at the rear. Furnishings included a plastic desk and a lounge chair that reclined, becoming a second bed. The lighting, on dimmers, went bright enough to read a paper form.

Philip searched early for a place to eat. Aside from vending machines in the VCQ, the cafeterias were in the activity buildings and at reception. The East Activity Building was listed closed. *The bus-people must be there?* Philip walked to the central cafeteria and took a cheeseburger and chips. He was pleased to find the chips were fried potato wedges. Lastly, he ate the raw green herbs recommended as a palliative for the meal.

After returning to his VCQ room, Philip realized he should have checked for activities available on campus. Already he could feel the long days ahead before he would see Ice. Unexpectedly, his wrist kom sounded three times. His message read, SECURITY CHECK. CALL IMMEDIATELY. Philip pressed and held his tab 7. A voice instructed, "Please look into your video lens and state your full name and your mother's maiden name."

"Philip B. Russell, and Marshall."

"Thank you. Your security link is confirmed. Also, please note your message from housekeeping that your suitcase is available in the VCQ's holding room."

Philip picked up the suitcase. Back in his room the evening passed slowly. He suspended komming and found his Crowley book. Breathing deeply, he was able to finish it before being weary enough to rest. *Forbidden topics and censorship have been around forever. No reason to expect them to disappear, our era being more about illusions than reality. So much media and so little information on anything other than the nebulous benefits of a global market explained in terms of dependent parameters. And how many of those dreaded gaps are being closed? How many gaps are listed with specific and tangible problems, milestones, means of remediation—none!*

And the religious and nonprofit entities that do share their hospital, educational, recreational, and social services are continuously pressured to abandon their beliefs and become part of the undifferentiated culture of prohibitions. Pressured to sellout and be turned over to the other. Like successful, high-tech startups, community doers are being destroyed. Then the commons are left happy admiring their local leaders as showboard managers of organizations that begin failing notwithstanding the said superior analyses and decisions made by the artificial intelligence driving their showboards. This Pystead Group must be a transnational that doesn't like prospects on land if seasteading be in their offing. And I must consider seasteading in terms of gritty realities rather than as a conceptual sanctuary. And hey, aren't black flags seen quite often on the Caribbean's offing?

✳ ✳ ✳

Again that evening his book, *The Forbidden Lecture*, proved depressing and he abandoned it for a program on natural disasters in the showboard lounge. He found the program informative though neither relaxing nor uplifting.

Today must have added to my awareness of reality. Must it always be distressing? No wonder so many choose both their texts and their variables with care. They avoid that dark, dream-like shadow, that dilemma in which they must confront the dreaded monster, Reality. It's more comfortable to remain as unreal as possible, to let public activists, whistleblowers, and decent people take the arrows! But the deemers and their creatures will overcome those few and come for you on some unexpected morrow. Yes, I live in troubled times! World over, creatures working for the deemers are bullies, scofflaws, and liars. Generally armed, they resent decent or professional people and worship their own oppressors! Can there be anywhere a sheltered niche of high-abstracting and decent minds? I must choose wisely for my next niche in the cosmos!

Philip adjusted himself to face a window. *For me the ivory tower is done, hence avoiding the greater world reality, the real world, is done. What I do now is done done! I must join something or perish. I should be asking how in touch with reality is this Pystead Group? An impossible question to answer. Have you nothing to say, my primary process? Let's contemplate Nevis island and seasteading with Pystead. What about South Holland or Utrecht? Possibly a restaurant in Florida with Rhonda as wife, she liked me. And her only secrets would be culinary! Still, can any place in the States not succumb to its gothic creatures? Cosmos, what of here?*

Back in his room, Philip fell asleep early with his primary

process surely swimming with recruits and goths in strange waters. Saturday morning when Philip woke he missed the scent of Mrs. R.'s bacon. He felt terribly alone without prospects of seeing Ice or Samantha. His Father's book, *The Forbidden Lecture*, had been disturbing. *This beginning again has lots of lows.* Knowing that breakfast would perk him up, he took the three steps needed to get to his bathroom door, before realizing that his suitcase was still packed. He stopped, able to remain positive by thinking about a hot breakfast, allowing negative feelings to recede into his subconscious dimension of mind.

Within thirty minutes, he was eating French toast and pancetta in the Central Activity Building's cafeteria. The hot latte was especially comforting. The only island fare he noticed were curried fish patties and pan-fried plantains, which he sampled. Before half-finished eating he felt good, finally declining the recommended pureed herbs in a small vial. He left the cafeteria determined to explore the campus and learn about the company.

Philip walked to the reception facility and looked through the gift shops. He found a dozen paintings from the Island Expressions Co-op, two painted by Ice. Then he checked out recreational facilities. Each activity building had tennis courts, handball courts, a heated pool, a jogging track, and cardiovascular and strength exercise machines. Posted signs reminded crewmembers to stand and move about at least five minutes of each waking hour, and to walk several thousand steps daily for the health of their cardiovascular system and brain. *Well, if less time here is wasted on ghosts in the machine and useless administrative chores, I'll have as much productive time and be healthier. I can play tennis and racquetball for those steps on many days.*

He found a chess tournament that drew forty players, including two grandmasters, three masters, and five experts. He saw musical and theatrical performances scheduled, including a junior high school play with a catchy number name, *13*. He found a string quartet available for group events. He discovered that Pystead's schools taught the liberal arts and the fine arts from elementary grades through college, including graduate-level programs in the humanities. *Possible opportunities for ex-colleagues?* Then he was ready to leave, like a fisherman with a full bucket.

That afternoon, after sandwiches and chips from a vending machine in the VCQ, a new concern surfaced. *How did that small-town Wheaton police department have the authority to act for United States Customs in seizing a dozen of my books? Before any attempt at leaving the country!* Philip took a few minutes and found access to the Net more comprehensive via the Pystead system than by his personal kom. Only by using its complete fifty-four-character address punched in manually could he find Pystead using his kom. For comparison, Philip walked to a campus showboard and found Pystead, but with a U.N. warning against access to avoid identity theft. *These symptoms must point to more than a censorship struggle. This niche of the world is under assault.* His neck tingled at the thought. *A dog's hair shouldn't stand up like a cat's.*

Back in his room, Philip returned to searching the public Net. He was presented with tracts attacking the Western enlightenment. *Did the Enlightenment ignore as much of human nature as do the Post Essentialists? Well, yes, the Enlightenment was borne of the Western mind, then and now in the minority. Even in the West it has failed to penetrate deeply enough. Western icons are perishing in the West. Yet here I feel most have decent Western values regardless of childhood origins! Pystead should have a high chance of producing a more perfect union.*

Still, I must decide if I might belong. I must seek an opportunity to probe for intentions and hope for the wit and boldness to take it.

At five-thirty Philip called Ice on kom to set a date for their walk on the beach with dinner afterward. Ice said Wednesday would be better than Tuesday and to use her apartment door at the back of the building, which faced a paved street. Next, he called Mrs. R.'s and made a dinner reservation for two at seven thirty. Inquiring about wine, he learned the R.s had Ste Wolls champagne obtained from Lamancha House, the local distributor, and he reserved a bottle to be safe.

SPECIAL FRIENDS

Philip dressed in a blue-and-white-striped shirt and his dark-blue Bermuda shorts rather than his new island clothing. He had decided to return to Mrs. R.'s and experience the first day of Spring Festival. He secured his new stick pin inside his shirt pocket. Using his campus app he found trams and shuttles and arrived back at the guesthouse by nine a.m., in time for the last of breakfast, fortunately with bacon still available.

After breakfast, time slowed, he wouldn't see Ice for four more days. At Mrs.R.'s suggestion he walked the town for sights and familiarity with his new hometown. The day turned into as much an exercise in walking as seeing the town. He returned for lunch, tired with mixed emotions. Rather than return to his room, Philip ended up standing on the screen porch sipping red sangria. Another guest entered the porch and came to stand beside him. "Hello, Philip."

Her voice was familiar. He turned his head. "Hello Samantha."

Only top two buttons open, pink blouse, pink streaks.

She said, "I'm pleased you remember my name."

"I should have asked you to dance."

"I was disappointed."

"So was I. Philip, I want to dine at Lamancha House before leaving Nevis, and have a purely platonic proposal if you are available Tuesday evening."

Platonic and how expensive? "I am."

"Good, good! I'm treating taxi, food, and champagne. I want you to escort me, eat, drink, and chat."

"Purely platonic?"

"If you're chatty, a sweet kiss goodnight and a date for next year if you're interested."

"No dancing, right?"

"Not this year. Next year is up to you."

"I'd like to go. What should I wear?"

"Just as you are, casual. Very few dress for dinner on Nevis. I'll wear a sundress."

Philip inquired with a grin, "A pink sundress?"

"Yes. You continue to amaze me, even if guessing pink is easier than guessing researcher."

"You obviously like pink, not to mention the pink streaks in your hair."

"My stylist would be scandalized hearing pink streaks."

"What then?"

"Dimensions of color, my dear, dimensions of color."

"Ah. Tell your stylist I think you have exotic, yet sophisticated, dimensions of pink."

"Flattery will get you everywhere—next year!"

"What time Tuesday night?"

"Here at eight-thirty. Look for the girl in the pink sundress."

"Proposition accepted, Samantha." *Did I really say that?* "Samantha, what are you doing tomorrow?"

"I'll walk the town for the first day of Spring Festival. It's completely different than the second day that's all energetic youth. Would you escort me, be my date?" She smiled. He accepted.

Philip returned to his room refreshed and read before taking a nap. He got through the afternoon searching the Net and worrying about the state of the Caribbean.

✴ ✴ ✴

Monday morning Philip and Samantha ate breakfast together and left the guesthouse to walk the streets of Charlestown for the first day of Spring Festival. Already musicians played at street corners, and residents played recorded songs from their doorways and porches. The music was mostly religious although Philip recognized only the Christian melodies. Near the ferryboat dock they noticed a colorful poster that pictured a yellow tree and a bald-headed old man with a long, white bread, dressed in yellow pants and a red-and-teal shirt, holding a book bound in deep yellow. Samantha took Philip's arm and both agreed the day was relaxing and spiritual. *And a safe island,* thought Philip, *except for any cupids on the loose.* Samantha tugged on his arm and they moved on, walking slowly, enjoying the relaxing music and counting the different denominations having Christmas scenes, all with the Christ child, plus Mary in a manger or with angels or wisemen. When returning to the guesthouse they came to a street corner covered in artificial snow with Christmas lights overhead for a colorful canopy. Just past the snow, a musician, an old woman with graying hair, stood just inside a doorway playing what Philip took to be a viola. Samantha accepted Philip's invitation to an early lunch and they found themselves in a cozy café decorated with colorful lights and flowers that their waitress said were violets and pansies. The café was upscale and surely for tourists. All seating was along the walls and they were seated side-by-side. Philip had a cheese steak sandwich without the hot peppers, and Samantha took a garden salad topped with tuna salad. When seated the song had been a slow, quiet version of Somewhere Over the Rainbow. It suddenly claimed their attention with a melodic riff that morphed into a slow I'm Dreaming of a White Christmas. They ate without talking, enchanted, even though not wishing for snow. They stayed for a second coffee when the song changed and was soon identified by the musician as Edelweiss. They walked back holding hands and sat on Mrs. R.'s screened porch without speaking.

After a few minutes Samantha said, "The second day of Spring Festival is all energetic music, costumes, and street dancing by the youth of Nevis."

He asked, "Is it better to stay downtown for that, or visit the botanical gardens?"

"It's better to do both. Begin downtown and take the circulator bus to the magnificent gardens. There will be dancing everywhere. Why don't we go together? We can be back with time to rest before dinner."

She sent him to his room with a smile but no kiss.

✻   ✻   ✻

After a peaceful night's sleep, Philip was downstairs early to eat breakfast with Samantha. To attract conversation at the gardens he wore a pale green shirt with a random design of large, white flowers. The friends walked the streets as the music was beginning. The songs were lively and soon young men and women danced by. The men in their yellow bird beaks and white-plum head feathers chirped, the girls swirling in colorful dresses with flowers in their hair sang songs that Philip could not understand. Soon, with music coming from everywhere and several groups of dancers in sight, Samantha took Philip's hands and swung him in a circle. Being bold, he continued the swirling dance for almost a block. Samantha hugged him and they rested, waiting for the circulator bus to the gardens.

The many bus stops added to the two minutes of riding time. They arrived at the gardens with music played by woodwinds and youthful dancers, all costumed as flowers, wearing green clothing, the men with tall red plumes on their heads and the girls as plants with large red and white flowers on arms and heads. Samantha purchased a few flowers and had Philip pin them on her shoulders and in her hair. She had known to wear a green blouse and complimented Philip on his flower-patterned pale green shirt.

The gardens were magnificent with flowers and plumes of all colors. There was a large Banyan tree with roots hanging from branches to the ground like the tree beside Philip's chosen apartment on campus. They saw two medium height trees, one covered with red flowers and the other in pink. There were a few strange blossoms that Philip and Samantha stopped to enjoy. One exotic flower was complex and large with maybe a dozen long white petals beyond their purple bases that formed an inner circle of color, overlayed with dozens of long, thin, white sprouts. The center was the most exotic part with two stacked sets of relatively bulky, chartreuse, wagon-wheel-like spokes. They found a strange brown flower and then a green, both with bulky, prominent centers of another color. Philips favorite was a lavender orchid having dark brown coloring as the base of its petals.

Unexpected was a desert hot house with cactus and a few tall Joshua trees in an area with rugged rock walls and hard, brown dirt dotted with a few types of twisted and bristled low plants.

By early afternoon Philip wanted to see the Hamilton House Museums. He and Samantha agreed they would return to the gardens another day. She asked him to walk her to the guesthouse.

Enroute, a sign caught Philip's eye and they stopped to look at cheese and La Mancha dairy goats. The cheese was mild and they bought sandwiches that were good. The goats were interesting, of different colors, sleek without horns, and at first glance without ears.

Unlike the big-eared goats in the San Diego Zoo. Philip tried a Net search for the goats, getting only advertisements. On a second try, he was presented with an opened advertisement. SEE STREAMING VIDEO OF THE FAMOUS GOAT MAN AND HIS ONE-MAN CAMPER WAGON. FOR YOUNG HOSTS AND ANTICS, CHECK 'CIRCUS'; FOR TOPLESS HOSTS CHECK 'ADULT'.

Samantha wanted to look. He told her, "Must-see advertisements even here." Philip soon told his kom, "Skip." The advertisement remained. He searched the screen and finally found a small tab: SKIP AD. "I'm sure that 'skip' did not appear up front. The People's Portal no longer has need of those searching for free or true information."

"That's my experience too. The news is served by bubbly anchors telling celebrity gossip, sports hype, tales of good dogs, and little hard news with no mention of negative public-policy outcomes. The free news ziffs are politically slanted policy illusions, strike-it-rich shows, and virtual games. The large companies buy a full spectrum news service. Few individuals can afford one. Even then, creating your own ziff for friends is illegal, and impossible without illegal equipment."

Philip's kom screen flashed: ENTERTAINMENT WITH AN ESCORT FOR TONIGHT. "Kom off." *Will I get an antisocial demerit for disrespecting another advertisement?*

Samantha searched for La Mancha goats and persevering for five minutes to skip ads found a photograph of a man Philip recognized as the man assisting with paintings at the Island Expressions Co-op, posted on a site naming Nevis's Pigs with over a dozen other evidently successful Nevisians.

The site jolted Philip. He recalled his friend Sandra explaining that they and their fired colleagues were all marked on social sites.

Samantha searched again and instead of La Mancha dairy goats found anything related to goats and another photograph of Isaac Lamancha on a site's home page that linked to Nevis's Pigs and to Antisocial Devils on Nevis, listing both locals and tourists with photographs, names, addresses, and family information.

A lump formed in Philip's throat and in his heart. *This island is corrupted with legalized assault. Nevis' Net is a home for dark money and its bullying creatures!*

Philip accompanied Samantha to Mrs. R.'s. He took a few cookies and told her he was in good shape and would continue to

Hamilton House and look closely at the old stone building. Too he wanted more local history before seeing Ice.

Samantha caressed his neck and kissed him goodbye on the lips, twice. "We are only friends, Philip, but let's be special friends."

The walk to Hamilton House was longer than Philip had anticipated. Increasing his pace he found he could see the museums and get back to the guesthouse for dinner with Samantha.

7

TWO SURPRISES

That evening Philip was on the porch five minutes early. The girl in the pink sundress was waiting. She patted the seat beside her. "Taxi is almost here."

Dimensions of color, the pink streaks are in different shades. Philip sat down and asked, "Have you eaten at Lamancha House before?"

"Last year, my only visit. My husband took me. I had a delicately spiced, plantain encrusted, Chilean seabass filet. It's still on the menu."

"Samantha, you have dealt me two surprises in one sentence."

"Honestly, Philip, I intended only one surprise per sentence this evening."

"Staying with the obvious, let me inquire about your husband."

"A fine husband who works out of Kitts. That suits since it gives me a few weeks alone on Nevis, shall we say, for inspiration." She smiled. "While in the West Indies we have what some call an open marriage. For us, island flings never go home or repeat."

"Oh."

"You are surprised, aren't you?"

"Sure."

"What the second surprise I dealt you might be, I cannot imagine."

"I thought Chilean seabass was an endangered fish and off menus."

Samantha pointed. "Our taxi is here. I'll tell you what I know about seabass over dinner. It's also known as Patagonian toothfish, found only in deep, almost freezing cold, salt waters."

The taxi turned onto a narrow road that ran up toward Nevis's peak. The scene outside was dark except for green foliage in the taxi's headlights. The inside scene was mostly the pink Samantha in dim cabin illumination. "Samantha, what does your husband do?"

She slid over to make elbow contact, reciting in a soft voice, "His work is company confidential. I don't know details." After a moment she asked, "Can you be discrete if I tell you a little?"

"Yes."

"He works out of Kitts for projects that are located on Nevis. His company pleases politicians by spending money on Kitts instead of Nevis. That spending, plus design secrecy, saves time and money on the projects."

Philip turned to look at Samantha. "In my Net searches I have found Nevis highly criticized."

She nodded. "The Kitts and Nevis union has always been plagued by sectarian antagonisms. The world these days favors Kitts. My husband stays out of politics because he's a Project Engineer and not a Project Manager."

"What kind?"

"That's part of the secret."

As Philip pondered the situation, Samantha remained silent. The taxi soon slowed, turning around a bend in the road. They were approaching a dimly illuminated yellow building trimmed in pastel blue. Philip counted four stories. "This must be the tallest building I've seen on Nevis."

"It's history plaque says it was the only four-story structure on Nevis when built. This site has tall trees, and the zoning ordinance required structures to be lower than the surrounding trees. The first floor is two meters below grade with those half-height windows— they go to the ceiling. We heard the original landowners were one of the so-called royal families of Nevis. The current owner's father, from Europe, married into the family and was allowed to purchase the land."

The taxi pulled around a circular driveway to the front entry, and their attention turned to details. Lamancha House had no doorman. Philip let himself out while the taxi driver assisted Samantha. She took Philip's arm and with two steps up they were on a wide front porch where guests lounged in rocking chairs with drinks.

⚹ ⚹ ⚹

They descended several steps to enter a grand lobby painted in light yellow and muted red. "Vermilion red," said Samantha. The furnishings, not modern, reminded Philip of Mrs. R.'s Guesthouse. He counted nine sofa and chair groups and estimated a dozen more single chairs. The lobby seemed half-filled. "Must seat over seventy people," Philip guessed.

Samantha pointed across the lobby. "They have one of the few elevators on the island. To our right is the dining room, called a

Tea Room." Samantha was holding Philip's arm and he led her left because he wanted to see the main desk. She followed without comment. There were photographs and a framed floor plan on the end wall that drew his attention. Samantha explained, "The second floor has very small sleeping rooms about three meters wide, I heard last year."

"Those rooms are certainly the smallest on this layout." When Philip looked at the staff photographs, he said aloud, "Isaac is the owner?"

"I'm sorry, what?"

"This photograph reminds me of the man I met when buying a painting at that artist's co-op you mentioned." Samantha took his arm, and they turned toward the lobby, taking only a few steps before stopping so abruptly that she was jerked to a halt. Philip stood watching as the owner spoke to a seated woman with very blonde hair. The woman stood and Philip saw her in profile. "Ice!"

Samantha said politely, "I didn't understand." Isaac and Ice walked into the Tea Room with Isaac caressing her lower back with his fingers. Philip and Samantha followed and she asked for her reservation while Philip hoped Ice would not look around. Ice and Isaac sat at the bar in the back of the room, facing away from the dining area. At their table, Philip took the seat with his back to the bar.

He was hurt and Samantha sensed his mood. "Let's have a drink, Philip."

The Tea Room was elegant with a golden-brown wood floor and pale purple curtains. The pale gold ceiling held several small crystal chandeliers. The wooden chairs matched the flooring and had silver-gray cushions. Each table was covered with a silver-gray tablecloth and held a short red candle. The elaborate bar, Samantha explained, was mahogany-red teak wood, the barstool cushions were dark gold. The restaurant's floor was also teak. All very expensive Samantha assured Philip.

Philip forced a smile. Samantha asked, "Did you see somebody you know?"

As Philip wondered how to answer, he remembered Samantha was being honest with him. "I'm sure I know the woman who walked in ahead of us."

"The couple. That is only one surprise per sentence." Philip didn't respond. "I should have guessed by now."

Without looking at Samantha, Philip said, "Our first date was a week ago, she's the artist whose painting I bought at the Co-op."

Samantha reached across the table and put her hand on top of Philip's. "I'm just not your type, am I, Philip?"

"I didn't know what to make of you last Tuesday, except that you were beautiful and potential trouble. You were too different. Now that I know you better, I like you."

"If you like me, Philip, that's perfect." Samantha rubbed his hand for a few moments before asking, "Do you think a man can be a special friend to a woman without sleeping with her?"

"I had a few close female colleagues."

"But not as close as your male colleagues?"

"No, but sociologists say platonic friendships have been believable since the nineteen seventies."

"If you slept with a female, even once, she would be much closer?"

"True, I'm sure."

"Maybe once will happen for us as special friends." Samantha withdrew her hand and offered a card from her purse. "This card uses my name, Moody, registered in Kitts-Nevis, California, New York, New Mexico, and Canada. My husband has his own last name. You may contact me in the States as a friend." She winked. "If you are smitten with that vanilla blonde overnight, perhaps over time you can fall into friendship with dimensions of pink."

Philip took the card. "I am falling in love with her, foolish as that may be after one dinner date."

"I'd recommend asking her to dance if you go to Pinney's boardwalk. The mambo is popular. Take a quick lesson."

"She seems to have a significant other."

"Perhaps he's merely a lover? She might drop him like a hot plantain for the right man."

"I feel like I must owe you for a therapy session."

"What are friends for?" Samantha held up her menu. "I know what I want. Are you in the mood to order, or shall I order for you?"

Philip picked up his menu. "I'd like the seabass with a side Caesar salad, and I'm treating."

"Then only the cocktails, I must insist. As a friend, Philip, may I say that I hope you have had that wrist looked at by a medic."

"Thanks. It's both wrists, Mrs. R.'s nurse says they are healing."

"You must tell me more on the ride back."

The restaurant's incandescent lighting—soft, red-spectrum illumination—highlighted Samantha's dimensions of pink. The ambiance was subdued. They chatted about Nevis and the chance encounters that provided Samantha with new experiences and emotions that she needed as a writer of amorous fiction.

The food was served, and Philip agreed the seabass was superb.

And the champagne, Ste Wolls, Samantha's favorite, was Philip's first real champagne and good enough to add enchantment to the word. He chatted, distracted, knowing that Ice was drinking with Isaac at the bar.

Before they were ready to order dessert, Samantha with her head down said, "Philip! Those two are getting up." After a moment she told him, "They left the room around the corner across from the end of the bar. Let's see where it leads."

"If you go first, I'll follow."

They passed through the dimly lit bar area and turned the corner. "A back-side elevator lobby and stairs to the guest rooms," Samantha observed. "Privacy for bar patrons."

The elevator light signaled a stop on the fourth floor. "The suites," said Samantha. "There can be more than one reason for that, Philip. She could sell paintings out of a suite. They could have a party."

"I'd say Occam would take them for lovers."

Samantha nodded. "Let's have dessert and coffee."

Philip mentioned Spring Festival and told Samantha she had looked gorgeous in her flowers at the gardens.

"Philip, do we have a date for next year?"

"I'd like that."

Back on Mrs. R.'s entry porch, Philip received a hug and long kiss on the lips from the girl in the pink sundress, who thanked him for a memorable evening and said he must see her again next year on Nevis or in the States. He floated up to his room without a clear thought and managed to set his wake-up alarm before falling onto the bed without taking off even his shoes. Before he slept, Philip recalled Samantha saying Ice might drop her lover for the right man. *If she acts like all is good between us, so will I.* Soon he slept, although primary process must have churned anxiously over surprises of the day.

SECOND DATE

Philip chose a maroon knit pullover and tan Bermuda shorts. This time he put on his new island sandals and his medium brimmed island hat, a beige colored tropical Tilly from Rebecca's Atelier in Charleston.

Confident that he was dressed well for the evening, he was still nervous, hoping to talk about cheerful island topics instead of philosophy. *Since I'm beginning again, I should learn to be interesting to women who aren't looking only for a husband. Sandra warned me. Irene's English-Lit friends tried to help me.* Philip found his compact umbrella, which he hung on his belt, ready for rain.

Philip's kom held the seventy-two-character address that would present a three-dimensional walk-through of his new apartment with access to furniture that he could place for appearance and fit. *Surely Ice will help with selections.* He had seen the island artists' paintings displayed on campus and read their profiles. Six women from Nevis were artists in residence at the Island Expressions

Co-op, and two men and one woman from Kitts were listed as artists in inventory. Ice seemed compatible with him based on her short profile, and thirty-two years old, a year younger.

He walked slowly yet arrived early at Ice's front door on the paved street—not picturesque like the shop's entry on the walking lane. After a check that his wrist's bandages were holding, he pushed the door button. He didn't hear a tone, but from the perforated circle above the button came Ice's voice, "I'll be right down."

When the door opened she was standing there in a white sundress. She held a cat under her arm. She was just as he remembered, yet Philip found himself momentarily speechless at the sudden presence of her very blonde hair, very red lips, very pale cleavage, and very black cat. He beamed and finally heard himself saying, "I missed you this past week." He gazed at her. "You make the most delicious picture I have ever seen."

She smiled and took the last step down onto the outdoor level. Her dress became less modest, and Philip took a moment before noticing the white jacket over her right arm. "I have missed you, too. I'm wearing my most scandalous sundress for you." He couldn't resist another look. She tilted her face up for him. He lightly kissed the red lips. "Help me on with my jacket, please." She held up the jacket. It was lightweight lace and sleeveless, awkward to put on while holding a cat. She finally turned to toss the cat inside and shut the door. Before turning back around she slipped into the jacket and fastened its three big buttons. "Now I'm ready."

"The sundress version was quite nice."

"It's an old sundress from the States. Here on Nevis the dress is illegal on the streets or a crowded beach. I went from west coast risqué to Charlestown scandalous."

"It's a good thing you found the matching jacket."

"I had it made."

"You designed it?"

"Oh yes."

Love that flash of her eyes! "I'm no fashion critic, but I do think it's perfect."

"You're sweet." She stood on tiptoes and kissed him on his cheek. Only then did he notice her very blonde, narrow, crocheted headband, not needed to hold her short hair in place.

"Nice headband."

"I wear it outdoors, almost by habit now."

As they started down the walkway, Philip remembered dinner. "Ice, I made dinner reservations for us at Mrs. R.'s Guesthouse, at seven thirty. Is that okay, or would you prefer to go elsewhere?"

"That's fine, although I can fix us a nice cold plate."

"We have the reservation, so let's go to Mrs. R.'s." Then, about to suggest champagne, he recalled that Ste Wolls was distributed by Lamancha House. Isaac caressing her back came to mind, and he was too distraught to mention champagne.

They took a circulator van to the town limits and began their walk. After a few minutes, Ice tugged on Philip's arm toward a dirt path. "This is the only way to OneWay Beach that avoids the foul odor of stinkweed. The town planted the first stinkweed to keep children out of an old landfill. Then a wealthy Asian created an artificial beach centered on the old landfill and extended the stinkweed to keep tourists out. The wind keeps the odor off the beach. The beach is not listed on Net. Only locals and a few wanderers get there."

Soon they were on a narrow footbridge crossing low dunes to

a narrow beach. Ice released his arm, loosed her three big buttons, and slipped off her jacket. They left her jacket and their shoes at the footbridge. Philip offered his arm. "You could have brought your cat."

Her voice was somber, "Somebody on Nevis is killing black cats. I no longer let him out. Cat's don't do well on a beach."

"Disturbing turn. Can you move to campus?"

"Yes and no. My situation is, well, in transition."

"Would that situation be related to the situation with your name?"

"The location decides the name, due to fancies of mind. Philip, do you prefer one name to the other?"

"No, and I'm quite fond of Ice."

"Perhaps aesthetics can inform the decision?"

"I don't think so."

"Good," she said with a toss of her head.

Weary of slogging in dry sand, they sat down on the beach and enjoyed the sun softened by wispy clouds. Philip asked if she had painted her cat in a beach scene. She had, using charcoal and ink. Now she wanted to paint him in oil for fond memories, then paint a scene of cats with fauvist colorings to memorialize the spate of black-cat killings.

⁂

Ice wanted to talk about art. "A lady visiting the shop yesterday asked if I painted for the sake of painting, or more for the money. She wanted to buy a well-known artist who is not a member of our Co-op. I wanted to know if she bought paintings for art's sake, or for the prospect of financial appreciation, but held my tongue. I told her I painted for personal enjoyment but would paint less if my paintings didn't sell."

They both turned to watch a small flight of birds. Ice kicked the loose sand. "More and more I'm interested in the topic of aesthetics. Especially what is fine visual art, and what is art for art's sake."

"The ontology of art is a subfield of aesthetics, popular in the last few decades. As to art for the sake of art, seems the Post Essentialists feel that fine art is fundamentally corrupting, because it's costly, hence materialistic and believed inescapably for the ego or investment of the rich."

"I suppose it's corrupting in that sense, as any collecting among a small number of items. In the year twenty-fifteen, an unknown landscape valued at five-thousand-dollars was authenticated as a John Constable and sold to an anonymous buyer for five million dollars—a thousand-fold increase for the name!"

"Wow! Ego driven, only to impress self and close friends it seems."

"My art professors claimed there was no purpose independent existence of art and questioned the concept of fine art."

The couple mused in silence before Philip decided, "I believe that art can be for art's sake, or for another sake, depending upon the mind of the artist, the beholder, or the buyer. Turner and Van Gogh surely painted for art's sake, and some must buy for art's sake. Most who visit the art museums do so for art's sake. I don't believe one person's mind should attribute such a motivation to another person's mind, or that one culture's preferences should be deemed judgement of another culture's preferences."

"Philip, a friend's husband, nicknamed Prince, a concert pianist, says that Rachmaninoff believed art must come from the heart and be directed to the heart."

"Ah, like Pascal, implying a non-discursive phenomenon of mind. And highly subjective, its emotional experience sure to vary among receiving minds! To attribute a corrupting influence to such inscrutable emotions is to deny our core humanity."

Ice exclaimed, "Perfect for salon talk!"

"The topic spans both my professional interests, philosophy and cognitive science. I believe the issues are related to innate human nature and can be quantified using neural brain scans. The actuality of the mind's machinations should get us around the problem of defining an open concept like fine art. Of course, many deny the existence of universality, of any innate human nature, or any core-dependent homonymy—rejecting funds for research touching the issues."

Ice smiled. "Oh, you must tell me more, I could have better conversations. Many of our Co-op's visitors are quite knowledgeable." They sat quietly, enjoying the breeze and the low sun disk surrounded by a yellow dome on the horizon, casting a broad stripe of yellow across the sea, dissolving at water's edge into tiny, frail fringes of blue. Ice gave his arm a tug. "Time to start back; the sun sets in about five minutes."

They returned along water's edge in firm sand, yet walked slowly, half watching the horizon. Philip observed, "The sunsets aren't the bright colors I'd expected in the tropics." He turned to enjoy Ice.

"We have been overcast for weeks. I have a copy of Renoir's 'Sunset at Sea,' and a copy of Théo Van Rysselberghe's 'Beach at Low Tide,' both with colors we're missing. *Beach at Low Tide* almost glows when viewed from three meters." Ice pointed. "The sun is setting." They stopped to enjoy the sight.

Ice went on to say she had been attracted to Portland for the artistic glassmaking there and in nearby Tacoma and in Seattle. She had left for warm water and weather, moving to Nevis at the suggestion of her parents. She would not return to the States because her parents were moving to Nevis. Philip asked where they lived. "Reykjavik now, recruiting for Pystead. With a few hours' review, Dad can speak fluently any of his eight languages, and my mom, six, including Icelandic and Persian. They were in France on their first assignment in twenty twenty-seven. I was seven years old and they took me with them. I didn't move to campus until twenty forty-nine."

"I was recruited by a young man named Patrick Coughlin," Philip recounted. "He was an abstract algebraist from County Tipperary. Wasn't interested in my professional qualifications, only in confirming my personal circumstances. After a required medical check-up, he talked me into an f-MRI brain scan by saying it would give me the nod over any candidate who didn't take it, and queries were innocuous if I were a decent person."

Philip paused, and Ice said, "Go on."

"Patrick asked if I had ever had a kidney stone, and then about sleeping and depression. He asked if I ever used an assumed name or sabotaged or bullied anybody for personal belief or gain. Did I ever slap a girlfriend, enjoy abnormal sex, or make a sex video. Did I have a child or a needy parent I was not helping. He asked if I would choose being famous, say an actor, or choose being a consultant to a billionaire, above being a college professor. Then he wanted to know if I had been a follower or activist in any non-academic group, or a member of any doctrinaire group meeting in person or virtually. A few questions surely explored the issue of schadenfreude. Lastly, he shocked me asking if I had any membership I-D chip implant in my body."

"Our schedules were accelerated and working hours increased last fall, with advantage given to the most vetted."

"I took a polio booster and two other vaccines with my medical exam to reduce the waiting period for travel."

Ice asked about Philip's parents and he hesitated before saying, "Both my parents were killed in a trainwreck almost three years ago."

"Oh, I'm so sorry."

"They were wonderful parents. I had a happy childhood in West Hartford, Connecticut, and they encouraged me in school. They left me investments including a house that I sold. After a semester off, I finished my dissertation and graduated with my second degree in philosophy. Then came my two years at Compton."

Ice continued her story. For her program in antiquarian art and design, she had avoided all but one philosophy course and one psychology course, both required even though they covered the same continuity of ideas in visual media, claiming that any painting of visual or conceptual interest was art, and aesthetics were relative to culture and bias. One professor let it be known that she admired only modern Western art because earlier art, before the Dadaists, disrespected so much of humanity. Ice lamented her experience with so many professors validating art based on their personal feelings, and teaching that only intermedia productions could be called fine art.

The couple moved into dry sand to avoid a sandcastle from child's play and paused. "Intermedia?"

"Oh, yes. Art produced by multiple disciplines, often

performance art or a follow-on installation. Though even a painting must have a concept person, a medium expert, and two painters."

"There must be teamwork?"

Ice nodded. "Multicultural teamwork. Proponents remind us that even the great Botticelli depended on a concept person for his religious scenes."

"And the talented individuals are not pointed out?"

Ice nodded. Philip said his formal courses were no better, with Western philosophers merely identified and criticized out of context. For his education, he had enrolled as an interactive auditor in History of Philosophy at Utrecht University, the school of his degree in cognitive science, and completed their online program a week before contracts were not renewed by U.C.C.

Ice frowned with him and tugged on his arm to walk. "I had to read about Clive Bell on my own, an important twentieth-century art critic. His theory of significant forms should have been discussed in class even if not embraced. After all, his theory anticipated abstract painting as fine art—now all the rage! Also, I found articles on family resemblance theories of art but hardly touched them because all would have been heresies in class, and I preferred painting and collecting artistic glass. I have come to believe that fine art, like a symbol, is impossible to fully define, yet there ought to be something tangible to say about a work beyond personally liking it. Something to say about why so many people like a particular artist. Something to say about the differences between art and craft, about elements that are visually present, versus elements present only as theoretical constructs of interpretation. After all, everybody knows it when they see it, even if they can't define it. There must be tangibles lurking if only in the heart."

"Aha, that's so! Evolutionary reasoning, Ice, concludes that our mind makes sense of lines and their arrangements and colors in order to make sense of objects encountered in the world. Our brains evolved specialized regions, hardwired modules, to interpret shapes and colors. To lead to evolutionary selection, these modules had to be useful, and became so with the mind that preferred certain patterns over others. Those primitive, hardwired preferences remain the basis for our enjoyment of both pictorial and abstract forms."

"Oh, good, there are tangibles lurking!"

"Yes, and functional brain scans confirm that vivid colors and pleasing patterns will light up the pleasure center of the brain."

Ice sighed and pointed to the sky. The sun on the horizon had been replaced by bands of gray on the horizon, shading up to yellow and orange. Philip studied the colors. "Ice, the low colors soften in the north and south to pinks and even a streak of blue-gray."

"Yes, due to the pollution from our industrialized neighbors like Mexico and Venezuela."

"On those tangibles lurking, Ice, if art evokes special feelings then it has an aesthetic mode of existence, implying a substantial mode of existence—Gilson, I believe."

"I do associate Gilson with modes, but again I read little because he couldn't be mentioned in class. One modernist, Rothko, had ideas I like about the colors of a work creating a psychological mood in the viewer. I really tried with his large, color-field work of magenta, black, and green on orange. I almost went to sleep, but I'm sure I never felt calm and contemplative as he intended. Maybe the lighting wasn't right for the colors?"

They slowed to wade in the ripples of water. Ice sighed. "I do think Rothko was right in relating colors and mood. Colors ought to affect our mood."

"I agree. I'm sure our primary process of mind associates and values color in emotional dimensions."

The water was warm and soothing, the slight breeze refreshing. The sun disk, unseen below the horizon, was changing the high clouds into scarlets and reds, creating a brilliant twilight. After pausing to appreciate sea and sky, Ice added, "My professors admired those who criticized Western art as Eurocentric and disrespecting of the Other, even knowing the West was influenced by Others. Why weren't the Others just as disrespecting of us?"

"Ice, I've come to realize that American culture is intellectually dishonest, especially at highest academic and political levels."

"I'm sure that applies to art critics as well."

"I call those type deemers."

"I call them watchdogs. Nevis has many, and they know little more about art than does a dog."

"As to art and mood, Ice, lots of abstract art makes me think I'd see the same thing on a construction site, or that I've been conned for the price of my ticket."

"Oh, yes. The abstract art form need not evoke warm and fuzzy feelings. It avoids humanity because there is no object nor implied story. That pleases our watchdogs."

Signifiers without troubling dimensions of a signified thing—Post Essentialist nirvana!

Arriving back at the footbridge, the pair found their shoes and Ice's jacket. *This would have been rare in California, finding either the clothing or the open-minded, educated woman. And I'm glad she has paintings of sunsets at sea.* They stepped onto the boards and brushed the clinging sand from their feet. Ice handed Philip her jacket for his help, but did not turn her back, producing a few moments of intimacy bathed in the red glow of twilight. And Ice thought the red evening sky could signal brighter blue days and a return of hottest burning rays, even in the tropics after days of unusual hazy skies. "We should not ignore the appearance of the sky, I've heard from Matthew," she noted.

As they strolled towards the bus stop, the sky darkened and yard lights began to come on. Ice assured Philip they would get to Mrs. R.'s on time. Their talk turned to island lore, island monkeys, and wine. Ice said Ste Wolls champagne was a favorite. She praised Mrs. R.'s reputation. Each step found Philip afraid he might wake and find himself alone. Are such perturbing states the lot of humankind, or does such existential apprehension denote a too abstracting mind? *Could Pystead be right for me? Might Ice be all that really matters?*

❇ ❇ ❇

Mr. R. greeted Philip on the porch and showed them through the kitchen to the dining room for locals. As a pleasant surprise, the tables were not crowded. The tablecloths were white, and each table had a small yellow candle. The ambiance though quiet enough was less than romantic. Both Ice and Philip ordered Grouper basted in American chili sauce, with an arborio-rice casserole. Philip was pleased to talk about wine and food, and Mrs. R.'s grits and bacon. Ice knew of grits but had never tried them. She said he would have to bring her for breakfast.

The fish was a filet served warm, butter browned, and flakey moist throughout. The whisp of chili topping was mild, which

Ice said was probably the reason for calling it American chili. The champagne was cool with a final moment of sweetness that made Philip yearn for another sip—as good as he could imagine wine being.

When Mrs. R. lingered nearby, Philip introduced Ice, who was obviously enjoying the evening. Philip sat enchanted, breathing lightly and waiting for the next happy flash of her big, blue eyes. They decided to skip dessert. Ice told Philip he should bring her for coffee and dessert another time.

Once outside, Philip stopped, suggesting an after-dinner drink. Ice tugged on his arm, "I made margaritas, and I have cases of wine for the Co-op's evening socials." Philip said he should provide the drinks. She whispered, "Don't be silly."

"I do like margaritas."

"I want you to see my apartment. I have paintings of mine and others, and if you know anything about art, you will be surprised."

"Ice, I don't know paintings except to think about art as an abstraction, or to walk through a museum and read the plaques. I discovered art in college, at the Centraal Museum Utrecht."

"I have a few famous paintings. An original N. C. Wyeth."

"I believe he's twentieth century American."

"Yes. I have a Miró print."

"Expressionist?"

"Yes. I have a knockoff da Vinci, Ginevra de' Benci, and one of Vermeer's, Girl with a Pearl Earring."

"You mean really good knockoffs?"

"They are magnificent."

"How can I decline and be deemed sane?"

"Simply invoke Pascal."

"Pascal tells me to go."

They walked arm-in-arm. Ice worried aloud about being uninspired as an artist because she didn't get out for big occasions.

Philip relaxed with the sound of her voice and the tug of her arm. "You are making a Pascal convert of me."

"You're feeling the artistic temperament."

O Cosmos, could you shield this wonderful creature and her cat from the gothic wirings of the world? Could you guide her through the labyrinth with enchanted moonbeams instead of sun's burning rays? Philip glanced over. Ice seemed happy. She was the laurel and the palm, beauty and truth, the winner of his golden apple, all that he needed or would ever need. *A touch of da Vinci, a touch of Keats, a touch of Gibran, and a new love shall bear me.*

"Philip, you should probably know that while in graduate school I dated over forty men, counting mostly single dates." She sounded serious. "For the three I thought of as marriage prospects, I had my father check their backgrounds—required vetting for prospective Pystead crewmembers. The first, who told me his art course was an enhancement of a philosophy degree, was promised as a minister supported by his denomination. The second, a commercial art major, was engaged with a banquet hall already rented by his fiancée's family."

"Both from art courses. And the third?"

"From the private club I joined for socializing and recreation. A jeweler, inherited his father's talent and shop, called 'Twenty-Two Carat.' He designed and crafted fine jewelry. I knew he was a playboy, but he gave me the rush and hinted he should be settling down—most men do, you know. Then I learned he was seeing prostitutes. The two I saw were tall with stunning figures."

"Guess I'm relatively unglamorous, Ice. Not a party animal I've been told."

She smiled. "Neither are my present friends."

"Well, Ice, since high school I have dated about two dozen women. Did not keep count and can't name many of them. None of whom I came to think of as a marriage prospect."

"Philip, your Pystead vetting report addresses personal relationships and finds no character flaws. It does not provide specifics."

"As a part-time employee, how did you have access to my vetting report, may I ask?"

"I have friends who are influential crewmembers."

"Good, fine, I can tell you anything you might want to know about my past."

Ice looked at Philip's bandaged wrists. "I only want to know why your last girlfriend tried to murder you!"

After his initial surprise, Philip managed, "She merely dumped me for a promotion, surely not even sleeping with our boss, a university Dean. The wrist wounds I received on my way here. I was detained as a witness by some rogue police department and jerked around in handcuffs."

Ice steered their walk to the right. "Oh, my, do your wrists hurt?"

"Not since arriving on Nevis. The nurse visiting Mrs. R.'s, Shanae, prescribed a good pain medication. She says my wrists are healing properly."

"She's an excellent nurse, part-time with Pystead."

"Which part?"

"Maybe sixty percent. She circulates among several hotels and is otherwise on campus for anybody asking for help at our gate. Ninety percent of my time these days is spent painting or tending the Co-op."

⁂

Ice opened her front door wide enough to peek in, announcing that her cat, Char, named for his charcoal color, was not on the stairs. She invited Philip in. The stairwell walls were painted red with yellow waves on one side, and yellow with red waves on the other side. Scattered on the waves were white, gold, and purple bubbles. "Nice, although strange, these walls."

"They are inspired by Rothko's color-field concepts and a few abstract wave paintings by Sharon Cummings."

At the top of the stairs sat a marble statue of some animal, probably a dog or pig, having sculptured wiggles for hair. The statue stood in front of a narrow wing-wall decorated with a large, beveled mirror in a yellow-gold faceted frame. Philip paused to look at the gray stone creature, but the mirror drew his attention. It was split into quadrants, each having a slightly different curvature and a slight off-set orientation to the wall. "It's a Tasmanian Devil, a dog."

"If you say so, and what do you call the mirror?"

Ice gave a little wave of hand for him to follow. "A gift." She stepped to a built-in bar across the rear of the main room.

The end wall and bar followed in a bold arc across the width of the room. *Nice aesthetically, I suppose.* While pointing out a little pantry, cupboard, and refrigerator, Ice poured two margaritas and set out a dish of roasted macadamia nuts.

They clicked glass rims, and she toasted, "To life."

"To life." *Italian?*

Ice took a long sip and set down her glass. "I'll be right back. Help yourself. Look around." She went down a side hallway behind the entry wing-wall.

Philip stepped over to look at the montage of photographs at the end of the bar. *The tall Indian and Isaac! The older couple, surely her mother and father. And Lois Henssen. Not an overstatement to say she has influential crewmembers as friends!* Philip looked around for a place to sit and joined the black cat on the beige sofa. The walls were off-white and held two levels of paintings. In a front corner with nothing above or below hung the knockoff *Ginevra*. Many of the paintings reminded Philip of local art, but some reminded him of the museums. *All the masters are knockoffs except for a Wythe and a Miró print—somewhere.* The cat did not move so Philip scratched the top of his head and was rewarded with a purr.

Ice reappeared sans jacket in her white sundress. She picked up her drink and sat beside Philip. Her presence electrified everything. He gazed at her. She offered him the nuts and he took a few.

"The margarita is very good."

"I make it to remind of California."

"Good, I'm not a fan of most island drinks."

"Have all you want, I made a gallon. What do you think of Ginevra?"

"Very fine, I once saw the original in the National Gallery."

"And Vermeer's Girl with a Pearl Earring?"

"She was captivating until you returned."

"You're sweet."

Philip took a sip of the margarita. The drink was good and the woman intoxicating. He shifted to see her and sipped again, soon finishing the small glass. She stood. "I'll get the pitcher."

Ice returned, leaned over, and poured his glass full. He couldn't help enjoying her very white cleavage.

"Something is slightly different about you, Ice. I'm sure it's more than the margarita's influence."

"Then you will have to conduct research to find out."

"I may become too intoxicated for the game."

"Maybe you will get lucky?"

Philip ate more nuts and sipped the margarita before telling himself, *You are supposed to play the game!* He put his arm on the sofa and leaned over. "Could it be the color of your eyes? Open wide." She did a big-eyed pose. "Still blue, I'd say."

"Yes blue, but what else could they be?"

"I was exposed to colors in graduate school, assisting with culturally oriented neural scan studies. I'm fine on the distinct colors, except I have a slight blue-green deficiency."

"I don't wear contact lens, my eyes are blue with no hint of green."

"Don't jump." He stroked her hair, parting it to the scalp. "Very blonde to the roots. No change here I'd say."

"Correct again, still not the answer." She smiled sweetly.

And she called her girlfriend Barbe a tease. Philip sat up, still gazing at Ice. She repeated her big-eyed pose, arching her back, causing him to sigh. "Lipstick looks the same cool red."

"Right again." She pursed her lips and slowly kissed the air.

"I hope you aren't trying to drive me crazy."

"Oh no, I'm merely trying to drive you wild."

After a few more sips of the margarita, he told her, "My focus seems to be waning."

"Oh my, how many possibilities are there?"

"Well, there are only five senses if one discounts balance and blindsight. But how can I test taste without an experimental kiss?"

Ice held up a hand. "You may taste in the old-fashioned, court style."

Philip took her hand and kissed it twice. As he released her hand, he noticed a change in something. *What is left?* "Aha, pheromones!"

Ice shook her head. "Simply a part of life, surely haven't changed."

He took her hand again. She wiggled her fingers for him. *Cute., but what has changed since our dinner at the ferryboat dock?*

"I never use pheromone spray, and neither do my friends. Pystead doesn't have users."

Philip guessed again, "No voice modification device?"

"Don't be silly."

That's colors, voice, and taste. A change in touch is as silly as taste since I've barely touched her. Perhaps not wearing a bra, although per-haps not before either? Best wait for a hint there. I've tried olfactory but failed. What could I be expected to notice about smell that is…one doesn't actually smell pheromones, one smells perfume!

Ice broke the silence, "Do I need to give you a hint?"

Philip grinned. "No, you will have to give me a fully earned kiss."

"The answer is?"

"Perfume."

"Correct, and what fragrance?"

"Don't be silly!"

Ice leaned over, pursing her red lips. Philip slid his arm around her neck and pulled her closer, exchanging visual for tactile, kiss-ing her firmly. Then she kissed him and he took her in his arms. As their lips parted, he found his hand high on her waist pushing against the softness of her breast.

She almost purred, "I hope the kiss was a fair reward for your effort."

"How can one kiss suffice for a man driven wild?"

She smiled. "Can you pick me up?"

"Pick you up?"

"Yes, lift me into the air."

"I suppose so."

Ice kissed the air before saying, "If so, you could give me a wild man's kiss."

Philip stood and leaned over to pick her up before realizing that in the movies the woman was standing when she was picked up. *She expects me to fail? Perhaps she has miscalculated by challenging a wild man?*

Philip bent his knees and reached his left arm under her legs. He pulled up and she locked her knees to hold. He caught behind her back with his right arm. "Oh Philip, I don't want to hurt your back."

"Wild men lift with their legs."

"Really, I was being too silly."

"I'm in the mood. Let me try."

"Don't drop me on the cat." He pulled up with his arms, which for a moment he thought would stall, but when aided by his legs brought a short gasp from Ice as she came off the sofa. He surged on with unexpected strength and

stood holding the openmouthed girl in his arms. He shifted her left and lifted her close to kiss. She drew up her arm and massaged his neck while he kissed her lips and down her neck. She relaxed and he kissed down into softness.

Her eyes were shut, her expression happy. He whispered, "Do you believe in love at first sight?"

"Oh yes, kiss me again." He kissed until the sundress blocked his hungry lips.

"You should put me down, but not on top of the cat." Philip looked around for the cat. Ice seemed to purr, "Take me down the side hall and to the right."

Her bedroom?

The wild man took his woman down the hall. He placed her gently on the bed, distracted momentarily by the unexpected curve of the bedroom wall on the living room side. He leaned over and kissed her, soon sliding his fingers under her far shoulder strap, nudging it off her shoulder. He felt her hand on his fingers and thought he was being chastened, until the strap slid off as she drew her hand and arm up through the loop. She was warm and soft and firm. She moaned. Philip passed from thinking to feeling, and from feeling to being, as would a wild man. They lay holding each other for a long minute after the climax.

Philip asked quietly, "Do you think you could fall in love with me?"

"Oh yes. So, Philip, there is a good chance you will stay in love with me?"

"I would ask you to marry me if you knew enough about me to make a decision."

"Do you want children?"

"Yes, do you?"

"One or two."

"Fine."

Ice pushed up on an elbow and said sweetly, "I accept your proposal of marriage."

Philip sat up. "We're engaged?"

"You did want to ask, didn't you?"

"Yes, just checking, you know so little about me."

"Oh, Philip, surely our chances are as good as any couple's? Pystead's vetting is worth months of dating insight." She smiled. As he began to get up, she caught his arm. "Why don't you give your new fiancée a kiss?"

Philip kissed and felt her gently, as if she might break. He sighed. "My most erotic kiss ever."

"For me, too. Now I have key lime pie, if you'd like."

"I would."

The painting in the bathroom gave Philip a jolt. A heart-shaped face softened by a rounded chin and smooth forehead, a mermaid having very large, pale-pink eyes without pupils looked out at him. She was painted with stylized hot pink lips and whorls of blonde and silver hair, with a silver loop of hair held by a golden comb. Her face and skin were pale pink, her nipples dark pink, her hips and legs pale pink blending into jumbled pink shades that shifted and overlapped, forming a skin of scales to her very-blonde tipped tails. She was lying on her side in shallow surf, pushed up on one arm, smiling. To her side at water's edge, a burnished bronze trident stood impaled in the sand. A naked man in the same style was kneeling in the surf, admiring the mermaid. He was broad and muscular with unkempt blue-gray hair and a short, brush beard tracing the contours of his firm jawline. *Must be Poseidon?* Above the mermaid's tails, farther up on the beach, stood another mermaid, a brunette, presenting red.

Philip ran warm water to wash up, feeling macho with mermaids watching. Taking a departing look at the central mermaid, he noticed her breasts sagged and the man's stomach was almost paunchy. He was circumcised and unaroused, almost, perhaps in cosmological terms beginning trans-Planckian adjustments. *They are both old. And in the distant surf?* In silhouette, a tall and slim mermaid, standing, flaunting her form and long hair. *Lots of sail for such a slim ship!* The painting had only one name, at bottom center, done in bold red ink using a calligraphy pen, *Amanda.*

Ice greeted him with a smile. "My painting, after the mannerism of Amanda Valdes."

"Were you the model?"

"Please, never admit to anyone that she's somewhat an older me. Pystead has a few genuine Valdes's—somehow better, especially the lips."

"Yours is captivating."

"Thanks."

"Who's the man?"

Ice smiled and quickly said, "Poseidon."

"I'm competing with a god for your affections?"

"You are after all, yourself divine! Now slip on your pants and let me serve you a piece of pie." She did a big-eyed blink.

Was that involuntary, a habit? Philip watched as she slipped into a pink lace robe.

"I'll get the pie while you put on your shirt."

His fiancée was alluring in her lace robe, and the key lime

pie was delicious. Philip paused with spoon raised. "Ice, is there a jewelry shop in town? I want to get you an engagement ring."

"Oh, yes, but I don't need a diamond ring."

"I would like you to have one. I'll buy a diamond I can afford without using credit. Would you wear it?"

"I would."

"When should we get married?"

"Anytime, Philip, let's keep it a small occasion."

"Perhaps we should wait for me to make crew?"

"Do you have any contagious disease or addiction?"

"No."

"Do you have reservations about Pystead as you now know it?"

"No."

"You're vetted, a fully functioning model, and clever. Why shouldn't you make crew?"

"I suppose I should, unless perhaps they prefer men who take adventurous vacations—hiking in Nepal with all those Bengal tigers about?"

"If you support Pystead in principle, but don't make crew, you will be eligible as my husband." Ice hesitated. "If we live off campus, I would not want children unless I believed Nevis to be a decent place for them to grow up."

"A sentiment I share, but how would we decide as a practical matter?"

"Oh, we would talk about it. I don't want to look at my child, or any child, living with fear in his eyes that he will be jailed or killed before becoming an adult, or not allowed a college education. Who daily hears bold-faced lies told about his parents and his community, saying society would be better off without them.

Psychological stress forecloses motivation and joy, it's thought detrimental even to the germ line."

Philip nodded. "Ice, what is your position with Pystead?"

"I buy art and ornamental glass. The old masters and pre-moderns in this apartment belong to Pystead, except for a few that are mine. Pystead will keep most of their paintings and donate a few to Nevis."

"Ice, what color is your lapel pin?"

"Oh, a modern, medium blue. My first pin was aqua." She said slowly, "Philip, my friend Lois Henssen, by coincidence the night before we met in the Co-op, called to mention you to me."

"Why so?"

Ice paused for a long moment, eyes half-closed. "Lois read your entire vetting report. She called to say you might be the man I'd been looking for, that she approved of your character, the laboratory approved of our genetic distance, and our palm reader was pleased with your palm." Ice leaned over and kissed him. "After that, I wanted to be special for you. I'm sure you are perfect for me."

"I'm surely not perfect, but I do love you. I'm curious, do you have a rank with Pystead?"

"Can you keep a secret?"

"I can."

"I'm a Commander, equivalent to Lois Henssen."

"You're a top officer?"

"Yes, but a staff officer, not line. I am not in the line of succession to a general leadership role. I am like, say, a medical doctor, a chaplain, a counselor, or a piano player."

"Do you know what my beginning rank might be?"

"Oh, yes. You will be an ensign for about sixty days, after which your promotions could come quickly because we are expanding. Your track could take you to lieutenant next year if you apply yourself to cross-training and want a leadership role."

"Would that be line or staff?"

"Depends on you and Security Branch."

"I like to do things I can do well. Either category would be fine with me."

"You need a minimum of five years' experience to become a Commander. A new criterion is that you must be thirty-five years old. Full service ends at age fifty-six, after which we can teach, mentor, and provide special needs assistance. Remember that a promotion means duty hours and responsibility without significantly more perks, especially at sea."

"What if I concentrate on my cognitive research instead of promotion?"

"If you remain an ensign and focus on your research, I will be perfectly happy. If you are happy, I will be happy."

"Okay. What time is it? I need to catch one of those shuttles."

"You have time. I'll get you up in the morning for a proper new beginning. Afterward, I'll make bacon and eggs."

"Sounds good."

"I cook my bacon just crispy."

"Make that for two." Philip took her hand. "So, Ice, there is a good chance you will keep me?" She did her big-eyed pose. Soon both were asleep, thought surely their primary processes dreamed about events of the day.

An aroma roused Philip, but a blink of his eyes found darkness, and he sank back with the thought, *Not bacon.* The bed sagged and the enticing aroma again beckoned. He drew a breath.

A sweet voice whispered, "Good morning, Poseidon. I promised you a proper new beginning." Philip opened his eyes to focus on Ice's face, then on her breasts. She leaned over and he kissed a breast. She pulled back his covering sheet. He flinched at the unexpected warmth on his stomach. "Let me wash you." He relaxed and enjoyed a warm birdbath. She slid into bed and he rolled over to hold her waist, soon exploring the curve of her hip, eyes closed. "Oh Philip, don't go back to sleep."

He opened his eyes and smiled, more at the golden comb in her hair than at her. "Right. You said we'd have breakfast." She looked away.

Philip sat up and kissed her neck. She turned back to him, tears on her cheek. "Ice, what's wrong?"

She looked away. "During my first year on Nevis I had a boyfriend, Sven, a blond, a member of the crew."

"Go on."

"Everything was fine until I wasn't enough for him." Ice put a hand to her face. "My rival had an incredible figure. He hurt me terribly."

"Ice, I'm sorry."

She wiped her eyes. "Definitely for my long-term best." She looked into Philip's eyes. "Do I excite you, Philip?"

"Of course!"

"I thought you'd take me as an appetizer for your new beginning."

"I'm enjoying you, my beautiful mermaid."

"I'm hot and wet for you, you should be hard for me. If you are going to need more than me, please…." She bit her lip. Her big blue eyes did not flash. "If you need a more shapely mermaid… please leave me now!"

"You are gorgeous, perfect, I want only you."

"You should want me now."

Finally understanding the morning, Philip pulled his mermaid close. He enjoyed his appetizer for a proper new beginning.

Ice left the bed first and too soon banged her spatula on the frying pan. "Why don't you take a quick shower? Breakfast in ten minutes."

Philip rolled out of bed and once in the bathroom again did a doubletake at the painting of Poseidon and the three mermaids.

When he entered the kitchen, his very own mermaid served him a hot breakfast. She was alluring in a red lace bra and matching panties. The bra's sea-shell cups were a single layer of lace not hiding her pretty pink.

Philip smiled. "You make an irresistible mermaid."

"Actions speak louder than words."

"Maybe you will swim by after the assembly?"

"You will have to call sweetly. Remember, it can take a minute or more to swim by."

"What's your name?"

"Oh, Amanda."

"What if my fiancée hears me calling?"

"Merely say I'm an appetizer."

"She'd run me off."

"Oh no! I know her well. She will always be here."

"But would she be true to me?"

"Oh, yes, she adores you."

"Doesn't seem fair?"

"Ice will explain, eventually! You know, soon we at Pystead will all live in a strange new world. Be sure to remember my name, Amanda."

"Right."

His mermaid swam away. Ice returned wearing a red lace robe. Philip looked to find highlights in pink. She moved close and whispered, "The lace shifts with movement. Color can peek through these two layers of lace. My cranberry lace dress happens to have its own meandering under-layers of lace in all the right places." Ice smiled. "Only you will know more than high cleavage. Phil, how is the bacon?"

"Good, just crispy."

"I'm pleased. Amanda liked it too."

"A cute one, that Amanda, sweet and mysterious."

"I could become jealous."

"She's merely an appetizer."

"Oh good, don't go putting on weight."

"Right." *I have no idea what she means.*

After breakfast, Ice produced a tube of hand sanitizer and told Philip to use it after contact with anyone, after touching a common thing in public like a handrail, and before eating or touching a hand to his mouth, face, or skin. She said that henceforth they must put clothes directly into the hamper when taken off, and then wash their hands, arms, and face using a disinfectant soap. She put her cat in the pet pod. She dropped a thick spongy pad at the door to step on when leaving and entering. Then she pulled on her very blonde, crocheted headband and told Philip not to look back at the bright blue lights that would come on as they left the apartment.

ORIENTATION ASSEMBLY

Ice accompanied Philip and they arrived back at campus on time and young at heart. Ice went with Philip down the R aisle of Administration's tank-building and asked him to choose their seats.

The high ceiling module Philip had noticed during in-processing was descending above the central platform with a separate video screen facing each of the nine seating sections. Below, on the platform, a lectern faced each quadrant of the auditorium.

Philip spotted a stairwell opening on one side of the central platform as a man emerged and stepped to one of the lecterns. Although he stood in an almost profile position to Philip, the screen clearly showed his face and shoulders larger than life. Several other men and women not shown on screen emerged from below and took seats. Each wore the familiar white jumpsuit. Philip checked the shoulders of the man on screen and found no insignia. His pea pin was green. *Henssen's pin is deep blue.*

Without speaking, the man at the lectern leaned to one side and made a low hand motion, producing a high-pitched ring, followed by two more resounding rings from a hat-sized brass bell on the lower side of his lectern. He stood erect and spoke without an island accent. "Welcome, recruits. My name is Robbie Markwaters, I am General Manager of The Pystead Group. This meeting is the first in a series of orientations that you must attend. We want each of you to understand our company so that you can assess your personal compatibility with us."

The Manager paused for a long moment before continuing. "I was recruited from Barrow, England, although before that I had lived in Santa Monica, California; Pascagoula, Mississippi; Newport News, Virginia; and Groton, Connecticut. Our Commandant of Administration, Lois Henssen, recruited me through an employment app where I had listed anonymously and below my professional level without giving my employment history by dates and titles. I was hoping for interviews and employment partially because of the engineers I could attract. When Lois contacted me, she knew my real name and had guessed my game."

Someone called out, "How did she do that?"

Markwaters replied, "I could tell you how, but then I'd have to shoot you." There followed scattered laughter. The Manager smiled.

A faux pas gone good.

"Commandant Lois felt that an easygoing Caribbean island would appeal more to me and my family than the hassle in the States." The Manager said pleasantly, "Our present crew and you recruits are here as individuals or as members from a nuclear family. We have no clans of kinship, nor do we recruit groups of any kind.

"Our culture is fair, free, and equal for all. It will remain equal until we can escape our zero-sum existence with safety and plenty for all. It will be fair so long as merit is allowed to rise while equity and kindness prevail for all. It will be free as long as each individual is allowed to choose his or her own way commensurate with abilities.

"Our policies have served the present crew for decades. To flourish in our little group, you need not be at variance against anybody to please the group. We do not submerge the individual. We expect to prosper with reciprocal altruism benefiting individuals and therefore the group. With honesty prevailing injustice has no place to hide, and our innate humanity responds with the empathy and trust required for a strong social contract."

The Manager reached down and rang his bell. "Ladies and gentlemen, you need to know that we keep religion effectively separated from policy. Our selection process necessarily rejects anybody with domineering religious or other ideological beliefs.

"We have few pure desk positions, and everybody should expect field work to learn a hands-on job and be able to contribute when needed. Those who design something should be able and willing to help build it, test it, and repair it. Entertainers should be willing to help design and build their sets. Mathematicians and artists should be able to do something hands-on, and the company is open to suggestions." He got a laugh.

The Manager grasped his lectern with both hands. "You are our first large number of recruits from North America. As of now, each of you and your family, friends, and pets are eligible for medical treatment at company expense. Per our policy, if you feel sick, if you run a fever, if your temperature drops, you are obligated to contact a company physician immediately, any time of any day or night." Markwaters took time to look around. "I know most of you leave medical care to the virtual physician of your medical insurance. In the U.S.A. most of you have had the same provider." The Manager waved to the overhead screen that showed the homepage of Medical Doctor Masterson. "You may have had different insurance and applications software, but in the United States you all had the same politicized medical care by a virtual physician, Dr. Masterson. His artificial intelligence often works with too few symptoms for days or weeks until generating the appropriate questions never asked by your diagnostics physician, real or virtual, who should have reviewed your medical case.

"If you are considering employment with us, however, you should know that we have a personalized approach to healthcare. The key difference here is that our medical doctors are real people board certified in either the European Union, the United Kingdoms, the Dutch Republic, or Russia. Their classroom and laboratory studies were residential and exams were proctored. We have osteopaths and naturopaths in research roles. You will have options in choosing a medical doctor. We do employ the virtual Dr. Masterson less the politicization as another opinion. I encourage you to compare our Dr. Masterson to yours for past or hypothetical symptoms. Here you will find access to good painkillers and biologics even if you have a high antisocial score."

The overhead screen showed video of Pystead's two hospitals, each a one-story, steel-shuttered building raised above grade a couple of meters on dozens of spring-mounted, steel columns supporting the building on large slip plates.

"Our medical care is by far the best available in the Caribbean and perhaps anywhere else. We have had no case of injury or death due to poor care or secondary causes such as infection. Our hospital has had only ten patients die, all from fifty being shuttled around by their own country's hospitals because of their high probability of dying. And those ten bodies were returned with all organs in place—a rare event as organs are routinely 'lost' during autopsy in many parts of the world. You have to hope those missing organs were not also the cause of death."

Philip squirmed in his seat. *An institutionalized practice of killing people for their organs has been beyond my imagination!*

"Also, we do not employ vacant-eyed technicians with marginal technical and no medical competence. We do not introduce scribes unconcerned with your medical treatment into your exam room— most are regulatory spies, error-input secretaries, or voyeurs. None bear any responsibility related to your recovery. Our strength is that our personnel are fully qualified, understand the importance of cleanliness, and care about their practice and your health. You will come to appreciate talking to qualified physicians and nurses, unheard-of as that may be. Our medical personnel will talk with you in person because they are knowledgeable and not afraid of being found wanting."

The Manager paused for a sip of water. He waited while the overhead screen ran through photographs of several doctors and nurses identified by their first names and specialties. "Although we do not advertise, our patients spread the word and the grapevine keeps our beds filled. Consequentially, many of our patients are rich and famous with profiles on the Net. We will allow you to select representatives to walk through our two campus hospitals and chat with them and our many charity cases. Get together and compare notes." The Manager stepped back and took another drink of water.

He continued earnestly, "The world is changing rapidly, ladies and gentlemen! I advise each of you to study our posted policies, ask questions, and become prepared to choose either seasteading with us or a return home." He paused while video of Pystead's three-tiered floating fish farm city showed on screen. "If we were to learn tomorrow that this campus would be brought under political control, occupied, we would sail within three days. Read our forward-looking statements on amenities, professions, and ports of call. You do not want to live in a circumscribed community not to your liking."

The Manager turned and nodded to the others seated on the platform. A woman stood. He introduced her as Mrs. Lois Henssen, rank of Commander and Commandant of the Department of Administration that covered personnel and meta studies. The screen view switched to Commander Henssen. *Yes, the woman from check-in—deep blue pea pin.*

Henssen surveyed her audience. "Everything said here must be treated as company confidential. Although it may not yet be evident, we have political adversaries. No proposed infrastructure modification or expansion goes unchallenged. Every challenge means expense, delay, and reduced future capability—as intended. Our having a monopoly of some sort is often heard but is untrue, and not the real issue as we have never faced competition. Nobody is interested in our old-era businesses! The politicians make fun of them. In the Caribbean others do only electronics assembly, banking, big data, movies, and imported or exported sand. Even so, we are forced to be security conscious to protect our old-era technologies, and we hire only those who will keep safe our proprietary information."

The recruits remained attentive. Henssen listed their four business operations as fish farm, medical center, water treatment, and waste recycling. A topic of political speculation and anxiety, she said, was the extent to which Pystead was self-sufficient. Pystead was financially sound without debt, paid cash for its needs, and abided by most international, national, and local laws, rules, ordinances, regulations, and rulings by local officials. She said transnationals could never fully comply with all localities.

She waved her hand. "You should know that the United Nations is an antagonist to our company! The U.N. believes that we have hundreds of refugees as crewmembers and is insisting that we allow biometric and D-N-A scans of the entire crew. As justification, they say that we constitute an illegal, intentional community. Their hidden agenda is to identify each of us so they can pressure our relatives and friends until we return to our countries of origin. Especially they want to identify our scientists and deter technological progress. We know of their plans in detail because of friendly ghosts on the Net."

Philip closed his eyes. *Perhaps I should begin with Lord Acton. If absolute power corrupts absolutely, then political philosophy should support pluralism. Here, I sense a general concern for pluralism in thought and freedom for the individual.*

He returned his attention to the Commander who was now saying that almost seventy percent of the recruits knew a member of the crew who would contact them if they did not meet naturally within the next few weeks.

Her tone mellowed, "Our policies respect personal privacy and discretion, the immaturity of childhood, the right to decency in common places, and the need for truth and civility in administration and politics. Each crew member and family member is a bona fide citizen of the group, having considerable liberty and not subject to dismissal, arbitrary management, nor nit-picking to find offenses. Everybody is treated equally and fairly.

"Pystead owes its nine magnificent ships and their financing to supremely talented members of the crew. Those members owe their daily security, creature comforts, and well-being to most of us. In our daily lives a good cook is as relevant as a technical prodigy. Together we create a successful and contented group. Our social compact is strong.

"I do not mean to imply that each of you will approve of our policies and culture. Here, every individual crew and family member has the same food, clothing, lodging, and recreational venues. You must, however, pass your own tests and make your own friends! You must choose carefully when joining our crew, just as we will take care in choosing you. And be warned if you fancy yourself a loner, femme fatale, or alpha male, as you will not find happiness here because after several months in a small community you will become known as an unreliable person."

Manager Markwaters reappeared, this time with his back to Philip. Without ringing the bell, he said he wanted to mention a few important points. For over four years they had grown enough food aboard the floating fish farm to feed five thousand people. The fish and other farms for the crew were inside the pontoons of the floating city, not below it like the fish for sale. He thought that Pystead served good food. Pystead had its own warriors, librarians, mathematicians, scientists, engineers, medical staff, musicians, farmers, mechanics, cooks, artists, entertainers, and all the specialists needed for self-sufficiency with a first-world life.

Also, he said Pystead was more egalitarian than most of the self-proclaimed virtuous societies or groups on the planet, most claiming kindness in principle, but in practice being hard on individuals. He believed that anyone who valued personal safety, professional scope, time for family and friends, and retirement security above high pay would be happy. He said he didn't want to be all positive—drawing a laugh. "Success comes at a price. We continuously watch for industrial and political spies, and we sacrifice some personal privacy and convenience for practical security."

I'm all for eliminating secret sweeties like my last girlfriend in Compton.

"Ladies and gentlemen, because of current events in the Caribbean we are compressing your training schedule from nine months to three months and asking family members to attend the orientations and policy presentations. The good news is that you will be paid for nine months! The bad news is that to understand our group, each of you will have to read our company policies outside the assembly presentations."

Fine, they want us to know what's what, at least their version of it.

✳ ✳ ✳

For their lunch break, Philip and Ice wanted to walk the perimeter corridor intending to eat a small portion from each of the nine food service stations. The nearest station, Space Food, was interesting with eight different meals sealed and marked fresh at room temperature until 2070. Philip shook his head and he and Ice moved on. In typical Russell style, he spoke to as many people as he could.

Most were engineers. One woman, Angela, exotically dressed in red and purple with much of her midriff showing stood in the same line and ordered a cinnamon-apple crepe, as did Philip and Ice. They ate together and chatted. She was from Brazil, a KAM theory mathematician, which meant nothing specific to Philip or Ice. Next, Philip ate a beef taco and then a small serving of broiled flounder and-French fries.

Once finished eating and outside, Ice said she would like to visit friends and meet Philip at the central column ten minutes before two o'clock. She kissed him goodbye, suggesting he walk the campus and begin learning his way around, even get a haircut.

10

SCRAMBLE

With well over an hour of lunch break remaining, Philip got in some of the daily exercise expected of a crewmember by walking to the east side gate—merely a door for personnel. To his surprise, laughter and music could be heard beyond the campus fence. A guard told him that some locals celebrated Spring Festival for a week, then asked him to wait a moment before leaving campus. Within seconds his kom buzzed and Director Henssen introduced herself and asked if he recognized her voice. He said yes, and that he wanted to visit a nearby Spring Festival.

Her voice took on a serious tone. "Philip, Interpol makes random stops to check koms for apps and links. You will be arrested if anything unapproved is found."

"I'm fine on that."

"Hold the seven key on your kom if you feel anything is amiss, including a policeman merely eyeing you or approaching you."

"Fine, I'll stay alert."

"Enjoy your walk."

Within two minutes Philip encountered young men dancing along a narrow street in bird-face masks having the same yellow beaks and white feather plumes seen before, and this time with many colorful streamers from their shoulders to knees. With them were a dozen younger boys maybe thirteen or fourteen years old, wearing white angels' wings and clothed in island beige T-shirts and shorts, each carrying a ceremonial bow and arrow set. The bows were curved as if drawn, but without a bow string. An arrow, clipped to the bow, was gold with a large, red, thick, heart-shaped tip. *Probably made of Styrofoam.* Philip followed the procession toward a few vendors' tents. The cupids waved their bows and arrows and danced, weaving among the older masked boys and the sparce crowd.

One of the cupids, he noticed, was holding back and possibly following him. Only when Philip realized the cupid was not dancing did he become alarmed. Philip held his arms up as if stretching to relax and took a zoom image of the boy. His bow was not drawn, but it was strung! Its arrow tip was red, but thin, possibly cardboard, possibly something harder. Recalling Dr. Henssen's warning that the U.N. wanted to identify Pystead's scientists a lump formed in his throat. *I'm a Pystead scientist.*

As if by reflex, Philip ran for a portable toilet off the road. Its door was open, and he knew a vendor's tent would block the cupid's line of sight. He pushed the toilet's door shut and circled behind the tent, feeling foolish. He didn't have to wait for the boy to pass because he was pushing to get ahead. The boy stopped at the corner of the tent, peering around it. When he turned to look all around Philip stepped back to avoid being seen, and a bird-masked dancer pushed him clear of the crowd in front of the vendor's tent. The cupid's wings shook. Philip said, "P.R. kom, hold tab number seven." By then the boy was staring at him wide-eyed. *That cupid is notching his arrow!* Philip rushed the boy, jamming him. The boy tried to use the arrow as a spear, but Philip caught it and snapped it in half, keeping the tipped end.

The boy slumped to the ground, crying. Dancers and vendors gathered. Philip's wrist kom vibrated and Dr. Henssen shouted, "Turn on your microphone so we can hear."

"P.R. kom, open microphone on high."

An island woman from the tent asked the boy if he was hurt. He blurted out, "A big man grabbed my mom's hair and said he would wring her neck like a chicken's. Help her somebody, please."

Philip's kom spoke, "Get a full-face photo of that boy, his name, and where his mother is."

Philip tried to speak to the boy, but the crowd made a point of keeping him away.

Philip shouted, "Get his name and his mother's location so somebody can help her!"

"We need a policeman over here," an island woman shouted.

His kom sounded, "Philip?"

"Here!"

"We just destroyed the camera of the local police drone that was watching you and directing your cupid and a few masked dancers. Our guards will make sure their policeman trips in the crowd. Watch for a knife from one of the older dancers. They don't want this boy talking to anybody but the police!"

"O Cosmos!"

"Philip, point or grab any knife arm so we can spot it—use both hands, shout knife. Stand to the side, away from his free hand. You have drone protection overhead that will respond within the moment, but we can't spot a concealed knife. You might."

"I'm watching."

In the next moment a tall woman pushed past Philip and the crowd to the boy. She took a photo and asked about his mother. When a dancer tried to intervene, a big man held his shoulders, shouting, "The boy asked for help for his mother. We need to know where she is!" The teenage dancer twisted free and ran.

Philip's kom spoke, "Philip, in about ten seconds two unregistered passenger drones will land behind the vendor's tent. Get in with one of our male guards, the boy flies with the other two guards. Go now!"

⁂ ⁂ ⁂

Within a minute of flight time the passenger drone dropped Philip on the concourse level of the administration facility, below the tall tank building. Dr. Henssen was standing beside the Poseidon statue near the central column, and he went to meet her. "I suspect you'd rather talk about your little stroll than return to the assembly?"

"True, but the assembly is mandatory."

"Rules are made to be broken. We break them when necessary, as you might have noticed. Let's find a quiet room."

Once he was seated, Lois handed Philip a chocolate almond bar. "You have a pin, call me Lois."

"Thanks, I need this candy bar. What happened out there, Lois?"

"We don't know. This is the third appearance of those cupids, and they always cause trouble. The police always look the other way."

"I'm sure they were after me!"

"We were worried. With facial recognition, targets can be changed in a moment. We put guards and surveillance drones in place before you got to the parade."

"How could you respond that fast?"

"The militaries scramble jets, we scramble armed drones and guards—a secret."

"Why would the cupid say somebody was going to kill his mother?"

"Because they will if we can't rescue her. That's how they coerced the boy to work for them. His arrow, if it hit, shouldn't have killed, and even had he missed the police surely would have arrested you for provoking a cupid. They wanted you alive!"

"Cosmos, goths everywhere!" A wave of fear seemed to pulse through Philip's body.

"The boy and his mother will need to live with us."

⁂ ⁂ ⁂

Lois waved to a large kom screen on the wall. "Philip, I'd like you to hear part of one more talk that was recorded yesterday for another group's orientation assembly. We are running two groups. Kom, play the Windsor talk."

On screen, the Manager introduced Mrs. Joan Windsor, Commander of Pystead's Security Branch. Commander Joan wore a beige, medical facemask. Once at the lectern she removed the mask. She was, of course, wearing a white jumpsuit with no rank or nametag. Her stick pin was bright red. She was attractive in red lipstick, with light brown hair pulled into a loose bun on the back of her head. She wore a necklace of several gold strands, plus one heavy, red strand that a passing view showed holding a red, wagon-wheel pendant. *I'll call her the Red Queen.*

The video zoomed in and Commander Windsor spoke softly, "As Manager Markwaters was kind enough not to point out, among other things I oversee intrusions into your privacy. If I do say so myself, I'm good at it." She got both chuckles and moans from the audience.

Well, we know who you are. And you're not living in my apartment as was Paula in Compton.

The Commander reminded them that many positions in the world beyond were more intrusive than those at Pystead. "Here, we do not track social contacts, what you eat, where you go or how long you stay. We do not conduct evaluations of our social life or religious affiliations. We leave your personal life to you and your friends."

Joan Windsor smiled faintly, but her voice tensed. "Like most Western companies, we are under attack. Unlike most Western companies, we do not have insiders selling our password structure and firewall mods to hackers. Each month we identify and do not hire one or two candidates who are political or industrial spies. Their failure to penetrate our company greatly disturbs our detractors. We are rumored to have psychics on the payroll. I must confess, I did interview a psychic, but had no confidence in her—not a virgin!" Joan smiled.

"Our ship's control computers have no downloads from the outside and are reserved for operating the ship. No one except longtime crew speaks with any of our over two hundred binary boffins."

The Commander raised her hand. "There is offered a fifty million *Marker-Chit* reward, about thirty million kicu, for hacking us. Impossible without considerable and coordinated inside assistance and luck across functions guided by pseudorandom choices. The reward hasn't touched us, but it has resulted in the street killings of two coders who tried to scam *Marker-Chit*." Commander Windsor pointed up to a video screen and her image was replaced by a target-like symbol of concentric blue and white circular bands having a black eye at its center. "The Blue Moti or Blue Nazar, our good luck charm!"

Pystead does have a tangible Third Eye: functional brain scans—unknown to recruits because they are illegal and disguised. Better than a psychic! Screening need not intrude into personal life to identify spies and schizoids, nor to spot exaggerated qualifications and expectations. Those who sign up here will have to forego immediate gratification for long-term goals, hence most will be high-abstract thinkers willing to work for delayed benefits. Rejecting the gothic seems doable. A bit of secret, neural scanning and voilà, a decent crew!

When Philip began to listen again, the Commander was saying, "There is a personal benefit to our security. No crew or family member has ever gone missing! On campus and at sea on the fish farm, doors often go unlocked, yet we have never had an incident of anything missing other than a cocktail drink during a party. We have had pranks played by children, and for that reason I would lock the door. If you have a question, please ask on the inhouse network Fednet."

Windsor raised her voice, "Please listen carefully! Each of you must check and learn the posted list of draconian local laws before doing anything else outside this campus!"

"Skip to next topic," Henssen instructed her kom.

"Unlike most judicial systems, our laws and procedures are posted and searchable. At sea we eliminate the local laws. As an independent check on our policing, however, we now pay for Nevis to maintain three officers on campus and three aboard the fish farm. Each location has an officer and two sergeants who rotate on about a weekly basis. The media complain that the police are paid to hear and see nothing, because in all our years we have prosecuted only one criminal case. For any death, we, along with a coroner from Nevis, perform an autopsy. In addition to the ten hospital deaths already mentioned, a few dozen have died of natural causes, and two men died in an industrial accident decades ago, Steve and Curtis." Joan stepped back. "Thank you for your attention."

⚔ ⚔ ⚔

Lois told Philip, "You are fast tracked and your security scans take priority over all but first orientations. I will send you an executive summary of the talks you miss." She stepped over to a printer. "Here's a copy of next week's schedule. Philip, we are quite Western in law and culture, taking the best of it as we see it. Too, we vet for acceptance of religious and racial diversity, and gender equality. In our present circumstances, there are no resources that can be used to escape the norm. For now, a circumscribed life is our fate—the dark side of Pystead Group. Yet, to quote our Manager, 'In the spirit of Renaissance polymath Fra Giovanni Giocondo, let me say that although at present we cannot give you that which you have not, here you may look beyond the gloom of the world, and in the daybreak of the Pystead crew you may have peace and take joy, and let your ghosts flee away.'" Lois showed a painting on the kom screen labeled DAWN ON NORDFJORD, SPRING LIGHT, BY KATHLEEN FRANK. It glowed in yellow: sky, clouds, snow, water, trees.

A daybreak to remember! An acquisition by Ice, I feel sure. All my experiences with Pystead have been positive. I should be compatible here, able to belong. Yet, if our ghosts are to flee, it is only on campus! Even that would be progress. Still, what's what? Well, how many press-gangs care to woo their marks into a voluntary signing? They simply take you. Soon enough you would realize you had been duped. Even if legitimate, will existence on the margins be better than my previous Dean's suffering in freedom? Does seasteading offer enough?

✺ ✺ ✺

At Lois's suggestion, Philip contacted Ice and arranged for them to skip lunch together and meet for dinner. Then he walked to badge processing for his Level-Two scans. The facility was open midday for fast-tracked recruits. He stopped in the men's room and removed his passport from the carry pouch. He found a Level-Two line with only two people ahead of him and reserved the number three appointment.

When called for his scan, Philip was surprised by another head hood and a screen panel that fit above the shoulders. Soon he was responding to questions about his intentions, his education, and his mental and physical health. Then he answered questions on family planning and his willingness to limit offspring to replacement level and to consider gene editing if a problem were found.

By the time the scan was completed, he was weary from wearing the virtual reality hood and having the screen around his neck Finally, he received his updated pea pin, still pale blue. One of his scanner operators had worn a pale blue like his, and the other a light green. *Perhaps the colors have nothing to do with job or rank?*

Some correlation with body metrics as a visual double check when needed? Philip got to his VCQ room late afternoon with time for a nap before dinner with Ice.

ARTS AND SCIENCES

The next morning, sixteen guides ushered almost three hundred PhDs and MDs through classrooms, exam rooms, and laboratories. Family members were not invited. The tour became a hurry-up-and-wait event. The classrooms were not state of the art. The guides presented Pystead's approach to college education. Professors were expected to lecture, and students expected to take notes and ask questions in class. The classroom presentation boards could save the markings of the professor but could not receive kom questions from students. Each professor had a small office also used for tutoring individual students as a formal part of pedagogy. Exams would be proctored, and student's answers written by hand into bound notebooks provided by the college. In all but computer courses, calculations were to be assisted by past-century slide rules or hand-held calculators doing arithmetic. Grades were based on individual performance. Teamwork projects required participation and success but were not graded. Classroom participation was encouraged but not graded. Tutoring sessions were not graded but allowed sufficient evaluation for the selection of fellows. Students could not substitute social work, field work, nor a special project for coursework. Assisting apps could not be used. *Aha! This must be the old format that produced educated people before the Postmodern era of education. For a diploma here, one must learn all that needs to be learned. In the sciences, application of theory and the solution of resulting mathematical equations will be tested—future scientists will be identified.*

One recruit was displeased. Listening to his third angry comment, Philip recognized the voice as the spokesman for the bus people—the man who a week ago had stood and shouted to the Pystead representative addressing that group off the bus. He was the organism man, and he could not imagine subjecting callow student minds to the whims and biases of too often callous content providers. He knew the U.N. would object to the loss of participation and motivation that smart classrooms and qualified facilitators inevitably produced. He knew that not having presenters enforce educational norms would result in a hostile learning environment.

All things are relative. Here teachers engage with students who will be able to apply what they learn because they will understand the material they are reciting. Philip kept his distance from the organism man, and chatted instead with others, all of whom were open to the prospect of interacting with students in class. *Pystead dreams of progress rather than of Maintaining maintained by subaltern classes of professionals and trade masters.*

For lunch, the touring groups assembled in four dining rooms having a common audio-video link to the hologram of a faculty member beside the head table, addressing all four dining rooms.

The hologram said the faculty at Pystead were content providers appearing in person. Philip watched closely as the hologram vanished and was replaced in a flash by an old and gray sage clothed in deep blues and greens. She appeared standing and explained that decades ago Pystead's first principal officer had known where the arc of probability cast the self-contented who could become an able crew to fathom the seas and reach the stars. She reminded her audience that a singular mutation could transform the germ plasm, and that a singular elect could improve the epigenetically expressed mind. She believed that God's plan told in myth and metaphor might yet cast out that malicious eye and release mankind from the temptations of Satan. She dropped Satan in favor of, "We will serve lunch, and when teaching as a crewmember you dine at the head table." *My first holograms.* The sage waved her farewell.

The dining room tables were set in rows with a head table at the front of the room seating four tour guides. Crew in jumpsuits served the tables with a meal of seasoned baked chicken. Passing the serving dishes, the recruits created something of a family atmosphere.

A tall young man soon entered the room and stood beside the head table. *We have the real person this time!* He introduced himself as Harold Corwin, an analyst in the Department of Administration. He wore a white shirt and denim blue pants. He spoke of difficulties in forming Pystead's envisioned crew. The company had prospered, he said, because it maintained a balance of resources and population, and their spectrum of talent matched their spectrum of duties. Now with a population of seventeen hundred and fifty people including men, women, and children, the company needed seven hundred fifty more people of certain talents, genders, and ages. The company depended on science to fathom the dimensions of the human mind, to select those rising above that evil eye of malicious envy, to employ self-satisfied and disciplined personalities who wanted to live in a successful and peaceful community more than they wanted to be promoted. Harold said The Pystead Group had pursued a viable means of progress on the margins, from its beginnings in Europe to maturity on Nevis. Next, floating about the oceans, they hoped to live in relative liberty and security and visit friendly ports of call.

As to governance, said Harold, after a year of training and experience, company management would transition to governance based on a system having separation of powers, checks and balances, and a legislature with thirty percent of its representatives elected by trained crewmembers. There was and would remain an independent justice department and investigative reporters within each of their nine administrative groups.

Still, the devil resides in the details, and both needs and details change over time. The devil is lurking, always!

"You should know," said Harold, "that our eighty-seven principals and their families and friends participate as unidentified members of the crew. All have retrained to a shipboard duty. They believe that representation rather than perpetuation of company management will be the key to a sustainable social contract. The principals trust that a live-and-let-live culture will continue in each of our nine ships.

"There must be, of course, a progressive transfer of responsibility from company to representative governance, and then, only to those qualified. For example: qualified electrical engineers shall decide on electrical equipment and systems; those with knowledge of countries' laws, attractions, customs, and risks shall decide ports of call; persons in good standing will be those promoted. Our principals have elected to entrust the future of their children to the collective judgment of their chosen crew and its descendants. There being no guarantees in life, they found no greater hope."

⚹　⚹　⚹

Harold paused, nodding. "If you have a reasonable proposal for research you will be given an opportunity to lead a team effort to see it to fruition. For a successful development, major contributors will have some patent rights once an economic model is agreed upon and resources for an expanding economy become available. Our draft economic model is long and only getting longer. We intend to reinvent an economic system by testing persuasive provisions of organization and regulation never before accepted politically."

Philip found himself nodding in agreement. *The United Nations has not helped the hungry nor replaced fish stocks—despite their rhetoric. There is no Minister Peel to repeal the modern-day corn laws that keep so many undernourished. And the U.N. makes no effort to free, or even identify, the probably fifty million people effectively enslaved around the world, many in government labor camps producing goods and services that benefit the party in power. In the U.S. the rich pay few taxes, the middle class is burdened by the costs of education, and the poor go hungry and uneducated. The ultrarich have implemented systems of coercive control modeled on those of their enemies!*

Harold allowed himself a slight smile. "As to professional expectations, I still recall what Manager Robbie Markwaters told my group of recruits, 'If you are thinking to come here as a big fish in a little pond, be warned. We have more than enough gifted people and geniuses, and then we have the bright ones, the prodigies.' Personally, I am content to live and sail in the magnificent ships created by our talented crew. I will not suffer should I not become chief of meta studies." He paused before adding, "We are a diverse group of refugees—many of us without papers. Most fear a return to their origins. We are fortunate in an era of perhaps a hundred million refugees, having our own magnificent, mobile homes. We must, however, survive and stabilize in our present form before we will have the resources or the time for different approaches to organizing ourselves."

Harold smiled. "Our tour of the facilities went quicker than anticipated. Please use our official network, Fednet, for questions. Please be aware that we do not foresee a happy decade, century, nor millennium on Earth. You should give your utmost attention to our present situation. Please review Pystead's recorded history. We take origins and ends as beyond the purview of the human mind; we take observable reality as our primary source. We believe the mind that benefits from reality is the one that seeks the truth of the matter, regardless of what that truth may prove to be. We believe that during peaceful times humanity enjoys a positive proclivity in society and evolution." Harold stepped back. The diners remained quiet.

Philip looked around. *Sums up the Cartesian mind, the human condition, and my circumstances. Still, the devil will reside in the details and in the leaders aboard. Personally, I am approaching a shadowed entryway to an unknown reality! Aware and moving slowly to be cautious, moving because I seek to belong in a safe niche of the cosmos. O Cosmos, may my primary process get lucky!*

Harold announced, "Several of our officers are listening in on the hologram system. Anyone with a question may ask it now."

After a few questions a man rose speaking loudly. "I am Dr. Orlando Murphy Taws Osgood. Of forty-seven persons sanctioned by the United States and the United Nations, I am the only one accepted as a temporary employee. Our organism is here under labor relations and competitiveness laws accepted as fair for global trade among nations. The dream of the U.S.A. and the world is from the many, one. We all say God is one. We are given knowledge to sustain felicity for all, with harmony and unity to follow. The world's destiny as one people is disrespected by this company!"

A stretch of Francis Bacon. Hyperbole on we. Implicit prevarication about extant realities. As for this world's destiny, the media is mute that the bio-wiring of the mind makes the difference between individuals and cultures, and mute on incommensurable mindsets. Mute that so many minds do not accept the rights of mankind long cherished in Western cultures. Mute that incompatible minds living together cannot agree on public policy, justice, or civil decency. Can never trust each other.

Even Rousseau believed that a common collective consciousness and social contract were necessary for a viable state. Saint Augustine believed that a state need be a multitude of rational beings united by the common objects of their love. Of course, a common consciousness requires a common appreciation of the human condition and basic rights and responsibilities.

Even the prayed for technological singularity would not resolve psychological and social issues! And without curbing the growth of world populations, humanity will need a divine intervention for sustainable salvation! Is it not sacred word that the meek shall inherit the Earth?

Who thinks a technological singularity can create virtually unlimited habitable space and resources on Earth? Well…mystics, intuitives, and those who want chaos as pretext for their great-man to take over! Those who keep the commons angry without hope, to become enforcers and soldiers in their deemers' quests for ever more power.

⚹　⚹　⚹

Osgood with raised arm stood shaking his fist. "Your Pystead Group is being afforded its last opportunity to demonstrate responsible world citizenship before sanctions are imposed by the Caribbean Federation."

He's certainly loud enough.

"Pystead's leaders owe all new hires a detailed explanation of why this company draws so much negative assessment from the United Nations and from so many governments. Your reverence for Poseidon instead of Hestia exemplifies your lack of concern for the common good. We demand an explanation of why our prospective employees sanctioned by the world have not been accepted as temporary hires!"

Dr. Osgood beamed with satisfaction and continued loudly, "The K.L.J.H. Organism is a manifest reality of all things interconnected, employing culture and technology to enhance life by overcoming the implicitly limiting biases of the human condition. K.L.J.H. is an aggregating platform in the Net of participation that brings empowerment to all the peoples of the world. K.L.J.H. is the first superorganism: functioning at a level of cognitive complexity above that of any other extant organism or eusocial group. I am maintaining optimism while waiting for your decision on hiring this group!"

Osgood remained standing. Philip sat trying to interpret what he had heard. *Let's not underestimate a Network power backed by police strewn round the world. Almost as frightening is an implied conformity sufficient to destroy the last vestiges of human spontaneity—last vestiges of the human spirit in society. Deemers at every level decry an individual focus, except when choosing their own friends, party members, and leaders! Osgood was not chosen by lot, nor even from among the ranks. He is not subject to the protocols of the Organism. He is different, and thus far the only thing apparently super about K.L.J.H. is his mouth.*

A flash of light drew Philip's attention to the head table. "Hello, I'm Lois Henssen. Dr. Osgood, my department handles recruiting. Since the U.N. and the world governments that you speak of have neglected to communicate any knowledge of this case to us, I know nothing to tell you, except that we did not interview nor offer employment to anybody in your group other than you as an ethicist, and not as a spokesperson nor engineering group leader."

Osgood boomed his reply. "I do understand that your communications with the United Nations and with the nation of Kitts-Nevis are less than adequate. Formal information can be had in the morning. We expect an explanation at the next meeting!"

Commander Henssen asked almost in disbelief, "Am I to understand that the governments of the world, acting through the United Nations, have dismissed many of our offers of employment and replaced them with offers to your group?"

"Precisely!" Osgood happily shouted. "The action is no different than other corrective actions taken to redress wrongs perpetrated for reasons well intended or not. The U.N. shall not allow the citizens of the world to be broken on your wheel of complexity.

You are a bully culture. If you were to calculate and plan less, you would have time to live more and care more."

Philip grimaced. *Occidentalism lives. Live-and-let-live tolerance does not live. If all must be thought of, why not think of this Pystead Group? Instead, the grand deemers decry gaps as if they were the ultra-rich's cross of gold. And why should the great deemer deem to allow us non-we to go floating about his oceans on our own? Merely paying sea-lane fees will not be sufficient tribute, nor sufficient control of the suffering non-we who must labor. Any cargo producing wheel-of complexity must remain fixed to a deemer's axle, spun only at the deemer's command. Enough for everyone is not allowed! The angry have their uses.*

Osgood knows that Pystead offers him the freedom he would deny all. I'm sure he is assisting Pystead's evaluation process. The mind that accepts Osgood's conclusions, Pystead doesn't want. Seems once again that freedom clarifies more than it obscures—among the high-abstracting! Voilà, another strange attractor favoring a decent and talented crew.

✳ ✳ ✳

Finally, Henssen replied, "It would have been helpful of the U.N. to inform us of our infractions of these unpublished employment regulations, and even better if done ahead of your arrival. Now, as I understand the situation, your group demands employment as an indivisible group, with you as spokesperson completing one employment application for all. Your group is evidently to be employed as a facilities' engineering department bringing their own computer. Would you agree this is a true statement, Doctor Osgood?"

"Yes! We have been performing as an engineering department for three years. We are fully sanctioned by the United Nations."

"Dr. Osgood, has the U.N. determined that these forty-six engineers are more deserving than the humans to whom we offered employment?"

"The individuals per se are not at issue!" Osgood sneered. "The issue is one of proportionality among human groups, to eliminate gaps proving the point that social injustices have been allowed to develop. In this case, without regard for the right to proportional outcomes in world society. The sameness in appearance among this assembly is proof of biased criteria. Your campus excludes Citizen's Room and Board, Public Fellows, and Public Trusties. The world does not like what it sees here!"

Commander Henssen spoke sharply, "Our recruits represent every modern culture on Earth, including, for example, the little remembered Bask and Roma. Also, we have Siberian and Canadian Eskimo families. Do you people from the U.S.A. ever consider such others? Aside from physical, emotional, and moral health, a talented and enlightened mind are our prime criteria. We hire individuals, not groups."

Philip looked around. *Yes, a wonderful variousness of probably decent, high-abstract thinking individuals. And unlike the U.S. Department of Guideways, Pystead hires Jews and Mormons as more than tokens and scapegoats, attractive blondes younger than grandmothers, and tall Caucasian males.*

Henssen looked down, reading, "We do not have facilities offering accommodations of the type you have demanded. We do not have a common living space for thirty-five with and an adjoining living space for twenty-five. We do not have one professional space for thirty engineers, adjacent to vendor spaces for five including overnight accommodations."

Here, no unqualified people to entertain and promote to making lists. Surely few here are hiding mimetic desires or a past of altruistic evil. Except Osgood, who must want a proportional share of goths, Maintainers, non-English speakers, whatevers? Our average antisocial score is high! The world doesn't like our instincts and choices in life!

And Osgood's critical theory seeks not explanation nor emancipation for Pystead, nor decreased domination where it obviously exists! His theory recites the one-culture-fits-all of the social sciences. A discipline that's intellectually dishonest easily, because it's not a science!

A male voice from another dining room was heard over the speakers. "Am I the only Japanese here?" Commander Henssen's hologram responded, "Among the established crew we have one hundred Japanese women and twenty-six Japanese men, plus a dozen children. Your group of recruits were all living in the U.S. with offers to over fifty Japanese. The least represented groups among the large nations are Mainland China and Argentina. It should come as no surprise that our highest percentage of established crewmembers are from our geographic origins in Europe, many from the flooding Low Countries and Venice, or from other countries having relatively little fresh water or arable land."

Will he be satisfied?

A hologram of Manager Markwaters appeared. "We do not know what to think of forty-seven people who claim to be a single organism, the K.L.J.H. Organism we are told. We do not understand why our people do not have a right to be as free as those Dr. Osgood claims to protect, nor why our small group's peaceful and productive existence need concern the global population, or even the Caribbean population. Our legacy for Nevis will be free facilities that do no harm. Be advised, Dr. Osgood, that Commander Henssen and I are not the only voices to be heard in taking this decision. We will not have an answer for you by the next meeting." The hologram vanished.

Now we see him, now we don't. Despite the potential for virtual prestidigitation, I believe done honestly.

"Listen to me!" Heads turned. Dr. Osgood was on his feet again, angry. "It is the duty of each one of you to push for the K.L.J.H. Organism. Do not accept employment without our inclusion. You may have to sacrifice for the sake of social justice! Narrow selection criteria are tantamount to a premeditated creation of gaps." He waved his finger. "The U.N. knows who you are! If you support this company without our inclusion, you will never again have professional work when you return home after the impending collapse of this company!" Osgood sat down.

How can this mouthpiece sanctioned by the U.N. feel safe threatening Pystead employees after the alleged brutality inflicted on a woman complaining less? I'll bet Osgood's own people beat that woman. Osgood doesn't look like he's ready for martyrdom! Not a disturbed or devout youth given a deadly mission instead of love and therapy.

Sage Harold stepped forward and raised his hand. "Kindly regard the belief of the late Yann Arthus-Bertrand, 'That we all can and should act every day for the future of our children.'" The young sage nodded, turning. "Being a diverse group, we must intellectually develop our identity." With a sinuous transfer of his lanky frame, he departed the room.

All was quiet, leaving Philip mystified. *Was not that proper… a young sage more contemplative than inspirational…no pretense of being a prophet. O Giocondo, I can take joy if we can take the isolation.*

Philip stood and his thoughts returned to Ice and the puzzle of her name. *I like Alice!* The conscious mind may take joy while the subconscious mind seeks still that elusive truth of the matter. The elect know that all have the power, and that those who grasp the truth are favored to have the glory. *O Cosmos, may I choose wisely.* Philip blinked his eyes. *There will be a crew! O Pystead, choose wisely. O Russell, be strong!*

⁂

Ice met Philip in the lobby. "Do you have anything else for today?"

"I want you to pick out furniture for my apartment."

"Do I get to live there?"

"Sorry, our apartment."

"Oh, good." Ice took his arm and they stepped outdoors. "Phil, where will we put Ginevra de' Benci?"

"She doesn't belong to the company?"

"No, she is one of a few great copies that is ours."

"We will have so little wall space, Ice, why don't we loan her to the art galleries?"

"I agree, her and Amanda, unless you object."

"I don't want everybody we know saying you must be the model for the mermaid."

"We will list the artist as unknown. Only you, my grand-dad, and close friends have ever seen her. Why suspect me as the model when Pystead has hundreds of blondes and has mermaid and Poseidon statues everywhere? Only Amanda Valdes should be suspected. If asked, I will say I'm younger, and you can say I'm prettier. If pushed, I will simply deny it. After all, I'm only loosely the model. I'm younger, more shapely, and not a honey blonde with very long hair."

"Fine."

"Pystead should have the icons, Phil, and a gallery can properly display the reverse side of Ginevra. That will give us wall space at home. I'll begin with Giacomo Balla's painting, Dynamism of a Dog on a Leash, to show that we should move along rapidly."

"Boldly go!"

"Phil, let's meet at the VCQ for dinner. I need to attend a meeting on disposition of paintings and other items in the gift shops. Once out of Nevis money will not be relevant, and most new crew will not have even one painting for their quarters. We artists will need to paint for others as well as for ourselves and the art galleries. Some children may not have a teddy bear or a new toy."

"Some adults may not have a photograph or any memorabilia of Nevis or campus."

Walking back to the VCQ, Philip approached a group of adults seated on statues around a showboard. A hand waved, seemingly for him. He stepped closer. A man identifying himself as Hector invited Philip to join them. They all looked in Philip's direction. They all looked slightly not from California, somehow differently exotic, especially the women. Then Philip saw, sitting on a dolphin with bare midriff and shorts, close beside a man, the Brazilian KAM theorist from São Paulo. She called, "Hello, Philip, we met at lunch. I'm Angela and this is my fiancé, Vielou, an expert on breeding and raising cattle. Please join us."

Philip took a seat on a marble cat. Hector introduced the group as mostly from Brazil. They were following United Nations' postings about The Pystead Group and wanted his opinion. Hector brought up a file of United Nations' comments on Nevis and Pystead going back years. Philip glanced down the list of pronouncements, all negative and familiar from his own searches.

The most recent item linked to video of the female activist in purple lipstick who had disrupted in-processing. "This is quite troubling," Angela remarked. The woman was seen trembling. Her eyes were black, her lips busted, and her nose was red and possibly broken. The U.N.'s post claimed that the woman, upon asking loudly for clarification during the in-processing procedure at Pystead on Nevis, had been detained, gang raped, and slapped viciously before being released.

Philip and one of the Brazilian women had seen the disruptive woman taken into the guardhouse and soon thereafter observed her walk to the bus. Philip was certain the woman entering the guardhouse and then boarding the bus was in good physical condition and was the disruptive female from in-processing. When asked why the U.N. would lie, he could only suggest their information was mistaken.

"I'm afraid," said Angela. "Who beat that woman?"

Philip proposed that they observe events on campus, read the U.N.'s pronouncements, and continue talking off Net and off Fednet. When better informed, they could ask questions via Fednet and see if Pystead's answers were timely and consistent with their findings and common sense. In the States, Philip said, the government in responding to an unwanted query would often contrive an answer later proving to be a lie. Such as claiming something found was a certain type of weather balloon pod, a year earlier than that type pod had been manufactured. And the pod was probably manufactured thereafter to imply the finding had been a prototype model. Time and money could overcome most any witness or interpretation of an event.

Hector found a Bible verse, "And if you gather within your cities, I will send pestilence among you, so that you shall be delivered into the hands of the enemy."

Angela said, "That explains the quarantine before going to the fish farm or becoming crew."

Hector worried that with all their eggs in one basket on the floating farm, one dirty bomb or spray of a nerve agent could kill most or all of them and drive any survivors back to countries of origin as outcasts. Others argued that terrorists would not waste an almost impossible to obtain dirty device on an insignificant target. The consensus favored seasteading because the future might turn on the gestalt of many small and unknowable moments as well as on the consequences of a possible big moment. And all future moments were unpredictable.

Still, although no signs have been given by profits, angles, or stars, might there be One Above who cares? One who helps without revelation? After all, Pystead has been helping Nevis's art collection without public awareness, and after our departure buildings will be left intact at no cost to Nevis. Not to mention for years paying living wages to locals working for Pystead.

They agreed to meet at the showboard each Wednesday beginning the last half of lunch hour, attending as often as possible to get to know one another and exchange information and ideas. As Philip departed for his room, he heard Angela exclaim, "Another post!" But he walked on with Ice in his thoughts.

An exclamation out of context can mean anything. Angela exclaimed at a new U.N. post saying that an influential official,

Admiral Telaobade, was a strong advocate for The Pystead Group receiving a seasteading license. Angela had earlier learned that Pystead had nine ships instead of one, and she felt that none would sink without immediate assistance. She believed Brazil would extend visiting and trading rights to Pystead, and that visiting during cooler months would avoid the mosquitoes.

After meeting in Philip's room, he and Ice decided to look at the apartment Philip had reserved and order furniture. They took a tram. Ice told Philip he should rest and she would get the apartment's app. His thoughts drifted back to the busman, to Dr. Osgood's interruption of his professional orientation. *Did not God breathe life into mankind in his image? In his likeness in spirit—manifest in subconscious primary process. There the moral essence of humanity churned inscrutably beyond the grasp of even the grandest of deemers. Perhaps no longer? Now a human can be kept in a void of misinformation, wherein his mental process churns only upon itself. Perhaps the human can be pressured to devolve into a protective consciousness of being in the moment, devolve into nirvana. Devolve and rest beyond tbe fray, feeling superior, without help to self or another!*

Modern technology may soon produce an ideal subject: a worker requiring no dignity nor desire for abstract thought. A mind controlled via mere words after the short-circuiting of its subconscious pathways of bio-wiring. Just give them bread and circus, and Blake's fierce Tyger burning bright. O Cosmos, so many who once loved the Lamb now love the Tyger!

"Phil, I have the app."

As the couple stepped onto their new patio, Philip's realism spoke, *How do you keep a freeman in the common group mind, after he's experienced The Pystead?* "Eh, Osgood?"

"What, Phil?"

"Nothing love, sorry, wondering aloud." *Worrying that in the coming global order there can be no informed subjects, no complaining subjects, few semi-free subjects like Osgood. A freeman's worship shall not prevail, eh, Bertrand? Worldwide now, either the billionaire class or one political party effectively prevails, as did kings and tyrants in days of old—sociopaths all.* "I was worrying aloud, Ice, I should say."

She hugged him, and they stood quietly looking at the apartment and the tree. "Phil, I like this corner location, especially the Banyan tree. Carry me over the threshold."

My beginning again is done. Now we have a proper new beginning—she and I together. The two young loves with one step entered their new apartment, believing for the best in all dimensions of mind.

Ice looked around and nodded in satisfaction, then said the unexpected, "Oh Phil, would you mind if we go by processing to see if you can begin your Level Three?"

"According to the schedule, Level Three screening does not begin until tomorrow."

"They will be preparing now. And you are fast tracked."

With no point in waiting Philip agreed, and they took a tram. More than ever he believed that beauty and truth, love and life needed a kindly niche in the cosmos, needed the protection of a Poseidon.

"Phil, we get off next."

12

COMMANDER'S CALL

Ice and Philip entered the badge processing facility by the front door, stepped on the antiseptic foot mat, and sprayed sanitizer on hands and face, eyes closed. Ice took two white, medical face-masks from a lockbox, explaining they provided better protection for the crew. She motioned for Philip to sit and went through the door marked for crew only. Minutes later Ice returned with word that Joan could scan him. Ice pointed. "The men's room is around the corner." Soon after Philip returned with his passport in hand, Commander Windsor appeared at the crew door in island clothes and a beige medical mask.

In the next room, Ice introduced Philip as her fiancé and Commander Joan as her close friend. The Commander said pleasantly, "Call me Joan, we are sure to become friends." Philip smiled.

After a few steps, Joan pointed, "No koms beyond here." Philip turned off his kom and placed it on the tray. "Because your kom has been in the possession of others, we need to test it."

She knows details about Wheaton?

Ice took a seat, and Philip followed Joan down a short hallway decorated with paintings reminding him of the island artists. He approached a watercolor of young men in festival bird masks with the white top feathers and long yellow beaks—shown dancing on a street. He slowed to look and Joan stopped. The background building was the artist's Co-op, and the oversized face in the window was Ice.

"Does Ice know this prominent dancer?"

"That's her friend Isaac. He's twenty-eight years of age in the painting. Young enough to participate as youth."

The man who took Ice to a suite at Lamancha House. Joan walked slowly, allowing Philip a leisurely look at each painting. *Isaac must be younger than Ice by at least a year or two?*

⁂ ⁂ ⁂

In the exam room with four scanning machines, Joan asked Philip to select one. Each resembled a sit-down hair dryer that might be seen in a women's hair salon. He took the first seat and asked, "How can this helmet contain a neural scanner?"

Joan pulled up a stool. He held still as she adjusted the bulky helmet. "Did I mention neural scanning?"

"No, but what else?"

"I was warned that you would question the helmet."

"Especially the even smaller helmet used in the guard house."

"Perhaps we consider only your button responses to the virtual reality presentation? Perhaps we watch your eyes and breathing?"

"My interviewer in California referred to my 'first' neural scan and sent me to an f-MRI facility rented by Pystead. Button responses alone would not constitute the scientific approach to selecting a decent crew that he mentioned."

Joan pulled out a stiff screen, which she unfolded and circled around Philip's stomach. She said the unexpected, "We know our secret could be out in all the wrong places. Pystead's first technical breakthrough was a room-temperature superconductor. The first application was for a compact and quiet neural scanner. You are fast-tracked to help improve the process now that spies are surely being conditioned to beat our system long enough to learn if it's functional scanning and hence illegal." Philip nodded. Joan told him, "Beginning at Level Four, we do use commercially available functional-MRI equipment. We are fortunate that our scan helmets are much better than anybody suspects, because except for medical purposes with structural scans, MRI is illegal to everyone but the U.N."

Well…with corruption everywhere, secrecy and lie-detection must be the only way to assemble a crew of decent human beings. "I look forward to the work."

"Now, please remove your medical mask and hold still for final adjustments. In these machines, we must fix your head position with restraints. This Level Three requirement is primarily one of fidelity. As we begin to share company secrets, we need to know that you intend to keep them secret. We have already double checked your public record or I could not proceed. We know you were recently detained by the City of Wheaton as a witness. We have not been able to determine how you got to Savannah after having your rental vehicle impounded in Wheaton."

"I was given a free ride in Wheaton's double-decker, police train car. They searched me and my baggage in transit. They dropped the issue of my being a witness without explanation and released me in Savannah."

Joan raised her eyebrows at his answer and stood. For the first time, Philip got a close look at the heavy, red-gold pendant on her red-gold necklace chain. She asked, "Why did they search a witness?"

"They claimed I was often driving on manual in a car with a special security system, that I could be a distributor and have traces of contraband drugs on my person or in my book boxes. It made no legal sense to me, but their intelligent police system required impounding the car and searching me because of an unrelated and closed case."

Joan nodded. "Wheaton knew the vehicle had secret compartments that had been sealed by California and Dagstra. We believe the police wanted a reason to examine the vehicle's engine. Dagstra North American told us they knew its prototype HHO engine had been disassembled and reassembled because all their microdots on bolts were misaligned. Wheaton needed time to bring in the required specialists and created the pretext of searching you to give them more time with the vehicle before Dragsta learned what was happening."

"Dagstra told me the vehicle was testing a prototype engine that ran on HHO gas converted directly from water. My leasing agreement would fine me ten thousand kicu for telling anyone, but couldn't anyone have looked at the patents for details?"

Joan shook her head. "Dagstra had not submitted a patent application for their new water removal system used by that engine. They submitted it only after the car's GPS location failed to update and they learned the car was in police custody. Before making their plans known, Dagstra hoped to have their financing in place and their production facility designed except for last engine details, because the technology for economically gassing water is in the public domain."

"Joan, did you learn that the State of California claimed the car's insurance was lapsing?"

"No, but one of our principals from California faced incessant personal and business problems with the state, was always in the right, yet she was never awarded attorney's fees. Harassment finds a way in California. They are awash in nonprofit organizations with money from untraced sources."

"In Wheaton too, I feel sure." *I feel inconsistencies lurking. Gödel would say I have an opportunity to learn more. What drives harassment from sea to shining sea—besides dark money?* Philip knew to insist upon cause and effect as common sense, perhaps the most fundamental trait of thought at any level. "Cosmos! Joan, how did a small town in Georgia know about this engine, or get specialists to check it out so quickly?"

Joan punched a few tabs, nodding her head. "Our follow-up leads us to conclude that the Wheaton World Center for Change is a multipurpose agency of the United Nations. The U.N.'s officials and W.W.C.C. share the same one-world view. They steal all the intellectual property they can while pretending to be neutral in matters of energy and technology."

Gothic minds everywhere.

"Philip, Ice told me the police in Wheaton damaged your wrists?"

"Yes, they strung me up naked by steel handcuffs and rubbed itching power on my private parts while riding me to Savannah in their double decker train car. They were women and seemed to hate me. I assume their showboard flagged me as a highly anti-social elite. They pulled me up to straighten my arms and got my toes off the floor. That and my uncontrolled jerking at the itching caused the damage. They never acknowledged my cut wrists and didn't treat them or give me an antibiotic."

"I'm sorry, and not surprised. We see physical and emotional abuse worldwide—a prime reason many of us are with Pystead." Joan lowered her voice, "Many crewmembers have significant others they are bringing to our group. The entrance criteria for family and friends are less demanding than for their sponsors who are to have the critical duties. We want to be assured that each crewmember has bona fide affections for their significant others, in the event we are ever, say, stranded at sea!" Joan paused before adding, "The Level-Three asks personal questions about relationships past and present. I want you to know this in the event the subject is broached in any context in the future. Because Ice is self-sponsored, I will omit those questions in your scans."

"Is this the norm, or are you making a special case of me?"

"A special case."

"Joan, I'd prefer to take the same scans as everybody else in my category."

"As you no doubt suspect, Philip, many of the queries are subliminal, and you will not be aware of them."

"I still prefer the norm for my situation."

"Your situation is not normal. We have nobody else with a fiancée they have known for such a short period of time. Our psychologists tell me that the complex emotions of attachment bonding may not have fully developed in such a short-term relationship."

"So, Joan, please test me and save the results. As a cognitive scientist knowing my own conscious mind, the scans should prove helpful to my own future research, and perhaps for others as well. Too, I'm interested in whether subliminal queries might evoke dreams." Philip thought Joan's face twitched at the mention of dreams. "I want you to be able to tell Ice I took the complete check. I'm certain that I love her in all dimensions of mind."

Joan seemed pleased. "Coming up, Dr. Russell, the full scan with results archived upon request of the scientist."

"Thank you, Commander Joan."

The scan helmet covered Philip's head with a visor over his face providing a visual display. *Better than any other virtual reality helmet I have experienced, aside from the head restraints.* For the first time the scan proceeded rigorously like a professional scan. During the initial few minutes of calibration, he wiggled toes, fingers, lips, nose, and hips as directed to establish his brain's physical regions. He read aloud, answered simple questions, performed simple arithmetic, and looked at a brief video for what he knew to be further mapping of his brain's functional regions. *I must be one of only a few who have any idea what's happening, one of few suspecting compact and noiseless resonance imaging equipment. Evidently spies don't get this far because this mapping would give the process away.*

Joan asked the questions. When an animal jumped in his face, Philip jerked against the rear head stop. *Surely there was an accompanying audio subliminal with that visual.* From the numerous lightning flashes, rolling claps of thunder, and animals, but hardly ever both visual and auditory distractions together, Philip knew subliminal queries were involved.

Then Joan asked, "Do you let trash, magazines, or anything else permanently pile up in your office or residence, or in your vehicle—things not kept labeled, indexed, on an appropriate shelf, or at least suitably boxed?"

"No."

"Do you recycle hazardous items as required?"

"Yes."

"Do you own a metaverse helmet?"

"No."

"Do you borrow one and spend time in any metaverse world?"

"Yes."

"Please explain."

"Once a month our college Dean held staff meetings in a metaverse office having paintings of Postmodern scholars on the walls."

Not long afterward Philip lapsed into a state of dazed responses as if his subconscious were speaking while his thoughts slept.

Joan decided he needed a break. She released his head restraints. Philip walked down the hall turning his head and blinking his eyes. After a drink of water, he returned to finish the set.

Joan asked that he select another scan station. The second series was longer, repeating many questions from the first set and adding queries about his medical history, asking whether he possessed perfect pitch, and if he were easily irritated by any type of music, noise, or tapping. He finished the process weary and hungry. *Evidently, they have not thought to have a flag for being peckish? Will hunger at some point affect results—must investigate.*

Joan asked him to give blood and urine samples in the restroom just around the corner. She pointed to a catalog of Pystead's paintings for his entertainment while his scans were being evaluated.

Almost fifty minutes later Joan returned and told Philip that he was a Provisional Level Three. His final Level-Three scan could be taken after an in-depth analysis of the first scans. He would return for a scan series administered by another person using different equipment. "We are quite serious about security. I must inform you that nothing about this process is to be revealed to anyone outside the company, or even inside below the rank of Commander."

"What about Ice?"

"She's a Commander. Now let me have your lapel pin and card for updating." Joan slipped each item into a computer port and within seconds pronounced Philip ready to go.

Still a baby blue dot.

"We will let you know by kom or personal contact when you may come for next processing. Probably by morning since yours is one of the first Level-Threes. We are expediting seven dozen others. May we call you as early a six-thirty in the morning?"

"Yes."

✷ ✷ ✷

Joan raised her hand, deterring Philip from turning for the door. "Your kom is bugged. A top-notch job using components not commercially available, including a firmware bug. Rather than destroy the bug, we would like to study it in operation. We believe it's designed to spread a worm to other koms and send coded signals and video." Philip frowned. "We will reimburse you for a new kom of your choice. You must buy it in Charlestown. Buy an expensive kom and register for the warranty, then bring the kom to us for alteration. Kitts-Nevis installs an active tracking app on every local kom: hidden files, illegal to remove, and impossible to secretly neutralize without expertise and special software and hardware. After we neutralize its tracking apps, use the new kom for all local contacts."

Philip nodded. "I understand."

"When walking around Nevis, Philip, for a slow kom vibration turn your face to the left to avoid a facial recognition camera, and look right for a fast vibration. If you get an X on your kom screen at any building location do not enter; we want no correlation between you and any company interest. If police stop you and ask for your kom, let your new kom hear you say 'I have two koms." That will signal security. Also, use your old kom for established commercial transactions. On campus, keep kom microphones on low volume, and keep the video lens turned away from Pystead personnel's faces, security posts, and technical details. Be aware that your old kom's bug is always on even with the battery removed. I will brief Ice and she can help. Should you inadvertently slip, call security and put the compromised kom in the shielded bag we will give you, or in a metal box such as a microwave oven, or wrap it in metal foil. Do not call security from a public showboard unless you must call for immediate help when in physical danger. Questions?"

"Why didn't Kitts-Nevis remove the Wheaton bug?"

"It's a United Nations' bug! Customs would have installed one if it didn't already exist. Interpol makes frequent and random street checks of kom software on the pretext of fighting terrorism. They are actively supporting the U.N.'s unauthorized surveillance programs, although not allowed to do so by their own charter. Your new kom after our debugging will pass all street-stop checks, including the exact memory size as installed and their unaltered code. It's all there but will not work when you personally use the kom because of blocking subroutines we will have installed. If the police force you to use the kom, use it without changing your location, or make a mistake and begin again. If they take the kom, tell them you think its GPS is off so that your kom can hear your voice say GPS. For personal use, begin a command by typing p-a-l-i-m-p, then take four long steps away, and finish typing with s-e-s-t." Joan paused.

"Fine, I know the word."

"You must practice on campus until the police-stop usage becomes easy."

"Will do."

In addition, security checks were needed of each suitcase, box, book, and personal item that Wheaton had taken possession of, including his clothing. Pystead would check for micro bugs and slow acting poisons. Philip asked for new clothes and said Joan should take everything in his VCQ room and at Mrs. R.'s Guesthouse to a lab. And they needed to image his person, which he too thought necessary since the police had given him a rectal exam, with itching powder.

Finally, Philip couldn't resist a long glance at Joan's red pendant. It was a wagon wheel with too many spokes. "I like your pendant. When I see anything unique these days, I wonder if Ice designed it."

"She did not design it, although she has said its sixteen spokes are too many. It's a childhood pendant, not real gold." She pointed, "Imaging is second door on the right."

The imaging scan was done in ten minutes. Five minutes later Joan brought in a flash drive cube for Philip. She explained that it would play his kom usage instructions and police-stop drills only in his VCQ room. "Keep the cube in your room." Joan smiled. "Ice is in the lobby. I expect to see you at an engagement party in the near future. It's nice to know that my good friend has a fiancé who loves her very much."

"Good, and thanks for the special handling."

"You are welcome. Somebody has to go first, even among equals."

⚜ ⚜ ⚜

Philip hurried to tell Ice the good news. He did not think to thank the mysterious cosmos. In the entry hall, Ice pulled down his face-mask and rewarded him with a kiss. "You were perfect."

"How do you know?"

"I'm a Cobalt Blue. I can know anything as soon as it happens! Let's return soon for your next scans because I'm dying to tell you things about our advanced technologies."

The couple sat, waiting for Philip's change of clothes. He told Ice he liked her painting of the dancing Isaac. She said it came out well because Isaac's face was obscured by the bird-beak, that she was not good with facial expressions and avoided portraits. She explained that she began paintings with faces, and if she didn't get lucky after a few tries she turned the head. They sat quietly, and sooner than expected Joan brought in new clothes, a security bag for his kom, and a soft, white facemask that was comfortable and his to keep. He left to change. When he returned, Ice said she was relieved that he had no body bugs.

She can know anything as soon as it happens.

The couple left arm-in-arm. They took a shuttle bus. Enroute to town Ice called a jeweler and asked if he could open his shop for her without too much inconvenience. They had to wait only ten minutes for the jeweler to arrive.

Both Philip and Ice liked his rings. She preferred a small, bright diamond to a larger stone of less quality, selecting a round, one-carat diamond, ideal cut, set on a thin yellow-gold band. They purchased matching wedding bands having little grooves reminding Philip of a peach pit's texture. Ice kissed the jeweler goodbye on his cheek. "A family friend, Phil."

Philip surprised her by suggesting they have an engagement party as soon as he had the full Level Three. She replied, "I thought Melita Rose was the only mind reader in town."

"Don't be silly," said the professor. *Thank you, Joan. Thanks too, Samantha and Sandra.*

On the way back to the VCQ, Ice told him the rings were from the jewelry shop favored by her grandfather, who knew a lot about gemstones. The little reassurance was significant to Philip, wary of most things including a price of less than expected for the diamond. He experienced a distinct pulse of joy as the sparkling stone flashed in his mind's eye. Compton's own Prince of Nevis needed to announce his engagement to old friends.

13

LEVEL THREE

Philip's second professional orientation was scheduled for Saturday morning. He followed the directions and arrived at a single-story, white-brick building. He strolled the building's perimeter looking for the entry and was soon looking for windows. At what should have been a rear entrance, shielded by tall shrubbery, he found the building's only door beside a mirror, which he took for the one-way glass of a guard station's window. When given no instructions, he pulled down his facemask for identification. A white dot shown on the mirror and he shifted to stand in front of it. The door opened, and he entered. A guard scanned him with a hand wand, handed him a paper receipt for his kom, and allowed him to pass through a steel door only to confront a second steel door that trapped him when the first closed behind him. Air hissed in and out of the chamber in strong pulses before a green light blinked and the second door opened. Philip stepped through and joined a small group led by a neurosurgeon named

George Snyder. Only Snyder and two others wore beige masks.

Dr. Snyder and his colleagues walked Philip and six other recruits through laboratories and offices, showing equipment and outlining programs and resources. The School of Cognitive Science consisted of an interdisciplinary team for mind and brain research and applications. Two traditional, bed-sized MRI systems were shown, with no mention of scan helmets. Dr. Snyder made clear that a full Level Three badge was required before their next meeting, to be held as soon as possible. In less than an hour the tour was done, and the seven recruits were released one at the time with instructions not to meet and chat.

Philip was third out and walking to his room when he received a text message on his old, bugged kom, informing him that his security processing could continue and would require two hours. *Perhaps we will be shown the building's emergency exits at full Level Three? I've always wanted no-nonsense security. This must be it, and it's creepy! Perhaps worth it as soon I"ll be trusted enough to know some of their secrets, and I'll better understand the place.* He contemplated the building, unmarked, called the Imaging Center, said one of the most secure buildings on campus. It was clad in a special brick armor, and its entrance scans were said sensitive enough to find micro bugs. It had four emergency exits somewhere, visible only from the inside. It was made of steel and tough plastic and glass construction, and though not visible from the outside it was earthquake resistant. The building was mounted on numerous half-meter diameter coils of spring steel itself the diameter of a tangerine. Its floors, walls, and ceilings were lined with silver or copper panels to block signal transmission.

Philip headed for his final set of level Three scans. *This notification came on my old, bugged kom! The Wheaton goths should be pleased with my progress and the continued operation of their bug. Hope I don't develop a case of cyber entomophobia. Yet, perhaps I should fear bugs and ghosts if I'm to live in the real world. Is modernity too complex and perilous? Can enough of humanity come to grips with the issues at hand? At some point, is my old Dean's 'maintaining' the only viable path? Is the unfettered idea of progress flawed, incompatible with the capacity of too many human minds?*

Philip arrived at the security processing center and was shown to an exam room furnished with four, three-sided cubicles set with a chair facing the cubicle's back wall.

The room's rear door opened, and a beige-masked young woman entered pushing a hand cart loaded with portable equipment. She introduced herself as Arlene Shaw, an imaging equipment engineer.

A scan helmet rested on the top of Arlene's computer processing unit. It was brownish-red, a color reminding Philip of a dried, red chili pepper. The helmet looked shallow for a scanning device, evidently covering above the ears only. On closer look, however, he noticed a front visor that could surely slide as well as an outer rim that would cover the ears if it slid down. A heavy cord hung from the ceiling above each chair. *Must be power and data.*

Arlene asked Philip to take any seat and began connecting her equipment using plug-in cables. A second woman entered, a nurse, who examined his eyes and told him that during the scans he must keep his head up and look forward, keeping his eyes open. He could not put on eyeglasses or contact lens. The nurse handed Philip a chocolate-nut bar. "Have a snack break when you'd like." Philip took a few bites before nodding for Arlene to proceed.

She said, "Let me place this little screen." The screen fit

snugly around his neck and unfolded to attach to the cubicle walls. Arlene leaned over and said, "Let me know if you feel uncomfortable."

This check for claustrophobia must be a subterfuge not to admit the use of a magnetic screen! But why shouldn't I feel uncomfortable in this black cave of a cubicle with my neck stuck in a tight hole? And where is that thermal imaging lens I must be looking into? Ah, this back wall has a surface texture of bubbles that must conceal dozens of imaging lens! Arlene didn't choose my cubicle and thereby did not select the thermal imaging equipment surely used for a double check!

"So, Arlene, you administer the scan? I thought you were the equipment engineer?"

"I design my equipment—applications level design. I select, test, design and install components. I maintain the equipment, set it up, and nowadays I administer scans. The scan questions are selected by the spooks, our security-side psychologists."

The test proceeded with the expected audio and video distractions, which Philip knew accompanied subliminals of the opposing sense to the distraction. With his head free to move and bearing no weight of the helmet, time passed easily. After twenty minutes or so, Arlene said they would take a break and she played a music video. She closed her eyes. Philip did the same, leaning back in his chair, suddenly aware of the helmet against the back of his head. *How does this helmet hold its position on my head without touching when held by that cord?*

They resumed the scans with questions that surprised Philip about Earl's Barbecue, Wheaton, and Dagstra. Then came a series of questions about whether he had ever abused, or wanted to abuse, a female friend. Had he ever encouraged a physical fight that he could have avoided? Did he take prescribed medicines when sick? Was he a member of any group having an illegal, physically strenuous, sexually revealing, or humiliating initiation rite? Did he use illegal drugs or get drunk?

After a pause, Arlene began a series of repeat questions, which finally ended in a series of flashing scenes and a light show that was almost blinding. While he was still blinking his eyes and gripping the arms of his chair, Arlene asked sternly, "Philip, have you ever known anybody you suspected of acquiring or selling a child outside an official adoption process?"

"No!" *That was unexpected.*

"That's all, please hold still for me to reach the helmet."

"Arlene, does your equipment automatically rate me?"

"No, and I don't see many results. Somewhere along the way, the spooks discovered I could read questions off a screen, and that was the beginning of my downfall."

"You have a nice voice."

"Thanks. Now take a few minutes, and when you are rested another engineer-reader will run another scan using his own equipment."

Philip headed for the men's room. As he approached the restroom, Joan opened a door and motioned for him. He needed to give samples of blood and urine. *They are completely serious about findings. This scan surely used the brain regions mapped before by Joan.*

❊　❊　❊

Thirty minutes later, Philip arrived back in the scan room wondering whom can you trust in this life? He knew how to use instruments to measure brain waves that would reveal whom a person trusted in terms of quantitative parameters of mind, but he also knew that minds could change and trust become misplaced regardless of best efforts of man and machine. *Still, might not this brain scanning process be an adequate Third Eye for Pystead? The secret to excluding the gothic bio-wirings of the world and hiring the decent? Their technology advanced enough to be used in secret.*

The next engineer-reader was a young man named Craig. He placed a screen around Philip's waist. His questions were similar to those already asked, and Philip was tiring when asked, "Do you know who is killing the black cats on Nevis?"

"What? No!"

There followed an inward spiral of silver-blue colors for thirty or more seconds, accompanied by an uneven series of background clicks. The helmet's visor opened and Craig produced a sharp snap of his fingers, commanding, "Crow like a rooster and flap your wings!"

As Philip opened his mouth in astonishment, he remembered a childhood game. "You didn't say, Simon says!"

Craig grinned. "Have you ever been hypnotized, even as a parlor game?"

"No."

Craig asked a few unmemorable questions, except for one about any loss-of-time event. Philip replied none that he could remember. Waiting for removal of the helmet, he asked if Craig knew know how long it would take to analyze the scan."

"No set period. I've heard two hours to weeks, depending upon the availability of analysts and any need for further background checks."

"Thanks. Too, I'm curious about the color of my stickpin. I have seen colors other than the light blue we both have, such as deep blue, green, red, and caramel tan."

The young man shook his head. "We engineers don't know, but rumor has it that colors are assigned pseudo randomly."

"Thanks. I'll try putting it out of mind."

"I believe it's random except for Commanders who get to choose. My wife received a yellow pin similar to a lemon-colored pin of hers. She complained and swapped for red, which was underused. The colors gold, silver, pink, orange, lemon, black, and white are not used. Turning black or white indicates a missing I-D card."

"Thanks, I feel better about my baby blue."

Craig nodded. "I assume the artists and the shrinks got together and spiced up the colors."

Philip put the pin color out of mind, only to have it resurface as he stepped outside. *Ice's pin is a medium blue, cobalt blue. She probably shouldn't have mentioned being able to know about anything to a Provisional Level Three? Best be mum about her mysterious Blue! I'll ask if she chose the color.*

Ice called to say she was working at the Co-op, and he should stay on campus. She would get to campus for dinner.

By late Saturday evening Philip was pleased to have completed his Level-Three scans. *Pystead is certainly working an accelerated schedule to vet us recruits. Well, world news isn't good.* Although late, he decided to see if the Brazilians were at the showboard. The group was soon in view, and he hurried. They were standing instead of sitting. *Exotic looking these women.*

As Philip approached, Hector pointed to the showboard, "Can you believe this?" Philip stepped over to read.

UNITED NATIONS ACCEPTS THE NATION OF KITTS-NEVIS INTO
THE U.N. PROTECTORATE OF OCEANIA, TO BE PART OF A GREAT
UNIFICATION OF RESOURCES TO MAINTAIN A ROUTE OF WATER FOR
TRADE AND CULTURAL EXCHANGE.

UNITED NATIONS TO MEET WITH EXTRATERRESTRIALS IN
FIRST EVER DOCUMENTED CONTACT. VIDEO TO BE BROADCAST
THE NEXT DAY.

UNITED NATIONS TO INVESTIGATE THE PYSTEAD GROUP ON
NEVIS ISLAND FOR SUSPECTED ILLEGAL SEABED MINING AND
HARBORING PIRATES.

UNITED NATIONS TO REVISE CRITERIA FOR SEASTEADING TO
ASSURE EQUAL PROTECTION ON THE SEAS AS ON LAND.

Angela's voice trembled, "There has been no warning. How can this be happening? How can we be safe anywhere?"

Hector found a U.N. post describing Pystead employees as anti-social, angry persons who should not be trusted with professional work when they returned home.

The news seemed to drain from Philip's head and fill his stomach. *The door slammed in our faces for taking legal employment. A new era of official intolerance begins, bought by untraced funds in a world that traces everything…well, everything except the deemer's spies, dark money, dark data, media lies, guns, and too-sweet business deals.* "Hector, what have you learned about the E.T.s?"

"Details will not be announced ahead of time. Media will be included with the U.N. delegation. Video of the event will be available afterwards."

After thousands of years of recorded sightings and anomalous events around the world, E.T. now decides to do business with one body of secretive politicians unelected by the people? Philip spoke up, "I suspect this will be a faked event unless similar events are being announced by the nations having nuclear weapons."

✼   ✼   ✼

Hector waved, "Let's walk." He moved to the walkway, whispering, "That showboard plaza may have listening devices."

"Yes," agreed Philip, "and not necessarily planted by our company."

The group proceeded down a walkway, past a cluster of mermaid and dolphin statues, away from the buildings, and across a wide and level lawn spanning fence to fence, the width of the campus. "This back campus lawn is listed as five hundred meters fence to fence," Hector told the group.

It was as well-kept as the other campus yards, with many small sculptures, but without showboards or fountains, without Poseidons and mermaids. They entered a line of trees and soon encountered a small stream flowing across the width of the entire backside, blocking access to an abrupt downhill slope of lawn to a high fence. "No stepping stones across," observed Hector.

"We are discouraged from crossing," said Philip.

Beyond the high fence, the downhill slope allowed a view above uncut island trees, out to sea under a clear sky. Hector provided a kom address for an aerial view that showed the area fenced on both sides, across the beach, and into the ocean, closing behind the ends of the railroad piers that ran from each side of the campus. The group chatted quietly, pointing to the visible ends of the two docks and enjoying a cool breeze.

Distracted, Philip kept asking himself what being a part of Oceania might mean. He could only conclude that the citizens of Kitts-Nevis were becoming the subjects of Oceania, and that their ghosts would not be fleeing away. He clenched his teeth. Hector quietly told Philip that they knew nothing more about the beaten woman or the K.L.J.H. Organism.

As they turned back toward the working campus, Angela insisted they needed to understand Pystead's culture and policies in more detail before seasteading.

Philip said he would linger a few minutes on the back lawn and listen for songbirds. After hearing several chirps and perhaps a distant song, his thoughts returned to the unsettling news. *This campus isn't a government facility. A private entity can't protect itself. The police are scant deterrents, arriving late for anything not likely to have political ramifications. What do the commons care for the security or extortion of the upper middle class? Will an increased U.N. role bring artificially intelligent police showboards and gothic wiring to Nevis? Didn't that W.W.C.C. showboard list a Caribbean Coordinating Committee? Yes! Sure, Nevis and Pystead are slated for a return to the norm of world vulnerability with tax increases to pay for it. This peaceful and picturesque campus of decent people lulls one into a false sense of security! Already on Nevis the Net and all apps are under attack and scrutiny. A teenager's bow and arrow is considered a weapon, except in the hands of a cupid. There is no way to shield family and friends! I feel the need for seasteading, like that desperate need for speed in a nightmare where your legs go limp, and you can't outrun the monster. Without even a small campus that we can protect, we are not free to be ourselves as a peaceful, productive niche of the cosmos.*

Philip started back, but stopped at a cluster of statues and stood with his eyes closed. He called Ice to tell her about his Level Three processing. *Of course, she already knows! Perhaps the bold pin colors simply mask her unique color?* So, he asked Ice if she knew about Oceania or the E.T.s.

"No, but Pystead is at an Orange-Three security alert, a high level. Please come directly to my apartment in town to see a special video. Hurry!"

⁂ ⁂ ⁂

Philip picked up his pace to a brisk walk. He heard a voice from above. "Dr. Philip Russell, Dr. Russell, Commander Ice Germaine has requested that we give you a ride to her quarters in Charlestown."

Philip stopped, looking up into thin air. *Who said that?*

"Your ride is behind the brass elephant statue to your right." Philip took another step on the walkway. The voice in the air above urged, "Please hurry to behind the elephant statue for your ride to Commander Germaine's quarters."

Philip was searching the air above when a familiar voice spoke, "Phil, this is Ice in your favorite aqua pantsuit, please get into the Egg craft on the other side of that elephant statue."

The elephant statue, of course, was too big to miss. Philip hurried to the statue and found a dull metallic, silver Egg over three meters in diameter. *Why didn't I see the bottom of this from the walkway?*

"When the door opens, Phil, get in and buckle up." A door slid open to reveal a dull metallic interior.

He said to the air, "Really, Ice?"

"Yes, please get in!" He moved quickly through the door and into a seat. "Buckle up, love." He found the seatbelt and fastened it.

The door slid closed.

"Swing over the two shoulder straps," said an unknown voice.

"Looking." He found the shoulder straps as the craft accelerated.

"Thanks, Phil. You will be here in four minutes, in time for me to brief you on a video."

Must have made the full Level Three! Philip did not think about who trusted whom, or why they should or shouldn't, or why the color of a pin. At times one must simply believe.

A screen illuminated on the instrument panel, providing an aerial view of the flight, revealing little except that he was flying above treetops and slightly faster than the slow vehicles on the road he was almost following. Ice spoke again, "Phil, because it's daylight the approach and landing will be abrupt. You will be jerked downward and immediately bounced hard to a stop. You must sit up straight, keep your head and neck straight. Push yourself firmly back into the seat and headrest."

"Okay."

"Welcome to The Pystead Group, Phil."

TASMANIAN DEVIL

Philip pushed back into the seat and felt a flow like pliable wax molding around his neck and head. *Must be happening. Now let's imagine my automatic pilot has an automatic copilot because I really distrust binary beings.* He closed his eyes to hear again that sweet sound of belonging, *Welcome to The Pystead Group, Phil.*

Interrupting his thoughts, Ice's voice told Philip to keep his arms flat on the armrests for landing. An artificial cockpit voice followed with a countdown, but he never heard zero, distracted by the jerks and bounces of the landing.

"Ouch, damn," he muttered. *Nipped my tongue.*

The Egg's door slid open, and Ice smiled for him. "I can make a grilled cheese if you're hungry." She was standing in front of her bed wearing her aqua outfit.

"Cosmos!"

"During alerts, I have my own shuttle to campus."

Some things simply cannot be imagined, like a secret hangar, for a secret craft, in a secret commander's apartment. If it were plausible, it would not exist. Philip smiled for her. "In that outfit, Ice, you should always be on alert."

She rewarded him with a kiss.

"Why use an Egg craft to fly me to see a video during a high alert?"

"The foo fighter Egg was being sent to me. Joan's security branch decides. What about a sandwich?"

"Sounds good."

"Would you bring the big-screen kom?"

"Ice, why aren't you more concerned?"

"Because we are prepared. Joan's secret surveillance discovered the U.N. Admiral's plan to visit the palm reader Melita Rose on Tent Street." Ice took out a frying pan and spoke to her big-screen kom. A blue border appeared around the screen with a header: **PALM READER ON TENT STREET—LEVEL-FOUR CLEARANCE, EYES ONLY.** "Joan says you know enough about us to see this event."

Philip pulled out a stool at the curved counter. The aroma of grilling reminded him of his youth, of his mother and father. A wave of sadness swept over him. *Those scans have asked nothing about my youth. Surely the psychologists do not leave the formative years unexplored? Must be covered at a higher level.*

Ice put a grilled cheese sandwich and a handful of corn chips on his plate. The aroma evoked further thoughts of childhood and his older cousin, Lauren, who had read stories to him. As they ate, Philip took notice of his fiancée. "I do like that outfit."

The screen beeped and captured their attention. The alert line read: **ADMIRAL TELAOBADE HAS ARRIVED IN CHARLESTOWN FROM BATTLESHIP UNS OCEANIA.**

"Define battleship," Ice said to her kom.

The screen posted: **BATTLESHIP OCEANIA IS THE FLOATING HEADQUARTERS OF THE U.N.'S OCEANIA PROTECTORATE, NOW REACHING FROM TARAWA ISLAND TO THE WEST INDIES. BATTLESHIP'S GUNS ARE ACTIVE. TWO OLD EXOCET MISSILE LAUNCHERS HAVE BEEN FITTED. THE SHIP IS COMMANDED BY U.N. ADMIRAL TELAOBADE, BORN IN TASMANIA, AUSTRALIA. THE ADMIRAL IS A CANDIDATE TO BECOME GOVERNOR OF OCEANIA.**

A photograph of the Admiral displayed: a tall man wearing a military hat and carrying a pistol on his belt. Text posted: **THE ADMIRAL HAS SAID THAT UNTRUSTWORTHY NATIONS AND BUSINESSES WILL NOT BE ALLOWED TO SAIL A SINGLE KILOMETER ON OCEANIA'S WATERWAYS. PYSTEAD'S SECURITY BRANCH HAS IDENTIFIED THIS MAN AS INVOLVED IN THE PIRATE ATTACKS IN THE CARIBBEAN. HIS BATTLESHIP IS SERVICING THE PIRATE'S MINI SUBMARINES.**

Over the years, has there been media or government to track sales of stolen loot or ransoms paid? Without pluralism and transparency, nothing is known but the party line. Now, along the world's new road of water for trade and cultural exchange, global justice is to proceed administered by an opaque bureaucracy of anti-democratic mindsets, enforced by a man involved in pirate attacks! O Cosmos!

"We must watch." Ice issued instructions to set up the video feed. She found Philip a copy of an art history book named Janson's "You might enjoy this old, wonderful, and long banished art book."

"Thanks."

✳ ✳ ✳

Ice's big-screen kom soon posted: **ADMIRAL TELAOBADE IS SAID**

HERE ON OFFICIAL BUSINESS. OUR SOURCES, HOWEVER, INDICATE HIS ONLY BUSINESS IS TO VISIT THE PALM READER MELITA ROSE. CREWMEMBERS ARE ADVISED TO REMAIN OFF THE STREETS OF CHARLESTOWN UNTIL FURTHER NOTICE.

Ice added, "Our alert remains at Orange-Three. At this level, we are concerned about something specific, although it's not expected to involve our campus or the fish farm."

Philip asked, "Why will the Admiral walk over a kilometer to visit a palm reader on Tent Street when he can visit one at the dock?"

"Because Melita Rose is the most popular reader in the West Indies. For years there have been rumors that she is psychic."

"What do you think?"

"She doesn't see for friends. She says little insight comes to her out of the blue. She doesn't deny it entirely."

"Is she a virgin?"

Ice scowled. "Don't be silly!"

"Right." *I'm sure I have no idea what she means.*

Ice called downstairs and urged the two artists tending the shop to get home quickly and stay off the roads leading to Tent Street. She and Philip took the interior stairs, and Philip looked at paintings while Ice attended to Co-op business.

Back upstairs, the big-screen kom issued a warbling tone and a warning that Admiral Telaobade and seven bodyguards were walking to Tent Street to visit a palm reader. The message told all personnel to monitor the alert status and advisories.

"Ice, doesn't this seem like an overreaction?"

"Let's see. Big-screen kom, ice blue, show biography of the Admiral." The screen filled with text. The Admiral was from Tasmania, having moved when a child to Arnhem Land outside

Katharine, Australia to live with a half-sister and attend school in the city. A good student, he joined the Australian navy at age twenty-three out of college. After fifteen years of naval service when a Captain, he was reprimanded for unnecessarily sinking three foreign fishing vessels in Antarctic waters claimed by Australia. He protested his reprimand, resigned from the Australian navy, and returned to Tasmania. Three months later he secured a commission with the U.N.'s expanding Oceania Protectorate.

When leaving Tasmania, Teloabade had created an altercation over a tribal mask and killed the mask maker. Now, Telaobade, a Three-Star Admiral, held the highest naval position in the U.N. and was Provisional Governor of The Oceania Protectorate. A final paragraph noted that off-duty the Admiral was an armed roughneck with bodyguards.

After fifteen minutes with Janson's, Philip heard the big-screen kom beeping. Ice brought coffee and they stayed at the counter to watch. The video showed close-ups of faces from street level.

"Where is this video coming from?" inquired Philip.

"Guard control?" said Ice to the room.

The room answered, "Aye," in an artificial female voice.

"Permission to show Guard B to Subject B?"

The room's voice did not respond immediately, and when it spoke, a live female asked, "Are you two in private?"

"Of course. My local security status is a-okay."

"Permission granted for basics only."

"Confirm okay to show Guard B and tell basics."

"Aye, permission to show B to B for basics."

"We will be quick."

Philip closed Janson's. *What's this?*

Ice pointed up. "I'm introducing you to your personal body-guard. Look up." She said to the air, "Guard B, present at counter without cloaking." As Philip watched, a spot blurred in the air and clarified into a floating sphere a bit larger than a basketball. Within several seconds, it showed clearly as a solid sphere of fine and short, fuzzy hair, except for a few small spots of dull metallic gray dimpled like a golf ball. "Your bodyguard, Phil, assigned with the concurrence of Joan and your professional chief, the neurosurgeon who led your seminar."

"A guard for me?"

"Oh yes, I kind of like you, Subject B."

"Well, Subject A, what does it do?"

"It flies and follows you. It tells me if you are misbehaving. It will alert security if you need help. It can stun or kill an attacker or dozens of them. You can ask it simple questions and give it simple directions. When you go through a door, keep the door open longer than necessary so the guard pod can go with you. The pod may proceed or follow you, so don't change your mind in a way that separates you from the guard. If your guard cannot follow without being seen, it will alert you via kom, or voice, or even blinking lights. Or maybe in your case it will rap your knuckles. Small rooms, low ceilings, unusual architectural features, chaotic color schemes, multicolored lighting, mirrors, hanging decorations, strong directional lighting, flashing lights, and smoke or water vapor are difficult or impossible for its navigating intelligence. You must not cause the guard to be put in compromising circumstances. It is procryptic, clever, and powerful, but not magical."

"Such a pod is providing the video from Tent Street?"

"Oh yes."

Love that bobble of her eyes. "Does my guard have a name?"

"Not yet. You can name it when Joan sets your personal interface commands."

"Right, and thanks, I'm sure. And how does it fly?"

"Smoke and mirrors, of course!" Ice spoke to the room, "Guards A and B, set to default control modified for audio and video privacy of Subjects A and B." Then she instructed Guard C to modify for audio and video privacy.

Guard C? She'll tell me when she can. More and more secrets are part of my life. Stranger and stranger this niche of the cosmos. Hope all these electronics devices have a backup. One appearance of a ghost in the machine and maybe my own guard shoots me? Philip looked around for any sign of Guard C, and when he looked back for his own guard, it was not to be seen. He searched the air, looking for a trace.

"If you know what to look for, you can often spot a quick blur that's your guard. Don't search in public because you could alert the wrong people that you have security."

Well, even if I have uneasy feelings about this or that, Ice showed me the perfect secret surveillance. She's not a secret sweetie like Paula was in Compton. And surely soon I'll be allowed insight into some of the technology behind Pystead's smoke and mirrors.

✵　✵　✵

Ice's kom beeped. Melita Rose's tent was in view with its two marble tigers and the very tall, white-robed Indian sentry. *That tent is too tall for a small tent. Perhaps tall for cooling, letting hot air rise?* Two customers were waiting. When the Admiral arrived, he stepped in front of them, hand on his pistol grip. The Indian remained standing with arms folded. The Admiral's bodyguards chased away the two waiting customers and blocked others from coming near the tent. The Admiral waited impatiently for the customer already inside to leave. The Indian zipped up his robe and adjusted his turban, turning it until a red spot faced forward. Ice pointed to the kom screen as the Indian pushed his bare hands into the pockets of his robe. As soon as the customer came out, the Admiral barged through the tent flaps. The Indian kept watch on the Admiral's guards, and when a guard approached to sit on a tiger statue, the Indian took a step forward and waved him off with a white-gloved hand. The Admiral's man hesitated, then retreated.

Their video feed switched to show the Admiral inside the tent, seen over the shoulder of a seated woman. He was standing in front of the palm reader, grinning. Running above the entry flap Philip noticed a line of small red and yellow annunciation lamps. The tent's ceiling rose about three meters above the Admiral's head. The palm reader stood and the video shifted to the side, showing her and the Admiral. Her hair was shoulder length, light brown. She wore a platinum-colored headband that Philip supposed was braided silk. Her platinum-colored dress had multiple, thin shoulder straps of different colors. A black stone flower hung below her modest neckline on a heavy chain.

"What is she wearing?" Philip asked.

"Five layers of voile. Each spaghetti strap is the color of its layer. She calls the colors irresistible cerise, vermilion, hyacinth purple, violet, and platinum."

Exotic, this voile. "And the pendant?"

"Black obsidian, a volcanic glass, on a platinum chain. Platinum is difficult to work. That chain cost much more than the black flower."

As the video ran on Ice's big-screen kom, Admiral Telaobade asked the palm reader, "Do you know who I am?"

"Admiral Telaobade."

"How do you know?"

Melita held up her arm to show her wrist kom.

"You are a fortune teller?"

"Merely a palm reader, Admiral. No cards, no candles, no tea leaves, no crystal ball."

The Admiral asked, "Devil's head charms?"

"No, Admiral, no charms of any kind, no chickens, no potions. No curses placed or removed."

"Tell me your name."

"Melita Rose Tsai."

The Admiral tossed his head. "We are under the impression that you and your surviving brother, now co-owner and veterinarian at Kruel's Sesquicentennial Farm in Connecticut, have the same name, Dezugi. He hides under the alias Leonard."

Melita Rose replied, "Tsai is a registered tradename that I have used for years."

"You must use your Roma name. Oceania's rules apply."

"If I must."

The Admiral stepped forward until he touched her desk. "The process to approve your new license could take a short or a long time. The bureau will have to confirm your birth name. Only birth certificate names and dates or a validated record of birth can be used in Oceania."

"November eighth is my name day for Mihail."

The Admiral sneered, "This is Oceania, not Romania! Didn't you learn anything working for that U.S. superconductor company?"

"I will apply as required. Did you come to have your palm read?"

"You should know! Your mother was a Vadona before she married, they had the gift. You are a seventh of a seventh, a white witch, the most possessed, a conjurer!"

The video switched to Melita. Philip was surprised at the black-eye image now seen on her platinum headband. Melita said quietly, "I can fathom the seas, I can reach the stars, and I know what the pirate doeth."

The view returned to the Admiral and caught a twitch of his jaw. He stood unmoving and scolded her. "We all know what the pirates do. Stay with those stars." His right hand reached into his pocket and came back into view holding a small penknife.

"Wait," Melita said for no apparent reason.

Philip glanced at Ice. "She told her guards not to shoot him. He's showing that he can draw blood and remove any curse she places on him."

"Joan gave her a guard?"

Ice paused before saying, "She sees drunk sailors every day. Her guard pod tells the sentry if she needs help. The pod protects her only as a last resort."

The Admiral waved his blade at Melita. "My men told me you were a looker. Give me something to look at."

"I look the way I always do."

"My lieutenant has seen you in one layer. He said color showed—illegal."

"That must be the drunk last week who grabbed my bodice."

"My duty is to check all complaints. I may overlook an informal accusation of you using sorcery to further the business interests of that company Pystead. You will have to remove all but the bottom dress for me to check."

"Pig!" exclaimed Ice.

Melita hesitated. The Admiral warned, "No look, no license. I can put you in jail even now for using the name Tsai. I'll let you keep that charm. You will be released but have one night to please the guards. You being a witch, your periapt will protect against consequences." Telaobade's grin showed full teeth.

Melita slipped four of her straps off one shoulder, and then off the other. "Pull the tops down, I'm not a stripper." The Admiral reached out his big hand and jerked down the bodices.

Melita helped the loose layers slip to the floor and stepped out of them. She told the Admiral, "You should take off your hat and stay for an off-the-record reading. Surely a man in your position could profit from, shall we say, insight."

Ice was furious. "I can't believe she is letting this happen!"

"Yeah." Philip refrained from mentioning that sorcery could be a capital offense, that evidence given against Westerners had included using magical powers to render a crime scene invisible.

Melita was left standing in a single layer of cerise voile, seen from behind clearly not wearing a bra. "My lieutenant may have been wrong. What do you see in my future, Missy?"

"How shall I focus my attention, personal or professional?"

"Personal."

Melita reached out and took the Admiral's large left hand. "Let me see your palm."

"What else do you want to see? I have a gift from my father as magnificent as your gift from your mother."

Ice exclaimed, "What?"

Melita said sweetly, "We should be generous to each other."

The Admiral pushed the penknife back into his pants pocket.

Melita reached up and pulled on a hanging rope. "My tent flaps are tied."

The Admiral unbuckled his belt and let his pants drop.

Melita told him, "As you say, I am of the knowing ones. I see stars in your future."

"We are talking personal, Missy."

"Shooting stars."

The Admiral grinned hideously.

Ice emitted a shriek clipped short as a roach-brown helmet lowered above the Admiral's head. Obviously, he didn't notice.

Melita placed one hand firmly on his hip and with her right hand reached back and squeezed an oily cloth hanging on her lavatory basin. She reached to caress his neck and then his shoulder. A silver sliver from the helmet flashed to his neck. He jerked slightly off balance, and Melita steadied him. He remained standing."

Melita kneeled and tugged down the Admiral's underpants. "Your turn," he said. She stood and pushed the cerise spaghetti strap off each shoulder. The Admiral grasped her bodice and pulled down. Cerise panty tops flashed in view as the video shifted up to her shoulders from behind. The Admiral reached out with both hands, obviously groping her breasts.

Melita said softly to her right side, "Run one." She practically sang to the Admiral, "How do I look?"

"You've got it, Missy."

"Yes, red is your favorite color."

"How do you know?"

"You said, Admiral, I have the gift."

In the blink of an eye, the helmet's visor covered his face. Melita told him, "It's as marvelous as you said." She whispered to her side,

"Run two." She looked up for a moment and Philip told Ice that Melita was watching the annunciation lights above her tent's door. One by one the little blinking lights were turning green. Another light went steady green and they heard Melita whisper, "Run three."

"Is she scanning him?" asked Ice.

"Must be. I recognize the scan helmet, although I didn't know it could fly. If guard pods can fly, why not a helmet?" Philip continued, "Melita Rose is evidently playing a virtual show and scanning him. The scan will use subliminals."

The Admiral's head bobbed up and then down, and he reached out, obviously fondling her breasts. "She should have gone private."

"Ice, we see only shoulders."

"Still."

The helmet's visor went up, and in the next instant the helmet itself was up and away. The Admiral was smiling. *That high ceiling holds more than hot air.*

Five separate times Melita's hands went above her head slipping on a layer of voile as the Admiral continued groping her with both hands.

When the video panned back down, Melita was dressed. She said calmly, "You must leave. One customer can't stay so long, not even an Admiral." She reached back and again squeezed the oily cloth hanging on her small, lavish, lavender washbasin.

Ice pointed. "A spot of blood." Before Melita touched his neck Philip too glimpsed the small red spec.

Melita was cooing, "For a truly satisfying read my house would be much better."

"You can count on it, Missy."

⚹ ⚹ ⚹

After getting his pants up the Admiral demanded, "You must tell me about my silver stars!"

"I hear a small ship in trouble."

"What goes wrong?"

"A sailor yells flooding. I see four stars circling in the sky. A large hand, like yours, reaches out but fails to catch them."

The Admiral was shifting on his feet and blurted out, "How can I get them? How can I find Pystead mining the seabed?"

Melita raised a hand. "You may find the proof in shallow waters."

"Where?" he demanded.

Melita frowned before saying, "I see a large, steel fish approaching a gap in a slope of sediment sand, swimming into the gap to eat. It's diamond-tipped steel teeth grind out a mouthful of cracked rock. It's steel stomach begins to fill, pressure builds and water is forced out into the sea." Melita paused for a moment before saying, "I see big guns firing at a huge ship in the fog—a ship flying the black flag. There are great, high flashes of fire and deafening booms, and smoke like a storm cloud." Melita raised her hand and paused. The Admiral was gritting his teeth before she continued. "The smoke clears. The round ship is gone. An officer laughs that she went down like the Hood."

The Admiral grinned. Melita told him, "On the other side of Nevis a robot submarine returns with video of the steel fish, west of Charlestown at fifty meters depth off the shelf. Divers with clamps are sent down to catch its tether line. The fish is half full of an ore. The big hand grasps the stars."

The Admiral straightened his belt buckle proclaiming, "At your house we will have a fair exchange of gifts."

Melita took the Admiral's right hand. She wet her own left hand's fingers in her mouth and stepped in to caress his neck. "A man in your position should take a reading every few weeks. Circumstances change rapidly."

"You can count on it, Missy."

"Admiral, you should not be recognized." Melita leaned over to her desk and jotted on a small piece of paper. "This code will unlock my back door after thirty seconds. My security system will tell me who is entering. Send in your men to secure the place. If your ship is off Charleston, I will be home by eight thirty. Surely you can find the address?"

"No problem, Missy."

Melita tugged on her door-tie rope. "Your hat, Admiral." The Admiral thrust the paper into his pocket and took his hat. He spun around with hat in hand and rushed out as quickly as he had rushed in.

✻ ✻ ✻

Melita sat down with tears in her eyes. Ice covered her face in her hands. The video panned up to focus above the tent's entry flaps. A narrow strip opened, revealing the row of little lights all green with one still blinking. A woman's voice said, "So sorry."

Melita responded blandly, "It had to be done."

The woman said, "All questions were probably answered. We have more analysis to do on a two versus three count and a few other points."

"Will he martyr himself?" Melita wanted to know.

"Absolutely not! We have clear reads on that."

"Then it was worth the revulsion."

Ice wiped her eyes. Her kom screen flashed to red text: **SECURITY TERMINATION OF POST-EVENT FEED.**

Philip sat quietly remembering that Melita was Ice's good friend. "I am sad for her, Ice, but glad she said the results were worth it."

"Why should she have to do this for us?"

Philip sighed. "There is something critical that we don't know and it's bad news. The U.N. has no practical reason for governing the small Pacific islands as a group, except for easy exploitation. If that Admiral is any harbinger of the wisdom of the General Assembly, small islands are in for terrible times."

"Joan has said for years that we will have to leave Nevis. We have been so good for them."

"Surely most of that event was above my level of clearance? Especially, when Melita spoke to the woman at Pystead."

"Probably, yes."

What am I missing? Philip closed his eyes. *Aagh!* "My guard is guarding more than my body!"

Ice nodded slightly, looking away. "What is it guarding?"

"My mouth! All that secret video, knowing about flying Eggs, guard pods, and secret scan helmets. Not to mention a palm reader who illegally scans for Pystead. In fact, Ice, I would not be surprised to be called to campus today."

"Whatever for?"

"My experience in correlating scan imagery with words and objects of thought."

"Want more coffee?"

"A top off. And, Ice, let's be ready to go. I was allowed to see that feed for a reason." *What is bothering me?* Philip mused aloud, "The palm reader must work at least part time for Pystead to scan for them?" Ice looked away. *Touchy subject? That makes at least four Pystead part-timers on the streets of Charlestown, and I'll bet Melita Rose is full time, having a special tent with guards inside and out. If an artist has a foo fighter available, Pystead surely has means to get a scanner out quickly and not take a chance on her being arrested. I'll bet both she and the Indian are full time. Both Ice and the nurse get around, so to speak. Melita's tent is adjacent to the woods, like Ice's paintings. That licensed passenger drone that lands behind Melita's tent must be a fair-weather ride. Her contingency ride is surely egg-shaped and lurking among the trees and bushes.*

* * *

There are reasons for everything. Of course, one might inquire about reasons behind the reasons, but that is not advisable. Only some of the elite who dare not raise questions glimpse those interior reasons. Western society directs its resources to remediation of the reasons given for its failings, with no hope of success, except, of course, for the success of the politicians and clerics who direct those resources.

The philosophers cringe at a public debate conducted in terms of dependent parameters instead of independent parameters, yet say nothing. After all, the commons have no concept of functions, of dependent outcomes resulting because of many individual and tangible independent things. Most pundits belittle arguments based on details and numbers as being wonky.

And there is a reason behind that. The deemers know of culturally wired, neural fistulas of brain that can short-circuit innate fairness and justify bias and cruelty. They spend and lie to keep active neural fistula circuits that can short-circuit innate morality and help maintain their influence. In the process, resources are drained from those espousing plurality and given to those supporting centrality and alleged simplicity, even if that simplicity produces a marginal existence controlled by a biased artificial intelligence.

Why is artificial thinking deemed good and human thinking bad? Over-thinking and most of the sciences, the deemers contend, have already done enough harm. The common man accepts any thinking affirmed by the big man. And the big man uses an artificial intelligence programmed to affirm his wisdom. To the commons, reality remains veiled and social contracts fail. The big man must step up and save the day. And most big men are sociopaths or psychopaths who save that day and all the days following for themselves.

"Phil, look, read about the Admiral. This Federation article combines U.N. and Japanese reports." Ice tugged on his arm.

"Right. The coffee is good."

According to the article, Admiral Telaobade, then Captain of a destroyer, had killed for preservation of the world's oceans and their fish and krill, and if need be, would do so again to protect the people of the world from predatory monopolists who in their profit motive of greed denied the people their opportunity to do for themselves. Rather than hitting one boat with one shell, Captain Telaobade sank all three fishing boats and left the survivors to die.

Overfishing can be stopped without killing entire crews of seamen. And when have the commons done for themselves, or controlled their deemers with regulations adequate to protect fish stocks? A lie about cargo or culture will trump common sense in the common mind.

Dare one think that the high servants of the one-world hierarchy would license the unredeemed of nature: the Paulas, Wheatons,

Osgoods, and Telaobades! Surely, only complexity and a lack of funds are the reasons for such oversights. A little more funding, a little more time, and even more wonders will befall humanity. So it is said, so it must be.

So much time and so many resources we non-we must expend to venture even a guess at what is true. And what do we know, except that we non-we are fenced like dogs and not serving our own family's interests. The deemers tear families apart, breaking the tenderest of human bonds, emotionally crippling children and adults for life. The unthinkable is unthinkable only to the unrealistic.

Are there reasons behind each professed reason that common sense might recognize if allowed a view? A view of history as recorded. A view of scientific findings and the rational implications of those findings. A view of the human mind as it can be fathomed to be. A view of crop circles as they can be photographed to be. A view of anybody other than as *AnalyticZiff* spins them to be!

Technology is smoke and mirrors to the uneducated mind, and with a little added obfuscation to any mind at all. Perhaps the truth may eventually be exposed by the collective primary process of humanity? Perhaps? And eventually can be such a very long time!

✶ ✶ ✶

Ice reached over and gently caressed Philip's neck. She did not speak, recognizing his mood.

I should have children who suffer so that eventually their distant and unknown descendants might enjoy life? Is that the way of nature? It does seem too cruel. And so, am I too a deemer of things, placing nurture above nature? At least I would deem there be many pathways with the individual allowed to choose hisher own journey. Yet, if reason may be applied only to a sure end, then reason may not be applied within the human domain that knows nothing of sure ends. It is written that humanity knows how to interpret the appearance of the sky. Knowing the sky prepares the mind to know truth when revelation is attained. And need the mind make defense for hope within the human spirit? Make defense for being created Cartesian and doomed to err in matters of faith and wisdom? For no sign shall be given! And many by word of a Godly man follow a false prophet. For what practical wisdom may the bounded mind know unto sure ends? Even Popes have proved fallible and cruel. Even an appearance of the sky or humanity has confounded. Belief in a divine hidden hand has seemed both plausible and implausible. Since I set aside childish things to reason like a man, do I now set contrary thoughts asunder and choose a wish like a child? To that ignoble end was I created?

Ice muted her big-screen kom. She asked, "Phil, please explain this functional brain imaging, the process correlating scan imagery with objects of thought." Before Philip could speak, she added, "Perhaps your funding committee didn't understand?"

He sat up straight. "Ice, my committee members understood only too well. I explained and offered to demonstrate the process by scanning one or all of them, so that each could personally confirm that my results matched his or her thoughts."

"How did they respond?"

"Not one agreed to be scanned, even using a preapproved list of questions."

"Oh gosh."

"I had used my computer system to show them typical video playbacks of actual scans. The screen shows an outline of the brain; the playback outlines the various regions of the thinking brain and shows its electrical activity in real time as the brain, the mind, thinks. My computer's signal processing unit handles research-level resolution. Electrical signals from the thinking brain are associated with their precise locations in the brain and saved as real-time patterns. Each individual spot of brain activity, about a quarter-of-a-million neurons, can be recorded and displayed as a dot on a diagram of the brain being scanned.

"The playback is slowed down and lets us see the places in the brain that are used and in what sequences they are used. If the brain is thinking of a number, a word, or even a particular scene, it makes use of the same memory neurons each time, activates the same MRI sensors, and produces the same pattern on the playback video. If we find that a certain local pattern means the subject is thinking of the number nine, for example, by knowing what number he is looking at and having him confirm that's what he was thinking, then we have a baseline pattern for that number in his brain. If we ask him a question later and that same memory pattern occurs, we have a correlation between his new thought and his known baseline."

"How could we get a baseline on the Admiral?"

"The dropped visor probably showed him a short series of numbers and recorded his reflexive mental responses. To overcome any confusing thoughts or processing signals between areas of his brain, surely he was also shown a sequence of dots, and then heard a sequence of the words for the numbers, spoken through the helmet."

"Oh, so he knew we were interested in specific numbers?"

"No. The queries were subliminal, too soft or too fast for his conscious mind to recognize, although his subconscious mind did recognize them, and by reflex thought of the numbers, providing his baseline, probably over a range of a few numbers."

"Sneaky! No wonder your committee members refused."

"Ice, they refused because of the sequencing information. If you believe what you are saying, your mind follows a certain sequence of thought, and if you are being evasive or lying, it follows different sequences to arrive at its response. The mind works harder to tell a lie! We can even tell if a thought comes from your personal experience, or if it comes from being told or having read about something. Generally, we can tell if you are being honest or duplicitous in your responses. My committee members couldn't risk being found to have political motives rather than academic motives."

"Oh."

No eye flash this time. "Ice, Pystead's helmet is advanced beyond any technology I ever used or read about. It's certainly the best I've experienced for virtual reality. With no weight on the head, it's easy to look anywhere and feel all is real. The virtual reality helmet showed the Admiral video that he thought was Melita, probably stock video that was computer animated to match whatever the Admiral should have been seeing or feeling. The subliminals were computer generated to work with the animation. Because he was emotionally and physically involved and drugged, the virtual audio-video should have captured his conscious attention allowing subliminal suggestions to be most effective."

Ice stood up. She took Philip downstairs and they tied a blue nametag on the support wire of each of her paintings, including those in storage. Then they used a different colored tag for each of the other artists. They packed four chests of canvas, paints, and brushes. Back upstairs after four hours of work, the couple relaxed eating boiled eggs, cold cuts, and chips. They drank the last of the margarita. Then they packed paintings from Ice's apartment into the foo fighter waiting in its concealed hangar. Just before one a.m. Sunday they got to bed.

15

TIMES CHANGE

Ice was sitting quietly as they sipped coffee. She hurried to respond when her kom emitted a series of irregular beeps. "Ice here."

"Can you bring Dr. Russell to campus by noon for a visit to cog-sci's computer center?"

"I can."

"Roman candles at ten-forty?"

"A-okay for ten-forty this morning with R."

"Roger and out."

Ice put hands on her hips. "Don't say I told you so. Only yesterday I said you were fast-tracked for some good reason. Now please help me select some digital images to buy while we have time. We are weak on grand homes and castles, especially interiors. I want our children to see the extreme differences that exist on Earth, and have an idea of the joy as well as the grief that abides here."

"I hope you have the grand old libraries, most are quite

236

impressive. The children should see the elegant old reading rooms. Some of the book stacks still exist."

"I knew you could help."

"Let's not forget the magnificent railroad terminals around the U.S. and the world. And the many finely decorated performance venues and religious buildings."

When their door chime sounded, Ice said she had expected as much. She returned with a bulky package. "Joan sent this jumpsuit for you. I'm wearing my baby blue pantsuit that is also half-Halo. Let's get you into this suit, and I'll show you how to close up."

The fabric was rather heavy. With pointers from Ice, he suited up and zipped up, ready to energize for half-Halo protection. "How good is half-Halo, Ice?"

"Joan says the jumpsuit's half-Halo is not half the protection of a real Halo suit, but how much either protects she hasn't shared."

"My suit feels fine even fully zipped. I suppose it's like the facemask, not uncomfortable, yet annoying after hours of wear?"

Ice only smiled. "Let's look at paintings in the U.S. National Gallery. There's a good virtual tour by a docent named Rosie."

❊　❊　❊

At ten-thirty Ice stood up. "Time to go, Phil."

The seemingly solid curve of the bedroom wall slid quietly open. The door in the silver Egg slid open without a sound. "Be sure to sit up straight," she told him, "we will go up like a shot."

"What are the Roman candles?"

"Distracting fireworks on the beach. We get a countdown to zero for departure." Ice looked over her shoulder and reported, "Have visual and green light on apartment door closed. Now for

Egg's door closed." She looked at the instrument panel. "Have all lights green. Ready on your count." A voice responded to standby for an early count. "Aye aye, ready now for the count." She turned to Philip, "Can you believe how good I have gotten at all these annoying little details?"

"Indeed, I have noticed." *Wish you could fly the thing.*

In less than a minute, the cabin voice announced, "Candles on the beach. No birds overhead. No gawkers gazing. Outer door shows opening. All systems are go for home. Ready then?"

Ice responded, "Have local video on outer door open. All panel lights are green for home."

The cabin voice asked, "Any pods to fly?"

"Two."

"Ready now," the voice continued, "Five, four, three, two, one, ze. . . ."

An upward surge hit Philip through his seat and he nipped his tongue reacting to the jump start. *Cosmos! Second time.* The view screen showed shops and street receding below. Upward acceleration ceased as forward acceleration set in. *Flying higher and faster this time. Campus within the minute? This certainly is a new niche in the cosmos, and I'm only a Level-Three novice. How many levels are there? What level can know the technological secrets of the Pystead?* Philip wondered aloud, "Where is my guard pod?"

"It's following us."

"Where is yours?"

Ice pointed forward. "It's leading us."

I simply asked for that. "How far can the pods go without refueling?"

"I've never asked. It's not an issue."

A key difference between staff and line. What is my calling in this strange niche of being? This veiled and mysterious niche of smoke and mirrors. I must observe carefully and think twice. Philip glanced at his wonderful fiancée and tensed. *Even if all they say be true today, what about tomorrow?*

Are there not many perils inherent in a floating city? The perils of outside intervention we hear and read about. What of perils from within? And what of those crew who now lead? Will they be apprehensive about boarding a floating city with the likes of us new recruits? Aha, perhaps an excellent query. We recruits are relative unknowns! Do all of us merely climb aboard and hurl ourselves into becoming, praying to the Fates we are a thing that's viable?

The cabin voice intruded on Philip's thoughts with instructions for arrival. Ice asked, "Phil, did you hear?"

"Yes, love."

"You have been quiet...are you feeling well?"

"Yes, merely preoccupied with all things."

"Just checking."

"Perhaps, Ice, we are all as ready for boarding as we can be!" Philip sat up and clenched his teeth. *Best think of my tongue in the moment.* For, in the real world, one must survive the moment to live to do again another day. In the real world, survival is the prime directive, and for the elect charity is the prime morality. Philip, the cognitive scientist, professional quantifier of mind, knew he was in zugzwang and could only await events and hope for guiding intuition via his subconscious process. He said softly, "I love you, Ice."

"I love you, Phil."

The cabin voice asked, "Ready for landing count?"

Ice replied, "Aye for countdown."

"Ready now."

Philip straightened up by the numbers. *Mind the tongue.* Tense for an abrupt landing, he was pleasantly surprised to find himself motionless. Then he realized that out of the public gaze there was no need to streak into a twenty-meter-long, dead-end hole of a runway.

⁂ ⁂ ⁂

Dr. Snyder arrived five minutes later wearing island clothes, a beige medical facemask, and sporting a turquoise pea pin. Ice said she would lounge around, maybe visit a friend.

Okay, time to get cracking.

Philip put on his white mask. By the time the two men reached the laboratory, they were using first names. Their first event was a lunch of sandwiches, and potato chips that Philip supposed were at Ice's request. George and his team then decided to try for a download of Philip's archived scan imagery through his lawyer, Will Smith, in Compton. Will, as usual, responded without concern for the day or hour, and asked no questions about George's requested set-up for transmission. He agreed to ship Philip's computer system to a contact in Toronto provided by George.

Philip's scan files were downloaded via a foo fighter hosting an onboard wireless server, a Pystead asset remaining in California from recruiting days. There followed a tense wait while the computer technicians copied Philip's files, checked them for hacking interference, and then converted them for use by Pystead's computer system. There was no protracted wait for mapping correlations between Philip's and Pystead's data because both used an Arthur Toga compatible format. They gave a little cheer at the thumbs up from the lead technician. Now, said George, the two independent baselines could be compared. Tension increased again because any disagreement between the two baselines could not be resolved. Philip held his breath as the first pattern comparison ran for the number two. He relaxed at the high sign for a match within three percent for brain location and thinking patterns. "We would take five percent," George told him. The analytics team relaxed and waited as the technicians ran comparisons for several words and numbers selected by George. All agreed within four percent.

George expressed relief that Commander Joan could now have more confidence on a few vital points. First, in several cases, the Admiral had thought of the quantity two, instead of one or three, although with additional thoughts probably of the word 'shell,' assuming an English subliminal evoked the use of English for the response. The Admiral's English as a second language made a reliable interpretation of his word thoughts problematic. Philip concurred that the Admiral had rejected each suggestion that he might martyr himself to be rid of The Pystead Group. Instead, he was confident about his prospects. And Philip, like the lead scan analyst, read the scans as confirming the Admiral believed all suggestions that he would become rich as Governor of Oceania. Philip found that the Admiral's responses did not produce scan patterns suggesting preconditioned thoughts, although his perhaps inadequate understanding of subliminals in English could have resulted in prolonged thought patterns. They completed the analysis with Philip reminding himself that English as a second language needed more study—and something else, yet unnamed, kept him uneasy.

Both George and the lead analyst, Richard, said they were pleased to have Philip's assistance. As his own unease became tangible, Philip cautioned, "My conclusions were based on a drug-free person, or I should say, a drug-free brain. As you know, I have not factored drugs into my analysis." Watching closely, Philip thought George clenched his jaw, but neither George nor Richard said a word. Philip continued, "I'm surprised you would risk deceiving the Admiral using only a metaverse reality, even if perfectly controlled."

Neither man replied. George pulled up his kom and used it in touch mode.

Philip looked away. *He must be using the Commander's know-anything-as-soon-as-it-happens channel?* Philip said, "Especially when usurping a face-to-face interaction."

George replied, "We are constrained as to how much we can tell you."

"Then you should be wary of my conclusions."

George and Richard exchanged glances. George spoke to the air, "Joan?"

"Here, George."

"Joan, Dr. Russell needs to know if we used drugs on the Admiral."

Joan asked, "Philip, you do know you are being cared for by a guard pod?"

"I do."

"Philip is Level Three and has security to assist in his not misspeaking. Tell him whatever he needs to know."

"Roger, Joan, but I have no confirmation on the drugs. That's still in Blue…"

Joan said, "I'm releasing it to you."

"This Blue processing," Richard quipped before his voice fell to an abrupt halt.

Surely caught himself because of me. This Blue processing what?

George's kom soon confirmed drugs and dosage, injected into the right aorta using a microneedle. They reopened the analysis, and within an hour decided the drugs had not caused the Admiral to be delusional beyond the first minutes of his transition into virtual reality. All agreed the sex and its show had captured the Admiral's attention, leaving him unguarded in his responses. George explained that experimental runs using test subjects had found no other humane approach for obtaining the needed information.

Philip, however, was still focused on Richard's guarded words. *Must save appearances and work around their wording. Blue processing was expedited for Commander George, although Commander Ice with her Blue screen border seems self-releasing? Must I also work around Ice's wording?* His stomach pulsed. *And haven't I had enough of secrecy within my own apartment in Compton?*

And Philip remained dissatisfied with the analysis. "George, did you ask any place questions?"

George shook his head and Richard explained, "We didn't ask any place or time questions."

"Still, let's check grid and place cells following the number questions."

"Philip, do you know what the numbers represent?"

"No, but most anything asked could have elicited a thought of place."

"The number is the quantity of atomic warheads the United Nations has recently acquired. Allegedly to make it an entity with the means to protect the Earth from asteroids, and to deter terrorist groups from establishing large, permanent bases."

"Great ghosts!"

"My thoughts are less genteel," offered Richard. "We also checked for any nerve agents the U.N. might have. At least that was negative."

George asked what words Philip would like checked. They analyzed the patterns. No response, however, matched a probable thought pattern for Nevis, campus, fish farm, floating city, or battleship. Philip requested a computer search for probable matches to a dozen other words, and correlations were returned for ocean and ship. The team concluded the atomic devices could be aboard U.N. ships.

The lead scan analyst, Richard, and then George each made backup copies of Admiral Telaobade's scans, two of which were picked up by security to be stored in different buildings. George reported findings and stayed in the laboratory showing Philip the equipment. Joan called and cautioned them to treat the scans as critical documents and have another crew double check findings in the morning.

As an off-topic query, Philip asked if working to separate the innate wiring of the mind from its cultural wiring might be an acceptable personal project. George foresaw no objections and thought it should warrant consideration as a formal Pystead project after completion of crew training. His positive response energized Philip with hope for a progressive niche in the cosmos.

Once outside, Philip considered events. *Was I helping or being evaluated? A concurring opinion must add confidence since my scan files could not have been faked to mislead. Probability is on the side of helping while being evaluated. Glad I was a bit assertive. And I'll bet they have already used subliminals to learn if I would martyr myself to raze the company! Joan accepted me early on, but covered her decision with a guard pod keeping tabs on me! A clever way to find me out if a spy.*

It's almost five o'clock on a Sunday afternoon! Was this timing planned to test my willingness to work any hours for a better life? No! The Admiral's visit to the palm reader established the timing. One has to be somewhere! What better use of my time?

⚹ ⚹ ⚹

Philip had no message from Ice and decided to continue his security processing. He was soon taking his first Level-Four scan, feeling refreshed without his quarantine mask and happy to lie down for a big, banging, commercial machine. After a few minutes, however, he decided, *Regression to this pounding machine noise is uncomfortable. I suppose building a full-scale, quiet machine was low on Pystead's to-do list.*

The technician told him the scans would be repeated at future intervals, normal procedure, and were required for promotion. *That palm reader has a guard, Ice said 'guards.' How is that? How can she have guard pods she directs and not be a Level Four or higher? How would there have been time for deep background checks on somebody from Romania? Ice's body language as much as confirmed Melita Rose was crew. Sure! They would never have relied on a hastily trained palm reader for a critical scan of a powerful official—to steady him and clean up blood at precisely the right moments. To know what to do if something went wrong! The Pystead staff empathized with her as a friend. This Pystead Group is too strange to be unreal.*

Although weary and hungry after his scans, Philip hurried

and arrived at Dr. Snyder's office for the summation briefing on the Admiral's scans. Joan and Ice were present as well as others new to him. He was surprised to see Joan wearing yellow-cream pants and a white blouse. *No red lavaliere, no red belt, no red boots, no red fingernails. Lip gloss instead of red lipstick. This is not helping my Red Queen image!*

Joan presented the case, beginning with the backstory that Admiral Telaobade was a rogue officer, servicing the pirates' mini submarines from his battleship, and probably directing them as well. The pirates were possibly rogue crewmembers from the battleship, which had two underwater docking ports for mini submarines of the type used by the pirates. The battleship had the docking ports, but the U.N. had never acquired any mini-subs. The battleship was, however, never more than sixty miles from an attack, and always proceeded in the direction of the attack to investigate, always without findings. Once suspected, Pystead's surveillance pods had easily confirmed that the battleship was servicing the mini-subs.

Joan reported that Pystead's Federation Council feared a new world order was imminent. The U.N. had not announced its acquisition of the nuclear weapons. Seasteading licenses expected by a half dozen groups had been denied. The U.N. had four old Exocet missile launchers and probably a few dozen missiles purchased from small nations around the world. According to Pystead's surveillance pods, the U.N.'s position would be that nuclear devices were necessary to create a bona fide power that could protect the Earth from an asteroid should no major power be willing to act. The U.N. would not rely upon findings of a near-Earth miss by astronomers not employing Six-Sigma quality protocols.

Ha! Even I know that a calculated specific point of impact on the Earth would be unreliable. The major powers would act. And a trajectory calculated by a dozen modern nations and universities is not a quality finding? Are we to believe the U.N. is now the Earth's astronomical authority? Philip clenched his teeth.

Joan said the rogue Admiral's record of acting on his own initiative had always been supported by the Security Council, even backdating votes to sanction his actions. The Admiral was influential, would probably become governor of Oceania Protectorate, and surely would support Kitts over Nevis or Pystead. Joan reported that Manager Markwaters thought the Admiral would demand monetary kickbacks from wealthy persons and businesses, and that criminal and civil justice would be replaced by his justice, or lack thereof. Joan was pessimistic about the future viability of working out of Nevis because Pystead had not received permission to use international waters, which were effectively United Nations' waters and off limits to all except approved member nations and transnational companies paying sea-lane usage fees.

George presented the findings of their brain scans of the Admiral. Joan asked for comments. Nobody spoke, so Philip asked, "Did the analysis attempt to determine if the Admiral was alarmed over the defeat of his boarding party on the recent sailing ship bringing Pystead principals to Nevis? Did the Admiral suspect that ship's guards were provided by us?" No one spoke, so he added, "Do we have a Jolly Roger flag?"

His comment drew a chuckle from Ice. Joan frowned and replied, "We have considered those issues, except for significance of the Jolly Roger, but could not scan for them. That flag could become a key to the Admiral's behavior after Melita's prediction that he would sink a ship under the black flag." Joan paused, "We all worry that dreams, as well as hypnosis and drugs, could reveal enough about our process to show it's illegal." Then she said, "Let's break for today. I believe we are making progress in defining some of these short and long-term problems."

George spoke quietly to Joan, "Thanks, we'd have nothing without your scans." She half-nodded.

Joan squints her eyes? As they were leaving the room, Philip again asked himself, *What have I not been told? What have I missed?*

⚘ ⚘ ⚘

Joan caught Philip's eye and beckoned for him to come over. She said he had received a small package from Cognitive Dimensions and wanted to know if it was expected. After a moment he recalled, "Friends in the States said they would send pills for me to experiment with. I don't know what's in them."

"We need to test them."

"Fine. They aren't medication. I have no use for them before my laboratory is established, also I should know the drugs used."

"Since we are busy, we'll put them at the bottom of our list."

Ice came over and took Philip's hand. She whispered, "My intuition tells me you are helping."

"My place or yours?"

"My place, Phil, we didn't bring Char."

"I get another chance to nip my tongue landing in your spacious runway pit."

"I forgot to tell you to keep your teeth together and your tongue back."

"Merely an annoying little detail."

"I'll make it up to you."

So it was that Philip Russell, effectively exiled from Compton, held Ice's hand and departed happy, if not jolly, having professional employment, a fiancée, and a cat—all in a promising niche of the cosmos. If his primary process worried about seasteading being denied, or secrets within his own apartment, the thoughts remained submerged. In the moment, Philip savored the bliss of belonging.

16

ON THE LINE

With the black cat for company, Monday they stayed in Ice's apartment checking Net news on her big-screen kom. According to the latest United Nations' announcement, Admiral Telaobade's demands to local officials on Nevis had produced a framework for security procedures that would almost immediately lead to reducing piracy in the Caribbean. Government, commercial, and residential sites on Nevis would be searched. U.N. Admiral Telaobade would direct operations under the auspices of the Oceania Protectorate. Martial law would be declared to carry out search mandates.

"Not good," concluded Philip. "They will begin with our shipping docks and end up searching for Halo suits in every room and box on campus and fish farm. We must dispose of all traces of our scans of the Admiral."

"How could they find those?" Ice asked.

"If history be any guide, they will interrogate and abuse everybody until they find virtually everything." Pacing the room, Ice paused every few steps to look at one of her remaining paintings. Philip worried, *What can we do? The news implies that pirates are operating out of Nevis, possibly from Pystead.* Philip clenched his hands and tried to relax his tense stomach.

A subsequent broadcast reported on the U.N.'s planned meeting with the Galaxy Saucer, originally set near the Ushtogaysky Square in Kazakhstan, now to be on one of the Tobago Cays. The U.N. had declared a large exclusion zone around the Cays and posted a statement that the E.T.s made clear they would not tolerate unauthorized air or sea craft in the vicinity of the meeting.

Already anxious, they both tensed when the big-screen kom emitted a series of irregular and loud beeps. Ice called, "Yes?"

"Ice, you must get to campus with Philip and your cat, and your favorite clothes and paintings. Wear jumpsuits. Bring all koms and all portable smoke and mirrors. Use your checklist. Remember the dog, the mirror, and half-Halo clothing. Do not plan on going back! Leave within the hour. You should get out before new radars and videos become operational. That is all."

"Roger to leave forever within the hour! I'll message you on items remaining for pick-up, including the one hundred thirty-five paintings hanging or stored in the Co-op."

"Wasn't that Joan?"

"Oh yes, I've never heard her so frenetic."

Ice sent Philip down to the Co-op for seven cases of wine. She called her artist friends and told them to never return to the Co-op because the police might be waiting for anybody with an entry code. She would cancel all vendors and Co-op events and contact each of them at home. She said not to worry about their paintings because her friends were saving them.

Ice threw clothes into her two suitcases and laundry bags. In forty minutes, they had loaded all they could fit into the foo fighter and climbed aboard with the black cat. The cabin voice began reading a checklist. Then a gray dog walked in and laid down beside Philip, who jumped by reflex. Before asking about the dog, he recognized it as the Tasmanian Devil statue. When the cabin voice finished reading the checklist Ice replied, "All items are visually confirmed aboard, including Guard C."

Security Guard C is the ugly statue—a robot!

"I-D tags report all aboard," confirmed the cabin voice.

Before the countdown, Ice said sweetly, "Oh, Phil, teeth together and tongue back."

"Aye." *Didn't miss her last opportunity to remind me!*

The kick through their seats sent them soaring. *What's to become of us? May smoke and mirrors be with us!*

The Pystead Group had suspended improvements on campus. Philip and Ice could not have furniture moved into their assigned apartment, so they moved into his VCQ room with Char Cat and Pig Dog, both as dubbed by Philip. Ice approved of her cat having a last name. Encouraged, Philip asked if he might call her Alice. She said she would like being Alice once aboard ship, and she also liked her future surname, Russell. Philip was surprised she didn't want to keep her maiden name. She wanted to take his name and use Germaine as a middle name for their children.

Next day, the media reported that *UNS Oceania* was at sea, and the Protectorate would delay inspections on Nevis. Upon hearing the news, Philip teased Ice that she should call Joan before Joan called her. Ice reached Joan, and only a minute into the call said, "Oh, that's fine." Ice went to speaker mode.

After a quick hello to Philip, Joan was serious, "Did you have a particular question, Philip?"

"A concern for the Co-op's artists on Nevis. They will surely be picked up for interrogation after the special features of Ice's apartment are discovered."

"Philip, the apartment's hangar was modular and built for quick return to original construction. Within two hours after you vacated, all the hinges, rails, rollers, power operators, springs, wiring, and instruments were removed and the roof nailed down. We even refilled the pit with its original dirt compacted to almost ninety-nine percent—difficult to do quickly and quietly. We eliminated the bar side door and framed out the bedroom door using matching trim and hardware. The hangar space is now a closet on both levels. We left dried-out paints, old shoes, and a half case of wine."

Joan paused, "Still, I believe the Nevis artists could become targets when it's discovered that Ice worked for Pystead. For weeks now we have known the U.N. is infiltrating Nevis's government and pressuring everyone to reveal the smallest detail that might lead to Pystead personnel. The U.N. has announced that our collecting art in this era of economic distress acted as a catalyst for divestiture and veils our black-market activities. The U.N. claims we are not helping cities and museums with our purchases, photographs, and copies, but are exploiting them. This when we bought no top-tier originals, and those who did are never mentioned. The U.N.'s perspective is completely without merit as we were hardly noticed in the market. The world is led to believe we were responsible for sales by curators who were finding funds for contemporary purchases required by law to close gaps in the fine arts. Officers at the Nevis museum will have to reveal the source for a dozen of their paintings, if they have not done so already."

Philip said, "I have met the artists. If I could get to their houses, I could warn them in person."

"If you and Ice visit the shop and then the artists, the trip could be done quickly enough, but you would need to use a shuttle bus there and back to avoid new and perceptive surveillance of the sky over Nevis. We don't yet know all their tracking capabilities."

"Will you offer the artist's sanctuary with Pystead?"

"Philip, why are you so fearful for them?"

"Because I was mistreated on the way to Nevis for no good reason, and in their cases there will be a reason."

"The General Manager, Commandant of Administration, the business managers, and a few psychologists are now discussing the general issue. I will relay your and my concerns about the five artists. We do acknowledge our role in placing them in a compromising situation."

"Joan, I believe you should also consider the Kehchens's Jazz Quintet who play on Tent Street. They sing about miracles, magic, and enchantment for Western tourists, and are surely as unpopular with the U.N. as are the humanities."

"I'll nominate them for consideration; we need another jazz group. Now let me speak with Ice."

Ice used text mode for a few sentences and then put Joan back on speaker. "Both of you may go. Ice would like video of the local beach. Philip, go to VCQ lost-and-found with your guard pod and both koms. We will swap your guard for a more powerful model and give you an introduction to capabilities and command interface. We have half-Halo island clothing for you. If you have difficulty with kom access, switch to channel Nine-Four-Six." Joan paused.

"Okay, Nine-Four-Six."

"We will provide each of you a tube of sanitizer, and a tube for each artist. You should leave a-s-a-p. The shuttle buses now depart on the hour."

"I'll be right down."

"Give Karl twenty minutes to get over with pod and clothing."

"Okay."

"And Philip, for the record, we never used black markets to move money. Our infrastructure purchases and funds have only recently begun to be traced. Most of our operating funds for three decades were moved using colored diamonds, synthetic gemstones, and industrial diamonds that were unmonitored at the time. Five of our nine pontoons, actually our ships, are leased to us by small manufacturing or shipping companies indirectly owned by us."

"Interesting, thanks."

"Ice, we must call each artist for her location while Philip is out."

�֗ ✗ ✗

Philip's new guard pod was larger than the first. It held four flying surveillance devices that looked and felt like short pieces of pipe. Karl called them six-centimeter rods. The guard pod itself was more powerful. Philip asked about its flight range and was told unlimited. *That's a bit much? But okay, I believe it, relative to tiny Nevis Island.* "Karl, when can I know something about the science underlying this smoke and mirrors?"

"Once you are aboard ship to stay, or at Level-Six clearance." After fifteen minutes of orientation to his new pod, Karl asked, "Philip, what is your clear channel if needed?"

255

"Nine-Four-Six."

Karl held out his hand, "Let me have your kom for a moment." In a minute, Philip had it back. "Nine-Four-Six will be available only if you need it, otherwise it doesn't exist. It's the highest numbered channel listed on your kom."

My very own ghost in the machine! Nine-Four-Six, Nine-Four-Six, number nine does flips for a six.

Karl handed Philip a soft package. "Protective civilian clothing. After you energize, it will stop a nine-millimeter. Avoid anything larger—a pistol that just looks big."

"You are expecting trouble?"

"Off campus we always expect trouble, and have always handled it, except for once being surprised by a cupid's arrow."

"I like that approach. Things are normal until they aren't."

Karl pointed to tabs. "Flip and press at any one of these six tabs to energize. The process is almost silent and takes only several seconds. You will acquire a heavy fabric look that security personnel will notice. Wait until needed, especially on the hat, but any adversary will be a good shot so energize the hood if you think anybody might shoot."

✶ ✶ ✶

The noon shuttle arrived. Ice pulled on her narrow, very blonde headband, and said she was looking forward to beach video. They were to make contacts together and in person. The Federation Council would offer each artist a crew position with cross-training required. Recognition analysis for surveillance video would be one of the jobs offered. Ice and Philip would ask each artist to return to campus with them, bringing pets, suitcases, and paintings as could be managed. Anything else they must have would be picked up for them by armed Halo guards.

How can anyone decide to go on the appearance of one friend? There is no general awareness of corrupt police and officials. We need an option for next year, after conditions have deteriorated. And what are the chances of Pystead being wrong about the future? Will the expressed animosity of past and present minds meld mysteriously into individual and institutional decency? Will the long-time, dirty-tricks political parties and nations reform themselves? Will terrorism abate? Will Den Haag stop cherry picking laws and venues? I don't think so! Once mature, most minds are done done! I know of no general success for the planned character rehabilitation of a mature mind. On the group scale, even laogai must be repeated in every generation to overcome the innate humanity of a decent majority. Philip lowered his head and peeked at his wrist kom. The expected blue dot surrounded by four blue lines showed at upper left. *My Kong One is active with all four surveillance rods.*

Before reaching town, they stopped for Collette. She was already saving to get out. Her aunt had moved from Kitts back to France last month. Collette agreed to meet the bus on Ice's return trip. They next stopped for Sophie, who said no way could she pick up and leave, but she accepted hidden addresses for requesting a later pick-up.

After returning to the bus stop the couple waited for a shuttle of Ice's choice. Upon boarding Philip noticed a few men wearing long sleeves, long pants, and wide-brimmed or heavy hats—looking suspiciously half-Halo capable. Midway back sat a police officer. Philip and Ice took seats, and before the doors closed the policeman shouted, "Driver, keep those doors open!" His footsteps thumped forward and without warning he had Ice by the arm, jerking her up. "You are under arrest. Come with me!"

Philip was half on his feet as Joan's voice rose in his earpiece, "Stay seated!"

"He's dragging her off the bus."

"Speak softly! Oceania is watching with a real-time link to police headquarters."

"I'm losing sight of her."

"Our pods have her on screen. She's fine. I'll put the video on your kom. Your Kong One is not involved and not needed. It's holding near the bus, staying with you."

"He's dragging her along off balance, on purpose. Joan, she's just an artist. He will hurt her for the fun of it."

"She is not just an artist. She's a Pystead Commander! Not highly skilled in the martial arts, yet trained to slip a punch and react, conditioned to be confident. She will energize if necessary. She has held her own pod's fire because our Halo guards have been present as a secret force in the area for almost an hour. This cop is one of a new breed of bad dogs on Nevis, and he will not be getting any assistance from friends. When he approached the bus, we noticed he was not wearing his body camera. Ice must be a case of mistaken identity. He wants to add a new thief and concubine to his harem, not physically harm her. You are in one of the areas of town recently gone bad. Stay calm and do not become a liability!"

Philip returned to his kom view as the man pushed Ice behind a shrub bush, taunting, "You little thief, I have you now."

Ice, head down, mumbled, "I have nothing stolen on me. Don't arrest me. I'll show you a good time." She unzipped her blouse and took the cop's hand, looked away, and brought it to her breast.

He grabbed her by the arm. "I have a house near."

"You don't have to jerk me."

He released her and pointed. "That way!"

Philip noticed a brown bug or lump on the underside of the man's wrist a moment before it flashed. His arm dropped limp, he stumbled, slumping to his knees. Ice ran. A curved line of metallic gray appeared in a bush ahead of her and spread into a crescent shape that Philip recognized as a foo Egg's opening door.

Still down, the man yelled, "I'll find you, little bitch, and make you beg me for it."

Ice stepped into the Egg. The door closed and the Egg became a rising blur of bush before vanishing among the trees as a slight rippling of limbs and leaves.

"What did she do to him?"

"She used a stun bug, ours, but available at Magic Corner."

"Where?"

"Magic Corner is a dark Netsite selling legal and illegal information, zapper bugs of all sorts, and pistols—to criminals only. They have a representative on Kitts-Nevis and use implants in people and pets to confirm membership. The cop knows what she did to him. He has his own stunners. We've known to watch the new hires on the force for several weeks."

"Ice is hurt?"

"No, she will wait for you in the Co-op. We have a rod following every cop in his gang. None will be going anywhere near you."

Philip lifted his head, looking distraught for the police's video on the bus. *Goths everywhere.*

⚹ ⚹ ⚹

One artist, Kathy, lived near the Co-op but was not at home. Another lived on the way to the beach, and another up the grade toward Lamancha House. They found artist Barbe on the beach way. She wanted to walk to the beach with them and take her own video. As they stepped onto the sand, three young boys ran from them.

"That's unusual," observed Ice.

"Yes," agreed Barbe.

Philip too thought it strange the boys would be frightened by adults, then noticed one missing an ear. He instructed his new guard pod, Kong One, to follow and video all around the heads and hands of the three running boys, and to copy campus with a flag for security. He noticed a blur in the air as his guard pod flew directly away from him without using a sinuous flight path. When he checked its video on his kom, the missing ear and a missing thumb were confirmed, as well as a missing little finger on the third boy. A lump formed in his stomach. Philip told Ice he would visit the remaining artist, Jane, since he was in good shape and could walk it quickly while she and Barbe packed and caught a shuttle bus. Ice agreed. He reminded her to let Collette know when to expect them. Ice kissed him goodbye.

"Follow me, Kong One."

"Following."

Philip took a connecting road to Lamancha and was soon climbing its increasingly steep grade. To his surprise he began to tire, his legs and buttocks strained, but he found Jane at home as planned. She called Ice and asked if her husband could be picked up after work. Philip waited outside for her to pack enough for a few days. He spoke to Karl about the injured boys.

Joan soon joined the conversation. "Months ago the U.N. complained that we were trying to attract Kitts-Nevis children to live on campus in a boarding school for use as shields to slow any needed police searches of the campus."

"Who maimed the boys?"

"We don't know who; we suspect why. Elite parents on Nevis want a year-round boarding school on Pystead's campus for temporary use as a refuge in dangerous political times or bad weather. Pressure is being put on them to stop the movement. The Oceania Protectorate requires that public schools eliminate the humanities, meaning all stories of kindness, mercy, cruelty, or suffering for a cause. Stories that encourage empathy and reflect human decency are not found in Oceania's schools."

Philip said, "It follows that without a cultural dimension of respect for the individual, many minds may be persuaded to altruistic evil presented as virtue."

"Admiral Telaobade, Provisional Governor of Oceania Protectorate, is already seeding Nevis's government with his lackies. He is surely behind the goons maiming children whose parents have not put them in a religious school. The Protectorate is a repressive entity! Oceania allows no text in English with any word not on its approved list of thirty-three hundred words, nor with any number higher than eighty-nine thousand or having a base other than ten. Home schooling is not allowed. Studying ahead the unassigned lessons is cheating."

"Cosmos!"

"Oceania Protectorate is coming our way, Philip. Isaac at

Lamancha House is a leader in Nevis's campaign for a school on our campus, even though not a parent."

"Okay."

"Karl is staying with Kong One. Stay alert."

As he sat waiting for Jane, veiled from the roadway by shrubs, Philip's unseen guard pod spoke to him, "Three beach video subjects are approaching on the road."

The three boys soon ran past. Philip opened the front door and shouted, "Jane! Jane, I'm running up toward Lamancha House. Leave something for me to carry inside the gate and leave the rest inside your front door. You go as soon as possible."

"I'll be out in five minutes!"

"I must go up the hill right now! And you must leave for campus! Take a Pystead shuttle or any bus to campus."

"I'll leave two small paintings and a rolling suitcase inside the gate for you."

"Fine, I'm off." Philip pulled up his arm. "Kom, set ringer to vibrate." Then to the air, "Kong One, deploy number one rod to stay, follow and report on this woman, Jane, who lives here. Pod, follow me."

His artificial voice in the air replied, "Number one rod with Jane, pod with you."

✻　✻　✻

Philip took to the road at a trot, but soon lost sight of the boys. *What can I do for them?* Tired, he slowed his pace, unable to keep up. *Somebody needs to know what happened. Surely I can use my new resources!* "Kong One, can you lift my weight?"

"Affirmative."

Fine, but how do I hold on to a fleece-covered ball? "Kong One, can you extend a rod halfway out on each side?"

"Affirmative."

"If I hold onto the rods for you to pull me, will it damage anything?"

The next voice from the air was Karl's, "You may use the pod with rods to pull yourself, Philip."

"Good."

"Are you in danger?"

"I'm following injured boys from the beach."

"I'll stay with you. Watch your kom channel, you know." Philip punched up 9 4 6, his special channel.

"You're good to go."

Philip's guard pod presented itself long enough for him to grasp the rods like handles. The assistance proved awkward, but both Philip and the pod learned that he should leap every third step and soon he was taking long flying strides. The boys came in sight, but his arms were tiring. He knew the hotel was around the bend in the road and kept going. The boys went up and sat on the porch, being still and quiet—unlike young boys. Philip slowed his pace to a walk and crossed the porch without glancing at the boys. He left his pod outside to watch and had two rods follow him inside.

Isaac came to the counter at Philip's request. Philip introduced himself and motioned Isaac aside to look at video of the boys. "These three damaged boys are sitting on your porch."

Isaac grimaced upon seeing the first injured hand. "I know the boy."

"Isaac, what happened?"

"We are told by a new candidate for office that all elite children must attend a religious school or suffer consequences."

"Which school?"

"Any religious school will do. There are Anglican, Roman Catholic, Mormon, Confucian, Baha'i, Rastafarian, Baptist, A.M.E., maybe others, except no Jewish."

"The boys ran from me on the beach."

Isaac frowned, "That's further indication the children are being maimed by adults and not bitten by monkeys while hiding in the woods to sneak a drink. We islanders know monkeys will steal a drink, but they don't bite and run. When alarmed, they hold on and rip up your face. An adult monkey is quite strong."

"Why would the boys run to your porch?"

"I know their fathers, except for the boy with the missing thumb, Norman, who's a well-known orphan. The orphanage cannot let him attend a private school by law. Please wait here and let me speak to the boys." Isaac headed outside.

✺ ✺ ✺

Philip stayed, looking around the magnificent lobby. He noticed a woman with long brown hair, and on second glance he saw pink streaks. *Samantha Moody, whom the R.s thought left Nevis.*

As Philip approached, Samantha put a finger to her lips. She looked frightened and certainly not herself. "Sit with me." She looked around before whispering, "Somebody kidnapped my husband off Kitts. His company told me to come to Nevis and pay cash for everything. Nevis is the last place in the Caribbean where cashcards are legal for accommodations. That ends next month. I'm staying here in one of the small rooms. I need to contact The Pystead Group and see if they can help me. Don't say my name."

"Okay. Maybe I can help with the company."

"Is that your company? The Netsite must be down."

"I'll find out what we can do."

Samantha shut her eyes. "Thank you, Philip. Please tell them about Albert Marino, thirty-six years old, from Sunnyvale, California. I have his biometrics ziff."

Before Philip could speak, the boys from the porch ran in. "Help him!" one shouted.

"Help who?"

"The Lamancha man! Two men grabbed him."

Philip directed, "Boys, please sit down right here. Lady, please sit too. Stay seated and watch each other!"

Philip went through the front door but could see neither Isaac nor two suspicious looking men. Not one person remained in a rocking chair. One man pushed past Philip to get inside, and others were leaving the far end of the porch. Philip called, "Kong One?"

"Here."

"Did you see a man abducted off the porch?"

Karl's air voice whispered beside his ear, "I was watching."

"Karl, you must send my pod to protect that man, named Isaac. And there is a woman, Samantha Moody, in the lobby who needs sanctuary because her husband was kidnapped on Kitts."

"One moment."

Joan's air voice soon spoke, "We have two rods staying with you, and your pod is finding Isaac."

"What about the woman, Moody, in the lobby? I met her at Mrs. R.'s Guesthouse. Don't know her, really. She says her husband has been kidnapped off Kitts, and his company advised her to contact Pystead for help."

After a few moments, Joan told Philip to bring her to campus. "When we find Isaac, we will bring him. Philip, where is Ice?"

"She's with Barbe. They should be on a shuttle and picking up Collette."

"I'll check. Stay alert. Karl believes the two men who grabbed… Isaac, are professionals of some type. We are feeding your pod's video to your kom. You can direct your three local rods using the kom."

"Fine."

"Karl is staying with you."

"I hope so, and Joan, artist Jane left a suitcase and two paintings inside her gate and more inside her front door. My rod one is staying with her."

Philip took a seat on the porch to watch his kom's video in private. After a few seconds of trees and shrubs, Isaac came into view held between two big men wearing tan jackets. Philip expected laser shots, but the pod held back as the men threw Isaac to the ground beside an ice-cream peddler's cart. One man stepped on an arm while the other pulled a strap from the cart and cuffed it to Isaac's ankle. Then the video showed two more men to the side of the cart, pistols drawn.

These goons are prepared, but according to my briefing they should be easy pickings for Kong One. "Kom, show rod one video." His kom view switched to Jane standing on a street corner with a suitcase and two paintings. "Kom, show video from Rod Two." Samantha was sitting with the three boys. "All rods, copy video feed to security." *Samantha's probably telling the boys a story.* "Kom, show pod video." The scene of men and cart flashed up. *Why no rescue?* Soon

Isaac stood and the men and cart began moving slowly into the trees. Red text flashed at the top of Philip's screen: **FOO FIGHTER ARRIVING FOR ISAAC AND PHILIP.** In the next moment a flash was seen from the cart and then nothing. Red text flashed on Philip's screen: **POD VIDEO LOST.**

"Karl?"

"That cart has a gun, hit your Kong One. Uses a very compact drone scanner—something new! Your number four rod survived; its video is up."

Philip held his breath. The two men with pistols were yelling at Isaac to stay down or get shot. A gun barrel was poked through an open port on the cart. The two men who had abducted Isaac were not seen. Then ripples of movement appeared in the trees on video. *What?* The scene switched, red laser beams flashed and the two men with drawn pistols jerked and fell without firing a shot. Red beams next hit the gun barrel on the cart and then the strap holding Isaac. A voice from above called, "Isaac, you are free! Run to your right, run!"

Isaac was up and running as the cart swung around, extending a second gun barrel from its other side. It fired and a tree in its line of fire exploded with bullets ripping through, sending bark and splinters flying. Beyond, Isaac was on the ground. Another laser beam hit the cart and it went still and quiet. A foo fighter appeared near Isaac. Within seconds a white-suited guard was out. He lifted the evidently unconscious Isaac into the Egg craft. Before Philip collected his thoughts, a message flashed: **TAKING ISAAC TO HOSPITAL WITH SHATTERED LEG.**

Karl's voice called, "Philip?"

"Here."

"Isaac is in trouble. Major loss of blood and in shock. Another foo is on its way for you, E-T-A about fifteen minutes to avoid new optical trackers. We dropped another pod before we knew the cart had two guns, and it took out your relief pod. Keep the two rods and three boys inside with you and stay put. A local outpost pod is on its way to you, now named Kong, about fifteen seconds out."

⁂ ⁂ ⁂

Philip turned for the front door, but his entire body pulsed and froze. Two big men in tan jackets stood on the porch steps. They turned in his direction. A reflex tensed his body. "Rods? Can you hear me?" No voice came from the air. Philip searched and found a pink light blinking as it moved across his line of sight. The rod's movement steadied to the point that he could make out a blurred form. He said, "Kong One rods, if either of those men near me lays a hand on me or pulls a weapon, ram him in the head at top speed." The pink light blinked like crazy. *Morse code?*

The men were quick, and as Philip headed to jump off the porch, both their heads jerked forward with thuds. They fell with blood in their hair, but one remained active, reaching into his jacket pocket. Philip called to his kom, "Rods, hit the man moving!" Nothing happened: no hit and no pink lights in the air. Philip checked his kom screen and found only one little blue line shown, and on the wrong side of his kom screen. *Not one local rod?*

He gulped as Sifu Kong's quick high voice from long ago Kung Fu lessons sounded in his head, *Go in!* Philip bounded forward as the man pushed up to one knee. *Go in, go in!* Philip stomped on the hand, but the man jerked free and stayed up on his knee. *Go in!* Philip kicked at the man's supporting knee. Nothing happened and time felt suspended before he again thought, *Go in!* Remembering form, Philip drew his foot to knee high before thrusting sideways as he leaned away to brace his own body as his leg straightened. The big man's knee buckled and he toppled over, keeping his good hand in his jacket pocket. *Go in!* Philip shifted to kick the man's arm and then slid forward to hold it. Although hurt, his opponent was too strong. Philip thought to hit the throat, but his attacker spun away with an anguished groan while kicking backward with his good leg. The kick struck without force on Philip's shin but stalled him as the man rolled out of reach and came up with a pistol. Philip threw himself down and forward without thought except to strike the throat. He hit the deck hard on his left side, punching forward with his right arm—into nothing. His mind screwed itself up for the bullet, yet, after a moment he was still alive and smelling something ghastly, something burning.

Philip opened an eye and saw a bloody head—eyes bulging out of bloody sockets. Karl's air voice told him, "Your relief pod blew his brains out. You stalled him long enough for us to get the shot."

"There were two of them!"

"The other's still unconscious. Get inside and brief Moody. We are expediting your ride."

Philip gagged at his next breath. He looked, and sure enough, the man's hair was burned off a charred and bloody patch on the back of his head. *Cosmos, the laser beam boiled his brain until it exploded.*

Philip's left arm moved without strength and he paused, worried. "Karl, where's that gun cart?"

"Literally blown to bits by the foo fighter. Your new pod answers to Kong—has no rods."

"Understood."

"You seem to have a limp."

"Most everywhere is sore."

"It will be worse tomorrow."

"A really good thing to know now?"

"We have pain pills where you're going. Your ride is seven minutes out."

"I'm moving."

"I've got your back. No need to hold the door for your new pod, your number three rod broke a picture window to get out. Your ride will be out back, behind the first row of hedges, or on the roof, or inside the lobby if necessary."

⁂ ⁂ ⁂

Back inside, Philip briefed Samantha on how to be quick for the pickup. Then Joan copied Samantha's kom address and her husband's biometrics file.

Philip asked, "Joan, where is Ice?"

"She's on our bus with a cart of paintings, two suitcases, artist Barbe, and a Siamese cat. That bad cop will get a Russell-rap upside the head if he approaches the bus when it stops for Collette."

"Fine, and Joan, watch for Jane, traveling alone, catching the first bus she can, probably at Pump Road and Craddock. My rod one is watching her. Her husband needs to get to campus after work." Philip sighed. Samantha asked no questions.

From zugzwang to Cosmos knows what? And I believe it. Philip asked the three boys to be patient and stay seated. He asked Samantha to move close and listen carefully. He began by warning her not to act surprised if he said something sounding like fiction, because truth was often stranger than fiction.

She snuggled up to him and took his arm, waving five fingers to a waiter. "Philip, I have recently gotten over life being routine." Before Philip finished his story about the boys and Isaac, the waiter handed each boy a glass of purple punch and produced two flutes of champagne. On a few points, Samantha nodded her head in understanding, being sure to smile. She said she was ready to go, her cards and kom were in her purse. She gave him a kiss. Then she wiped his lips with her fingers, "There's not a speck of lipstick on you, friend Philip."

They sat and sipped Ste Wolls, waiting for their rescue call. Philip noticed that Samantha kept a furtive watch for anyone entering the room. He used his kom to reach Karl and learned that his two local rods had blood on their lens and had risen to altitude on automatic to send distress calls. Karl said he was programming them for black-jack hits, and would try to find water or clothes on a line to clear their video lens covers. The number four rod was unaccounted for.

Samantha tugged at his arm, "More champagne?"

"No, let's stay alert. Be sure to let me know if you spot anyone suspicious."

"If I kiss you again, it will be to whisper something serious."

As Philip finished his champagne, the need to stay alert sent a cool tingle down his spine and his senses heightened. *This dog is alert.* The same reaction in a cat stands its hair on end.

Samantha took her last sip and whispered to Philip, "One of the boys, Norman, is an orphan. He's afraid to go back because they are going to whip him again for drinking in the woods, something he did not do. He says Isaac told him to stay here."

Philip stood up. He knew that Pystead's Pawson Medical Group could probably regrow the boy's thumb. *Isaac wants to keep him.* Philip turned to the boy. "Norman, do you have a brother or sister, or an aunt or uncle, or any family member here on Kitts or Nevis?"

The lad shrank back. "No, mister."

"Do you want to stay with the manager, Isaac Lamancha?"

"Yes, mister, he asked me."

"We are his friends, Norman. You can come with us, because our friends have rescued him, and we are going to see him now." Then Philip remembered his charge to sanitize. He pulled the tube of hand sanitizer off his belt and used it as all watched. "Everybody going must use this on their hands, arms, and face with eyes closed."

"Yes, mister."

"Lady, please take these two boys and leave them behind the desk with instructions to call their parents. Be assertive—be quick—be quiet. Come directly back here and sanitize your hands and face."

Samantha smiled. "Yes, mister." She took each boy by the hand.

Philip spoke to Norman, "Young man, we will leave in a strange car with no wheels. You must do as I say and be quick to come with us."

"Yes, mister."

"Don't run off. I may not have time to find you."

"Yes, mister."

"Okay. Let's sit and wait for our ride and sanitize our hands."

"Yes, mister."

"You're going to like your new home and friends."

The lad half-smiled.

So, now I propose we become bona fide kidnappers? Surely, we will not send the boy back to lose more fingers and be whipped for each loss, never to receive regenerative treatment? Am I doing good, or simply changing the name of the child who suffers? Is it my right to intervene? On behalf of whom? Only this boy? Perhaps even Nevis's judges would rule against us? Should mercy in the moment be so analyzed? Can it be fathomed by less than a divine?

We should have a pod find these terrorists and their political leaders and blow out all their brains! Aaaha—no wonder dark deemers hate Pystead. To them, there is nobody worse than an honest cop, a super-hero, avenging angel, even a missing dissident. Certainly, any subaltern capable of secretly eavesdropping with video and bestowing a fatal rap upside the head of anybody, any deemer included, is intolerable! A new era of over-mighty subjects will not be allowed on land or sea or in orbit—nor on the Moon! Pystead's disruptive technologies that have allowed them to exist in relative security are becoming known, at least suspected.

Philip caught the back of his neck with his hand and wondered if he had thought twice. *Why should Norman belong to going-gothic Nevis more than to Isaac and Pystead? Why? What about that transparency in governance that I associate with liberty and honesty? Pystead is opaque to the outside world, even to would be professional informants, shielded by secret brain-scan technology! I have become part of a new and illegal wave of secrecy!* Philip noticed Samantha watching him closely. *In this real world a secret dog must remain an alert dog, wary of everyone from cupids to cops.* "Lady, I'll explain later, but I must step over to the water cooler and chat with someone."

"Please don't abandon me!"

At the water cooler, Philip asked his unseen guard pod if he could speak with Joan.

Seconds later her familiar voice asked, "Yes, Philip?"

"Commander, we ought to save an abused orphan boy, but it could be called kidnapping by the wrong judge."

"The future is not ours to see, but do not concern yourself with worldly judges. I'll explain later."

"Roger, expect three to fly—sanitized."

"A Pawson Group team will be standing by for the boy." Philip closed his eyes and let a slow relaxation sink from head to toes. He drew a deep breath and turned to observe Samantha and Norman. Joan's voice spoke, "You should energize for half-Halo if you haven't already."

"Energizing now." *How did I forget this? Best hold the helmet and look almost normal. Now stay alert, doggie. In this moment you are as real as you can get, but not as dead as you can get, and not a cat with nine lives. Norman and Samantha need you.*

Samantha, upset, met Philip halfway back from the water cooler. "We heard at the counter that four police drones are arriving from Kitts. The local security guard is instructed to detain a woman with long hair named Moody and any friends. After we had walked away from the counter, the guard, a friend of Isaac's who I know, told me we must not tell the desk staff, but we had to hide. He took off his badge and told me to go to the roof door and wait for him."

"Why?"

"He didn't say."

"How many drones arriving?"

"Four."

"How many outside doors in this place?"

"One each side, four."

Those kidnappers sent a distress signal when we found them. Philip looked around. "We are sitting in line-of-sight of three doors right now."

Samantha told him, "The Tea Room has a door, and the bar area is dimly lit. Takes time to adjust to the dim lighting after you enter from outside."

"We should have access to the stairwell. The roof may be our best chance."

Samantha nodded. "There's an entry to the stairs and elevator for bar patrons only, on the back side of the elevator."

Philip pointed and said softly to the air, "Kong, go to the restaurant room to our right side and scan for weapons. Report to my kom." Soon his kom posted an all clear for the restaurant. Philip stood, "Let's move."

Samantha took Norman's hand and they started for the Tea Room. When almost there, the front door banged open and a male voice bellowed, "Police! Nobody move! Stay where you are!" The three ran and shots rang out. Philip was thrown forward onto the floor. Samantha dropped with him and lost her grip on Norman's hand. The boy hopped onto a high-backed chair. Philip and Samantha crawled beside a couch and then a credenza into the Tea Room. "Everybody, get on the floor on your back—now!" shouted the policeman. "Face up and visible or I'll shoot you on sight." The boy, Norman, trembled and stayed in his chair. The policeman began crossing the room. Shoes clomped on the floor and rugs. People were crying and a child was screaming to be let up.

Watching from the dim floor of the Tea Room, Philip could see no chance for Norman to get to the stairs. "Kong, protect the boy, Norman, in that first highbacked chair from us, in the lobby."

"Aye."

"Return to me here or in the stairwell, maybe at the top. Front entry to stairs in the lobby; rear entry to stairs from the Tea Room's bar area."

"Aye."

The policeman turned toward the elevator and stairs and spotted Norman in the chair, and a few adults on the floor on their backs. He saw blood on the boy's hand and approached. He pointed his body camera. "Identify this boy."

The response was, "Fugitive."

The policeman took a step towards Norman. "Please, mister, don't hurt me, please, please." In the next instant, a shot rang out and Philip flinched. He could not see the policeman's arms and legs go limp as he crumpled onto the floor.

A man sprang up from the floor with pistol in hand that he put in his pocket. He took Norman's hand, pulling him forward. "Up the stairs!" As they entered the stairwell, the side door was flung open and another policeman from Kitts entered the lobby but stopped short seeing the officer on the floor.

The Tea-Room fugitives hurried for the back-stairs entry. Behind the elevator on the stairwell platform, Philip and Samantha ran into the man and Norman. "Kong protect," ordered Philip. But there was no threat and Kong did not fire.

Norman told them, "This man shot the bad one."

"I'm house security. The Kitts police will kill me if they find me. We can hide in the attic using a secret roof entry."

They scrambled up the stairs. At the second floor, Philip opened the stairwell door and left it ajar. He asked, "Karl, how many seconds for Kong to cut the bolt on a metal storm door?"

"Allow twenty seconds."

"Too long," said the guard. They climbed and Philip again turned the stairwell door handle and left the door ajar. Again, at the fourth floor he tried the handle but the door was locked. "The desk has put the stairwell in late-night security mode, locked from this side." They heard heavy thuds behind them. "Kong, stop the men behind us and return."

"Aye."

Then the lights went out. "Cosmos!"

"We can see a point of light at the keyhole—kom lights not needed. It's a special old lock, and I have a key that opens it without alarming at the desk."

"Norman?"

"Yes, mister."

As they turned the next corner around the elevator shaft, shots rang out and Philip pulled the boy along, feeling the slickness of his hand. Philip's heart pulsed. He instructed, "Kong, be quick. Disable them all and return up the stairs. Does your hand hurt, Norman?"

"No, mister."

The security guard unlocked the roof door and looked out. "All clear."

"Wait! Clear until they send up their drones. Let's wait for my flying laser."

Samantha whispered, "My hand hurts."

Philip turned on his kom's flashlight. She wiped blood on her slacks.

"A bad nick," said the guard.

In the next moment, Kong's artificial voice informed them, "Three down, no pursuit."

"Kong, come to the top of stairs, and then check the roof for men and machines. Shoot down any drone that's not ours."

"Roger."

Philip's kom announced in Karl's voice, "Your ride is approaching for the roof. Philip, I put your guard pod in offensive mode. Mr. Lamancha Security, you must leave your pistol to go with us. In your lighting we cannot confirm facial recognition."

"They will learn for sure my gun shot that Kitts policeman."

"Drop your pistol on the roof. A pod's laser will hit it. Kitts should think you fought us and were captured."

"That's better."

"Brian?"

The man answered, "Yes?"

"You have been approved to stay with us, if you don't mind seasteading the rest of your life."

"Well, I'm single and I'll be alive."

"Your friend Isaac is with us."

"Count me in."

"Karl, we need a medic for a gunshot wound to Samantha's hand—a bad nick."

"Will do. To get you all in easily, Philip put the boy between the two front seats. Tell him to expect the bulky white suits."

"Roger."

"Your ride is on deck. Go!"

They ran. A rising police drone turned toward them with a man leaning out of the cabin bubble. Philip and the guard pushed their group behind the foo Egg for cover as bullets bounced off its hull. The guard leaned over and shot repeatedly.

"You hit him," Karl's air voice told them. In that moment Philip spotted a drone rising to their side. A dense red laser beam fired from the foo fighter, exploding the drone in a flash of heat. Philip felt a hot pressure pulse against his eyeballs, but he could still see. Then he was aware of the sharp boom that had come with the fireball. Another drone rose, and a red beam sprang from the foo fighter hitting its control panel. The drone tipped over, rotors tearing at the roof with terrible shrieks and sparks flying, its occupants' mouths wide and screaming. The drone twisted and flipped onto the roof deck. A bloody-faced man began crawling out of its cockpit bubble.

The foo fighter's door opened. Philip helped Norman in. "Crawl over the first man and sit between them. Be quick! Get in, Samantha, to the rear. Brian, gun on roof, then to rear." Philip followed and pulled over the net that served as their seatbelt. His pod flew in and the foo's door slid shut, blocking out the horror on the roof. Acceleration set in.

The cabin voice said, "Keep pressure on the wound."

"I am. It's beginning to throb."

A white-suited arm reached back with little packages. "Put the salve pack on the wound and keep pressure on it. Swallow the two pills."

Philip asked on his kom, "How is Ice?"

Joan's voice answered on the cabin speakers. "Philip, your fiancée arrived safely back on campus and is being entertained by her grandfather. Now you must let me speak with Samantha and Brian."

Philip hardly followed the conversations. He felt his heart racing and took deep breaths to calm down, regretting having first sent his guard pod to stay in the Tea Room. He did hear Joan tell

Samantha that Pystead would find her husband. For the first time, Samantha wiped away tears. Philip noticed that her hand was no longer bleeding. To the security guard, Philip said, "I'm Philip Russell. How do we know your name?"

"Your company keeps close tabs on Lamancha House. They know us all, even the desk staff. Back there I'd be dead or hiding in the attic. Kitts has hated me ever since I threw out a goon looking for Isaac."

"Seems we're also on Kitts's short list."

"Lamancha House has provisioned, bullet-proof hiding spaces known only to Isaac and me. Kitts came in almost without warning this time and caught me by surprise."

"What of the desk staff?"

"They know nothing, but the new man must be spying for Kitts."

17

SOFT SERVE

They flew a low, slow, and circuitous route, arriving on campus with Samantha unimpressed with the egg-shaped craft and distraught over her missing husband. Brian and the boy were impressed and quiet. Joan greeted them wearing a beige medical mask and carrying white masks for the new arrivals. She explained to Norman that adults were wearing a medical facemask to protect from airborne germs, but that since they were wearing masks, he could wait for his. The boy nodded his understanding. Joan handed out packets of sanitizer. She said a friend of hers would take Norman and Brian to see Isaac, and then accompany Norman to a doctor for a look at his thumb. She told the boy he would receive his own medical mask and meet Issac for ice cream. She suggested Brian have ice cream with Isaac. Turning to Samantha, Joan mentioned that Pystead's chief of water services knew Albert, and the company was using all its resources to find him. Samantha put her hands to her face, "Please save him. He's a good person." A nurse with long hair arrived to care for Samantha.

After the two nurses left with their patients and Brian, Philip reminded Joan that he did not know Samantha well. He was pleased to hear that Pystead had been trying to hire her husband. Joan explained, "He's a bio-cavitation specialist for water purification. I believe the attractiveness of our employment offer is improving."

"Do you know where he is?"

"Not yet, but his kidnapping was caught on video. It may take a day or so, but we will find him."

Philip ventured, "Maybe there will be a ransom request?"

"No! After he has told them all he knows about people and technology he is fish food. We must move fast. Fortunately, Admiral Telaobade has focused his attention on the alleged E.T. meeting, giving us a few days' grace. We will not be staying in Kitts-Nevis and we are not at all playing by the rules of the game. We are monitoring officials and specialists, street traffic, police, even residential houses."

"What of Isaac, the man shot in the leg?"

"He's in surgery with no risk of dying, but his leg is shattered, evidently hit obliquely by a twelve-point-seven millimeter bullet— a size illegal to use directly on personnel, although used by all the special forces."

"What did he do to anyone?"

"The police probably came to the hotel looking for Samantha and found Isaac first. He's one of the influential Nevisians resisting the creeping growth of central power in daily life, including pressure on public school curriculums. Once the elite children are out of the public schools, the humanities can be dropped without public awareness. The proponents of change want to provide every child a large-screen kom with applications, forcing many interactive hours of virtual life on them. Later, elite children can be driven back into the public system discrediting and financially wrecking the religious schools. That's the main line of speculation. We may never know because our Federation Council has voted to leave Nevis."

Philip's eyes almost blinked shut. *Does Pystead have a license for floating about? Do we recruits have nothing but persecution awaiting us back in the States? That intuitive presence in my head wants to know if I can belong here enough to be happy as well as physically safe. I must help my small voice of primary process, and soon! How? Can I recognize an opportunity that allows insight? Nothing ventured, nothing gained in one's career, friendship, or love. To evoke signifiers I must be bold.*

Joan led Philip to a sheltered bench and produced a tube of sanitizer. Philip knew the drill and applied it to his hands and arms. When they sat down Joan removed her mask, motioning for him to do the same. "May I have a word with you?" He nodded. "Thursday morning there will be an assembly on our agora. We will serve soft and hard ice cream along with hard information. You must come, and you should bring Ice."

Joan waved her hand around. "This bench is sited and designed to be audio and video screened from the general campus. The assembly tomorrow is to announce a change in plans due to circumstances beyond our control." She spoke quickly, "We are pulling out of Nevis, foregoing the floating city and seasteading, and moving all the way off Earth."

Philip did not blink because he could hardly get his tense eyelids back down. *Mind that normalcy bias.*

Joan took a moment before saying, "Private entities are not

allowed to stage equipment or supplies in orbit or on the Moon. We escape that need because our scientists have made breakthroughs before others. Worldwide, nations have rejected the type research that would lead to what we call aether energy. Mysterious deaths of scientists, refusals to process patent applications, contradictory government funding decisions, plus economic distress have contributed to a dearth of research and product development worldwide." Joan managed a half-smile. "That lack of technical progress has allowed us to forge ahead in a few key technologies. Others have done little more than maintain their capabilities for research, whereas we have been fortunate to make technical progress and have managed to secretly pre-position expendable materials on the Moon. We hope that picking up those materials will allow us cover to place a secret communications satellite at L-five, and a decoy orbiting the Moon, sure to be found."

Philip asked, "Seems that Pystead must have developed technologies faster than others usually do after a scientific breakthrough? Good fortune is often the difference?"

"Yes, and our good fortunes in science and technology often came in mysterious ways."

"How so?"

"Several of our scientists and engineers had dreams leading to seminal ideas."

"Dreams driven by intuition?"

Joan shrugged. "Our ships can easily reach orbit."

"Even in orbit, how can one company hold off the entire world?"

"We can't, but we will prevail in small battles to escape from planet Earth. Nearby and entirely defensible is orbiting with the Earth at a stable Lagrangian point, say L-5."

"Joan, how long could we live in microgravity?"

She nodded. "We can spin the assembled ships, the Wheel, and get by with good gravity at our outer rim with much moving of equipment and crowding of venues and people. We must leave before that rogue Admiral gains control of a nuclear warhead. Once he has one in his rocket launcher we would strike and become hunted criminals."

"Even the Admiral could never bomb Nevis."

"He can attack the campus with his men. If we and our military robots prevail, the attackers will be called a U.N. inspection team. If the attackers prevail, they will be called pirates so the spoils and cruelty need not be accounted for."

"Sounds right to me."

"The Admiral doesn't have the power to defeat our ships at sea, either as fish farm or mobile floating city, unless he uses a nuclear warhead. We are not so advanced that we can assure he will never get a warhead within easy range without ourselves becoming criminals. Once he has a torpedo conveniently nearby all he must do is wait for proper weather conditions, and he has the entire crew conveniently assembled for destruction without deadly fallout to others. He is the most respected voice in favor of granting us an international waters license."

Joan paused while Philip looked around, before again looking her way. "Philip, the Admiral is afraid of our technology, as you once suggested. Fortunately for us, he seems willing to give up his dangerous sideline as a pirate if he can become Governor of Oceania Protectorate and take what he wants with impunity. Already he is developing a list of hundreds of fees that will be due for every so-called minor privilege, from an outdoor light to placing a flowerpot on your porch. Under Oceania rules only citizens can own real estate, and everybody will have to apply for citizenship. New and non-hazard related housing code provisions are already law in Oceania. Homes not brought into compliance within ninety days, even if funds or contractors are not available, will be fined and fines may be increased each week thereafter until in compliance. One can anticipate that anybody not pleasing Admiral Telaobade will quickly lose their home. There is no appeals process."

Joan frowned, looked around and continued. "Telaobade plans to revoke professional and trade licenses not issued by Oceania, and all business licenses not issued by the World Trade Organization. Details on any type of research or product development must be published to Oceania when first envisioned by an individual or a company other than a transnational. Approved private companies will be allowed to use non-compete agreements even for warehouse workers, tying employees to jobs like indentured servants. Luxury items not affordable by ninety-five percent of the population will not be imported, including fruits and spices. Vitamins, herbs, and raw walnuts will become prescription drugs. Large burial stones, and any stone, plaque, or obituary memorializing a life's accomplishments will be abolished, along with funeral processions, except for worthy leaders. All private and non-elected government employees will be paid on a basis of team performance. Without government approval, no person can make a statement about a public official or policy, a public service, politics, science, religion, or about any registered group or person. Even more court proceedings will be sealed and most government actions and policies classified secret, as now done pervasively in your U.S. to hide failed policy, unwanted evidentiary findings, corruption, and political retribution."

"Joan, I experienced the trends in my work and daily life. In the public sphere I read about egregious events drawing no political or public outcry and forgotten without consequences or relief to victims. I knew about outright false prosecutions and theft by judicial taking—ruining individuals and families! I hoped the Caribbean would be an escape."

"Not anymore!" They sat in silence. Joan was first to speak, "We know that Telaobade intends to rule Nevis as an autocrat. That prospect is giving us several more days of routine policing on Kitts while he seeks favorable publicity befriending E.T.s. Of course, to feel secure he will have to have our Halo suits and whatever else he can find. The island's kom transmission towers are being fitted with radar, infrared, and optical trackers. The Admiral is looking for unseen flying objects over Nevis! He surprised us with a compact drone scanner that found your guard pod at Lamancha House. If captured, we would fare no better than the Templars in the fourteenth century." They sat unsettled, reminded of that ancient and first Friday the 13th.

"Yes," Philip agreed, "I would take my chances on the ship, as far from the new-order Jacobins as possible."

Joan's hand went to her chest and she said firmly, "You must not utter one word about Pystead leaving! Our abandoning campus is top secret." Philip nodded slightly. "Philip, are you listening?"

"Yes, Joan. I have learned too soon about leaving campus and cannot mention it to anyone."

"Don't slip up!"

"Right."

Joan's voice softened. "Then you will sail with us?"

"Yes, I have no viable option, and I can't leave Ice or you."

"Don't go for me, Philip."

"I need to belong among friends since I must be alone existentially."

"You belong and will have liberty aboard ship, including choice in your vocation. You will remain healthy because we have exercise, medical, and other ways to work around the loss of Earth's gravity. Trust our ways and trust Ice. Welcome to Plan B. I want you to cross-train as a Line officer if acceptable to you. I believe Ice has mentioned Line versus Staff positions?"

"Yes. I want a job I can do well."

"I believe you have a talent for the Line. I should know!"

"How is that?"

"Oh, Ice hasn't told you?"

"What?"

"Never mind."

"Please tell me, Joan, or I'll lie awake wondering what I'm missing."

Joan straightened herself. "You will hear soon, anyway. The secret is that I'm also the palm reader, Melita Rose. You know, she has the gift. She tells me you are right for the Line."

After a moment to regroup his thoughts, Philip said, "I really want to pursue my cognitive science research."

"Not incompatible. You can be Reserved Line."

"Do you, as Melita, really have the gift?"

Joan smiled. "Melita's intuition is uncanny, occasionally with images appearing on a swirling clay disk being thrown by an unseen potter."

"The sailors think she has the gift."

"Yes, so does the Admiral, although there Melita enjoyed the advantage of considerable surveillance."

"I have assumed for years that successful psychics must use facial recognition to look up backgrounds of their customers in real time."

"Some do, those also working for Kitts. Melita doesn't. I provide her with pod surveillance of the Admiral. Often real-time coverage when he's on a weather deck or on the streets."

"Joan, what happens on Melita's clay disk?"

"The images move outward with the expanding clay, acting out their stories. Melita says that some dream stories are astonishing, yet those for her regulars must have value because she has many repeat clients. Her rates more than double the average, and the merely curious choose a less expensive reader."

"Can Melita see beyond the edge of the clay?"

"For a full story she will see an image slung off the edge of the clay."

"Slung to where?"

"Off and vanish. Some go whole, some in pieces, some stretch. Some flash brightly, some glow, some go dark. Some shriek, some moan, some sigh, some sing, some sleep. All are caught up in a swirling vortex and vanish."

"Ah, this vortex. Swirling in or out?"

"Simply swirling."

"Speaking of vanishing, I hope your brother is coming aboard?"

"He is. Joan threatened to have him kidnaped. He agreed to come peacefully with his two girlfriends, two large diamond rings, and six of his horses in the deal. The girlfriends, twins, and his favorite horse get to live at his place!"

Philip and Joan enjoyed a smile together. *She's beautiful as either Joan or Melita.* "Joan, don't you think a Line officer should be better at facial recognition than I seem to be, such as not recognizing that you look like Melita?"

"As a guard or operative, but you've had only a few glimpses of Melita on video. You could become a good strategic and tactical officer. Learn the ship's systems and your natural discipline coupled with your resourcefulness should serve us well."

Minor prosopagnosia not a disqualifier.

"Let's consider the immediate future, Philip."

"Fine."

"First thing, direct outside communications will not be allowed tomorrow after the assembly begins. You should take care of last business and personal calls. Of course, be most careful not to give away our plans." He nodded. Joan continued, "Samantha Moody will be taken to the ice-cream booth at the rear center of the off-campus area for the morning assembly. Unless I call, please stay rear center and find her. You are the only person she knows."

"Will do."

"Aboard ship, those exposed to off-campus environments, such as you and Ice, and myself as Melita, will have to wear masks outside our quarters for a few weeks or be quarantined in an off-campus neighborhood. The boy and Samantha, whom we cannot rely on to be so careful wearing a mask, will have to remain in a quarantine neighborhood. Once aboard ship, however, you should continue to check on Samantha."

"Fine."

"You will learn the quarantine protocols, and Ice can help you understand the mentoring relationship. If we find Samantha's husband, your efforts should become a nominal kom-call checking." Then Joan asked, "What else must you remember all evening and tomorrow?"

Philip grinned, "Aside from not eating too much ice cream? Not to mention one word about Pystead leaving campus, or my not being available after tomorrow."

"Correct. A matter of life and death."

"I shall think twice before I say anything to anyone. But, Joan, surely anybody speaking at the assembly can be heard well beyond the quad?"

"You really should cross-train for Reserved Line! We need backup talent for the five new crews to be trained."

"Reserved line sounds interesting if compatible with my cognitive-science work."

"Compatible, yes!" Joan smiled. "During the assembly, Philip, our loudspeakers will not be heard outside the quad because we have low volume throughout the quad and sound cancellation speakers covering the perimeter and the ceiling. The sound system is technically sophisticated. The inside speakers are time delayed based on their position for clear, low-volume sound throughout. This makes complete cancellation possible outside. Costs much more than earpieces would have, but our psychologists want a secure presentation with no doubt that everybody is hearing the same thing."

"Pystead has the best security I've ever experienced."

"We wouldn't exist without it. I'll try to see you and Ice later this evening. Remember to make last minute contacts using your new kom."

Philip turned to watch a bird, thinking, *Joan is beautiful.*

She reminded him to visit Brian and Norman as he would be one of their only familiar faces from Nevis.

"Fine."

"Philip, we expect to come up short on crewmembers for Plan B. Once leaving Earth, we will have no safe means of recruiting. If you know of potential crewmembers without chronic medical or psychological conditions, you should inquire about their relocating within the next few days. Experience is not critical if they are willing to cross-train, but don't ask, rely on your judgment. Be sure they stay alert with their koms. Confirm their physical location if you can do so discretely."

"Alright."

"Describe them to Fednet even before making contact if you believe they may be readily persuaded." Joan closed her eyes. "We have ship's design capacity for five thousand people. We would be better off with ten thousand for genetic diversity. Eighteen thousand are recommended for the colonization of Mars with all specialties and human diversity. Therefore, we need crew who can and will cross-train and have good judgement. We vet for a crewmember having considerable personal discipline and perseverance, and for general social compatibility. That Covid-19 pandemic of year twenty-twenty alerted us to the lack of personal discipline found across all classes of society."

Philip nodded.

"Too, we select those who can appreciate and vote present circumstances instead of received dogma and hatreds, and who can perform their work to professional standards. We are not taking the world's problems into spacetime with us!"

Philip glanced at Joan and almost sighed, then he almost smiled.

Joan relaxed. "Is that a quizzical look, Philip Russell?"

"Sorry, Joan. looking beyond the misery."

"At what, may I know?"

"Never mind."

"Please tell me, or I'll lie awake wondering what I've overlooked."

He smiled. "If you must know, I was noticing how beautiful you are."

"As long as you were listening, I'll forgive you for staring."

"Definitely, I listened." *Is she a friend or a Commander in search of a trainee?*

"Philip, there are many variations on living life, intended or not, working or retired, whether single or married. Some prove difficult, some unhappy, some disappointing, some happy, some strange. Aboard ship we must remain open minded, accepting, and not take each other for granted."

"I try to be considerate."

"In our strange new circumstances you should know that women are often promiscuous during ovulation, expecting certain genes for a child."

"The reason for all the single mothers?"

"That, career mobility, lack of mature role models, plus the ease of living alone in a city if you don't mind social services raising your children."

"Sounds reasonable."

"Philip, I suspect that you have led a sheltered life. Perhaps you will need another few conquests before you are ready to settle down?" Joan paused. "No response?"

"You are too strange."

"I live in a strange world."

"I love Ice for so many reasons."

"You'll need only two reasons to kiss me."

Is Joan a potential friend having too much fun, or an analyst testing me—or both? In either case I should be bold, respond in kind and hope for insight. "What would you do if I tried to kiss you?"

"You should find out."

"Surely not." *Wimp. A kiss might separate friend from analyst!*

"Good. This flirting has gone too far on my part—beyond any approved mentoring relationship. I simply must impress upon you that our circumstances will surely result in a strange new culture. Be thoughtful, be tolerant of yourself and of Ice."

"Thanks for the warning."

Joan smiled. "Be solicitous of Ice."

"I am."

"Be charming, flattering. Although you have her heart, now and then try anew to win it. Try seducing her occasionally."

He nodded. *Did I learn anything new in that exchange?*

"Philip, I met our first principal, gold sash and all, when eleven years old and reading palms in my front yard for a coin. From the first reading I fell for him, a case of puppy love. The third day he came around, my mother came out, and I learned that he had met her eight years earlier. They went inside and didn't come out for half an hour. The next day he came by and mother introduced me when I was my second personality— unknown to me at the time. Mother soon took me to Bucharest for a medical checkup with an E-E-G. Thereafter the man, Comte, visited often with his colleague Lois, and they talked to my mother and father in private. For weeks, I was allowed only the pleasantries of hello, thanks for the chocolates, and goodbye. Then Comte and Lois began tutoring me and my brother Frank in English, history, and algebra. They ended their weekly visits but sent tutors for years. When I was fifteen, Mother asked me to help her read the palms of Comte's recruits. I would make a card on each one and say if I thought the person was being honest with Comte. The next year, religious mercenaries killed my father who had never hurt anybody or been active in politics."

Joan stopped her story and looked down. She wiped her eyes and remained silent although she seemed to Philip to be whispering, head still down. "Mother appointed Lois my first-in-line guardian if she would come live with me. Then a cold winter with pneumonia killed my mother who was working too hard on our farm. A social worker came by for three days until Lois moved in to take care of us. Lois got Frank help with our small farm and found me a job as a waitress to foreign scientists in their company dining room. I watched for Comte and found an unhappy superconductor scientist, whom Lois hired for Pystead to work with the first scientist that Comte had recruited in twenty-ought-two. The next year I turned nineteen and in February of the next year, Frank turned twenty-two. We both went with Lois to live on Nevis."

"But only you began working with Comte?"

"Yes. Comte felt that he and I were on the same wavelength, fortuitously entangled when working together! He sent Frank to Connecticut with his twin girlfriends and six horses from Romania. Pystead bought Frank part ownership in a ranch and soon had him in veterinary school and in training as a farrier. I would have moved to Frank's ranch, but for the stories he told about his neighborhood. One toddler was bussed by law to day-care at twenty months old, there ignored by the adults except to scold or change a diaper. A model student and pleasant eighth grade boy was forced into some Rocker Rehabilitation program on the advice of his teachers, while children who set fires in the toilets and shoved teachers remained in academic classes. The boy was required to provide three hundred hours of community service before he could graduate high school."

Joan shook her head. "Also, Melita learned that Connecticut had criminal laws against disparaging comments made against dozens of protected groups, and college students had been arrested for using contemptuous language even when overheard talking privately on campus. That and not being allowed to raise and protect my own child was something I vowed to avoid.

"The Pystead campus was then a small but complete community, and Comte easily recruited me as Melita. He told me that long ago Mother had made him promise not to mention the dissociative or dual aspects of my personality—to avoid iatrogenic stimulation. Mother had promised him not to allow me to be hypnotized unless I began to have symptoms such as self-abuse, identity disturbances, or out of body experiences."

"Cosmos!"

"The duo of Comte and Mother put psychosis and a few known anomalous examples together and anticipated my dual nature when multiple personality disorder was controversial."

"Yes, that was before dissociation was confirmed by functional brain imaging."

Joan smiled. "I have little cross-over awareness yet maintain continuity of time. I hear no internal voices, I'm not manic-depressive, have no phobias, and no substance abuse—I'm lucky." She wiped her eyes.

"And I' m lucky, Joan, to hear your story."

"Comte asked me to choose a first name for my alter, and he sent me as Joan Windsor to college studying the liberal arts, psychology, linear systems analysis, basic physics, chemistry, electrical circuits, and the eternal golden braid, grooming me as the analytic and managerial alter." Joan raised her hand. "By the way, Philip, I am watched closely. As Joan, for example, I may not recognize somebody I met as Melita. According to prevailing theory, I would be easy to hypnotize. If audio-video in my tent shows a customer with shiny jewelry or an affected speech pattern, I'm warned. I cut the reading short, and I'm scanned in the tent for any trace of hypnotic suggestion."

"Are you scanned as both Melita and Joan?"

"Well, yes...you might be interested to know that each personality has minor traits that differ. Our core instincts, diets, and passions, however, are the same. We both adore you!"

"I'm fortunate to have you as a friend."

"As a friend, you should watch us closely for signs of impairment such as the wrong alter being conscious for circumstances."

"I'll do my best."

"Please be vigilant even in social circumstances. Watch especially for a male seducer with Melita, and for any possible hypnotist. Anybody who snaps their fingers at me or anybody else, for example, alert security. I feel sure you will be able to hold my attention. Say that you need to keep me close at hand for a few minutes and talk about our future and strange new variations on life."

Philip nodded. *O Cosmos, state secrets, mermaids, duals, psychics. Well, we ought to be sui juris.*

For a long moment, they sat in silence. "Truly, Philip, life in our future may seem strange as we confront new realities, relative crowding, perhaps boredom, all in a ship so much smaller than this tiny island. I trust most will adapt to the adventure."

"I've adapted quite a lot already."

Joan pursed her lips. "I would have let you kiss me, hands off."

"So, kiss me at our wedding reception; thereafter my potential variations on life should prove less numerous."

"I'll have to kiss you once for me and once for Melita."

"You'll have to let your hair down for Melita."

"Actually, I'll have to put my hair up for Joan." She smiled. "In your chosen variation of life, you'll receive one passionate kiss from me, and social kisses from me and Melita."

"That variation could be a tiny bit disappointing." *A sufficient test in boldness?*

"We will all want to create happy, future variations."

I'll call this a draw. And you my primary process get cracking and figure out what's what.

"Remember, Philip, one day we will both live in the same strange world."

"Strangeness, Joan, will be highly subjective."

"Yes, and I am, fortunately, deliriously happy with my divine and introverted Prince."

"He sets the bar quite high. I hope Ice doesn't expect so much of a sheltered mortal."

"I'm told that Ice confided in Melita that you are divine." Joan leaned forward. "Soon, Philip, you may kiss me as a close friend, divinely. You may not, however, kiss Melita Rose on the lips."

He sighed loudly. "I live in a strange cosmos."

"I'm sure all will have many variations to sort through in a developing culture."

"My imagination fails me."

"Wait and see, divine Philip, wait and see." She winked, "All will be revealed in its time."

Does Joan know about mermaid Amanda? Do the other two mermaids in Ice's painting have names or models? Could Joan be the second mermaid? She has broached intimate topics. I'll ask once I know her better. "Joan, I have the impression that I'm chatting with an analyst."

"Not so! You are chatting with a friend and mentor. Wait and see."

"If I could have kissed you a moment ago, I want to kiss you now. I'd like a variation on life with two passionate kisses instead of one." Philip slid over and took her hand.

"Hands on my waist only." She leaned forward and he kissed her lips, catching her waist. She leaned forward for a second kiss, and his hands slipped up against her breasts. She caressed his neck with one hand and kissed him again before leaning back.

Philip sighed. "Joan, I hope we are close friends."

"I wouldn't have kissed you hands-on without wanting to be close friends."

"May I relate to you independently of Ice?"

"You may, and I may."

"I will cherish your friendship."

"You are fondly in my heart, Philip, regardless of career choice. Do not cross-train line for me! Promise?"

He nodded. "Much as I enjoy your company, I find it strange that you can afford time for me at this moment, given the mention of nuclear warheads and a Plan B."

"My deputies are completely capable and need experiences not led by me. Your intuition for the line is good. New tactical options are being studied. I will review them. And I must wait and see you marry before we kiss again."

"As friends, divinely, in a happy variation on life."

Joan whispered slowly, "Hair up…hands off…eyes closed, excepting one more passionate kiss."

"Divine."

"Bear in mind that hands-off lasts a very long time."

Naturally he nodded, as the quiet voice in his head whispered, *I can belong with Pystead.*

✳ ✳ ✳

Joan stood up. "If orbiting is not desirable because our ship is too small to spin for good gravity at all decks, and too small to forever fight off nearby Earthlings, where shall we go?"

"We have been led to expect seasteading with an occasional relocation by flight to avoid immediate danger. But to escape a determined U.N. we'd need to be on Mars."

"Yes, at least."

"Joan! Mars?"

"For certain! In the year twenty-nineteen our final phase of design began, and we made the final conversions of our farming and living pontoons into spaceships. We call each ship a key. An outer hull, engines, computers, and the many other ship's systems were added. We also began four completely new ships that the world thought of as more pontoons. Our Key Logos *was* designed and built with our crewmembers working among all specialties, beginning construction in twenty-thirty-four and completing in twenty-forty-five. Our technology can easily take us to Mars and sustain us there."

After long moments, Philip found only Vanderhought's refrain, "I can believe it."

"Each of our nine ships has been to the Moon, and two joined together took a slow, fourteen-month trip to Mars and back, confirming recycling and atmospheric quality control in a closed system." Joan smiled. "Also confirming successful procreation with three healthy babies conceived and born in space."

"Your daughter?"

"No. Cici was sixteen years old. Prince and I stayed here with her. We will all go live on Mars and decide on another planet for permanent colonization before the U.N. can build a fleet to attack us on Mars. We have the necessary technology and resources." Philip nodded. "Not a hint to anybody! You are the first new crewmember to know. Our true plans must not leak and incite a U.N. attack."

"Understood."

"Your guard pod is helping you."

"Fine."

"Hear Plan B. You will learn that Pystead has carefully prepared for living in space, including gravity." She smiled and waved her hand for him to go.

Philip walked slowly with thoughts of strangeness playing in his head. *Joan is strange enough in the present, secretively being two people. And not a hint from Ice about her dual personality. Nor a hint from Ice about her own secret Blue role, aside from that one slip about being able to know anything as soon as it happens.* As Philip neared their room, he shook his head. *Commander George had to wait for Joan to release information not ready for the network, yet Commander Ice simply releases her own need-to-know information. Ice has special access! Does Joan even know? What would be Ice's need to know?*

Secrets again inside my apartment? He sighed. *I thought this a kindly niche for myself and children, but have I thought twice?* Mars seemed a moot worry.

⁂ ⁂ ⁂

Wednesday morning Philip woke to Ice's voice talking to Char Cat. She came over and sat on the bed. "I was worried yesterday when I couldn't find Joan for status on your return from Nevis."

"I thought you could know anything as soon as it happened?"

She frowned. He said, "Surely you could find trip results on your Blue channel?" Ice did not respond.

Seems Commander Joan can be untraceable when she wants? "Well?"

"Oh Phil, you are not supposed to know. We can't talk about it, and you can't mention Blue to anybody." He pulled away from her and snapped, "I'm supposed to live with secrets in my own quarters?"

"You know."

"But I don't know what's what. And I wouldn't know if you hadn't slipped."

"I slipped because I love you. I haven't said I misspoke because I love you and trust you. It's a strain for me to hide even a small part of my life. I would like for you to know everything now, but I don't make all the rules."

"I thought I was marrying an artist, not a spy."

"I'm not spying on you or anyone. I report on dubious happenings, generally not on individuals. I am a Commander as well as an artist. I told you my rank after you proposed."

"George Snyder is a Commander, but he couldn't access unprocessed information to confirm what he already knew. Joan had to release it."

"She's Security Branch Commander."

"Yet you, as Commandant of Fine Arts accessed her unprocessed information. Your access is special and secretive! Does Joan even know?"

"Phil, many people here and in the U.S. have confidential information and secrets they don't share even within their families. Don't you trust me?"

"I trust you. The trouble is from within, living with the unknown. How could I bring a child into an existence perhaps dangerous, and frustrating for me personally, perhaps…not enduring?"

"Oh, Phil, I love you so much. I really can't yet talk about Cobalt Blue in more detail. I have put you on the vetting list to know."

"When might my case be decided?"

"After a month or so aboard if you will agree to unannounced scans."

"Of course I agree! And what's the longest my case might take?"

"Nothing I do should affect our relationship, nothing. Please trust me."

"I do, but I feel our future might be unsuitable for raising children. Thinking about it, my head spins, swirls, spirals! I can spiral in and be caught at an immobile, ringing hollow. I can spiral out and never slow, or perhaps slow and stop. It doesn't matter in a cosmic gap whose only virtue is being lost to harm's eye."

"Don't leave me, Phil, I need you so much!" *The lineage of Saint Germaine needs you!*

"You didn't tell me the worst case to know about Blue!"

"Oh Phil."

"I need to know!"

"The very worst case is twenty years."

Philip stood without moving or breathing. "Say something, Phil."

"I don't know what—thoughts are fragments."

"I have never lied to you about anything. There is nothing extraordinary to fear."

"The heart is irrational."

The couple spent a strained day and night with few words.

❊　❊　❊

The next morning, Ice served blueberries and milk for breakfast. They ate in silence until Philip stood and announced, "We must attend the assembly and hear Plan B." Ice wiped her eyes and reached for his arm, but he stepped to the door. "And the Manager needs to admit a few of his own secrets if he expects people to trust him. Let's go early rather than sitting around here." Ice said she needed to find her artist friends who were finishing medical checkups and Level Two scans. Philip said he'd go on and be rear center.

Philip arrived at the Main Quad and like others was intercepted by guards and told to wear his mask unless eating, and not to talk while eating. Dependents and children were being given masks and assistance. He was directed to a gate for off-campus personnel. Philip noticed an unpainted statue of Poseidon, and sure enough, spotted a Poseidon with a trident at each of the four entrances to the quad. The crowding increased as everybody funneled into one of five lines leading to ten security-scan tubes. Upon exiting a tube, Philip was handed a small packet of sanitizer and observed while he wiped hands, neck, and face.

Finally at large, he counted thirty-one ice-cream stations, each visually spoiled by the server's beige facemasks. *Joan talked to me without a mask. Ice and I have not been compromised. We hardly got out in public, especially where we could have been anticipated, or in a crowd. The guard pods have watched our backs. The sanitizer Ice introduced days ago, and I've had recent blood and urine tests with my security scans.*

As Philip looked around, the urgency of contact with friends struck him. *Must not reveal that this may be my last day to call.* He found a loudspeaker box on the lawn and placed his new kom on top of it while he held his ice-cream cone. He felt a slight coolness and looked around, satisfied to find eight, two-man high, slow-turning fans at the perimeter circulating air around the quad.

Philip reached Stuart by kom and asked him to please listen carefully. A groggy Stuart asked if Philip realized he was in a much earlier time zone. Philip explained the possibility of joining The Pystead Group. Stuart was interested, saying for a decent job in a decent neighborhood they would move to Mars.

"Stuart, I'm almost certain we don't have facilities there."

"Then Nevis will do fine. Also, I have a chemist cousin, female, who would like to relocate."

"Both of you keep koms at hand—literally."

"You sound serious. For my cousin, too?"

"Very high chances. Pystead teaches elementary school through master's degrees and offers doctorates for their fellows."

"Irene and I can teach subjects through ninth grade, including algebra."

"Do you have a lawyer to handle close-up details?"

"One of my second cousins."

"Brief him today. This very day! I'll contact you again as soon as I have details. Send me your chemist cousin's kom and house addresses and a photograph of her face. Be sure to use my new kom address!"

"Philip, where are you?"

"Same place, Nevis. You must call both your cousins immediately. Stay with your koms twenty-four-seven. Time is of the essence for this selection process! Goodbye for the moment."

"We'll be waiting to hear."

Success, he took me seriously. And why have I not thought about my own cousin? Will she remember me fondly? Maybe she thinks of me as the younger cousin who disappeared without caring if she needed any help or family? I lost family ties after leaving for college. She wanted to be a dermatologist. Philip searched for his cousin, Lauren, and after paying a fee found her as a nurse and medical student. Taking his own advice to call immediately, he succeeded in reaching her. She remembered him, and after their conversation he relaxed because she had accepted him without reprimand. She was interested in a career that could escape the protocols of Six Sigma, which Philip could not find mentioned by Pystead's Fednet.

Now for Rhonda, possibly difficult to locate. Then I'll surely find Dennis or Sandra. Best hurry, only a few minutes before hearing Plan B. And where is Samantha? So, for a few minutes Philip became a dedicated kommer, his mind on prospective crew and a few good-byes disguised as hello from Nevis.

He did not think about his guard pod spiraling above, unseen but seeing, relaying his kom's transmissions. Pystead's secret server resources were dedicated to that greatest probability of adding to their crew. Time was of the essence. The difference between Philip and the typical new hire was the extent of his briefing and the high priority status given to transmitting his messages. After all, equal treatment of unequals is an unequal thing, and perilous when survival is at stake. Because of that stark reality, there were those, including Dr. Orlando Osgood, who were not briefed and who were experiencing the usual frustrations of censorship and slow traffic on the public Net.

Still, Philip wondered if sanitizer and medical facemasks at a lawn assembly were signifiers of something amiss. He wondered if he should be entangling family and friends with dreams of entelechy. In the final moment, however, he regretted not offering the chance to escape to his lawyer and the R.s.

ICE-CREAM ASSEMBLY

His komming done, Philip actively looked for Samantha. The grass smelled freshly cut on the large lawn between the buildings: Business, Administration, Facilities, and the Central Activity Building with its large cafeteria and gymnasium. While enjoying a vanilla-chocolate -twist cone, Philip studied the tall poles supporting the sky-blue tent top covering the quad. *Prepared for the rain.* Deciding that the fourteen large poles were sufficient support for the top cover, he returned attention to the ground where he contemplated the seats and the platform outside the business offices facade, mostly located in his off-campus section. The platform provided a speaker's lectern in front of five tiered rows of empty stadium seating. All around, loudspeakers could be spotted on the tent poles or as freestanding units on the grass. He took note of the many serval statues near the front platform.

Masked children by the score were sitting on or hanging off the large faux marble cats. Most of their masks worn properly. In a receiving line on each side of the platform stood several Pystead officers in their white jumpsuits and beige medical masks. Philip took time to go through his area's line and meet the General Manager, Robbie Markwaters, whom he found personable. Neither Lois Henssen nor Joan Windsor was in either line. Returning to rear center he watched for Samantha. Ice called, she was walking over with her friends.

Philip spotted Samantha in a red-striped blouse. She was not alone, talking with an older Indian woman wearing a pink sari. Both wore a white medical mask and looked ominous, as did the entire masked crowd. Samantha recognized Philip and waved as he approached.

"I hope you're feeling optimistic, Samantha."

"My mood swings wildly."

"I wish I could help."

"You are the person who helps most."

"That's what friends are for."

"Philip, this is Rathy Salcmann, a crewmember. Your friend Lois introduced us."

Rathy said, "I've heard about you because my husband is a colleague of Ice's."

"Harinil, the curator of modern art?"

"Yes, the elusive Harinil."

"Ice showed me the modern galleries on screen. His paintings of women were good, I thought."

Rathy rolled her eyes. "Men like naked women, even the abstract ones. Why don't we have some ice cream?" She added, "No talking with our masks up."

Did Lois send Rathy to keep tabs on Samantha? We're certainly controlling the germs and genes going to Mars with us. Must be mum—top secret.

Philip and both women went for ice cream and asked for a soft-swirl cone. Not ice cream, but a custard, Rathy told Philip. When they pulled masks down to eat, Samantha surprised Philip with a kiss. He replaced his mask for a moment to tell her that his fiancée, Ice, the woman they had seen at Lamancha House, would be arriving soon with her artist friends. "I want you to meet her."

Rathy pulled up her mask and Samantha did the same. "I want to meet her." Samantha leaned over and whispered in Philip's ear, "Of course, meeting her now could preclude our getting to know each other more intimately."

"We will get to know each other, Samantha. Let's be friends who enjoy each other's company and talk about anything in the whole fantastic and strange cosmos."

Samantha nodded. "I hope so, special friend Philip."

"What a wonderful relationship you should have," Rathy said. "On this little island good friends are so scarce." They finished their custards and adjusted their masks for chatting, with Philip telling Samantha she could have confidence in Pystead's technology. His kom sounded. Ice had him in sight.

Philip received a masked kiss from Ice. She greeted Rathy, and soon all were introduced. Philip said, "Ice, did I tell you that I met Samantha at Mrs. R.'s Guesthouse. She has no friends on Nevis."

Ice was welcoming, "Samantha, stay with us for the meeting."

"Thank you. Now that my husband has been kidnapped, Philip is the only person here I have known for more than a day." Ice instinctively put her hand on Samantha's shoulder.

Philip asked Ice if she wanted an ice cream. She wanted a scoop of strawberry in a cup. "I'll be right back." Rathy was leaving with Harinil when Philip returned with the cup of ice cream for Ice. They found seats.

⁂ ⁂ ⁂

A crisp sounding bell rang three times. The recruits knew the Manager was about to speak. He was not wearing a mask and began loudly, "I am here to deliver a far more serious message at an earlier date than we had anticipated. Although surprised by the timing of events, we are still prepared for circumstances." The Manager paused to take a slow look around. "Please give me your utmost attention for the next few minutes on a matter of being or not being for this company—a matter of life and death for many of our present crew, no hyperbole involved." He paused. The crowd was quiet enough to hear his sip of water. "I will make the case as I see it, and each of you will have to decide by the day after tomorrow. That is not adequate time for a decision of the magnitude I must propose, but that is all the time we have."

The Manager took an obviously slow and deep breath. "If at first you want to disagree, please be patient as I hope to get around to saying something that rings true. Please bear in mind that when time is the problem, we are all vulnerable. Keep in mind that we do not yet know you much better than you know us. Like astronauts, we will have to make personal relations a priority in our immediate lives and get along even when interpersonal chemistry is less than desirable. There are worse fates!"

He almost smiled. "As some of you already know, seventy percent of you recruits were pointed out to the company by a present member of our crew. That type of personal networking built our organization and was so outmoded as to be forgotten—the reason we evaded political notice for years, decades—until about two years ago. If you have not yet met your sponsor, that person will try to meet you later this evening. We want each of you with a sponsor to have assurances that our company is capable, trustworthy, and considerate of the individual."

Markwaters rang his bell. "Ready now?" He began distinctly and slowly, "We have evidence from the news, from our own secret surveillance, from the actions of the United Nations and its officials, and from the movement of military materials and troops, that this campus will soon be attacked by armed forces. Whether they be marines or pirates is of no matter because they intend to take the campus by force. Many seek the destruction of this company for political reasons. If history be any indication, crewmembers found here will not be treated well. That is my belief."

Philip looked around. *Good thing I'm not still enthralled by the normalcy bias. Neither is Samantha. Ice is okay.* Views of the floating fish farm were projected on the walls of two buildings. *Impressive, but should I be going? What's to happen with ninety days of planned training ending after fourteen days? What established crew preparing to sail the seas and the cosmos wants just anybody who can fog a mirror?* The professor sat among those he wanted to love and protect yet knew not what to think. So, he sat and listened to the Manager, eyes often closed, while his fiancée sat shifting nervously in her seat.

The Manager proposed to offer confidential information and the tour of a ship as evidence that Pystead's capability was commensurate with its goals. Each recruit could use their kom to list names or descriptions and facts about people they wanted to tour the ship on their behalf and experience the proof of capability that would be demonstrated before ending the assembly by early night. The Manager's instructions were simple, the computer powerful, and within fifteen minutes one hundred and five persons, Philip included, were asked to tour the ships at sea and bear witness to the assembly.

The Manager assured everyone that computer-driven sound cancellation speakers around the perimeter were keeping everything said within the quad from being heard outside. The tent top and its sides held a conductive mesh that prevented direct signal transmission in or out of the quad. Kom transmissions were being screened and relayed by Pystead's servers. To maintain security, all witnesses and anyone remaining in the quad to hear the presentation would have to remain for two nights on campus.

As proof that their ship had flown, each witness needed a drop item that would not be returned. The items would be dropped at some identifiable location where the media could show and report on them. Samantha gave Philip a wide-eyed look.

"Sounds all right to me."

The Manager's tone became somber, "Our flight will draw attention because many nations have radar and telescopes trained on the skies to catch a glimpse of E.T.s. The U.N.'s Oceania Protectorate will be furious and will say we must be stopped. Thus, before midnight we will hear your witnesses' testimony. You will have two nights and two days to remain on campus, ask questions, and consider your options. By Saturday evening we will have completed boarding our ships at sea. All doors and gates on campus will be unlocked and open for all to leave.

"Anybody who thinks they may want to sail with us must— must—stay on campus. Already, several ferryboats are parked at

Kitts, loading hundreds of people to come here and protest our unjust treatment of the islands and our harboring of pirates! Can you believe it? We have inside sources telling us that they will block entry to the campus and beat anybody wanting to enter.

"If you have family or pets and did not bring them to campus as advised, then make contact and get them here immediately using the shuttle buses. The buses will run every quarter hour until the ferryboats arrive. If you need assistance, contact Administration. The campus gates will surely be blocked by this evening.

"For all other unfinished business, use your koms and attend to final banking and legal matters. Then confirm your wills; I strongly advise a signed and notarized amendment to your lawyer and beneficiaries with instructions for immediate execution as a prophylactic measure. We have proposed texts and links to notaries in all your states of residence. You must sign and deliver your amendment via your registered kom to have a legally binding document. We will add your GPS location after clearing your message. I advise confirming to your attorney and each beneficiary that you made a will before leaving home, and that it should be executed if not revoked by you within, say, a week. This is important because the U.N. or your state could refuse to confirm your death, and after a two-year absence legally seize your entire estate."

After a long pause filled with the muffled tones of conversation in many languages, the Manager continued, "Aboard ship, you will not need kicus nor gold."

So many without insider friends or experiences, no soft served warning, nowhere decent to go and children to care for. Many are crying. So much for rational thought, this decision is a call by primary process!

"We have enough floor pads for everybody to sleep on campus.

During the witnesses' tour of a ship and their flight, we will intro-duce our new operating plan, Plan B. Those of you who remain in the yard will have video of the witnesses' tour shown on the sides of two buildings and by our inhouse network Fednet." He raised his voice, "Now you must call for off-campus people and pets, and call Administration for any needed assistance."

Philip turned to Ice, "Have you experienced everything I would get to see?"

"Yes, and more."

"Then I don't need to go."

Ice took his hand. "You had forty-two votes, the most of any-body, next was thirty-seven. Pystead needs you for those people and their friends—your future friends. We need every qualified person."

The Manager waited patiently before announcing, "We have one hundred and three acceptances. This list of names with back-grounds is available to every registered kom address checked in for this meeting."

The Manager waved his hand, waiting for talking to subside. "We need a unique article of clothing, accessory, or jewelry for each participant to take and drop off to establish a record of the flight in our private, non-commercial craft. Anything that is easily identifiable from a photograph, and that is relatively unique and difficult or impossible to buy off the shelf is ideal. Strong colors and bold patterns show up best, as will, of course, larger articles. Knee-length ponchos are available at each food station for main-taining personal modesty. Remember, the donated article will not be returned. For your estate's protection, remove any name or iden-tifying address from the article. We have scissors at the ice cream stations and up front for removing labels before departing."

The Manager paused, looking around. "This demonstration will confirm our ability to transport personnel and equipment as needed and quickly. Our craft fly very well and are far safer than current aircraft of any type, excepting the low and slow helium filled airships in good weather. We will drop your articles at a place where we believe the media will video and report on them, and where anybody will have difficulty tampering with them.

"We will then demonstrate orbital flight. Yes, the kind of flight that reaches into space above the earth. We hope the ease with which we perform this trip will provide sufficient proof of our technological capability to allow you to make the decision to join us as permanent crew. More on that later.

"For now, each of you who is to participate as a witness, please raise your hand." Hands went up. "Would those of you in the presence of each witness please furnish a suitable article for the drop marker. Please be quick! Remember, wiitnesses, you must stay two nights on campus even if not sailing with us."

✳   ✳   ✳

A woman standing beside Samantha called to the local crowd, "Here, here, this must be a designer blouse, this pink and red striped." She waved her arms high and shouted, "Poncho here! Poncho here!" A poncho arrived via overhead hand conveyance.

"It must be unique," Ice agreed. Samantha pulled the poncho over her head and took off her blouse. Ice raised her mask and kissed Philip farewell, tears in her eyes. "Think about me, the woman who loves you so very much."

Samantha handed her blouse to Philip as the Manager called, "We have some drop items up front. Travelers, witnesses, move

316

quickly to the front platform in your area for video. Crowd, please give way!"

Philip joined the trek of witnesses to the front. The Manager announced, "For those who remain, we will present video of the trip, and you may come and go during the day. The video begins soon with train and ferryboat rides to a ship. When the witnesses return tonight they can speak. Tomorrow, Friday, beginning in the morning, we will hear the details of Plan B. You will have to decide, probably by noon Saturday. After the last ferryboat departs Saturday evening, this campus will be abandoned with all doors and gates unlocked."

The Manager's voice changed to one of urgency, "If you know now that you are not going as crew, my advice is to leave campus now." Again he rang his bell. "Please everybody, during the day watch an hour or more of the live trip. By one-thirty this afternoon our seasteading ships should be in view. You will see the ships and equipment and observe our talented crew in action. Here in the quad, sandwiches, coleslaw, fruit, crisps, cookies, ice cream, and sweets will be served all day, and the cafeteria is serving hot meals."

Again, the Manager rang his bell. "When your witnesses return before eleven o'clock tonight, you really should be present to hear them! It's your decision, your life—take it seriously!"

Manager Markwaters stepped back as an intruder stepped through the doorway to the tent and stopped. He was holding a megaphone, and boomed, "Attention, everybody! Give me your attention!" The crowd became almost quiet, and the currents of movement slowed except for the trickle of volunteers to the front. "I represent the K.L.J.H. Organism, a group of U.N. approved persons constituting a fully qualified engineering department. Although we have not yet been hired, we are living on campus. It is my duty to make each of you aware that this Pystead Group does not take the precautions known necessary to achieve a high degree of reliability in engineering or in hospital services." The shouter lowered his megaphone momentarily, as if consulting his kom, then raised a hand and shouted, "This Pystead Group does not have a Six Sigma quality management program in any venue! Six Sigma, however, is mandatory in China, the United States, Mexico, Argentina, Brazil, South Korea, many others, and will be mandatory here when Oceania assumes oversight of the Kitts-Nevis Federation. The U.N. will have a responsibility to protect you from foreign and domestic threats, which will include protection from the malfeasance endemic in this organization. Each of you should be wary of utilizing facilities or hospital services until such safety regulations can be implemented and verified. The more one hears, the more one fears, that the Manager here trusted so well, has only one notion for sailing the ocean, and that is to tingle his bell."

No attribution when he knows few will recognize the paraphrase.

The Organism's speaker shouted with renewed fervor, "Do not forget that each of you has the duty as a citizen of the world to report non-conforming practices and suspicious activity directly to local U.N. approved officials. You must help the U.N. help us all maintain a world without gaps. There are rewards for reporting and penalties for withholding."

In Oceania everybody becomes either an unpaid spy or a criminal for withholding, or a liar for profit. The U.N. must already pay for reporting in Middle Georgia! The entire Wheaton police force was abusive, and the officers had to know their artificially intelligent police system was either wrong or corrupt.

The intruder lowered his megaphone and stepped back outside the enclosure past the clear plastic curtain separating the side walkway from the assembly. *Not allowing his group breathing rights with us. After all, an easy way to stop us would be with germs.*

The flow of witnesses came to a halt at the front platform. Philip wondered why such a grand quality assurance program had not averted the trainwreck that killed his parents, nor found any reason for the accident. *Six Sigma must be more public policy not worthy of public discourse, yet mandatory! Why aren't these wonderful regulations posted in a Cloud so all might benefit via common-source wisdom? Private positions must post a detailed job description matrix. Professors must post almost verbatim their lectures. Yet governments post nothing but prohibitions!* Philip looked back for Ice. *Can't see anybody I know!*

The Manager spoke, "Yes, I have a bell. To those to whom our culture has appealed, ask not for whom the bell tingles, it tingles for you! If you want to know where we are going, why, and how, you must hear Plan B. You should see and hear the live reports of your witnesses tonight! Once settled for the night, you can use your kom to clarify points and ask questions." He rang his bell. "If you leave campus today you will not be admitted thereafter unless you are a registered hardship case, and then you will have to get back before early evening, before the paid protesters and goons arrive from Kitts."

Philip heard a current of murmurs in a foreign language from the front row seats. *People revert to their native language in a crisis. Our off-campus group is large compared to the on-campus group. Sure, I live on campus, but with off-campus exposure. The Brazilians I know live on campus, but their talking to me has exposed them to the outside environment.*

From their rear center location, Ice and Samantha lost sight of Philip. Ice offered to show Samantha to her overnight building, then remembered that she had no friends. "On second thought, you should keep me company."

Samantha put her hands to her face. "Your lady, Joan, told me she is looking for my husband and wants to hire him."

"That's good news. She will find him. Stay with me a while longer. Do you recall the name of your building for tonight?"

"It's the East Activity Building. My suitcase is already there, a small one. I've had to travel light since Albert went missing. His company thinks his abductors would like to get me too and erase a troubling long-term memory of Albert."

"Oh no! I'd invite you to stay with us, but we have only one tiny room, and you must remain positioned to hear instructions and board the ship. Let's get your suitcase and you can come back with me for a hot shower and change out of that stylish gray poncho."

The two women were in sight of the VCQ when Samantha said, "You are kind to help me. You are Philip's fiancée?"

Ice's thoughts froze. "Oh my, were you and Philip lovers?"

Samantha hesitated. "No, never, but I wanted to seduce him before I met you. I warned him that our meeting would interfere with getting to know him intimately." Ice opened her mouth, but no words came. Samantha rushed to say, "Philip said we would get to know each other well. He means a platonic friendship. I cherish his friendship, please don't drive him away from me. With my husband gone, he is my best friend on all of Kitts-Nevis."

Ice nodded. "Agreed. He is your platonic friend and my fiancée."

"What about Isaac?" inquired Samantha.

Ice stopped walking. "What about him?"

"He's going to be aboard ship."

"How do you know that?"

"The same way I know that I can go. Your officer Joan told Philip we could both become crew. Philip came to Lamancha House following three young boys in trouble and ended up rescuing me and Isaac."

"Oh, Samantha, Isaac was my boyfriend but that is past. I said goodbye to him recently."

"At Lamancha House over a week ago?"

"How do you possibly know that?"

"I had begged Philip to escort me to Lamancha House for dinner that Tuesday evening—strictly platonic and on my account. We saw you and Isaac entering the Tea Room and he was caressing your back."

Ice put her hands to her face. "Oh no."

"Philip told me then that crazy as it might seem, he was in love with you."

Ice smiled faintly. "I'll introduce you to Isaac. He's an interesting person. I kept him at a distance because I wanted to marry a member of our crew. My relationship with Isaac worked for years because he always had two or three girls. I was willing to sacrifice holidays, making his juggling act easier, assuring there were always two of us." Samantha seemed to be smiling under her facemask, and Ice added, "I am not sharing Philip!"

"Albert will have all my attention. I thought Philip called you something sounding almost like the word 'ice' that night we saw you at Lamancha House, now I realize that's your name."

"For now. I'll become Alice aboard ship."

"A sweet name." Samantha sighed, "My husband is such a fine man."

"There will be chances for late pickups for days after Saturday. Also, just before we sail you could be returned to Nevis or Florida."

"Thank you, Ice, thank you so much." Samantha hugged her. "I will sleep better tonight, even on the floor."

AS GOOD AS IT GETS

The witnesses were separated into two medical-masked groups, with the on-campus group wearing beige departing east, and the off-campus group in their white masks departing west, each group taking trams to a waiting train. The train, positioned to back down the grade to the dock, surprised Philip. A heavy steel ladder ran between the rails. One of their group knew that cogs on the train's axles meshed with the rungs of the ladder and kept the train from slipping on the steep incline down to the dock.

Once in motion, a soft, metallic zinging rolled slowly downward with them. A weak jolt from the tracks brought back for Philip the trainwreck that killed both his parents. *What's what? Life in the coming Oceania Protectorate, if one thinks about it, will not only eliminate trust in society, but will put anybody at risk of any charge a deemer cares to bring with a paid witness as proof. Just buy a lie to drive results on your favorite police showboard.* Philip looked out the window at the trees he was passing by. *Few know enough about*

The Pystead Group, the Oceania Protectorate, the U.N.'s increasing isolation of Western countries from each other, or the U.N.'s unknown presence in Western countries as with the Wheaton World Center for Change in Middle Georgia. The Manager can't provide such information on the free world's multitude of problems in time for favorable opinions of Plan B to form. He can only count on our personal fears to date and hope that enough individual's primary processes of mind will have them pilgrims by Saturday in their tormented moment of decision. O Cosmos!

At sea, the ferryboat ride seemed as slow as the train ride had been. *How are we supposed to escape in slow motion while that hostile Admiral looks on?* The top of the fish farm came into view, and one-by-one each lower tier rose, revealing the three-tiered, taupe gray structure peaking at center, as shown on Fednet. Now there floated nearby an unattached pontoon. *That liberated pontoon must be our ship?*

Without its superstructure the single pontoon took on the appearance of a wedge-cut piece of pie that got thicker as it narrowed towards its tip, its rounded-off blunt tip. *Assemble such*

wedges into a pie and it would have a small, scalloped hole at its bulging center. If that pie slice flies, why not fly it to the dock? Ought to think about this in case Joan tests me for an opinion. Perhaps the water is too shallow, but even closer would be better! Did the Manager make clear that we would fly in the same ship we would float in? What else? What would a saved crew do without a saved ship?

Philip glanced around the ferryboat and estimated a third of the witnesses were women. As the ferry approached the towering ship, the public address system explained that each witness having a drop item of clothing should take an expandable frame to keep their article recognizable after the drop. There were clear plastic bags for jewelry or items that might break or fly apart upon being dropped from some height. Philip passed on a few frames and then used one to turn Samantha's blouse into a pink-and-red striped flag having a center line of white buttons. He fit the frame's strap loop around his wrist and felt secure.

The ferryboats veered to opposite sides of the loose pontoon at its low, circular edge. Even this low part of the ship rose above the ferryboat, and from there continued up on a good incline toward its far forward tip. Public address speakers announced that the outer rim was nineteen meters above the water. Slung over the tapering and blunt-edged sidewall of the big ship was a flexible ladder hanging free from halfway up. Philip glanced at his kom. *Almost forty minutes at sea. A slow trip.*

The ladder confronting Philip was narrow and less than perfectly still, its hanging framework of steps quivering at random intervals. *At least we have an enclosure with mesh backing. Maybe they want to remind us that we are not on good ole terra firma? Perhaps the psychologists decided this little climb would cull out those who shouldn't be making the trip? I do trust the equipment and maintenance—based on nothing more than knowing Ice and Joan.* Philip tightened his grip on the drop item. *How could I tell Samantha I lost her blouse off the boarding steps?* He concentrated on each step. When the hanging steps rounded over onto the top of the ship's blunt front edge, he looked down and by reflex tightened his grip on the railing. *O Cosmos, must focus on the task at hand and underfoot.* After several difficult steps, the ladder was resting firmly on the tapering topside hull, and Philip stepped onto a small, level, platform area offering relief before the steps that continued upward as a red carpet resting on the sloping, metallic surface not meant for standing. The walkway of carpet had loop folds that might be called steps, and it could be seen ending at a door in the first steep rise of the topside hull. Along Philip's left side at waist height ran a single red rope line tied with grip knots. The supports for the rope looked flimsy, and Philip gave it a test tug. *Okay!*

I feel no motion or vibration. Can't see or hear the ferryboats. He heard an occasional muttered expletive not always in the official public language. One particularly loud, four-lettered English word was followed by what looked like a heavy turquoise necklace in a plastic bag skidding down the deck.

Would even a submariner call this a deck? The topside of a slippery pontoon would be apt. Philip looked around. Here and there he saw a large, rough looking area. *Are those lots of little flat, polished rectangles with something between them like screwdriver tips, or merely painted designs? We certainly won't be having ice cream out here.* Philip peered across the water to the sea's horizon. *All looks calm—no swells apparent.* Still, in the moment he felt terribly small, high, vulnerable should anything move. He recalled video of a sailboat heeled over and grasped the rope line. *This is like entering a cathedral that you know should fly like a wheel within a wheel, but without the assurances of God. At least I know Joan! These other flyers are the ones with true grit. Cosmos, if I feel this vulnerable and insignificant on Earth, what will I feel like off Earth?*

Toying with the rope line, Philip's thoughts narrowed to the moment. His knees steadied and his grip relaxed. Surely his primary process experienced a dimension of being without thought of becoming. *I've reincarnated. Still a dog, but a hunting dog, a breed that runs without making the music, although I could howl at a full Moon. Stay in the moment, doggie!* Philip shifted his gaze up from his feet. His balance held. He blinked and stayed in the moment.

A welcomed public address voice instructed everybody to proceed up the red steps and through the door. The voice assured them nets were out to catch anything going overboard, including a person. Movement remained slow, hesitating, as though progressing down the aisle at a wedding. The speaker advised everybody to wave or smile for the video camera beside the door. When his time came, Philip managed an uninspired wave of his colorful flag.

He took three steps to pass through the wide doorjamb, the depth of the ship's three pressure hulls enclosing its two hull tanks. The public address said to continue down the hallway. After several more steps, the group turned into a room divided by a clear plastic screen and having a raised speaker's platform at front. Philip glanced around and found no paintings on the walls and no ice-cream stations. The few doors in the space had rounded corners. The on-campus witnesses from the other ferryboat were already assembled.

✴ ✴ ✴

As the last witness entered, a man of mid-height stepped into the room and onto the low platform. Over his right shoulder, across his chest, and under his left arm he wore a wide golden sash set with large gemstones of every color and clear gems like diamonds. His shirt was of ivory color. He was well built with a large head, handsome, and clean-shaven. *Surely those gemstones are too large to be real? Even from here they sparkle.* Not one person spoke, making audible an ambient sound of flowing white noise. Philip shifted for a better view.

The bejeweled man seemed to look at each of them before beginning. "Welcome to our only ship designed and built with majority crew participation. Our designs are occasionally original but are usually based on established products in consultation with manufacturers. We call each individual ship a key. You are aboard Key Logos. I am Comte Saint Germaine, one of eighty-seven principals of The Pystead Group. My role has been to bring the proper people together at the proper times to do the necessary things, beginning in the Czech Republic as far back as November of nineteen ninety-four."

He must be over eighty years old. Looks mid-forties?

"Most of our financing principals, seventy in all, were committed by the early twenty-first century as world policy turned increasingly to anti-austerity and public mourning as magic wands for fixing problems without having to define them. Our principals did not accept the touted examples, such as a small country printing money and not repaying creditors as evidence that Keynesian economics was a viable world-wide economic model. Finally, year two thousand and thirty brought our last financial principals, and year two thousand and thirty-eight brought increased commitments and sufficient funding for completely outfitting our nine ships. After that, we received a little frosting on the cake for luxury items such as grape vines, Oriental rugs, and copies of fine art. Our financing, management, and scientific and technical guidance has been provided by principals and senior crewmembers. Even a few of every type tool and instrument used to build this ship were made by our crewmembers. Some of our materials and metal alloys were developed by our crew, and have properties not suspected by any contractor."

Saint Germaine is pleased with their accomplishments. A crew as complicated as the ships!

"Most of our interior partitions for quarters aboard the sea farm, comprising seven of our nine key ships, were prefabricated by the only shipyard in the world still building and repairing cruise ships. They took the work and did a fine job using lightweight materials, believing their government would never support seasteading by any private entity. When their government sees those walls and cabinets leave port, we can only pray for those managers of that shipyard who declined to come with us."

Saint Germaine shifted his stance and spoke faster, "We have organized, worked, and adjusted; we have learned to do for ourselves everything we need. We have deep redundancy of specialists in the core disciplines and skills. We have become self-reliant. To build the campus and the ships, over the years we purchased, disassembled, and relocated many items of extremely heavy equipment. We have spent the equivalent of well over ninety-thousand million kicu on investigations, studies, agents, land, tools, materials, designs, inspections and tests, sea trials, personnel, and contractors for our campus, ships, defenses, supplies, and education—over the past fifty-eight years. We have carefully monitored all construction even when contracted out.

"All our funds were legitimately earned, except from one principal. His family had an automobile wreck in which his wife and daughter died. He and his son left their country for medical treatment, carrying bank account codes for twenty billion kicu that had been stolen and placed in overseas accounts by his country's leaders. Of course, our mini surveillance drones had allowed him to acquire the necessary information and codes. None of our other funds came from organized crime, gambling enterprises, leaders for life, con men, retired generals, or high politicians or clerics. Completion of our financing was facilitated over the years by the onset of terrorism, cultural unrest, economic and environmental problems, and lastly by the virtual suspension of foreign aid and military alliances by the United States. Many of our materials and pontoons, now inner hulls, were acquired at low prices during years following the various financial downturns that began in the year two thousand, eventually bankrupting seventy-six of the ninety companies having space programs. Even better than the availability of materials was the easy recruiting of experienced personnel."

Saint Germaine frowned. "Over the years, many of us have lost family and friends to old age." He paused and the witnesses whispered among themselves. "For those perplexed by our company, our secrecy and plans, please reflect upon the reality that most people who acknowledge the world's many problems including overpopulation, will lament gaps in social justice, and even the loss of strong democratic values. All without voting for needed reforms! They must feel that suffering in chaotic times is unavoidable, and that the United Nations, though sympathetic to authoritarian regimes, is necessary to maintain relative peace in the world and in their lives. Most remain as if meditating in a wood after their dog has begun to growl. We at Pystead, however, have unlocked our pieces and are headed out." The witnesses stirred, heads turning as if searching for a thing sensed but unseen.

"Please note that natural developments together with disruptive politics and technologies, including some of our own, have made the security of persons and investments at Pystead relatively viable. Our principals and present crew are among those who believe that disruptive world and national changes will inescapably bring harm to their lives and the lives of their descendants. The external threats to Nevis are little less than elsewhere, but our group's weaknesses are minimal, our strengths and opportunities superior. At every stage of development, we have been able to show proof of concept with something amazing. Disruptions to world stability, together with decades old frustrations of youth everywhere, provided us with ample opportunity to attract personnel from the United Kingdoms, the European Union, the Dutch Republic, Russia, Ukraine, the two recent Indias, and various small countries and regions. For the past several years we have offered flights in one of our key ships, attracting a wide range of young talent."

Saint Germaine paused. The witnesses remained quiet. "A few years ago, we discovered the United Nations' plan to spin off Pacific and West Indies members of the Alliance of Small Island States to create an Oceania Protectorate. We concluded that Nevis would become closed to Western newcomers, and probably to us as well. Needing full crews for all ships, we initiated and rushed recruiting in the United States. Most of you here today are the result of that final effort. Our company, however, came to the attention of the United Nations and is now watched closely and disparaged relentlessly despite no specific violations of law. We are told that The Hague is investigating us for inculcating discontent among those who must return to contingency employment cultures—the Westernized countries. They say that we waste energy on transportation from abroad instead of hiring locally. We have yet to hear whom we could have hired locally. Like a military or French court, however, international law enforcement has little need for compelling facts, discovery, or opposing arguments. A crime and venue that pleases the powers that be will be found for us!"

O Cosmos, one more reason we must flee!

"Recently, we extended our working shifts to eight hours, which the U.N. considers brutalizing. Our environment is characterized as hazardous even though we have had no industrial or traffic accident for over three decades." Whispering among the witnesses increased.

The public address speakers beeped, and Saint Germaine paused as general quarters was announced. He said, "We are about to fly." He continued with his former serious countenance. "As for internal company security, each crewmember and adult family member, including myself and every principal, takes the same security brain scans as do you recruits. Although we trust each other, we guard against the possibility of intervention. We do not pretend to know all that may be known about the human mind, especially under the influence of disease, coercion, hypnotism, subliminal suggestion, drugs, or perceived virtue. We also do not pretend that our instruments and computers, or our personnel, are infallible. We do our best to manage our human condition and avoid the hostile beings all too often encountered."

Saint Germaine shifted his weight and a few jewels flashed in Philip's direction. "Here, I can promise that you will not encounter passive-aggressive colleagues and improbity among leaders. You will not be doing your job and your supervisor's job. On a daily basis you will be professionally self-supervising. Supervisors will be technically helpful and double checkers. Managers will be project oriented, qualified, and involved—not schedulers of unnecessary reports, socializing meetings, group-hug retreats, and awards for everybody but you. Here, your colleagues and retired crewmembers will participate with you in an ongoing quality assurance process that is remarkably effective." Saint Germaine smiled.

Saint Germaine looked around and turned toward the on-campus group in beige facemasks. *Perhaps posing for video being sent to the ice-cream assembly?* Philip adjusted his position and caught a glimpse of a slot in the floor in front of the platform. Then he found a similar slot in the ceiling. *An air curtain. Surely the equivalent of a medical facemask. Neither Joan nor the Manager wore masks at the assembly. Joan is certainly critical in the immediate future.*

"We hope each of you will appreciate this ship. We, the crew, design and construct much of our equipment. We monitor it continuously when built by others and assure testing is performed to the letter of specifications—not easy tasks even for the qualified and dedicated, not inexpensive either. Try to imagine any large, complex project done on a specific performance basis for each and every item—costs are sky high and schedules always slip! Our Pystead crew maintains and operates everything.

"This ship, Logos, was designed and substantially handmade

by our scientists, engineers, and the many non-technical types who volunteered. I grew diamond crystals used in making heat dissipating substrate for diode rectifiers and for semiconductors used in our backup computers. They are less powerful computers, but more shock and heat resistant than the main computers." Saint Germaine seemed almost to shake his head. "To recant a bit, all but twelve of our thirty-three main computers aboard all ships use some commercially manufactured components because of our accelerated schedule these last few years.

"Also, you should know that we have a quantum computer designed and built entirely by our crew. It is being studied for reliability. It's capable of magically fast analysis. A life-saving tool for designing individually tailored medicines. Its mere existence is company confidential."

Saint Germaine again paused, and Philip shifted. *I'll be surprised if scan helmets get a mention. Perhaps brain scans are best forgotten? Will there be enough variation in brain's innate wirings among the crew for my research? If I must abandon my innateness research, what will my vocation become? Brain-scan specialist? Humanities professor? Seems the reserved line option should be my cross-training! I'm interested in ship's systems and there's enough there to fill any available time. I feel vulnerable not understanding anything about the equipment. No doubt a follow-on from learning how to handle Vanderhought's fourteen-meter sailboat with its sea charts, depth finder, radar, short-wave radio, rules of the water, quarantine flag, sailing basics, sails, auxiliary engine basics, fueling, batteries, dingy, electrical system, anchor. Not to mention food, water, kitchen appliances, and bathroom fixtures. Would certainly be comforting to know how to open the door on an Egg craft, how to fly it to a landing.*

The bejeweled man's smile was fading as Philip looked up. "You should know that we have a formal quality assurance program, although not a Six-Sigma program. Our program is most effective because each crewmember is qualified to do his or her job, is alert, self-disciplined, and temperamentally dedicated to safety and success. At Pystead, we know that our safety and success are not mutually exclusive. We also know that some things, such as engineering designs, are too complex and require too much experience and judgment to be reduced to a piecemeal design process constrained by politicized criteria and mind-boggling administrative and workplace burdens. If you are not professionally competent to do a job, you do not become competent during a refresher briefing. You simply frustrate the professionals who must continually take the time to brief you and clean up after you. We hire only those who are truly professional in their specialty.

"We avoid the waste, oversimplification, lost time, and frustrations attendant to the Six-Sigma process. For example, we are mindful that medical devices or factory equipment checked by unqualified people are often unsafe—especially medical x-ray equipment. In the U.S., many of these certifying technicians have fake credentials, but only a handful of states confirm those credentials, while never hesitating to ruin the career of a senior doctor for some trivial violation of a Six-Sigma regulation. They will rehire the doctor as a nurse practitioner at a lower salary, reporting to the subordinates who testified against him and received promotions. He will then do his old job for less salary while the others receive increased salaries for doing their old jobs. Creating reliably dishonest leadership is more important than maintaining standards! The long-range planning, political, judicial, and media support needed to hide dirty tricks in politics and business have long been understood by the very rich. They learned from failures, and over several decades cured their weaknesses. A feat of management unimaginable to the general public.

"Here, ladies and gentlemen, we triple-check everything. Strategic decisions and supercritical details are confirmed at least five times. We hope that many of you will be signing on as crew to support and extend these efforts. To that end, we offer this tour to demonstrate capabilities commensurate with our objective. In the future, even a floating city may need to relocate on a moment's notice and float in another place, say to avoid a two hundred kilometers per hour torpedo, perhaps relocate even into orbit of the Earth or Moon."

Saint Germaine asked, "Any questions?"

"Yes, Mr. Germaine! Why design equipment if time and money could have been saved by hiring design and construction?"

"To keep the secret that our pontoons were being fitted out as complete ships—as more than seaworthy living and farming platforms. Most of our designs are based on some proven item and adapted to operate underwater, upside-down, weightless, hot or cold, and in the reduced gravity and increased radiation of space. You might like to know that by overall design none of our valves can be installed backwards. Our sealing rings are free from any Grignard reagent—no cost-saving steps in manufacturing. Our ships are capable of orbiting and extended space flight. Hull materials were selected for long life in a cold and high radiation environment. The outer hull is made of superalloys of nickel, titanium, and beryllium—very expensive materials—capable of operating hot for sustained Mach-Four flight. The hull's forebodies are coated with a phenolic impregnated graphite resin for heat rejection and tensile strength during an above redline flight condition."

Saint Germaine waited but did not get another question. He said, "All ships are fully armed and provisioned—ready to sail, fly, and fight. We have fighter planes using zirconium and hafnium diboride shells that can sustain Mach-Seven flight. Those materials are not unique with us, but our fighters with a vastly greater operating range, greater speed, and superior maneuverability are!"

Maybe he won't mention Mars to us recruits until the night before boarding? Why do I already know? Melita must have told Joan I needed special handling. Perhaps I did—still do? Why? For assuming the worst as a way of imagining that I can manage the real world. Here or there, I'm quite real and vulnerable. And I must get real in my whole mind.

The bejeweled speaker stepped to a door that opened and motioned for all to follow. The guards directed the small on-campus group to go first. *Providing the best air for the least exposed. After all, off-campus types could have been purposely exposed to most anything. Why take a chance when you can take precautions?*

The overhead speakers broadcast Saint Germaine's voice. "Please keep track of your drop item. Your tour of the ship will not be comprehensive because time is limited and you are not yet cleared to see all things. For instance, although we will not tour an engine room, you may rest assured that we have main engines— eight of them, large and widely separated. We can fly and maneuver at any altitude using any four engines. We can maintain flight using two engines, and land without cracking the hull using only one engine."

What about cracking our heads against the uncracked hull?

"You should know that should the ship's primary control system and its primary backup system fail, we have a secondary backup system that is direct and structured so that one person can understand it—we have a dozen pilots already trained to fly and fight using that simplified control system. Even then, our ships outperform any others."

My kind of binary being that system.

"We will depart from the flight schedule announced in the quad. We will not drop the items and then fly into orbit. We will fly to a low orbital altitude and soon descend to drop your items. We will fly in this ship and not in another craft. Misinformation on scheduling and what might fly was a security precaution. We will climb to orbit using a flight profile intended to confuse any trackers. Our propulsion system is advanced enough to allow us to do that in complete safety. We fly like an airplane even to reach orbital velocity. All other craft reaching such a velocity follow a ballistic trajectory."

The tour stopped at a food kitchen where meals were being prepared. It was bright and clean. Next, they visited an art gallery with interesting paintings. A short walk brought them to a wide concourse that Saint Germaine explained would connect all nine assembled ships. They passed food kiosks and small parks along its way. Off the main concourse the tour soon entered a residential hall with a dozen apartment doors open for quick looks around. The living quarters were small but nice. Nearby were exercise rooms, performance venues, and lounges that felt spacious enough to Philip.

Saint Germaine raised a hand and waved it about. "You cannot sit in a closed room and know that you have gone anywhere. We have several observation stations, and we will spend good time in one so that you may be persuaded that it is more likely that you have flown than that you have been deceived. Today we will not have the element of surprise needed to land and let you verify your presence in a distant place. We will, however, open ports and have you toss out your marker articles. We hope these will be shown by independent parties as proof of a bona fide drop at a place remote from Nevis, made at a time well before you could have arrived using a commercial aircraft, or even using a military aircraft. We have decided against person-to-person interactions with the local population to avoid reprisals against anybody who might say what some powerful group would not want to hear. We will, however, retrieve a public item: a unique rock sculpture made of Scottish rock, having a flared hole through it. The rock is already purchased and prepared for moving. This will be a proof of our presence in the event Net censorship is imposed, which we anticipate world-wide within an hour."

The bejeweled man took a long breath and almost seemed to sigh. "Regardless of what we do or show, we might be called E.T.s or pirates by the media. If we attract a crowd, we will drop one-quarter ounce Gold Pandas as a way of preventing authorities from seizing everything and saying it never happened. As you will probably agree, authorities the world over deny anomalous events, except when they hope to benefit, as with weeping statues, haunted houses, or the U.N.'s extraterrestrials, no doubt to be faked. Now please follow me down to a viewport lounge." Philip found himself agreeing.

The tour proceeded, splitting into a dozen small groups to board elevators to reach the bottom deck of the ship. Something was troubling Philip. The cosmos is unknown, unexplained, irrational to the human mind in its mere existence, yet not perceived as anomalous.

One need not admit its strangeness. Although each step in the too-large-to-fly ship felt more disconcerting than Schrödinger's Cat or the origins of the cosmos. *Should this dog be barking at that cat and this ship? And what about that historical figure called Saint Germaine, acknowledged only by those called fringe historians? Known from the fifteen hundreds onward via the diaries of European royals. He appeared for hundreds of years, wore large gemstones of unknown origin, and could speak on any subject. Such a genuine being could inspire a company such as this. The commonsense conclusion, of course, is that he is an imposter, unless I set aside the normalcy bias. Or not? There are both ancient and recent accounts of long life and suspended aging. How little is known about anything! And 'he' could be a 'lineage' of sons!*

The witnesses arrived at a room with a large, round observation viewport in the floor, and a temporary plastic screen dividing the room and viewport. Two rows of segmented handrails circled the viewport. Comte confirmed, "We are on the bottom deck. This port looks directly down and out. There is a metal pressure door above, and one below, the glass viewport. The viewport is made of a clear glass stronger than steel, able to catch all jumpers."

He drew a few chuckles, and one muttered, "Not so funny."

Ice's last name is Germaine, pronounced the same even if spellings differ. Definitely, I'm not dreaming, although confused. I'm normal even if what I'm seeing is not. This must have been Descartes's state of mind? I must save these appearances for contemplation. Wish this dog knew more about that cat...and that fringe legend of Saint Germaine.

"Above you, the four internally illuminated globes of the world will display a bright blue dot to trace our route. We hope some of you will recognize a few features of land below. Our flight takes us first to fifteen kilometers altitude at subsonic speed flying like a passenger jet. Once off radar, we will climb to one hundred twenty-two kilometers and go supersonic at Mach-Two. Then we climb to a very low Earth orbit for an experience of weightlessness. Our orbit will be in the thermosphere and too low for a commercially viable satellite—too much atmospheric drag. Consequentially, at our chosen altitude of one hundred sixty kilometers, there is little orbiting junk and we will be much safer than at three hundred kilometers and above. We will use acceleration levels comparable to jet fighter aircraft, and most of our flight across the Atlantic will be either accelerating to speed or decelerating for our visit to Edinburgh in order to drop your items on top of a large white tent near Holyrood Palace."

Philip's thoughts were interrupted by an abrupt upward motion. A host of unfinished conversations spoke for everyone. Someone nearby couldn't believe such a huge ship could fly. The receding scene in the observation port was familiar to Philip, like those from his Egg-craft flights, only higher and faster. First, the ferryboats and fish farm, then even the islands of Nevis and Kitts began shrinking and fading into ocean blue and cloud white. "Please hold on," cautioned Comte's voice.

Philip stood with his legs apart and his teeth together, but the acceleration posed no problem—except to one recruit sprawled over the viewport railing, caught by his armpit. *That was me on Wheaton's hanging bar, not so long ago. Focus now, focus, doggie. Try to speak to Saint Germaine.*

After a few chimes and apparent changes in their direction of flight, Saint Germaine spoke again and explained that the entire world was primed, watching for E.T.s. He added that if a missile were fired at them their laser cannons could easily destroy it.

"What if it's nuclear?" someone asked.

"We have selected our route to avoid nuclear missiles. If we were to get a missile from any location, we would change course, accelerate, and leave behind automated craft to shoot it down to protect both our ship and others in its trajectory. This ship can be fast if necessary and can change course on a dime, much quicker than any missile. Because of our curvilinear shape and smooth surfaces, our radar signature is too small to attract attention as anything other than a small drone or failing satellite, and then only when one of our acquisition radar covers is open for maximum sensitivity. With our hull's large antenna covers closed we return almost no radar signal at any frequency. Our engines produce no infrared heat signatures."

Cosmos, this niche of reality is confounding. Internally kind based on appearances, if one discounts secret, high-tech equipment and secretive Commanders. We are told by the old movies that the lives of secret people and their families are often lived in peril of becoming pawns in the great game. Why would that be different here? Perhaps little is different here, except my potential family exposure to the game could be greater, living with an especially inscrutable Commander? How could potential involvement and apprehension lead to a psychologically neutral place to raise children? I could only wait and see and hope—simply knowing what I do not know now would not reduce family exposure! And too soon now I must choose the devil I know, or the devil I don't know.

Philip sighed. *I fear going back and I fear going forward. I have a choice. Doesn't mean either is good. Consistent with my apprehension about the real world. Hey! Getting real, reality is well served by staying in the moment. I'm taking this ride to observe for myself and others. Saint Germaine said crewmembers are to be daily self-supervising.*

Seems I need more of that personal discipline I wish for others. Evading the moment via contemplation must be a form of delusional living?

A tall woman dressed in a white jumpsuit entered the room. She stepped onto the platform and spoke with a pleasant accent, "Hello, my name is Sasha Gutkin, Manager of this ship, Key Logos."

Russian accent?

"Should conditions change such that decisions must be made on a crisis basis, I become known as Captain Sasha. As Captain, I would make decisions unilaterally until conditions became suitable for discussion. I much prefer being a Manager to a Captain. During this flight, we will be in management mode unless we are continuously tracked by radar. For that we have established terms of engagement, which favor evasion and retreat rather than having to defend the ship. Your chance for high adventure is low. Relax and enjoy the flight."

Philip was listening with his attention distracted by acceleration and a view of Earth's arc across the entire viewport. The witnesses exclaimed in several languages, some wondering about the view being genuine. Philip, a professor who believed in remembering and questioning what he was seeing, and in applying Occam's razor, found himself at loss for a conclusion. *Looks real and a lot like the video ads for commercial shuttles, though we do fly rather level and change directions, unlike videos from the rocket powered flights. Vanderhought once said there are often rotational errors when showing man in space, as far back as the first space odyssey movies. How would anybody here know?* Philip called loudly, "Is there an astronomer in the group?" *No response!*

"You will hear the details of Plan B on campus tomorrow," Manager Gutkin told them. "Now, each of you please take a seat in the balcony as we must accelerate to a speed of seven-point-eight kilometers per second. Once at orbital speed you will have a few minutes of free floating. Use the seat clamp to secure your drop item. You'll want both hands free when weightless."

After about fifteen minutes, the witnesses were called to viewport level. Philip caught a railing with his hand. "Please hold on firmly for final acceleration to orbital speed. If we were flying a typical aircraft's free-floating parabola, you would experience a period of double gravity on the upward arc, although if seated you might not notice. Earth's horizon line would disappear and constantly change on the way down during apparent gravity-free time, which would be about fifteen seconds." They all held a railing in silence. Manager Gutkin soon confirmed, "You are now experiencing microgravity and free fall in orbit. Please observe that Earth's horizon line will remain steady in the viewport. If you feel ill, please ask for a bag. Float on this level only as we return to gravity within a few minutes and begin deceleration to stop for Edinburgh."

Philip took a gentle hop and had to catch himself by the foot at the top handrail. *Half of us at a strange angle, feet off the floor! Two floating low—they push gently sideways, not up.* Within a minute the space was full of floating and eerily rotating bodies. *No one's talking.*

"Please, somebody, catch that man rotating…thanks. Note our steady horizon line. We return to gravity in thirty seconds. Get your feet ready to stand."

As feet found the solid floor, Manager Gutkin asked that everybody go promptly to their balcony seat and reclaim their drop item. The viewport transitioned to a white screen and a projector shown from overhead with a view of the assembly on campus. The interior of their observation room could be seen projected onto the wall of a building. An almost jovial Saint Germaine remarked upon the continued good attendance on campus.

Background music and deceleration began. Gutkin's voice was heard, "Attention, please! In fifteen minutes we descend to drop your marker items. Each of you, please take an adhesive weight and clip it to your drop item. You can soon return to viewport level. When we are over the tent, we will open small ports along this room's wall. This ship has three pressure hulls, and we are inside the innermost hull. Since we will be just above tent top level, opening a few windows to the outside world is not dangerous. You will notice a slight breeze outflow because this room is now pressurized to above one atmosphere to avoid ingress of local air, a standard precaution."

✳ ✳ ✳

Manager Gutkin raised a small handheld bell and produced a few rings. "Our flight approach will be almost straight down to above Dynamic Earth's tent top. Do not worry about the hill to its side or its tall, extended tent poles. We see them! Once your item is ready, line up at a porthole position. We don't want to linger on site. Toss your item and move away for the next person. Some of you should wait at the viewport to observe and video the first items fall, but please watch the line and keep it moving. We do hope for good initial Net coverage though even the Clouds can be purged—well, especially the Clouds can be purged.

"This tent is a long exhibition hall called Dynamic Earth. We have adhesive weights that will stick your items to the tent top. Guess we will need to send a hundred thousand kicu to cover

345

cleanup costs and ticket refunds. For now, please focus on the observation ports and the flight. Those of you at the front viewport railing, please rotate clockwise and to the rear at the chime to allow a front row view for all. Take your own kom video."

After the first chime, Philip rotated to the front row without concentrating on the view. *Could this man be Ice's uncle, cousin, brother...grandfather?*

Philip waited to video a few falling items and then took his turn at the porthole, surrounded by its own solid glass railing. He hurried back to the viewport and spotted his red-and-pink striped blouse. People on the ground could be seen peering up, some of them police officers. The ship shifted from directly above the tent, and crewmembers began dropping gold coins through the floor ports. Manager Gutkin instructed the witnesses to return to the balcony and buckle their seatbelts.

A buzzer sounded, a ring of red lights flashed around the viewport, and the viewport glass retracted with a pop and outward air flow. A large, padded hook descended through the open viewport. Once down, the hook swung into the hole of a reddish rock sculpture sitting along the circular road in front of the huge, long tent. The hook began to rise holding the sculptured rock. At the same time, a metal cylinder was lowered, although not from within their room. Gutkin explained, "We are leaving a package weighing well over a ton. It contains our clean-up payment and three Nevis policemen who insisted on remaining aboard this ship. Only the government will be able to retrieve the package. We have advised the policemen to wait for rescue rather than exiting uninvited. As for the rock, our agent bought it so that we are not stealing it. Cost us a small fortune! We were scheduled to pick it up today—the reason for the two video trucks."

On the ground below, people outside the tent began running, including police. Manager Gutkin concluded, "They must think our package is a bomb. We'll give them a call and try to alleviate fears." The sculptured red rock rose through the viewport opening and crew swung it over onto the floor. "Now, witnesses, you should come down and examine this rock, take a kom video, and return to sit in the balcony."

Philip pushed on the rock and found it too heavy to budge and its surface rough. "Seats, everybody, be quick. We are clearing out." The acceleration was strong and felt straight up. The ship crossed the rocky hill and a maze of buildings before flying low above pastures and trees with the ground seen passing as a blur. Soon they were over water.

After a few minutes of flight the ship turned toward a large yacht with five tall masts. Although still in daylight, *Key Logos* turned on spotlights. "You may come down and take any video you want." The viewport soon transitioned from clear to a white-screen mode. Video from above revealed the yacht's bow and name, before panning up and over naked party goers dressing or running on the deck. The view zoomed up to the wheelhouse, revealing faces clearly seen through its front windows—date, time, and coordinates were included in a by-line before a bright flash. The view then panned around to a side window where a series of flashes followed. An interior view of the wheelhouse with startled expressions on faces showed on the viewport screen.

Saint Germaine's voice informed them, "One of our scouts, we call it an Egg craft, is providing this video as proof of presence.

Other video in laser light is being taken from high above to document our ship's presence relative to the yacht below. That's better than no video."

Once well out to sea, the witnesses returned to the balcony, and Saint Germaine spoke again, "We are turning for a passenger liner. After that, we will fly a circuitous route below one-kilometer altitude with speeds up to Mach Three if needed. We have a vanishingly small radar signature and will avoid sustained tracking, and probably not be sighted even once. A meal will be served. We should reach campus by eleven o'clock."

Their spotlights came on and the scene on screen zoomed in and panned across the ship's name, waterline marker, and passengers dining on deck, before rising to the wheelhouse. After the expected bright flashes, their public address system announced, "Ladies and gentlemen, we will serve our typical shipboard meals for you to sample. Please try two or three different entrées even if eating only a few bites of each."

The meals were warm and all agreed good. Philip sat and listened to the quiet conversations around him but overheard only that flying in orbit showed Pystead was capable of seasteading in orbit. *What livelihood could we pursue in orbit? Offer vacation rooms with a view? Can one even perform surgery in microgravity? Would the U.N. charge orbiting fees? Why allow orbiting if not allowing seasteading? Ah, Joan told me we would have defensible orbiting possibilities, not a kindly niche for orbiting!*

When soft instrumental music began, Philip, like most others, closed his eyes and rested. Then he suddenly sat up and sent a message to Ice saying the trip was amazing and he wished she were with him. He watched a video on the ship's public facilities and looked quickly through an e-book of Pystead's art. When Comte Saint Germaine took the speaker's platform below to introduce Plan B, all but a dozen seemed to listen. *He's simply telling us what he's going to tell us in detail on campus tomorrow.*

⁂　⁂　⁂

After a long flight with several abrupt changes in direction and acceleration they landed in darkness far from the floating fish farm. The big ship seemed to pause on the surface before slipping and rocking twice to a stop. A crewmember told the travelers that seven United States military helicopters were approaching. Philip began to contemplate the sloping red-carpet steps and long ladder down to the ferryboat, with or without hostile helicopters. Then Saint Germaine waved to them. "Everyone, come down and follow me, with the on-campus group first. We have a deck at ferryboat level. We can use a cargo door for departure. If we hurry, you can be aboard your ferryboat before the helicopters arrive."

The witnesses boarded easily, and the ferry pulled clear of the huge ship. Only then did Philip remember wanting to speak to Saint Germaine. *If the Manager and Comte Saint Germaine say these ships will serve our purpose, I believe them. Comte, Ice, and Joan assure me the crew is as complex as the ships. Would I believe all this if I didn't know Ice, and Lois, and Joan? This huge ship must be powered like an Egg craft and a guard pod. For an afternoon proof of capability, I must say the flight was convincing.*

The beating of helicopter blades could be heard. As the noise increased, the helicopters took on shape in *Key Logos'* spotlights. Without warning from *Logos* flashed several incredibly bright and narrow pulses of light, producing reflected pulses off the helicopters. The lead chopper fell sideways and soon hit the water. The remaining six choppers wavered but continued. After circling Pystead's ship the six helicopters departed, without picking up survivors from the downed helicopter.

Only then did Philip worry. *If we appeared in places before current commercial or military aircraft could have made being there possible, we are really in trouble! How can seasteading provide security after that? We will surely be sealed off and declared off limits by the U.N. We shouldn't last much longer than did Tesla after his speech on free energy. If an actual flight we are in trouble with the world. If faked we're in trouble with the company. Seems the individual recruit is in trouble? Osgood told us the U.N. knows who we are! He and Hector report we are no longer to be trusted with professional work when we return home. My stomach isn't great, but why don't I feel worse? Why haven't I considered this issue before? Maybe I'm beginning to feel worse. Still, given circumstances, Pystead's proof of concept flight must be as good as it gets.*

* * *

Aboard the ferryboat, tension abated as the military helicopters held steady for the horizon, turning on their silly red and green blinking lights. Except that Philip, having disposed of implicit beliefs that normalcy would once again prevail, was prepared to believe that anything might conceivably, or even inconceivably, prevail. For the more one knows about the cosmos, the more one can believe that less is inconceivable every day.

The public address system spoke, "May I have your attention, please. This is Larry speaking, your ferryboat Captain. Regarding the helicopters, four carried marines, and three were gunships.

They thought they would have no problems against an unarmed ship, but our unexpected use of tactical stunlights temporarily blinded the lead pilot. That lead copter was a gunship with four men aboard—technically boys, all under twenty-one years old. We picked them up only seconds after they hit the water. Nobody was seriously injured—they were wearing crash helmets fitted to the individual. Each one wants to defect to us! We believe the marines were not prepared for our sloping deck and unseen doors, or they would have attempted to board us. They will return prepared, and we will be ready, as we were even this time. We can easily shoot them down or tilt the ship over after they are on deck, but why do that to young people who have no say in the matter? We can force helicopters to abort by melting the tips of their rotor blades, which we will do early on if there is a next time. Now fasten your seatbelts because we want to hurry back for your reports on the flight before the assembly loses too many."

Philip fastened up. *I ignored the Egg craft thinking it merely a techy passenger drone. That flying key ship is certainly more than a techy airplane—it's special. And melting blade tips on a military heli-copter, no problem, must be something special.* Philip tensed. *Back in Middle Georgia I ignored Earl's warning to get out of Wheaton before dusk. Why? Now with experience does my primary process warn me that returning home, even to West Hartford or Boston, is my worst option?*

The ferryboat picked up speed. A familiar voice spoke, "Hello, travelers, witnesses, this is Comte Saint Germaine speaking to you from Key Logos. We are sending sponsors for those of you who have not yet met yours.

"We need your opinions on the ship and demonstration flight presented to the assembly as soon as possible tonight. Individual testimonies will take too much time. Please group yourselves as like-minded on a score with an agreed upon message and a spokesperson. An overall score will be tallied using a scale of zero, three, four, and five. Hence, five hundred fifteen will be the highest possible score. Upon landing, four numbered areas will be available. A score of five should reflect satisfaction with the validity of the demonstration, and zero a belief that the demonstration was no more than an elaborate deception. Brief comments should be made to explain scores of three and four. Thank you for participating."

Philip relaxed, pondering events. He decided on the top score. *Could I be the only five? No, not among twenty percent space hounds.* He closed his eyes, yawning. *This Plan B will be challenging, with hot seas and recent capitalist principals having wings. The floating city proposition is challenging although within normalcy. But huge orbiting ships as normal? Living in spaceships on Mars? Cosmos, the ships will eventually be going to another solar system says Joan! Are starships within the norm? One can, however, believe in strange new variations on life after experiencing this Pystead Group! And that K.L.J.H. Organism of cyborgs certainly keeps Pystead on the human side of the strangeness scale!*

Philip rested. He knew that the cosmos rewards on its margins, evolving with least survivable entities—one reproducing pair being sufficient. From the one, many, as told by the ancient myth of Adam and Eve. *Flying or not, one may be carried away in speculation or delusions of mind. Is all a slippery slope without the normalcy bias? Is the idea of progress riskier than…maintaining? Is hypocrisy a virtue if one advocates maintaining? Is it best to forego critical inquiry so that the original state of humanity remains bound in babble? Should we lead a hard and unexamined life without luxuries or modern medicine, and die hard without a trace like a feral dog? Why is the original state of tribal life, inevitably a life of hardship, of infanticide, not characterized as the natural form of social Darwinism? When did tribal life not manifest as live and let die? Only with education and philosophy is the savage and his worship of brute force overcome!*

⚜ ⚜ ⚜

Philip glanced over the railing to confirm again what his inner ear and observation of the other ferryboat told him, and said aloud, "We are indeed, silently slipping above the sea."

The public address system announced, "Two long boats from Key Logos are overtaking us to starboard and request permission to come aboard. The boats bring two dozen crewmembers to meet those of you who have not already met your sponsor." All looked with amazement as the boats resembling large canoes approached, flying without apparent means of propulsion. Philip watched closely as they rose majestically, one landing on their ferryboat's deck. Personnel stepped out clad in white jumpsuits, each holding a beige facemask. Hands waved and names were called.

Not recognizing anybody, Philip sat back as the seat beside him was taken and a clear voice said, "Dr. Philip B. Russell, I presume?"

That voice held Philip frozen until he asked, "Vanderhought?"

"Believe it!" A hand shook his shoulder and Philip found himself face to face with Arthur Vanderhought, eyes only above a beige mask. The mask quivered, "We have stories to tell each other. I hope you join us. I was right about space energy; got me fired and almost killed. Pystead saved me. I disappeared on that ocean dive, but into an airlock equipped cargo Egg. Pystead was already extracting energy from space, what we now call aether energy. Philip, I need to get back to Key Logos. I'm their Commandant for Propulsion Systems. We are beginning red-line power certifications for the last four of our eight main engine-drives. The last ship to do so. If you have doubts about signing on as crew, call and I'll get to campus tonight and try to answer your questions. Okay?"

Philip nodded. "Okay. Arthur, do you know Janice Germaine, or Ice Germaine, or Alice Germaine?"

"No. I have never heard any name associated with Germaine other than Comte."

"Ah, well, it's reassuring to see you. Thanks for sponsoring me. I'll call if I need help, otherwise I'll be aboard."

"Couldn't think of a better person for the job."

"Arthur, do you have a blue channel on your kom?"

"A what?"

"Not sure, had an occasion involved with Blue Processing."

"That? The computers process to check facts and classifications and add cross-references before posting to a network—standard procedure."

"Thanks."

Arthur stood and pulled his medical mask on top of his head, took a deep breath, grinned, turned and started up the ladder to the ferry's roof.

Philip stepped up onto a side railing bar and was not surprised to see an Egg craft waiting. *I believe it.* He sat down, closed his eyes, and rested. His primary process may have rested too, with Compton done and Plan B seeming kindly.

I'm flying home.

THE SCORE

Philip debarked from the ferryboat and rushed to stand in the area marked 5. *Since the Net confirms the drop items, why not a five?* The five area became quite crowded on both sides of its clear plastic curtain. A showboard showed each voting area. Three people were standing in 0. *Wonder how many already have a friendly bet down on the score?* Philip's group grew to sixty agreeing on the top score.

Arriving back in the quad after surprising bursts of train and tram speeds, the witnesses were shown to the five rows of stadium seats facing the assembly, with on and off-campus groups separated by a plastic partition so that facemasks were not worn. Fresh air flowed from behind their heads outward. Philip could not spot Ice nor anyone he knew.

Manager Markwaters made a brief statement explaining that free expression had resolved far more problems than it had created at Pystead, and nobody need be concerned about speaking their mind.

The female architect representing their score of five said the group worried that boarding would take too long and give hostile forces time to react and stop departure.

The spokesman for four, an aerospace engineer, said Pystead's ship handled well, but asked how the company would be able to obtain enough fuel if ostracized from the world community, given that their guide had assured him the ship was not nuclear powered. He noted that the U.N.'s Netsite complained that a large ship had interfered with the Tobago Cays' exclusion zone, and that the E.T.'s mother ship, which was seen twice over the Atlantic, had refused to attend the meeting in the Cays. The man smiled. "We must have traveled to somewhere, and probably managed to be in two places at once! He got a laugh. He continued, "If not, we were still seen in one remote place having a small rock mountain, a castle, and a huge tent. Also, our ship's size and shape should make it stable in a stormy sea, and if structurally sound it should survive a tidal wave."

Cosmos, I didn't speak to Saint Germaine.

The speaker for three points admitted the ship was impressive, hence they voted three points on the merits of the ship for seasteading. They were not convinced that flying on a moment's notice could keep them from harm's way. More explanation was needed before risking one's life on the ship.

Okay, reasonable.

The man speaking for zero insisted they were deceived through cross-sensory perception. Faux sensations of acceleration and deceleration could have been felt if the room had been tilted, because with visual and video references remaining fixed, the inner ear would be tricked into a perception of acceleration. Showing an unchanging horizon while raising a spongy, clear plastic floor under people's feet could have felt like zero gravity in the confusion. Walls seeming to ripple like they might be a slow waterfall and surreal tones were experienced by many. Very Low frequency sound would cause some people's vision to blur, even causing some to see ghostly images, all without being aware of the sound. It was weird audio and illumination effects, and vibrating sensations that induced cross-sensory confusion and took many into an alternative reality of the anticipated zero-gravity event. The few people who seemed to float were holograms because one could see through them during a moment of concentration. As for Network coverage, it could be faked or paid for, including the blogs. The speaker asked why they should believe in a magical ship unknown to the rest of the world, including the first Mars group that would have had all the latest technology. He concluded that the demonstration flight would be a good platform for testing a person's inclination to distinguish between illusion and reality, but not a reason for seasteading.

Another ferryboat and two long boats flying alongside without apparent engines—not considered? Seven military helicopters in the middle of the ocean only five minutes after an unscheduled landing from a very low altitude approach? Not to mention the U.N. claiming the ship in Scotland was merely a helium airship while claiming at the same time we interfered at Tobago Cays causing the E.T.s to abort the meeting? The people wanting to rule the world can't find a huge, slow, and low-flying dirigible or its remains someplace near Scotland? And our three zeros can't believe their lying senses! Must be psychologists! What of the rock sculpture hoisted aboard? What of the two ships at sea that according to the U.N. must have seen us? These zeroes believe in a known lying U.N.'s acceptance of E.T.s over the Atlantic rather than us bringing back a popular carved rock from Scotland?

Markwater's voice intruded, thanking the witnesses, saying the score would be calculated. *Guess the U.N. forced every Netsite in the world to cancel the news videos of what they surely called fake news. Anything happening can be rendered irrelevant because the deemers' cure for reality is so effective that their high political defenders are rarely needed. Today's social-scientists routinely discredit science and rational analysis, accustoming the population to pseudo propositions, ill-posed questions, and binary thinking in terms of dependent parameters—finding the usual scapegoats for every problem. And the very rich? Seemingly above it all, uninvolved and managing their businesses, keeping production and employment in the very best of hands. So it is said; so it must be.*

Philip watched calculation of the score as displayed on two building façades. The tally was 453 out of the possible 515 points, for 88 percent affirmative. The Manager thanked the witnesses for their participation and the audience for their endurance. He rang his bell and announced, "May I have your attention, please! We will now present our Plan B in detail. Childcare is available in the activity center and adults may listen via headset while staying with children. Food will continue to be served. If you need assistance with any problem, say an off-campus family member or pet, contact Administration—immediately!"

I suppose those not believing in the critical nature of our circumstances will find this late night assembly a burden. I suspect Pystead hopes they stay on Earth. As Philip was making his way down from his seat, he recognized Ice's masked artist friends standing in a group.

PALE BLUE DOT

Several steps from the stadium seats, Ice greeted Philip. "Welcome back, traveler!" She was wearing a red outfit as alluring as the aqua that he liked. Made of crepe silk he had learned. "Our friend Joan liked your comment implicitly about the slow ferryboats and loading time."

"Why does Joan think that was my comment?"

"Don't be silly, you know she's also Melita Rose."

"Yes, I forget."

"Joan wanted that weakness in the plan to leak. She takes you noticing as a good sign."

"A crafty one, this Joan." *Ice's eyes must be as red as her pantsuit.*

"Our mechanics are buying casement winches to exacting specifications, rigged for pulling our heavy cargo bay doors into sealed position, although the doors work fine."

"So, the word is out. Could be expected to slow departure." He looked again at his fiancée in red. "You are beautiful even in that puffy white mask."

"I'm glad you like the red for a change."

"Ice, under this mask I'm smiling. Tell me, which key do you want to live in?"

"I really want to live in Key Bury Saint Germaine."

"Are you related to the man, Saint Germaine?"

"Oh yes, my paternal grandfather."

"You are related to mystery as well as Blue secrets!"

"I know you are psychologically ready for any family mysteries Comte will discuss with you. Now, Phil, you may mention our relationship with Comte only to very close friends. According to Pystead culture, we are supposed to live without public knowledge of family ties to principals and high officers, to avoid subconscious favoritism or discrimination in both performance evaluations and social life."

Philip mused, "I'd say the policy could produce its own problems?"

"Comte believes we are a singular group and will adapt to the norms of present culture. His hope is that among equals we can value each other for personal integrity more than position."

"So, a technician who does the job well would be more respected than a manager who does the job poorly?"

"True! Comte hopes that in our future a person will not allow himself, or herself, to hold a job that he or she cannot do well. Too, for any one manager or technician there are others well qualified. For planning and efficiency, somebody needs to be first among equals at any given time."

Philip nodded. *Rousseau, paradoxically, would agree; Aristotle would approve; John Rawls would disapprove via an alternative phrasing of the issue. Regardless, a live-and-let-live culture must imply self-acceptance. After all, the green-eyed monster is more of the ego than the id, more nurture than nature, and surely not because of a biological need via some unknown and quick means of emergent evolution! Yet what welcomed theory needs no more than a believer's gut reaction or existential want to be held among the social sciences? And today's culture in the States favors an undefined social justice with contempt for personal effort—a meme of the Maintainers. Our diapause naturally followed, like a Lysenko echo.*

"Phil, please return to me! Why such intense thought? Let's have dessert before the presentation."

"This Plan B must rise to cosmic proportions. I suppose I'm trying to imagine the human dimensions of our situation. Life on a huge boat with few friendly ports of call will be depressing for some, perhaps enervating for many. How many recruits are ready for a marginal zero-sum existence for who knows how long? Even if each tells the self that heshe is ready, their primary process may disagree in a future moment of truth! Cognitive science has confirmed as much via brain scans conducted over decades of people's lives."

"Oh Phil, I do wish you and Granddad could have gotten to know each other by now, but he has been too busy. He feels we will have challenges born of limited resources and continual threats from Earthlings. Simply living in a circumscribed community should bring change. He feels that close physical proximity aboard ship will result in child support from parents that leads to mothers in their early years of graduate school. He wonders if that and increased mingling in public will have overall positive consequences."

"For me, initially, the human dimensions of life and change

were conceptual, without specifics. Now, being practical, I wonder which of many possible and unexpected variations on life might befall us."

Ice said softly, "Comte believes we should expect changes, and that in our lifetimes they will be discretionary. With nine ships and administrations we are bound to have cultural variations among ships. We can move if you are not happy in Key Bury."

"I want to be happy, but I can't help worrying that a future with crucial family secrets would result in an unsafe life for children."

Ice closed her eyes, saying calmly, "We don't have to sit with the others." She gave his arm a little tug toward the activity building.

"We don't have time."

"We can walk and listen. A good pastry will help you listen." Philip nodded, but without smiling and without taking her hand. Ice wiped her eyes.

"Ice, can you tell me generally what you do with this Cobalt-Blue duty?"

She was silent for several steps before saying, "Not yet."

"Commanders only?"

"Oh, not entirely. Are you upset, Phil?"

"I don't want to be, but I guess I am."

"The duty is highly classified, not listed, unknown."

"How can I truly belong if we are to have such secrets?"

"I know you trust me."

"Still, you will be part stranger, and I will not know our exposure to trouble."

"Countless families on Earth have a member with security or professional secrets, even about well-known and normal things. Joan says that overall secrecy shelters those with the vital secrets."

The mass of bobbing white facemasks suddenly startled Philip and he snapped, "It's a sensitive issue with me!"

"My secrets will not make us part strangers. Since you have agreed to no-notice scans, you may know within a few months. Feel better?"

"A bit."

"You must never say anything about Cobalt Blue, or any Blue, to anybody except me or Granddad, regardless of rank or position! Some seamen are Cobalt Blue, most officers are not. Not being is not a reflection on anybody. The group is small, formed on an ad hoc basis. We may continue to use my Blue screen as before."

"That's because you slipped and let me know, isn't it?"

"Yes. You know more than your sponsor, Vanderhought. More than all but a dozen or so Line Commanders."

At the activity building Ice pointed to their left. "Let's use the crew door."

"Will there be an alarm if I enter? I'm not fully processed-in?"

"No, but you are with me. I'm Cobalt Blue for both of us."

An operative with special access. O Cosmos!

In the crew's lounge, they waited in a short line for the dessert table. Each took a chocolate éclair. "I will be marrying into more than one mystery."

"All will be revealed."

"Should I live long enough of sound mind."

"Philip Russell, do not say that!" Ice tapped on the bench, "Knock on wood."

"I didn't know you were superstitious."

"I'm sure I'm really not, usually, anyway, I have no wood handy so I'm not a fanatic."

"It's the many unknowable future variations on life that concern me. Beyond contemplating, imagining, perhaps fraught with perilous variations when vital secrets are involved."

The public address system spoke in the crew lounge, "Robbie has ended the assembly. It's too late for families with children. The details of Plan B will be presented beginning at ten-fifteen in the morning."

"Phil, after we are married, you will be my guide in all things not Blue. We will be happy and grow old together. We agree on so many things."

Facing a long time until fully belonging is better than were my prospects in Compton. And once I know, will I be part of the reason some others do not truly belong? Belonging is a messy concept, beyond discursive formulation. The peril of circumstances to children beyond knowing. But the time between now and revelation will surely challenge my primary process! Will I merely exchange old ghosts for new shadows? Does this mean Ice and I are not suited? I love her for so many reasons. How many reasons will I need not to have her?

"Phil, please return to me." Ice took his hand.

Must every issue be messy! Should a novice adventurer be going— going wherever, daring whatever! Well, going wherever forward does seem more reasonable than going anywhere backward. "I'm here, Ice." He looked at her. "I'm worried, dealing with so many strange and inscrutable issues: Osgood's threats, colonization conundrums, the shadow of Cobalt Blue."

Ice covered her eyes with both hands. "Please let's sit."

They sat with Philip ruminating on his fears. "In the States, children are punished for bullying because a classmate with an emotionally troubled past drops out of school. Adults and children are taught they have free speech and then punished for speaking freely. Employees and bureaucrats are taught there is whistle-blower protection only to find none lasting longer than thirty days before some misuse of official records or other improbity is discovered. A case of languishing in jail for seven years while magistrates and marshals neglect and botch their duties with impunity is not deemed worthy of punishment nor of lasting concern by politicians or media. The case of a public activist being successfully sued for millions because her cause affected an existing business contract is alarming neither to the public, nor to their political representatives, nor to media pundits! Not to mention of no concern to the government's judge. And for one's peers as jurors they allow scofflaws, the willing homeless, the uneducated, and incommensurable mindsets. Likewise, unjust is attorney-client privilege that extends to allowing the conviction of an innocent person rather than the coming forward of any-body's attorney! Lying officials, incompetent officials, scapegoat-ing, crudeness, social and economic dissolution are the American way. Tainted water and medicines may kill and maim, structures may fail because of faulty construction, police may shoot you sitting in your pajamas chatting on your kom, your child may be falsely arrested and become mysteriously ill even before seeing a judge, but no officer, official, or rich person will be indicted. People should get out of most places on Earth if they can find a kindly niche!"

Ice frowned. "The U.N. does its best to prevent there being a single sanctuary niche. The U.N. overlooks countries that dis-criminate against peaceful minorities living there. Still, we might find a few small enclaves that are livable."

"Ice, you would be giving up too much to stay on Earth."

"How can I be happy without you?"

"How could you be happy with me? On Earth I'm challenged by reality. Aboard ship I'll worry over family secrecy."

"I'd be happy because I love you. Don't you love me, Phil?"

"I want to. I'm still here."

Ice's entire face seemed to expand, and she shrieked, "I cry day and night for you!"

"I am here."

"You are not mine! You only want to love me."

"I do love you! Is future family happiness so apparent?"

Ice's eyes watered and she spoke as if to herself, "You see no future with me and our children."

Philip stood, his heart wounded by her tears, requiring a response as would the crying of a baby. Suddenly aware of people staring, he hesitated but took her hand. "I love you. My worries are about the world to come. I need time to understand life in a new context."

"Oh, Phil, there is little time."

"Let's take a brownie and go home."

"Phil, consider that somebody at Pystead needs to help assure that our ten networks are honestly reporting events, have independent voices, and allow a voice to all. Didn't Americans once believe that constant vigilance was the price of liberty? Don't you believe that pluralism is necessary for constant vigilance? Don't you believe in ghost busters? Don't you believe in me?"

"I do believe in you."

She once asked me to leave her if I would need more than her. What if I can't please her? Marriage would be unfair if already I disagree with her on having children! The glow of one moment is no guarantee for the long term. One's intuition must agree for longer than a moment.

Philip closed his eyes. *Should a pale-blue-dot marry a Cobalt Blue?*

22

PLAN B

Friday morning Philip sat with three of their artist friends from Nevis while Ice was finding the latest arrival, Kathy. Philip wondered about life aboard a ship so much smaller than their tiny island. His thoughts skipped to future family vulnerability due to Ice's secret duties, and then, as usual, he had second thoughts. *We are relatively secure because of the transparency brought about by brain scans. Does that simply make a coup attempt more desperate and vicious? Our vetting process is designed to eliminate problematic minds, but how much confidence can one have in only two turbulent weeks of a mind's contemplations? Would I experience a never-ending subconscious nightmare over secrets that others may want to know or suppress?*

Philip went for chocolate nuggets and returned. The artists chatted quietly. He overheard a woman behind him say that gifts would be scarce for perhaps the rest of their lives.

Why shouldn't I give Ice a present, if not for a wedding, simply a gift? Has only part of my subconscious mind entered the real world?

Is facing the real world my problem? Have I come to grips with Kurt Gödel, Lord Acton, Blaise Pascal? How compatible their implicit attractors: incompleteness, pluralism, secrets of the heart. I must remember that conscious thought serves directly only our discursive dimension of being. Too, one need not believe everything one thinks! And what of Joan's warning about strange new variations on life? Do I expect to live in space without cultural changes except for a pervasive lightness of being? Am I capable of accepting the unknowns that must be faced? Would I be ready in my heart to do the things that needed to be done? O Cosmos, can I truly belong?

Since Ice was not in sight, Philip quietly called Administrative Assistance. After mentioning art supplies, he was asked to hold. The next assistant said she painted as a hobby and explained that the established crewmembers were spending all their money since it was not used aboard ship. If anybody later decided to stay on Nevis, the company had remaining assets and would reimburse them.

Philip estimated that 4,500 kicu would pay his debts to Will, and asked for 6,000 kicu worth of canvas, oils, brushes, thinners, and whatever else was needed in balanced amounts for oil painting. The woman helping him was reassuring and ventured an opinion that an artist would want the gift and would like acrylics as well. Philip agreed, and remembering a comment by Ice, inquired about getting the assortment of oil pigments in a base form for mixing one's own colors. His assistant thought that a good idea. He remembered to ask for paper and ribbon to wrap one small box for public viewing. Then he texted Will with the authority and passwords needed to sell his modest investments. He felt better thinking about the proceeds of his small estate that he had bequeathed to ex-colleagues whom he felt were most in need.

Philip's kom beeped. Ice was returning with her friend Kathy and fiancé, Bill. After introductions, Ice mentioned that Pystead still needed two hundred forty new crewmembers. Lois, their administrative officer, estimated only five hundred recruits would remain on campus by the end of the Plan B presentation. Of those, she expected only sixty percent would want to join, leaving Pystead about sixty more recruits than needed, yet without enough choice to balance specialties, ages, and genders for the overall crew.

"Why so many?" Philip asked.

"Because each two ships, called a sector, should become self-sufficient. Because some positions require multiple shifts for alertness on duty. Robbie says that even with an ideal crew we will need considerable cross-training for triple redundancy in all four ship's sectors."

"Ice, are you cross-trained?" Philip asked.

"Oh yes, as a practical nurse. Also, last year I irradiated and cooked food for processing and long-term storage. I operated freeze-drying machines." Ice frowned. "Lois estimates we'll have less than the anticipated acceptances because of the lost months of training and interference by the U.N. Only seventy-eight percent of those expected arrived on campus. Lois is organizing a referral type recruiting drive with last minute pick-up possibilities."

O Cosmos, may my friends be among those possibilities. "Ice, will we leave without a full crew?"

"Not if we can hide someplace safe."

"There is a Plan C?"

"Oh no, only options for implementing Plan B."

Then Philip noticed her glancing repeatedly between her kom and the speaker's podium. *Is Ice now upset about operational concerns, or only upset about me?*

Manager Markwaters finally stepped to the lectern, smiled, and rang his bell. He apologized for being late, saying he had waited for Pystead's latest security update because the topic was about life and death for the company and many established crewmembers. He reminded his audience that further outgoing kom transmissions would not be allowed without approval of security. After pausing while a few families departed, he asked everybody to chat with each child in their vicinity to be certain there were no unattended children, including young adults under twenty-one years of age. Then he advised that children ages four through nineteen be taken to daycare, where a video with audio headset would be available for adults who stayed with them. There followed a flow of families to the activity building. Markwaters asked for word on remaining children under twenty-one, and soon reported all with an adult family member.

Many seats in the quad were empty. Philip had no estimate of how many were in daycare. *All this niche needed was a good leaving alone! Without political opposition, Pystead could have had the ideal number of ships and pilgrims for planetary colonization. But, hey, this is on the real side of the academic wall in an era when only the establishment can innovate or succeed bigtime.*

Manager Markwaters pushed his bell and explained that Plan B would not be available by kom except inside a building. He said that as a change of opinion on security, anybody could now leave campus, but within another ten minutes all remaining at the assembly would have to stay on campus for the night. Making another attempt to communicate, he said loudly, "Commander Joan, secure the campus according to the protocols established for departure."

Joan stood up wearing her red accessories and a beige mask. *The Red Queen lives! The Manager seems to have a glass breath shield. His face is certainly more trustworthy than a mask of any color.*

The masked Commander spoke, "Ladies and gentlemen, in ten minutes the campus gates will be closed to all persons remaining in this tented quad or in an adjacent building. This is your final opportunity to depart this assembly before you will have to stay another night and day on campus." Joan took her seat.

For the unconvinced a moment of truth in which primary process will choose!

Markwaters stepped out and stood in front of his lectern. He said that although he was the General Manager, Commander Joan was responsible for security, and anyone who later had an emergency need to leave campus should contact Security. "Don't call me or Lois Henssen, call Joan Windsor at Security."

After shifting about for a moment, waiting for stragglers to get out of the quad, the Manager pointed to video now projected onto the sides of two buildings, but he did not speak to his audience. Instead, staring at the walkway he yelled, "Do not come closer!"

Heads turned to see a large group led by a man carrying a megaphone. Pystead's guards allowed the man to step just inside the plastic barrier separating the assembly from the outside walkway. He shouted, "We are here to protest our treatment and your total disregard for the norms of the civilized world. Your actions rise to the level of discrimination and bias intimidation!" The uninvited group continued to advance toward the doorway. Philip expected many guards in white suits, but only a few guards met the group and kept them behind the clear plastic quarantine screen along the walkway. The Manager moved to stand behind his lectern.

Guard pods will be covering this event. My own guard pod is here. The Poseidon and serval statues must be robot guards.

The intruder shouted, "The U.N. will hold each of you personally accountable for supporting this illegal Pystead organization!" The large group crept nearer, still behind the clear screen along the walkway.

The Organism!

Their leader again raised his megaphone, calling loudly to his group, "What do you want?"

His group responded, "Sigma Six!"

The megaphone called, "When do you want it?"

They yelled, "Right now!"

"What do you want?"

"Sigma Six!"

"When do you want it?"

"Right now!"

By this time the Organism's members were jumping up and down waving their fists in the air. Children of all ages were conspicuous among the agitated adults.

"What do you want?"

"Sigma Six!"

"When do you want it?"

"Right now!"

The Organism turned and began departing while maintaining their chant.

Sad with heavy eyes, Philip wondered, *What prospects do those children have? Uneducated, living on a depleted Earth with cyborg parents posing as engineers and awaiting the arrival of cargo. O Cosmos, I'm so very fortunate to have a way out!*

⁂

Markwaters addressed his audience. "They are the K.L.J.H. Organism…whatever that means? There are fifty-seven of them, including children. The working engineers refuse to demonstrate the slightest capability using our computer and have refused all cross-training and study of our technical manuals. None can write or read script; only a few can print. They only message using an assist application. They don't even like us, yet they want us to rely on them as an engineering department. They claim that is the way to Six-Sigma reliability for us!"

Markwaters shook his head. "Ladies and gentlemen, our hospital, including its engineering and maintenance support, is superior to any Six-Sigma hospital on the planet. That fact is of no consequence to their, its, way of thinking, or I should probably say to its way of not thinking." The Manager shifted his gaze to the walkway, then looked down at his lectern. "The Organism is around the corner of the Facilities Building. Evidently, any of you who do not plan to go with us should catch up with them for maximum credit with the U.N." The Manager stepped back. A few families hurried after the Organism.

Anyone with close relatives staying behind must worry about their guilt by association—in this most-progressive-ever era.

The Manager resumed speaking, "Ladies and gentlemen, like most business plans, Plan B will have different meanings for different people. I'm sure for most of you it will hold elements of optimism, boredom, and apprehension. For some, Plan B will provide moments of disbelief, even knee-jerk rejection. My advice is that since you cannot leave campus, you may as well stay for the full presentation. If you endure, we might get around to saying something you can accept. Even if not, you would have tales to tell.

The presentation itself began silently with video of the ships, including the view of a main engine, described as an aether-energy powered, field-resonance space drive, located on the bottom of the ship, one in each neighborhood section of each ship: a smooth, oblong area dimensioned at 17 meters by 28 meters with each engine having seven circular areas of flickering white centers within a swirling blue rim. *And that rippled blurring seen beyond the engine is not explained—waves of hot air—distorted spacetime?*

The Manager stepped back to his lectern and reminded the assembly of their witnesses' eighty-eight percent approval rating for the demonstration flight. He motioned to the newly acquired red-rock sculpture on the platform, an imposing presence at more than twice his height. A Netsite video of the tent top in Scotland was shown—one of two sites that could still be found. More easily found was video of the ship's claw picking up the sculpture, with the U.N.'s complaint that the event was a theft by airship.

A mere helium filled dirigible implied. And no mention of a flurry of Gold Pandas, or three policemen from Nevis!

"Only one Netsite has acknowledged that the sculpture was purchased by a foreign agent and scheduled for removal," noted the Manager. When the tent top was again shown, Samantha spotted her pink-and-red blouse, now a nice color panel among the many other colorful and out of place articles adorning the many sloping sections of the large, white tent top.

Shouts of recognition were heard. Philip stood and shouted, "I see my pink and red striped shirt!" He sat down, relieved about doing his part, yet embarrassed. *That's not me. Do I now have a practical side? If I could only accept more of the risks of being in the real world. Our future niche in the cosmos may be strange, yet not unhappy nor unsafe. But with Ice's secrets abounding would my family's niche be more problematic than average, or perhaps more informed and secure? And getting real, any coup that succeeded would eventually affect all our lives…just as here on Earth.*

The Manager outlined their choices as fight, flight, or return home. The only way to fight, since they could not fight the entire world, would be to hide and fight as pirates, terrorists. They could use their stealth technology to assassinate leaders and their key supporters and officers until they got leadership willing to live and let live. Even if so, who wanted to live such a life in such a world? Otherwise, the recourse for established crew was going home as non-professionals, or flight, said by some the choice of the fragile. "I must warn each of you," Manager Markwaters almost shouted, "the fragile must not flee into spacetime with us!"

He frowned and continued, "Beyond our fence, we have much to fear. We have powerful defensive weapons and engine technology that governments and the U.N. would kill to have. All our weapons are illegal for us to possess. Also, if known, our engine technology would be said to infringe nonexistent or backdated patents and would be confiscated and classified secret. Since our compromised attempt to buy helium-three a few years back, we have been the subject of intense U.N. scrutiny. We were not identified because there was no transfer of money. We paid in gold and silver that could later be claimed as a find of long-lost treasure or be used to make jewelry. Still the U.N. came to suspect us. Thereafter we had difficulty finding enough pure helium and platinum-group metals for our projected needs. You should know that we use helium-three in some of our nuclear detection devices, Geiger counters. We will need to be able to detect any fissionable material brought near our ships at sea or in a port, or anywhere."

Manager Markwaters raised his voice, "We know the U.N. plans to overwhelm us through the auspices of the coming Oceania Protectorate that is being forced on Kitts-Nevis." He gave a little palms-up gesture. "We know the U.N. has three atomic warheads. We will depart before their most extreme elements can garner the political or surreptitious means to use one of them against us. Please note that if they can force us to an immobile fish farm, there would be relatively little or no collateral damage to others from a small nuclear explosion if they waited for suitable atmospheric conditions. They need not admit their attack by simply claiming that one of our nuclear reactors melted and exploded." All heads seemed to turn as the crowd buzzed. The Manager waited.

Philip, Ice, and friends all exchanged eyes-only glances. "He's finally being forthcoming about our situation," said Philip.

Markwaters continued, "We now use only thorium fueled reactors, which do not have enough fuel in them to explode or melt down. To our advantage, because thorium does not produce bomb-making material as a by-product and is more prevalent than uranium. Thorium is less controlled and less expensive than uranium."

I'm beginning to trust you.

✶ ✶ ✶

A pitched female voice, not through a mask, screamed from the crowd, "You have put us in the position of joining or going home to be interrogated and blacklisted. You lured us with promises of great things. You said we could go home anytime. You lied, lied, lied!"

"Ma'am, tomorrow is the same as today. You are not yet a member of the crew! The U.N. does not yet know about our armaments, and we will soon be gone. This morning we dismissed a small group of misfits, including a few spies working for the United Nations. They will know that none of you learned about our plans or resources. Those of you who decline crew status should become heroes with new information about us. And you will receive nine months' pay from us as promised, plus relocation expenses."

The woman shrieked, "If they don't know, why do you fear them killing you?"

"Ma'am, we are a model of plurality in thought and being. Treasonous values to the U.N. Our present crew has long dared to exist as a self-determined group of decent people! Enduring the isolation of being a secret community for the sake of their children."

"How do we know you aren't the pirates?"

"I ask you, how does anybody know U.N. resources aren't being used to support terrorists and pirates, or to avoid catching them? If the U.N. is justified in ruling the world, why after many years have they not been able to stop these pirates in the Caribbean? At the beginning of the nineteenth century, a relatively much weaker United States put an end to the first appearance of pirates in the Caribbean. And why does the U.N. need nuclear weapons except to extort others like a few puppet nations? You should consider that the U.N.'s pronouncements make clear that we will not be allowed to sail the oceans as seasteaders, only that we may live on our present fish farm." Markwaters paused, seeming to shut his eyes.

"The U.N. has already said they will occupy this campus and bring justice to all." He tossed his head. "Justice to all but this crew, that would be! And to make matters worse, several high officials already hate us for one of a few reasons, such as our refusal to sell the fish farming business and the medical center. Others are corrupt and willing to do harm for easy money."

The Manager raised his hand. "How do you know a pirate when you see one? Do you think the culture experienced here would be a viable culture for terrorists and pirates? Would you rather go with Dr. Osgood and his human drones? Have you read the U.N.'s pronouncements about our treatment of the K.L.J.H. and compared them to what you and friends have witnessed? Have you read recent U.N. statements about anything? Have you read our policies: posted clear, searchable, cross-referenced with no hidden zingers? Try finding United Nations' policy in any depth. They claim it's their copyrighted policy and will not let anybody post it." The Manager looked around and threw up both hands in disgust. "Try finding out about the quality of life in the places they most directly control. You likely cannot get a visa for even a group tour. If you do, koms will not be allowed: they will not risk unapproved video in or out. They censor as much as possible to maintain illusions both inside and outside their domains. Neighborhoods, shops, hotels, and restaurants are preselected for any visitor. Those public and private spaces will have hidden audio-video spying, even in bathrooms and bedrooms!

"Try envisioning a safe place to live anywhere in the world beyond our fence. Did you feel free to speak your mind to the media? Did you live in a safe neighborhood, and how would you know with the police selectively reporting crimes? I'm sorry to say that if you have not compared us to them over the last two weeks you have little basis for judging who we are versus them!"

The woman and her daughter left, almost running.

Wow! She's certainly not getting off campus tonight. I can't help feeling that she and her daughter are the unlucky ones.

⚹ ⚹ ⚹

Loud and deliberately Markwaters told them, "We did not anticipate the U.N.'s explicit threats on campus, nor their preparations for an immediate assault on this campus. We are, however, acting in time to get you out as a crewmember or home with funding. Recall that your funds are held in trust in your country of origin. You are to be paid upon presenting your passport and providing a bank account of your choice. Otherwise, we have authorized that after thirty days the funds are to be deposited into your account at your present financial institution's Network."

The Manager raised both arms as if a referee making a call. "You must hear the details of Plan B to be eligible to sail with us! We take only informed and accepting people. Any hardship case must register for a video replay because you must hear Plan B. Because we were interrupted by that K.L.J.H. group, the details of Plan B will be heard after lunch. Let's take a lunch break and provide a few minutes for anybody who needs to place an outside call." He stepped back and sat down.

For entertainment, the assembly sat eating and watching white-suited guards in hard helmets scan the walkway and grass over which the K.L.J.H. had moved. Security announced that the guards were collecting mini spy drones dropped by the group.

Ice tugged on Philip's arm. "Were you listening?"

He spoke slowly, "Yes, but we have little choice. I have no known prospects for employment, and you should not leave family and friends and this kindly niche of the cosmos."

Ice turned away crying softly. "Please have lunch." She stood and dashed off.

Philip watched her pass the nearest food service booth. He turned to the artists, "Where do you think she's going?"

Barbe shook her head. "She hasn't been herself recently."

Philip remained seated as the others were leaving for a hot lunch.

"Are you going to be crew, Philip?"

"Yes."

"Good," Barbe told him, "you virtually promised to take all of us out. Remember?"

"We'll certainly have time for that."

I left Compton following a considered course of action, yet none of my thoughts prepared me for what has happened. Over the years, my decisions have been of no help beyond matching my talent to the work available. I didn't manage to avoid the goths or deemers of the world, and now my childhood memes of mind have almost vanished. Plurality and a sense of justice, our imperfect Western culture done. Mixed into pseudo memes said respecting of all, producing a culture of prohibitions, striving for nothing except the closing of gaps! Philip pulled back his feet to let a family pass quickly. *Getting out of the way of others getting out of your way. No incentive to desire more than one's daily routine. A life of balm on automatic if you ask no questions and aren't deemed an antisocial dog. We non-we were concerned about artificial intelligence and robots when we should have noticed the deemers of politics and industry taking over the robots and everything else!*

Philip decided on a return to his VCQ room. *Not like her. Well, she hasn't been herself. Neither have I. How can anybody remain normal facing such a daunting decision?* He stood up. *Are the mysteries hereabouts sufficient to engender taking the risk? Only the high church requires miracles. Perhaps smoke and mirrors is sufficient when the medium of travel is via tangible ship.* He walked slowly. *Of course, a tangible ship needs a tangible crew. At one time I thought myself a perfect match for Ice and crew. Now thoughts are muddled, my psyche tormented. O Cosmos!*

✳   ✳   ✳

Primary process makes the fundamental decisions as to who we are. The mind's innate instincts and complex common sense, plus its self-aware imagination are the essences separating human beings from showboards—separating dynamical organons from algorithms—separating emergent properties from corresponding properties. Conscious ego makes our secondary-level decisions: the implementing decisions. The process of the whole mind is inscrutable because it is nonlinear, entangled, chaotic, imperfect, unpredictable. Results may be good, bad, or ugly. Contradictions occur.

Ice is crying, and I with hollow stomach and stiff upper lip more than tears. With more sorrow for her than for myself. How can I face her? Why can't I make the leap to Romantic and please the woman I love? Have I no help from the heart within and the Cosmos without? No guiding intuition via philosophy? Perhaps I'm only a dog?

Philip took a deep breath and opened his room's door. Ice was not there. Momentarily he stood stunned before entering. Without thoughts of where she might be, he soon had his slippers on and his facemask off. For almost the first time he wanted to drink alone. *Long ago, sweet Sally chided me for not having a real man's drink.* He skipped the wine and found their bottle of scotch, a Speyside single malt that Ice had kept for a couple of her colleagues. Philip poured a two fingers' glass and dropped in ice cubes.

Before his first sip, the door chime sounded. Philip opened the door.

Joan in a jumpsuit, not wearing her medical facemask said, "We need to talk. May I come in?"

"Of course. Have you seen Ice?"

"She is why we need to talk." Philip gestured to the chairs and they sat down. "Melita and I communicate best exchanging voice messages. Melita herself should tell you." Joan reached up with both hands and undid her hair bun. As Philip half-smiled, she shook her head and pulled her hair to let it fall. She unzipped her top until her white bra showed.

Melita winked. "Philip, you know that Ice and I are best girlfriends?"

A sweeter, lower voice than Joan's. He nodded.

"Ice has been upset for days because you can't accept her having secret duties in a family setting."

"My past fears, especially from my treatment in Wheaton I suspect, keep surfacing. So many have no qualms about hurting or killing others. How can I know how I will feel in the future about having children?"

"If that's a hint for Melita the psychic, please know that I never see for friends."

"Is it fair to marry if you have differences on crucial family matters. If secrecy's implications are troubling, how can I promise to bring children into a marriage with potential targeting because of vital secrets?"

Melita closed her eyes. "You know that we have eliminated the dangerous personalities! We scan twice a year for a change of intentions, four times for a commander or commandant, or for a supercritical duty."

"I know there are no guarantees in life, yet don't we owe our children the best possible environment?"

"Philip, how can we know what's best?"

"That's the problem—not knowing! The best I can do is follow my intuition and thoughtful analysis."

"Philip, my personal intuition, albeit more insightful than Joan's, may be merely a function of past and present extrapolated to near future events, except for the few inexplicable dream-like stories."

"I have come to appreciate that much is unknowable, guided by Pascal and Gödel. And those unknown things need not be good."

"Surely we can expect more goodness than on Earth. We have few or no sociopaths! All are educated and can vote on principle because nobody leads a substandard life or fears losing what they have to a hostile administration."

"I have accepted Pystead's apparent misrepresentations of assets and weapons. I accept that decent people should evade the bad cops and politicians. I accept that a great leap of faith is required because I love Ice and trust her judgment and her friends. I have accepted that we will be more citizen than subject, and that we will have a fine chance for survival on Mars, even of coping with endogenous issues. For me, that is getting quite real. Also real is the possibility that someone could try to get to Ice through her children!"

"I don't know where risk-aversion turns from prudence to paranoia. I ask you to consider our eighty-seven principals who are trusting the futures of their children to this vetted crew rather than to any nation and culture on Earth. They are intelligent and realistic people, even if generally not the easiest personalities. They trust in our world to come."

"Melita, have you ever seen future images of yourself or Comte?"

"Can you keep the secret, even from Ice?"

"O Cosmos, is she involved?"

"No. I feel the topic could worry her."

"What if she asks?"

"Promise not to lead her to ask?"

"Yes."

"If she asks you may tell her, noting the uncertainty of the future."

"Fine."

Melita looked upwards and spoke softly. "Comte and I go through life together and vanish from the edge of the potter's vessel at the same place and time."

"That's all?"

"Yes. No events in our stories. We are not slung off. We peer over the edge. We are at peace. We have passed our time, a golden wave descends over Comte."

"If I have survived, I will think of you and Joan together and often, as will the others."

"Perhaps you are meant to be a friend of Joan's."

"A surviving personality?"

Melita nodded and smiled. "I haven't seen you take one sip of that drink. Please go ahead."

"Would you like a drink: gin, scotch, wine?"

"A sip of yours would be nice." She took the offered glass and a sip. "Light, mellow, let's drink together more often. Of course, being Ice's dear friend, my relationship with you cannot be better than her's." Philip frowned. Melita said, "Joan is merely a good friend and would continue drinking with you."

"I wish I could be realistic without being paranoid."

Melita returned the glass. "May I use your loo?"

"Yes." *I could zap a few brain receptors in the D-2 complex and surely accept the ambiguities haunting me. But then I wouldn't be me! If I should not believe everything I think, should I believe everything I feel? If I transgress my feelings am I transgressing innate morality? Is the human the measure of all things, or is one human the measure of some things, with there being many different measures? The Post Essentialists surely interpret Protagoras as accepting the many gods of the Greeks, implying different humanities, hence different measures—although not admitting any differences? Is one human's innateness not another's?*

Sipping the scotch, Philip waited for Melita. When she reappeared her hair and her neckline were up and her lipstick red. "Joan?"

"Yes. You and I must talk after departure. Melita messaged me about your problem with secrecy and about your scotch." Joan stepped close and tilted up her face. "Your marriage is too distant." He kissed her divinely, hands off, eyes closed. She put a hand on his bicep, giving him a quick finger massage. "Hands off lasts a very long time in our strange new variations on life."

"Thanks for stopping by—both of you."

"What are friends for?" Joan smiled. "Philip, you may have supreme confidence in our technology. Our energy source and space drives are reliable even though not described mathematically. We believe that space energy results from a flow of what our scientists call aether energy, perhaps constituting spacetime itself. The hypothesis is that atoms draw a continuous inflow of energy from space to power their subatomic agitations. This space energy increases in density approaching a mass, becoming a spheroid-of varying aether density that is mathematically equivalent to curved spacetime. We are working with some success for an isolated mass in space, to convert an assumed spherical inflow of energy into a directional flow that will produce local gravity in direct proportion to the aether energy density at its absorbing surface. That would give us the means to produce local gravity without constantly accelerating or decelerating the ship, or without using the inadequate remedy of spinning the ship."

Philip nodded.

Joan said slowly, "Also, you should have supreme confidence in your cobalt-blue fiancée!" Joan was out the door.

Philip sat down feeling unreal in an uncertain room, gazing without apperception as through a window to fleeting smiles. He still had the scotch in hand when Ice entered.

"Phil, I'm so afraid."

Philip closed his eyes and his words came. "We can fathom the seas, we can reach the stars, and we know the heart has reasons."

They sat together as the cosmos, vast, unknowable, awe inspiring, coursed softly and sweetly through the circuits of their being. "Phil, are your heart's reasons to merely go, or to marry me?"

"My heart loves you and wants you to be happy."

"How can I be happy without you as my husband?"

"For decades, Ice, I have thought my life guided by keen observation and critical thought. I have done my best at the conscious level. Now I must wait for intuition's guidance, wait to feel that our children could be safe leading normal lives."

"We are at the mercy of the Fates?"

"Yes, it's too late to go on thinking. Unless we know of a flaw that must be shared, we must go. As Melita says, we must wait for all to be revealed."

Ice closed her eyes. "It will be my fault if you are unhappy.

I lured you here because you were my dream come true."

"Ice, you have been honest with me. I required no special lure."

"I said that Pystead was an upright company, but we violated international laws on armaments and disclosure of assets."

"I knew after the proof-of-concept flight, if not before. I chose you and your friends over the deemers of the world. You are my dream come true! We have both done our best. Now the Fates decide. We do have a chance for dignity and glory."

"Glory?"

"Survival of our children and their children, as far as the mind might imagine."

"Then you are optimistic for us?"

Philip's heart seemed to skip a beat. He whispered, "I must be on the cusp of becoming a Romantic."

"Oh Phil, the art world took fifty years to transition from Neoclassicism to Romanticism before its fling with Realism. If you want children by me, you have much less time." They kissed sweetly, eyes closed.

Pystead will have its crew. Poseidon will rise again. The crew will take joy. The ship will sail. And what of us? What of me?

Philip offered the scotch. Ice took a sip. "Phil, many of the trained crew are already aboard a ship. Let's board this afternoon. We can take Char Cat, our four suitcases, and a few paintings in the Egg. We may as well ride it to the ship."

"I have three suitcases and four boxes of books at Mrs. R.'s."

"The movers will bring your luggage and books, the cat pod, the wine, and anything else we need."

"Fine. I'd like to get video of you sitting on a tiger statue before we leave."

"We have them on campus. With the facemask?" They laughed.

"With and without, for all the children." Then Philip remembered Plan B. "Ice, I'm required to hear Plan B. I have to stay on campus all afternoon."

"You can listen while you move and unpack. Joan told me that you know and accept that our destination is Mars and later an exoplanet. She said she introduced you to our energy technology with the approval of Lois and Robbie. I'll set your kom for topics of interest: life aboard ship and questions from recruits." Ice gave him a quick kiss. "If you want to hear the pep-talks about the farms and ships' systems, you can also listen to those. You will be rewarded with a farewell dinner tonight, without facemasks."

"Great." *What a mundane beginning for such an adventure into the unknown. No family and friends to hug goodbye. No gifts of keepsakes and good luck charms. Merely a hasty departure of the forgotten and the hunted. The world for a long time has denied too many the right to a full life. Getting out does seem the thing to do.* Philip sighed. *History records that those who wait for an unmistakable exit sign have waited too long!*

In proponing probabilities, who knows where apprehension might wayward wander? A thing seeming once right may seem twice wrong. Yet the self-selecting of the vetted have reasons to moderate their fear of flight. For Philip, his Wheaton number, P18616HG, still replays and speaks for itself. The mind knows next time could be worse. The heart has hope, sweetened by speed. Speed is power, speed is armor, speed is courage. For Ice, the heart chooses family, friends, and duty. For Saint Germaine, the choice is family and friends, and a long sought human dignity through innate morality.

Did the myths and metaphors of ancient times judge that along the arc of becoming at some propitious juncture, a right singularity would certainly arise, inevitable as the evolving of a self-conscious, carbon-based being? The ancient myths and metaphors did judge that Satan would ultimately be proven wrong. The human difficulty is that actuality trumps potentiality, said since Aristotle. After rolling the dice, one must do or die. Philip stretched out his arms to relax. *Man the ship and cast off. Keep an eye on the Delaware. Cross the Rubicon. O Cosmos, deliver us from those evil eyes of malicious envy and greed. Tomorrow is our day one. Call it…after Earth, off Earth, out of Earth?*

Ice's voice interrupted Philip's thoughts, "Let's take Pearl Earring, I know you like her. The girls in white, one by Whistler, the other by Brate for name-day celebrations. Then Wythe's wind-blown curtains."

Liking 'Pearl Earring' is not getting real enough. I must take the girl in white and accept the chaos. Must take joy at my window of opportunity and hope for a wind instead of a gale. Philip took down the Wythe. *I need to grab a line and lend a hand for the ship. Here or there, I'm real enough. Every man has to die.* Philip paused and swallowed only air, feeling his realness. *Time to face it, every man has to die!* He grimaced. *I should be so lucky as to go quickly with my boots on—more likely on Mars.*

✕ ✕ ✕

Philip caught Ice's arm and gazed at her. "Since you become Alice aboard ship, this is my last day with enchanting Ice."

"I suppose packing will leave her a bit weary."

"Send me off now with a lasting memory of my only true love."

"We were up late. You'll fall asleep."

"You may wake me with cold water. I want you so much, Ice."

She tilted her chin up and pushed her eyes wide open. Philip kissed her and almost drew back when she didn't return the kiss. A voice in his head told him to try and win her heart all over again. He kissed her neck and reached to undo a button. "I love you, Ice, and I need you more than you know."

She gave his belt a tug to unbuckled it. He got her blouse open and smiled at her sheer lace bra. She whispered, "Get naked for me, Phil, then have me to suit your mood."

He pushed off her blouse before he undressed. She smiled and arched her breasts up for him. He surprised her by unhooking her slacks. "I want to see you in your underwear."

"Me or Amanda?"

"She never crossed my mind."

"There is a resemblance!"

He moved close and reached to unhook her. "Without the lace, you will be my original woman." He felt tenderly for her shape, whispering, "You thrill me."

"I've noticed. Now kiss me properly for memories of Ice."

He caressed her breasts and kissed them, and then began his play again. She indulged him until he picked her up and put her on the bed. After another kiss she moaned. "I love it that you want my breasts." He kissed again, distorting her shape. "You can caress me later." Finally, they made passionate love, and afterward Ice rested on her side while Philip caressed her.

As his eyes began to close, he remembered their schedule and gave her a quick pat. "We have to pack!"

Ice stood and did her big-eyed pose. He whispered, "I adore that pose."

"You're the only man I've ever posed for. I'm so glad you wanted me with life still normal."

"Perhaps you should keep your name, Ice?"

"Oh, no! New gravity will produce a new shape. A new name is appropriate."

"Do I get to remember Ice every now and then?"

"Lois says we will have some full-gravity nights. You can call me Ice those nights, although my hair style will be different."

"I like your hair as it is."

"I've already let it grow out a few centimeters. You haven't noticed. Let me vary for a while. Call it a new variation on life!"

"At least it's a variation you can control."

"Yes, unlike over the generations when Pystead's children will evolve a light blue tincture of skin coloring, according to Granddad."

"For this he has a reason?"

"There are precedents on Earth, both genetic and chemical. His idea is more intuitive I believe."

"I'll guess that intuition is from your close friend Melita?"

"Oh, my, then it will happen!"

At what generation on her spinning clay did one Melita Rose foresee this transition: Poseidon to Lord Rama? Being relatively homogeneous our present group of many within several generations could evolve into one self-identity. Even one that's tinctured blue, however not so strange with precedents on Earth.

The couple packed clothes and keepsakes and ate sandwiches from a vending machine in the VCQ. Then Ice sent Philip for a baggage cart. While he was away she changed into her aqua pant-suit that had first attracted him.

PRIMARY PROCESS

The Egg's video revealed the fish farm with a missing section and floating nearby a liberated pontoon without any superstructure from the fish farm. Philip thought the separated ponton must be Key Logos, which had given the witnesses their ride. The cockpit voice informed Ice that she was cleared to land on Key Bury Saint Germaine. Ice pointed to their video screen and a green light began blinking on one of the fish farm's decks. After a slow approach and smooth landing on the superstructure, their Egg craft rested in a docking cradle. Philip said as if to himself, "Yesterday residential pontoons, today spaceships, tomorrow starships!"

The couple stepped out wearing their facemasks and found themselves outdoors under a canopy with their guard pods waiting visibly above the Egg. Philip opened a lightweight baggage frame. They pulled out suitcases and paintings and loaded the frame. With a few commands Ice had a guard pod pick up each end of the frame.

She reminded Philip not to associate them with Saint Germaine, Joan, or Lois. She warned him not to be surprised when Joan was referred to as Melita by those in the know—not in public.

"Phil, please be careful with that carry bag. I have a surprise in it."

"For whom?"

"For our party, our probable engagement party. Want to guess?"

"It's heavier than I'd expect. I haven't a clue."

"You are such a clever creature."

"Favors for the probable guests?"

"Sort of, but more not, too conceptual anyway."

He grinned. "I will rule out margaritas."

"Clever creature. Let's find check-in. I don't know these ships well. Now, lover, no jiggling that carry bag."

"Merely adjusting my grip. Ah, insight, coasters with scenes from campus."

Ice sighed. "I should have thought of that, I'd have enjoyed doing monotypes. It would have been clever of you to bring them."

"I feel bad about that. I have never been the one to give the party."

"I hope our dinner tonight will lift your spirits."

"Since food stores are surely marginal, should we begin with a party?"

"We brought in our own food and wine for this meal. We will serve on faux china plates from a galley. For all departure parties the food and drink is not from ships' stores. In the future, parties with treats will be events like weddings or key accomplishments, and they will not be extravagant. Our food supply is quite adequate."

"It's on the tip of my tongue!"

Ice winked for him. "I'll dance for you after our probable party if you guess in your next two tries."

"Will you wear a fancy lace bra?"

"I'll borrow one of Amanda's."

"Give me a minute."

"You have until after dinner. No asking for hints."

Once inside the ship, after an incorrect stop, they found the in-processing window. The guard issued each a palm-sized stun gun and instructed that their guard pods should not go with them outside quarters except under a Grey-Four or higher alert status, with White-One being the highest. Ice's robot dog was pulled to serve the ship. The guard installed a map of the ship on each of their koms and on each guard pod. The maps could not be transmitted and required a seven-digit access code for other than emergency use.

Not everybody gets the same map? If Ice can find her way to all art galleries, she must have corridors for all nine ships. Surely we all do, because anyone can use any venue in any ship. There are places to locate in other ships, friends, venues, and refuge stations!

The guard began confirming Ice's status. Philip thought of the unmarked Imaging Center on campus. *There must be unmarked doors, even secret passages on some of these maps! The engine rooms, flight decks, maintenance shops, Egg-craft hangars, laser cannons, laboratories, seed storage vaults, all need-to-know only spaces like my imaging building on campus, unmarked with no windows and only one door. Maybe here as well? Cosmos, that implies high secrets for my job and me. How did I overlook that? How many at half-Level Four have their own guard pod and stun gun? Am I already a novice Cobalt Blue?*

The assisting guard explained that apartments were assigned

pseudo-randomly within personnel categories, considering duties and proximity to family and friends. Their category was staff officer with one child. Philip refrained from asking how long they would have to produce the child. "Commander, your apartment selection is complicated by duty-related restrictions." The guard made several selections on his screen. "You may need to change quarters once all are aboard and the family members from keys Marianas and New Ionia move out. You are, however, confirmed for permanent quarters in Key Bury." He hesitated. "Please wait a moment." He looked up. "Please have a seat, this apartment will be ready for occupancy in about twenty minutes."

Philip and Ice were soon following their baggage frame to quarters while taking a close look at the ship. Their pods knew the way and would return the baggage frame once unpacked, which should be done promptly. *Already limited resources are apparent.*

Ice pointed to a faint hair-line trace on the corridor wall. "Phil, this must be a door." Ice knew how to enter and they found a cozy nook with two padded benches. When Philip couldn't find it on his kom's map, Ice explained that small vending and seating areas were not listed and would be discovered mostly by locals. With dim lighting in the corridors for evening illumination people wouldn't be able to see such slight door lines. Only locals who knew the corridor well should find it.

When they continued walking, Ice gave Philip an earpiece for his kom and told him to use his channel 946 to hear Plan B. He could listen anytime and would get a beep for her selections. They were walking slowly when Philip got his first beep and Robbie's voice, "Those of us who stay with Pystead cannot become a fixed target at the fish farm! We were denied a seasteading license, so where do we sail without being called pirates even if we never fire a shot?" He paused. Philip glanced at his wrist kom's screen and saw Robbie on video at the quad.

A man shouted, "If we can orbit the Earth, can we go to the Moon or Mars?"

An audible gasp was heard from the crowd. Robbie replied calmly, "Mars is our best option. We could orbit near Earth or build on the Moon, but the U.N. would find funds to attack us. We don't want to kill to stay alive, nor have our quality of life sapped by the resources and hardships of constant readiness to fight, or to flee, at a moment's notice."

Markwaters paused, raising his fingers while keeping his hands on the podium. "Orbiting is problematic because our ship's radius is too small to spin on its axis for good gravity at more than a couple of adjacent corridor levels at any one time. A huge ship with a radius at least three times our length is needed to reduce the gravity differential from foot-to-head to an acceptable level for long-term health. As to colonization, Mars is a more habitable place than the Moon or Pluto. Orbiting at L-5 near Earth is a short-term option if we must return to Earth, say for our uranium, silver, or gold, but we expect to have everything aboard tonight."

He said happily, "We must go where no human has gone before." He waited for his audience but got only a few laughs.

Only a few watch the old shows. You must search for them and pay extra.

"As pilgrims, we can expect a comfortable life." Robbie happily added, "Not to mention our superior medical care and easy childcare opportunities."

Philip glanced at his kom screen. A man was standing. "The

U.N. has a science station on Mars. Do you think the U.N. could use it to attack us?"

"Not within a decade. We will be the vastly dominate military power on Mars. Our astronomers have a dozen candidate planets in other solar systems to evaluate for colonization, but we are not ready for such a long trip. Also, the planets known to date are probably gray-brown dots having no atmosphere, although within a temperature and gravity range suitable for terraforming—if water is present. Before we jump for any planet, we want confirmation from our scouts of water and farmland present, and of techno-signatures absent. We have the technology needed for scouting and for terraforming. We are in a relatively more capable position than were any of Earth's former pilgrims to new lands."

Lots of assumptions there, like finding beavers and corn instead of locus and germs.

Ice nudged Philip to turn right. The Manager continued, "The U.N. will find the funds to attack us on Mars, but they will need a decade or more to launch a fleet having any hope of success. Before then we will leave the solar system. Over thirty years ago we deployed unmanned probes to several candidate planets. We will not be sailing on a hope and a prayer!"

The couple waited for an elevator. Philip's program continued with Commander Henssen explaining that if families would limit reproduction to replacement levels, the group could stay on the ships for decades, almost forever—estimating fifty Earth years before a ship would need a general overhaul, which could be done in space, one neighborhood at a time.

"How will fuel be obtained?" called a fremitus male voice.

"We use an energy source found in all known space as our

primary fuel. We discovered this through our investigations of Tesla energy. After Tesla's mysterious death, his theories were rehabilitated by Dr. Nikolaos Simos, so that we recognize both as leading indirectly to aether energy, not to be confused with zero-point energy nor Tesla energy. We have learned how to extract this energy from space and use it to directly generate electricity. Our ships have already been to the Moon, and to Mars once, with aether space energy always available. Our latest probes in interstellar space have found the same energy present. We are now and will be existing in a vast tank of energy. Our thorium nuclear and H-H-O energy sources are kept to power emergency electrical systems, and they can power our main engines although we do not know why that might become necessary."

Ice asked, "Are you hearing all right on the move?"

"Fine, although I'm not sure this elevator is actually moving. I'll pause until we get out of the box."

✳ ✳ ✳

Because Ice was a Commander, their apartment was in one of the housing groups reserved for postgraduates. Their location was on deck five down from the top, in the neighborhood at the high end of the ship. Ice explained that at its outer rim, the ship was only one deck at twenty-seven meters high, which if their nine assembled ships were spun on their axis, could became a floor wide enough for doubles tennis at full gravity, and could provide space for ship's facilities that required good gravity. This emergency gravity deck was almost four hundred meters from their apartment. Ice pointed out the nearness of a small exercise room they should use almost daily. She said that according to her granddad, their unlimited supply of fuel would allow the ship to accelerate or decelerate continuously, providing good gravity throughout.

Better read up on our ups and downs in space.

Besides, all trained crew knew that the assembled ships, called the Wheel, would not be spun except during rare events since problems arose with spinning, including that the radial halls became gravity wells and had to be sealed or converted into elevator shafts by relocating the elevator cabs. If spun, local access between adjacent corridors on the same deck would then be via the now unused, horizontal ladder-tunnels that would become spiral stairs between the vertical levels created by spinning. Since a wall would then become a room's floor, and its floor a wall, any sustained spinning would require reconfiguration of spaces.

Our space travel will not be normal travel. Still, we have dwelt long enough on an Earth of tears. We must seek the mercy of the cosmos and be strong enough to deal with vexing new realities. This elevator is moving again.

The couple entered a residential corridor and passed a few doorways before the yellow light on their baggage frame began blinking green. The light went steady green at door number 25, in gold numbers. Philip reached for the doorknob but hesitated. "I know, Phil, but surely we will adapt." She kissed his cheek.

He pushed the door open. They were looking between off-white walls on each side of the doorway, and took a moment to appreciate the short wing walls creating an entry. "I expected a direct view into the entire space."

"Granddad told me all apartments are small and similar, except the units for Line Commanders have a secure office with a dedicated kom station."

A step in revealed the main room to their left having pale-lemon walls. "Ice, do you like it?"

"Yes. I expected off-white, but the hint of color isn't too strong."

"I like the rose-red and cream furniture." Philip counted seating for seven. Ice took his hand. The kitchenette to the right was set across the end of the room, separated by a tabletop pantry in a wood-grained, pale orange finish. Ice soon led Philip to the little square hall almost across from the tabletop, connecting the remaining rooms.

She wanted to see the bedroom. Philip was surprised by an enclosed canopy bed. A hidden latch that Ice knew to look for released the outside edge of the mattress, which pulled up and folded in to reveal a shallow drawer under the side of the bed. Ice said the drawer was primarily for a stun gun and jumpsuit. She found a second drawer on the opposite side.

"Ice, why a canopy bed?"

"It seals and keeps us alive if the room loses pressure or develops a toxic atmosphere. Gives us time to get into our jumpsuits, which then give us more than enough time to help children and get to a refuge space."

"Everybody has these canopy beds?"

"Not yet, we are leaving too soon, but canopy and jumpsuits are priorities. Children's jumpsuits are tubes with wide openings for arms and legs to serve over several years of growth."

Philip noticed a door on the outside wall of the tiny hall space.

Ice knew it was the second way out that all units had. They returned to the hall space, barely wide enough for two. Ice looked in the bathroom and said it was a lighter violet color than the bedroom. Back in the main space, they found another door midway of each side. The door off the kitchen area was another entry to their bedroom. The door off the seating area led to a small, off-white room that Ice said was to be a child's bedroom or an office. They went in and found a narrow door into the bathroom. She remarked, "We have a second way out of every room."

*   *   *

Philip heard another beep and stopped to project his kom's video on the wall. A woman from the audience spoke, "We expect to live long lives. Is the ship large enough for children and parents, or do multiple generations become packed in the same apartment?"

Lois answered, "Ships' apartments will be no more than forty-five percent occupied upon departure, with a total of fifty-two hundred units. Our quarters are livable sizes: college dormitory rooms are twenty square meters; one-bedroom units are eighty-five square meters, and three-bedroom quarters are ninety-five square meters, which is over one thousand square feet. For events like triplets and adoptions we can merge rooms from two apartments. For single adults we have what we call a Graham Hill efficiency unit at forty square meters, with a fold-up bed and desk. We will start out in the largest units and give them to younger families, our children's generation, as we retire or downsize. Our smaller units in retirement will become available to young couples, our grandchildren, upon our demise or sharing in old age. That cycle works with our initial population that will be between twenty-three and twenty-five hundred people, including children. We will be comfortable with family planning and long lifespans. We will be well fed with farming capacity for five thousand, giving us surplus fresh food to store each year. We can use the extra storage capacity of the Tank Building, which can float and fly by itself, and is coming with us. This Tank is a storage and factory ship having life support systems for working crews."

Commandant Lois spoke loudly, "If ten thousand people are considered necessary to maintain genetic diversity over many generations, how shall our descendants thrive? With family planning! Within days of departure, we will ask for saliva, blood, and skin samples, and fully sequence each person's genome. We will post a genetic type for each person aboard. With few exceptions, other things being equal, same type couples will be approved for only one child, and the most diverse of types might be allowed three children. Gene editing can resolve many concerns. Overall, our population must not grow beyond four thousand until a stable colony has been established—this not on Mars! We and our adult children must be content with replacement levels in order that our grandchildren can comfortably reach a colony planet beyond this solar system."

Lois said slowly, "Remaining on Mars is not realistic because the U.N. already claims Mars for Earth, and they will surely not relinquish that claim within our lifetimes. Interstellar travel to escape the Earthlings is very doable with our technology, once a destination planet is chosen, and by that time already scouted by our unmanned probes! The difficulties of our group need not last forever and ever. Those of you who sign on must want to join us, not change us! On Mars we will find materials to help with construction of a temporary colony, but not enough materials or time to support building another starship."

When Philip looked around, Ice was wiping tears from her

eyes. He froze. She said, "We can get office furniture for the extra room." She looked away from him.

Philip said softly, "Ice . . ."

"Just let me be."

Philip heard another beep and listened although he could not concentrate. *Why did we have to hear about children at that moment?* He shook his head. *Getting real, it's not the timing, it's me!*

✳   ✳   ✳

On his screen a woman stood. Philip pushed off the video projector and speaker. The woman sounded loudly in his earpiece, "Will you abort all but designer babies?"

Lois's voice answered, "Our policy addresses the complexity of our situation. We require intervention and abortion to avoid compromised babies having a serious birth defect or very high probability for chronic disease. For genetically predicted traits not detrimental to the germ line, the prospective parents may decide to carry the fetus to term. We recognize the constraints of our situation and have chosen long-term genetic quality as the greater good." After a pause, Lois added, "Our brain scans have checked all here for the onset of neurodegenerative diseases, and you may recall that we asked questions about abortion for sex or color of hair, et cetera. We dismissed those favoring such a highly personal reason for an abortion."

A young woman stood. "Commander, this family planning could intrude as much on personal feelings as did the old prohibitions against marrying divorced or lower-class people that hurt the lives of many European nobles and royals! Have you thought about that?"

"Marriage of a close genetic category is discouraged, not prohibited. Even then having two children could be possible if gene editing were feasible."

The young woman insisted, "Your restrictions coupled with mistakes and unplanned pregnancy could be devastating!"

"We do our best to screen out those not ready for new variations on life, of which we have cited examples." Lois turned and spoke to the entire assembly, "Space exploration is not for the faint of heart nor mind! We have mentioned a few possible problems: imbalances between the numbers of men and women, hence needed polygyny or polyandry, temporary sharing of quarters, family planning and genetic issues, a life circumscribed by limited physical space and resources, a life needing physical exercise. A life where luxuries are experiences among family and friends instead of consumer goods." Lois raised her voice, "If living with any endogenous issue raised by us, or imagined yourself, is beyond acceptance then you must stay on Earth!" She took a moment before saying, "Once in space, you have no reasonable hope of returning!" She showed a settlement dome of red glass planned for enclosing farmland on Mars.

Yes, it is written the meek shall inherit the Earth! Yet who among us can truly know if heshe is ready for strange new variations on life? I suppose, however, each can know if not ready? A case of proof favoring the negative. And for myself? Well, my intuition has me here, so now it should help me become a spaceman in full—and soon!

After waiting for a follow-up that never came, Lois continued, "We recycle everything with almost complete efficiency so that our initial provisions alone can sustain us for decades with little farming. The two spaces between our three pressure hulls are storage tanks. We have water with its hydrogen and oxygen. We have stores of carbon, calcium, ascorbic acid, nitrogen, and many other elements and molecules. We have farms. We have fish and livestock. We produce marbled meat protein quickly, abiotically.

Lois paused before saying, "Moreover, we can regenerate many human organs, fingers, et cetera. Whole limbs can be regrown as done in a few cases already—without public awareness of course. We synthesize genetic and molecular medicines tailored to the individual. We synthesize super antibiotics that kill all the known superbugs. We do not have to stock nor manufacture the myriad number of drugs now available for medical treatment. We do, however, have a fine stock of traditional drugs on board, and samples and formulas for most drugs even if the drug itself is not aboard in quantity."

Ice sat down on the sofa still in its plastic wrap. She wiped her eyes. Philip's eyes were watering. He said, "The apartment is small, but I like the arrangement and colors. I suppose we should unwrap the furniture?"

Ice rubbed her eyes and stood up, not crying, but her voice trembled, "Not yet. The furniture is only stored here until assigned a location. We can request to keep it."

"Where will we put the cat's pod?"

"Char will be delivered in his pet pod equipped with an automatic feeding and waste cleaning unit." She paused to wipe her eyes.

"Perhaps we should put it against the wall across from the entry, out of the way until we need the spot for another seat in the main room." They looked again at the space. "Ice, the entry's wing walls fold back. We can seat eleven using the counter stools."

"Enough seating for many of our art gallery staff meetings."

Philip again looked around. "I think the place will look cluttered if we hang many paintings."

Ice nodded. "I agree, we will need to rotate except for Vermeer's *Girl with a Pearl Earring* that will fit nicely in the loo. After we see other units and check the catalogs we'll know if we want to change anything. We can file an exchange request as elaborate as we'd like. Ask for a new location or neighbors by name, ask for different furniture. All requests will be considered when next assignments are offered, after we rendezvous with the two ships now in the Pacific Ocean."

"All that on top of location criteria for ship's duty personnel, and the computer has quite a puzzle. I'm satisfied if you are."

"Phil, we should begin thinking about furniture for an office lounge."

Have I nothing encouraging to say? "Ice, what if we begin with office furniture, but want to swap for a child's bedroom?"

She did not smile. "Could be in stock or available from somebody else swapping."

"Good."

"If not, all furniture can be melted and recast."

"Right, Lois said we recycle everything."

"Too true."

She must be feeling better? "Ice, should we stow our stunners before we forget."

"Let me show you how to operate the security system for the bedside drawers—watch carefully."

"This item of equipment you're handling?"

"Granddad has drilled alerts, security, and safety into me over the years, but you must help me with the pet pod."

"Every appliance has posted and screen operating instructions."

"You are good with those kinds of details, please help."

"Of course, but you must learn too."

"Be patient with me."

"Ice, be patient with me and my ways. I'm slowly becoming comfortable with strange new variations." She nodded slightly without looking his way. Philip wanted to say all would be fine with children. The words did not come.

He tightened his upper lip. *How can I trust Markwaters without trusting Ice? Vanderhought doesn't know about Cobalt Blue. Markwaters may not know about Blue! If important crew don't know, why do I feel a right to know after fifteen days? Cosmos, one can belong without knowing everything. It's Ice's secrets and our children's safety that worries. Obviously, there is no hope for descendants without some risk. How do I decide for a child? If I bring children into known miserable circumstances…am I any better than a god who allows misery to abound?*

Would a caring god have created sentient creatures cast in lot with psychopaths and gothic creatures of the deemers? What if a god created the cosmos but vanished, transcendent, although bringing into becoming a humanity both rational and spiritual, empowering each to a synthesis of the rational and irrational, perhaps elevating humanity beyond merely instinctive and causal thought? God's a spiritual immanence secure in primary process, although his creatures suffer both physical and emotional pain. Given a Cartesian mind, who's to say?

Philip stopped his Plan B program, shutting his eyes. *Metaphysics can only be about things beyond the pale. Hey, I'm not going to be within this pale but one more day! Tomorrow night I'll be in space or Davy Jones's Locker. Tomorrow everything changes! I must choose wisely.*

Ice said going was her second biggest decision. Have I made going my first big decision with all else to be determined? Going one day off the edge of Melita's spinning vessel. Going with the woman whose first big decision was living with me. I ought to be going with her! And I ought to respect the decisions nature has chosen her to make.

Ice stepped into the loo. Philip heard her speaking to somebody. *She hasn't screamed for me to get out of her life. Perhaps she should. Perhaps I ought to get real and please the woman I love. Thinking is so much easier than doing. I suppose that means my primary process is still churning? My subconscious self is in limbo! I am here because I fear going back. I'm in limbo because I fear going forward with children. The fear is intuitive, from the heart, from primary process wired by nature and experience. Yet according to my own concept of subconscious and conscious dimensions of mind being entangled, this should be an instance where conscious thought informs the inscrutable machinations of mind. Have I not grist for the mill?*

In the loo, Ice said loudly, "What a relief." She came out and told Philip that Samantha's husband had been found and was scheduled for rescue, and Isaac was recovering as expected.

Philip gritted his teeth. *Once I promised we would talk about having children and almost implied she would decide. That was primary process speaking before my concerns about secrecy and children. Too, Ice said I would be her guide in all things not Blue, misspoken because she loves me. She wants children. I can rationally conclude that our world to come will be much safer than today's world. Who am I to come here and choose the end of lineage? Who am I to know Blue after fifteen days? Ice, please be patient with me.*

Philip's kom beeped. The topic was artificial environments being well understood, including the function of insects in the food chain and microorganisms in the water and atmosphere. *I believe it! I'm sure Vanderhought believes it. I'm sure many scientists want to hear it.* He glanced at the list Ice had set for Plan B and deleted it. *Details enough.*

Ice said that after boarding was settled, they must visit her mom and dad, Isaac, Norman, Brian, Samantha, and their five artist friends. She called her granddad and asked when her parents were arriving. The answer was soon and all was well. She seemed to relax, but Philip couldn't relax. Seeking a pleasant topic, he asked about their paintings. They decided to hang only six paintings since they might relocate.

When the pet pod arrived with Char Cat, Philip gave the cat to Ice and downloaded the User's Manual. *Why did I think this cat house would be simple with an on-off switch and four hold-down clips? Seems I'm not yet a real-world person. I'll be real enough to check waste disposal before feeding the beast. Goodness, already both are napping.*

Philip's kom beeped several times. *Must see Plan B?* He projected the video on the wall. The Manager seemed to be frowning. He said he would be brief. Early Saturday morning, one ship would be waiting on the back-campus lawn and two at the ocean docks. Loading should take about twenty minutes. There would be late pick-up possibilities, but they would be problematic, and individuals with the most useful education would be given priority. After tomorrow morning, for a few days, there would be a few opportunities to get aboard. Those wanting to stay on Earth could be put off just before departure. *Ice said we could go into hiding if we needed more time. And she was certainly right about boarding early. I'd rather watch the commotion of general boarding than be part of it.*

Ice woke from her catnap before Philip finished reading about cat-pod features. He was worried. "Ice, Robbie was somber during his last talk."

Ice called Joan and learned that she expected an attack intended to stop their departure. Philip could think of nothing appropriate to say, so he asked about the dinner that Ice had mentioned. She seemed to force a smile and told him their company would include Granddad, Melita Rose and Prince, Lois and Dusan, Harinil Salcmann the curator for modern art, and his wife, Rathy. Sasha Gutkin, the Manager of Logos Key, would attend without her husband. The entrees were provided by her Granddad—Chilean sea-bass, synthetic rib-eye roast with Bearnaise sauce, and spinach.

Then avoiding Philip, Ice investigated linens and the pantry. Philip's thoughts returned to the surprise items in her carry bag, but he could think of nothing new. He did decide not to mention the first thing that came to mind, to evaluate before answering. He helped unpack at a leisurely pace as if in some motion malaise. They worked well together, but Ice would not look at him. He wanted to put his arm around her, to say children would be fine, desirable, but the words did not come.

Ice said she would get ice cream from a food kiosk on the main concourse and be back soon. Philip tightened his upper lip. *A great river of being requires only survival and reproduction. I think of human nature as the essence of the divine, an innate goodness in primary process beyond the grasp of deemers. And idea compatible with pantheism and ancient Spinoza's god in nature. True enough in the past, but innate goodness is no longer beyond the reach of deemers using functional brain-imaging and cyber-knife surgery! Already does the burden of keeping divine goodness alive fall to nurture and consciousness? Are we entering an age of deemers? Am I fast-tracked as a deemer to work for the free side of nurture? O Cosmos! Are there more dimensions to our future life than imagined in my philosophy?*

After the ice cream they continued unpacking and reading appliance manuals. They passed the day with perfunctory conversation. Ice chose a chartreuse dress for dinner and changed in the loo. Philip felt alone, miserable, and haunted by an incessant voice in his head wanting to be heard. *Is it Gödel? Pascal? Melita? No, no, it's my mother! Mother regrets not giving me a brother or sister, reminding me that I have a close cousin and should keep in touch. Reminding me that Lauren is a child of big emotions and will help me become a more extraverted and warmer person.* Philip smiled knowing that Lauren wanted to join them.

Another four hours of reading followed as they avoided each other. Philip was miserable and assumed the same for Ice, the only woman he had ever truly loved. And he was the cause of her misery. His heart had reasons, yet his primary process told him not good reasons. His mind swirled and his heart ached at not being right for her.

On their way to dinner, Philip and Ice passed a large crew party in one of the galleys. *No parades, but we do get final festivities—without masks.* Philip asked about Joan's husband. Ice said that Prince, as they called him, was named Ewen Beata Ossowska, a concert pianist, who had cross-trained as a sous chef to make food requisitions from farms and stores, and to prepare menu staples. An introvert and on the prudish side of socializing. On Nevis he would not attend dance parties with Joan, nor allow her to attend beach parties in a modest two-piece swimsuit. Ice added, "He accompanies Joan when she is Joan. When Joan is with our little group she is primarily Melita, and Prince has attended only a dozen times, I think, over the years."

"Stranger and stranger, your friends. What about Sasha?"

"Her first husband was killed three years ago in a terrorist bombing during a routine trip to buy supplies. Sasha finally rebounded to her warm, extroverted former self and remarried a few months ago to an engineer named Woody. He drew top quarantine status and is attending a special, masked party."

"What about Dusan? How did he meet Lois? What's his specialty?"

"Phil, is there an assumption that Dusan is Afro-European?"

"I suppose so."

"Dusan is Eritrean. He's here because he provided medical care for pregnant wives of the opposition political party and had to flee for his life. He crept across the border in the middle of the night. A resourceful and brave man. He's now a Western-educated medical doctor, cross-trained as a specialist surgeon."

"I believe Eritrea has returned to its previous clandestine support for terrorists, and to once again banning the meningitis vaccine."

Ice nodded. "Long ago, Dusan got out just a week before an intense campaign of agitprop and border patrols."

Surely a long-ago manifestation of dark money. Approaching the dining room, Philip wondered how off-campus and critical crew would dine together. *Tables at six meters?*

⁂

Why do friends gather? When are they willing to gather? Would you dare a group video that might mysteriously make its way into the public domain and displease some ghostly hero for a cause? When freedom coincides with some seminal event, however, a ceremony is natural and needed to mark the human heart. For better or for worse, memories warm or chill the heart and influence the circuits of the mind. From the shape of pheromones to circuits of instinct and culture, solace may be found among friends. Happiness in the resonant sharing of beauty, joy, longing, and suffering. Among friends, instincts meld and people thrive. The heart has needs. Belonging is one of them.

In the dining room, Melita Rose, unmasked, waved them to the left and said masks could be removed, but to use the disinfectant lotion. She smiled warmly and bestowed a kiss on Philip's cheek. She was wearing a white jumpsuit unzipped down a dozen centimeters. Her accessories, lipstick, and nails were all lustrous platinum. *No red this evening. Still, the jumpsuit allows transformation—zip and voilà, Joan! She must be Melita because her hair is down.* Then Philip realized that Melita Rose with her hair down had again not reminded him of Joan with her hair up. *I should recognize the same face regardless of hair style. Could my fusiform gyrus be going?*

Speaking of strange! A clear plastic curtain hung in an arc, dividing the large round table. On the smaller side, Comte and Lois were seated, with Dusan sitting beside his wife, and Sasha beside Comte. Without handshakes or hugs, Ice sat beside Dusan, across the dividing curtain, and Philip sat across the table from her. Prince and Melita sat beside Ice. When Harinil began to sit beside Philip, Rathy in a jumpsuit waved him over a seat before leaving the room.

Wondering about the source of a slight hissing noise, Philip discovered a clear tube with many holes lowering above their heads. *Must be entraining our breath for added protection.* Having searched for the slight hissing without provoking comment from anybody, Philip realized he might continue searching for pin colors. Soon he knew. *Ice has the only cobalt-blue stickpin, yet all belong. What about me? Well, I suppose that depends on me!*

Philip noticed a distinct area of smoothly finished flooring in one corner of the dining room. He asked about it. Melita answered, "This café is for intimate dining and dancing. Unmarried adults, twenty-five to thirty-six years old, are allowed up to two extra glasses of wine per week when dining with a bona fide date not a steady. The oldest couples thirty-six and under have priority for reservations and seating."

"You could bring me to dance, Phil."

"I should have lessons first."

"Dancing lessons are available," Melita said.

Two servers who arrived with platters of food for the table were greeted as friends. Next, they brought bottles of red and white wine and poured them into two large flasks set beside the table. From those two flasks they poured glasses on the table, red or white as requested.

After first sips, everyone heard a loud knock, knock, knock on the dining room door. Comte said loudly, "Come in."

A woman entered, veiled, dressed in white island clothes, wearing a straw hat and carrying a small white suitcase.

Comte asked, "Where are you coming from?"

She answered, "Earth."

"Where are you going?"

"I want to go to Mars."

"Welcome stranger, please join our farewell dinner."

"Thank you, patriarch. Thank you all."

The woman took the seat beside Philip.

Ice leaned over to Philip and whispered that Harinil and Rathy were in the off-campus group because Harinil traveled to buy art and consulted with the Nevis Art Gallery.

The woman pulled the veil over her head and added, "His last trip was to India proper, my home country, and he wouldn't take me."

"It was a whirlwind trip, Rathy, with transportation problems and no time for visiting."

"He is obsessed with paintings, especially his own."

The woman turned to Philip. "I'm Rathy Salcmann, we met briefly at assembly wearing those dreadful medical masks." Philip smiled. They were all smiling.

When Rathy passed the salad dish to Philip, she whispered, "He paints nudes using live models who he sleeps with, so he leaves me on campus."

"Ah." *Not a happy spacegirl, this Rathy. I'm sure Ice isn't close to Harinil. Seems he's outside our social circle except for big groups. Lois and Rathy must be the close friends.*

Philip soon realized that unlike the chardonnay and syrah, the grilled Caesar salad and entrees to come drew little comment. Melita even lamented that although they would be drawing nearer to heavenly spirits, they would be receding from the Earthly spirits. *Ice has brought wine for the engagement party.* Then he remembered not to decide hastily. *Must keep listening. How many spirits are there? Beer, sake? No. Champagne? Of course, Ste Wolls from Lamancha House. Any problem with that?*

The platters were passed, and a second wine glass brought to each place. Philip ate slowly and sipped the Earth wines. *Perhaps I could cross-train as a vintner? This unoaked chardonnay is fine with the mild fish. And I'd say the beef is perfect and the syrah, mellow for a red?*

As Philip savored a sip, Melita stood and bounded out of the room. Conversation ceased and wine consumption increased. Within two minutes she rejoined the anxious group, reporting for Joan, "The Admiral's battleship has changed course. Evidently he is willing to call off his meeting with the E.T.s or let somebody else handle it. Or perhaps there is no meeting, not even a fake meeting. Regardless, there is nothing to be done now. Joan says to enjoy our meal."

Comte remarked that although the dinner was a bona fide farewell to Earth, he also had enjoyed a penultimate farewell last week on the back-campus lawn, to him a magical moment with friends amidst the Earth's calming deep greens and blues. He reminded his friends that thanks to the efforts of astronomers and scientists, the cosmos, if still mysterious, was no longer foreboding. Comte mused aloud, "Here my jewels are impressive. They should be as bright throughout the Milky Way."

Sasha raised her glass. All followed her lead and drank an unspoken toast to the brightness of Comte's jewels.

⚹　⚹　⚹

With a smile seldom seen, Comte began, "Long ago, awakened by a vision on a clear night, I began a quest. Having read The Book, I went out and looked up to Jupiter and then beyond unto the cosmos. I counted the stars, not dismayed as we would have no constellation, and trusting in my dream I reckoned it to our merit." He nodded. "Since my first permanent recruit, Lois, we have sought a place where a live-and-let-live culture might flourish over time. You and others of the crew are the culmination of that work. The window of opportunity has been marginal, yet adequate."

Comte spoke softly, "We are a talented and moral crew who will cooperate for the common good. We are The Pystead Singularity! We are the diviners of the deceivers on this Earth. We are knowledge and power. We are the elect offspring of the fertile valleys. We are the nemesis to the high mountains. We are the true conjurers on this sphere, and we shall open a doorway to the cosmos and close it behind us. We are seeds of glory, to be numbered as the stars. Let us say, Amen!"

"Amen," said they all.

Comte savored a taste of wine, emulated by all. "Too many on this Earth are without moral emotions. They banish the fine arts and writings and rule without wisdom. They have altered the arc of becoming so that our memorials are unjustly forfeited from the Earth. Yet do not deceive yourselves that you go to better humanity. You go alone to be alone, for yourselves and your descendants. Anything more is unknowable. Be worthy. Be true to your legacy that your future generations might inherit integrity of self. Keep well my cordon and the diadem, both intact. Remember me."

✺ ✺ ✺

Each raised a glass and drank with Comte. Philip noticed that Ice closed her eyes. *Does she know? I did not. There will be no return from Mars because of the U.N.'s hostility, nor later from a far planet because of time's arc to potentially advanced and hostile Earthlings. O Comte, set us on a true arc. O Pystead, be clever. O Russell, be strong.* Philip gazed at his wonderful, probable wife and her friends and Granddad. He closed his eyes, shook his head. He glanced afresh at his new world of people, at his new home of metallic silvers and off-whites. *Ice can be mine to have and to hold. Thank you, mysterious Cosmos. Thank you, Saint Germaine, for your many mansions. Thank*

*you, friends. I must get real in all dimensions of mind to have a full life.
And I've never seen the diadem!*

The evening proceeded with good food and affectionate
exchanges. Philip learned the Chilean seabass came from Pystead's
fish farm. The exquisite roast was grown abiotically. The cows
raised aboard ship were milk cows. The cheese was from the
Pystead dairy aboard ship. The romaine lettuce was grown in
rooftop gardens and aboard ship. Philip learned that grape vines
in shipboard viniculture should produce enough wine for one glass
every other week per adult. As Comte put it, when spending bil-
lions of kicu, why stint on grape vines? *Aha, Ice has champagne in
her carry bag. She knew I would be handed the answer. And I'll need
a toast.* Philip thoughts froze. *I can't ask her to dance for me when
she's unhappy, and rightfully so!*

Melita stood again. "Excuse me." She was away five minutes.
"The U.N. battleship is tying up three foo fighters and four top surveillance pods because the Admiral has a nuclear warhead aboard.
It was loaded onboard two weeks ago during the night. We have
independent confirmation from sensors on two foos and all pods
that the warhead is below decks and not in a missile launcher. We
have video of non-crew technicians boarding the ship an hour
before it sailed. That surveillance is the good news."

"What's the bad news?" asked Lois.

"Bad is that we cannot afford to be nearer than six kilometers
if the nuclear warhead blows."

"Surely troops have been put closer to atomic blasts than that."

"Perhaps, but in foxholes. Our three hulls would not provide
complete protection from the gamma-ray burst if it were colum-
nated. We don't yet have aboard all the water needed for good

shielding in space. We are transferring our onboard water to the hull tanks above the waterline and shielding critical spaces with hydrogen-enriched polyethylene blocks."

Ice exclaimed, "How can he sacrifice the battleship without martyring himself, which I thought he would not do?"

Melita explained that the battleship was carrying two mini submarines as well as rocket launchers. The Admiral could send the bomb closer in a sub, or he could escape in a sub and sacrifice the battleship. He could say Pystead sank his ship and caused the stored warhead to explode. Melita continued with a frown. "We have been demonized enough that most of the world is ready to believe anything."

And with only one source of information, who could raise a question or check a fact?

Melita remained standing. "Line Commanders must join the Federation Council to discuss tactical options. We could return to campus tonight for the pick-up, but surely that would be felt as another high-pressure tactic and frighten off still more recruits. We could sink the battleship, but that would kill young seamen and put our recruits staying behind at increased risk. We could destroy the Admiral's two mini-subs and hope he would not martyr himself, but we will not risk our lives on a hope. The Admiral could be assassinated by another officer who would martyr them all."

Melita took a step backward, and then again back to the table. "There will be an alert! Go to quarters and prepare. Do not worry as we are not about to take a bullet. I would, however, be careful to secure loose items and drawers. Double-check floor latches on the furniture. Help your neighbors, especially those with children.

Call your new friends. I'd sit down at Grey-Four, we could escalate quickly. Now I need to get my brother help with his horse."

Melita turned, but before taking a step she stooped over, reaching for her glass of wine. Keeping her head low for the dividing screen, she said, "Let's drink to a better life out of Earth."

As they bumped glasses on their side of the hanging plastic, Philip knew, *Ice brought champagne!*

Comte put on his medical facemask. All followed his lead and stood.

Comte drank wine, but I don't think he ate more than a few bites of salad and fish. Philip asked Melita, "Wouldn't Joan be doing humanity a service if she could find a way to kill that rogue Admiral?"

"Yes, but for the sake of acquaintances left behind and for our descendants who might visit Earth generations from now, we don't want to be labeled killers."

"There may be an acceptable way."

Melita thought for a long moment. "A surveillance pod tells us the Admiral plans to visit me at my home on Nevis."

Philip advised, "A pointing by his tribes root man, herbalist, will not reveal a cause, even with an autopsy."

Melita replied, "Excuse me, all."

Before she could move, Lois asked, "Melita Rose, what's new under the sun?"

Melita raised her eyebrows. Her voice answered sadly, "There is nothing new under the sun. Consider the English poet Edward Young, inscribed at the American Library of Congress, 'Too low they build who build beneath the stars.'"

⁂

Melita put her glass on the table and pointed to Philip. "Please step over here for a brief chat." The step-over ended around two corners. Melita pulled her hair into a pony tail and looped it with a red ribbon. She zipped up her top. Her smile faded. "Now I'm Joan. As your friend and mentor, Philip, I must tell you that your scheduled career path involves security investigations as a member of Federation Watch."

He was surprised by the topic but responded, "My manager, Snyder, says the same without the name."

"Do you know you will have secrets to keep? Can you keep your secrets from Ice? Would you have the courage to pursue troubling leads close to home, involving people you might know?"

Philip said slowly, "Ice will have no need to know."

"Your brain scans would be a threat to would-be usurpers of management power. You missed Lois's mention of Duty- Site Committees in Plan B. Any problem reported by three or more crew-members will receive an immediate and through investigation."

"A form of pluralism that I believe good."

"Good, until abused, say with easily organized, small front groups to incite, to vitiate, as part of a political movement of dirty tricks."

"A real-world issue."

"Very! If a conspiracy was suspected, an investigation with scans would be necessary, conducted by crew emotionally fit for the task. Secrecy would be vital. In a coup attempt, physical attacks could occur. Whereas Ice, a member of the unknown League Watch, indirectly investigates an organization or a team, your scans would be of individuals. Your decisions on whom to scan and when could be the first elements of an investigation. I suspect you could have a problem with that. You will have to think about the situation and come to terms with yourself. I will have to scan you again, friend Philip, for the sake of the crew. You could transfer to pure research, medical support, or aptitude assessment."

Philip faced her with a blank stare, finally saying, "Good points. How can I have children and make targets of them?"

"Perhaps that probability is lower with your help at detection?"

"Kurt Gödel implies we can never know enough. Who's to say?"

"Certainly not Melita Rose!"

Joan pulled down her facemask and then Philip's. She took his right hand, brought it to her waist and stepped in smiling. She kissed him before stepping back and pulling on her facemask. "As your friend, Philip, I want you and Ice aboard as a happy couple." She kissed him on the cheek through her medical mask.

"Thanks, I needed that."

"You promised not to cross-train reserved line to please me, remember?"

"Yes. I want that for myself."

"In our next variation on life, Philip, we can be close friends with my hair up and your hands off."

"Divine. I will grow to love you, Joan."

"I hope so."

Then Philip recalled that the Melita-Joan dual retained continuity of time, but not of events.

Joan, I thought you wanted to chat about a root man?"

"Were you just talking with Melita?"

"Yes, about the Admiral."

"Melita hasn't messaged me about a change of topic. She must have expected you to continue the conversation."

"Recall, the Admiral's biography said when he last visited his tribal home in Arnhem Land he bought a tourist mask, but he took a family mask, a much finer, ritual mask. When the mask maker tried to stop him, the Admiral choked the man to death. As a child, the Admiral lived with the tribe and attended school near Katharine, Australia. Based on his scans, he may retain a primitive entanglement of subconscious morality and physiology."

"Psychosomatic?" Joan asked.

"Yes. Melita said the Admiral has plans to visit her for a reading at her home on Nevis. If you can find his tribe's herbalist, root man, he will point the Admiral who will die within hours to days! An anthropologist should be able to tell you which tribe he comes from."

"We have reservations about killing the Admiral."

"Melita told me that. In a death by pointing an autopsy will not reveal any cause!"

"If I can spare Melita a so-called visit by the Admiral, and spare the people of Oceania his abuses, I'll do it. I'll have to become a Valkyrie. Let's return to dinner."

Joan walked Philip back to the table and picked up Melita's glass of wine. Philip noticed that Lois took Dusan's hand and seemed upset as she turned to go.

Am I already in line as a future Cobalt Blue? Would I rather reside behind the walls of academia and not worry about the fate of academics in worse times? Still, am I suited for this realm of physicalism beyond the walls?

The Line Commanders threw goodbye kisses and departed with Comte for Council.

Ice asked, "What was that pointing talk about with Melita leaving the table and returning as Joan?"

Philip said, "A long story. Let's get home first." Then he inquired, "What was that under-the-sun question about?"

"Oh that? Melita always answers with the same essence. The exchange has become a ritual."

Philip asked, "According to ritual, who asks the under-the-sun question?"

Dusan answered, "Lois is worried by Melita's answer. Lois feels that Pystead is not poised to succeed until the answer is positive."

"Ah!"

"A year ago was Lois's turning point, when she mentioned our unique and secret aether-energy engines and resonant-force propulsion drives. Melita told her that our technology was derivative from an old space energy idea and newer spacetime-resonance concepts, and that the technologies could be discovered by others at any moment."

Ice added, "Lois knows Melita is not a Sybil. Still, Lois is fifty-five years old and doesn't want her twenty-two-year-old daughter growing up without a safe place to raise a family."

Rathy asked, "Philip, do you know that Kali Key has a philosophy club that covers Eastern philosophy? Epic tales, Sufi poets, with Sufi and Hindi poetry in dance."

"Interesting."

As their friends departed, Ice called after them, "Remember to help your neighbors. Be sure they aren't isolated during alerts." Hands waved.

Philip and Ice walked slowly. "I enjoyed the dinner party, Ice."

"I wanted you and Comte to have time to chat."

"Can we have him over?"

"Oh yes, let's."

Finally, her big-eyed bounce. I've missed it. My doing. Philip asked Ice about the Council and Comte's role.

"He is Chairman."

"What's the difference between the Council and the Board?"

"Each ship has a Board of Directors consisting of its senior Line Commanders and a few representatives elected by the crew. The four ships of original crew, the fully trained and informed crews, send their Boards to meet as the Federation Council to make policy and strategic decisions."

Long ago tyrants began killing humanists. Even today, governments, groups, and individuals often target schools, students, and faculty. If Pystead has culled out virtually all goths, we may well live without usurpers. Our spec of humanity should be sui generis, favoring moral progress. As an isolated group we become a single source river of being, eventually via germline we become a subspecies. We non-we, like a divine, must not overly respect the individual. The great rivers of being only are sacred. It is written, "I have set before you life and death, blessing and cursing; therefore choose life that both thou and thy seed may live." Build high, choose glory, say amen. As good as it gets! Welcome to the real world and may your guiding stars burn bright.

✠　✠　✠

The couple continued toward their quarters, not holding hands, each feeling a stricture in the head. Time is precious to both mind and body. And beware, for there are bandits of time, as well as of truth and solace. Where these things may be taken or denied, one may well find a human heart. Take care, for the heart may break.

And the Cosmos is impartial, reliably unhelpful and unforgiving—too cruel, say some. You need not pray to the Cosmos nor to the Buddha. Pray thee to a friend. And where time and liberty abide, gather while you may.

I was ready for my farewell dinner. Philip tensed as a wave of sensation pushed all the way up to his ears. *I'm not ready for my next dinner! Don't I want to be a salty dog, a cut above Laika who went up in Sputnik Two and died?*

On the main concourse, as they approached a small nature park, Ice slowed their pace and pointed to a squirrel. In the next moment, a few birds flew away from the squirrel and landed near three blue jays. "The reddish birds that flew are house buntings, songbirds."

"Nice. One can imagine being on Earth in some rural setting close to nature." The park was peaceful. "Ice, we should come sit and try to hear those songbirds."

"I'd like that."

They stopped. Philip observed, "This seems like a retreat to nature. I like the rounded-top trees. And we get animals that are rabies free, no wildcats nor mad dogs."

"Those three trees, Phil, are Weeping Japanese Snowbells. I'll have to show you a semitropical park with three-meters-tall, scarlet plants, poinsettia."

"I've never seen a tall poinsettia! And you know, I'm wrong to think of this as nature. This is eviscerated nature. This tiny park doesn't hold the reality of nature found on Earth."

"This park does have poison ivy, ragweed, and dozens of species of mostly unseen creatures like ants, spiders, bugs, worms, snails, snakes, and others I can't recall. Also, we have water parks with frogs and salamanders. We have a bamboo park, and a bamboo garden. Some parks are dark and grow mushrooms. My favorite is brightly lighted and grows dozens of wildflowers that I knew as a child from Oregon's Cascade Range. Quite beautiful too are the butterfly parks. It's said that evolution can be seen in the pattern on their wings."

Philip was looking at three small pink and blue statues, puppy dogs, sized for young children. He said, "Fine, but these parks don't make up for loss of the woods, their mysteries—their perils, even in this dim evening illumination of the corridor."

"Phil, we are here for tranquility."

"Children must learn of the woods in all their dimensions. We must teach them the lessons that cannot be learned within this simulacrum of the Earth."

"Oh yes! Also, we must also be sure they smell our few roses and see video of Earth's rainbows."

"Ice, you should paint a very large canvas, a mural, of rainbow sky for children to have as a memory."

Philip expected a smile, and when Ice only wiped her eyes he felt sad, ill, hollow, likely to vanish alone without a glow. He caught her hand. "Please, Ice, let's sit for a minute."

"There is little time before the coming alert."

"We must talk now. I want to live in the real world but realize that I also want the physical security of academia in good times."

"We all do."

"True. Yet some crew have jobs that are less than safe, and some have secrets that could make them targets."

"We live in the woods?"

"I'm afraid so."

"Phil, we will have stories from Earth, parables, fairy tales, and classroom lessons that warn children of the latent evil within humanity."

For a minute they stood and gazed at the small park. Philip reached for her hand and thought for a moment she was refusing, but she held his hand.

He took a breath and nudged her to sit. *Belonging is essential. A bird of what feather am I? Of what feather should I be, can I be? And Ice, whom I take to be all about the fellowship and happiness of the crew, readily agrees we must warn our children. She knows she lived protected by a fence with guards at the gate and guard pods protecting crewmembers off campus. She knew to expect trouble when we took that bus into town to warn and recruit her artist friends. She was trained, armed, and briefed. She and all the crew have dared to live daily with the risks I seek to avoid. I'm the one afraid to live in the woods, unfit to be a Commander or know the secrets of the Blues! I stumbled into rolling an eleven after a seven, and still not good enough? Not even in a niche of like memes of mind? This niche like all niches is real, therefore not a guarantor of life as it should be. The human condition. We must secure our own life, liberty, and peace. This time I must be part of the we.*

"Phil, Phil?"

"I have been delusional, Ice, not a real-world person." He shook his head almost violently.

"I love you as you are."

They removed their facemasks. Philip's words came spontaneously, "On many issues I no longer trust my own judgment. On one issue, my intuition has surely spoken. I can imagine myself in the woods happy, alert, no cognitive dissonance." Ice tensed and Philip squeezed her hand. "Ice, you are the love of my life. I can't imagine living without you and our children. Will you marry me?"

For a moment, she was puzzled, speechless. Then she opened wide her reddened eyes. "I will marry you, Philip Russell. I want only your children, and all of your children."

He leaned over and kissed her divinely, eyes closed. "I promise, and I'll no longer worry about your special duties."

"I want you to keep track of me, Phil, not because of danger, but because I like you looking after me."

"I'll take hints when I need to back off."

"Perfect."

They kissed, and Ice sighed. "You have made me truly happy."

Philip stood. "I am finally contented. I know we should be going."

The secret Cobalt Blue wiped her eyes and took her fiancé's hand. They stepped into the corridor, into their new reality of metallic silvers, whites, and grays.

O Russell, be strong, be brave enough to live in spacetime's woods! He took a deep breath. "I'm ready for your world, the real world."

Ice struck her eyes-wide pose. They enjoyed a smile together. *Young sage Harold was right.* Philip squeezed her hand.

Life is a kindness/to those who know the touch of/love from another.

ABOUT THE AUTHOR

For the technical background of this story, Pryor drew on his experiences as an electrical engineer and as an officer and classroom instructor at the USAF's Aerospace Research Pilot School. His world view has been influenced by a diverse set of experiences and friends, including friends of his wife, a British historian. To inform his natural curiosity, Pryor has traveled, read, and taken continuing education courses ranging from child development to cultural, historical, and scientific topics. Pryor has lived and worked in Georgia, Virginia, California, Mississippi, Texas, Florida, and Maryland; he currently lives with his wife in Baltimore County, Maryland.